Bryan Islip

More Deaths Than One

A Novel

For Delia
With whom no man could be an island.

'And the wild regrets, and the bloody sweats,
None knew so well as I:
For he who lives more lives than one
More deaths than one must die.'

Oscar Wilde

Author's note:

I call the prologue *Shrapnel* partly because a 38 page prologue could be a book all by itself and therefore deserves a title, and partly because it is the exploded, still red-hot and dangerous fragments of a man's past life.

The man is Thomas Thornton, through whom *More Deaths Than One* is narrated in its entirety. You do not *need* to know how Thomas Thornton came to be what and where he is at the start of the novel proper. The information is dribbled out in hints and allusions throughout the narrative in the customary way. So you can start with the prologue or you can skip to the thirty ninth page of this book, which is page one of *More Deaths Than One*. No problem either way. But if you do the skipping you may feel like coming back to *Shrapnel* after you've finished reading the novel. Which I guess could make it an epilogue of sorts.

Whatever, when you finally put down the book I hope it may leave a little of itself with you. Some small new understanding perhaps.

Bryan Islip

Shrapnel : A Prologue to *More Deaths Than One*

(November 14th 1970)
'Bye 'bye, Belfast

He's told to wait there in front of Miss Hunter's desk; she's writing something. There's the warm-iron taste of blood in his mouth but he remembers about not crying and about standing up straight like a soldier because that's what his daddy always says. That makes him want to cry even more because they'd killed him, his daddy. It smells of polish and old lady in here. His face hurts and the other bits where Clinty Saunders and the rest of them had hit and kicked at him. Both hands hurt as well where he'd hit them back and his knee is bleeding where he'd gone down on the gravel; he can feel the stickiness on the inside of his torn trouser leg.

Miss Hunter puts down her pen, looks up, says, "Now then Johnny, we simply cannot be having this. You cannot go on fighting with the other boys, certainly not with so many of them. Now, what do you have to say for yourself?"

"Nothing, miss," he mutters. He can tell it doesn't please her.

"Well then," she says, "Let me say it for you. I know how difficult a time this is for you but you have to be brave, Johnny. And you may be but eight years old but you have to be careful, too, because the others simply do not understand about what happened and because of that they are frightened. Sectarianism! Now, that is when some people think they hate other people and attack them. It is what is happening here in Belfast these days, out of fear and ignorance, you see. Sectarianism is a difficult word for a difficult problem, but it isn't you they really hate, it's just what they think you think about them, it's what they have been told you believe in or don't believe in. You understand that, I know you do."

"Yes, miss."

She sighs. "Oh, go on now. Go and ask your grandmother please to come in. Wait outside 'til I call you."

He can't tell whether Grannie Mac is going to cry or not when she sees his face and his trousers but she gives him a hug and goes in and he takes a very deep breath and stands still, in the corridor.

When the lady who's taken in the tea and biscuits comes out she leaves the door a bit open. He can hear some of what they're saying. Miss Hunter is asking how he'd been at the funeral and Grannie Mac is telling her that he'd been too quiet and about how they are now going to live in England with her daughter Ellie and her well off husband and about how all the neighbours shall probably say good riddance to the last of the MacRaes, "Bloody turncoats they will say; oh yes, so they will." She's definitely crying now. "'Unionists!' he hears her say. "Union between the devil and the grave, maybe." She goes on to tell Miss Hunter about his mother. "Blown up while my poor little Thomas was but a baby," she says.

"I'm so sorry. You have had too much of suffering," Miss Hunter says," But 'Thomas'? We have always called him Johnny here at school, so we have."

"I call the boy by his middle name, Thomas, because John is an unlucky name for us. My daughter's married name in England is Thornton, so Thomas Thornton the boy shall be."

Miss Hunter comes out, then, to ask him back in. She gives him his father's poem on the piece of paper she tells Grannie Mac she'd taken off Clinty Saunders. Clinty had stolen it in the fight. "Here you are, Johnny, or Thomas." she says. "Look after this. It's very good, so it is. It is your father's work, I believe?"

"Yes, Miss." he says.

Grannie Mac has her hankie out and she's dabbing it at her eyes. She says, "Yes, thank you, Miss Hunter; I'm very sorry."

"Miss?"

"Yes, Johnny?"

"I'm sorry, too, Miss."

"Then that makes all three of us. Remember what I told you, 'though, all right? About that awful word, 'sectarianism'?"

He says, "Yes, Miss, but my daddy isn't what they said. My daddy is a good man." He holds his head up like his daddy always tells him to.

"Yes he was, Johnny, I do know that," says head teacher Miss Hunter, "I can tell from that poem; a good man. And so are you - Thomas". She shakes her head, silver curls stiff, shiny, unmoving. She's quite a lovely old lady when she smiles at you. "Listen, come over here and shake hands with me now like a good man, Thomas Thornton," she says.

Close up, she smells like the bunches of flowers on the pile of fresh earth on his father's grave.

Aberford

Now they've arrived he's a bit scared. Actually, quite a lot scared. He really doesn't want to get out of Uncle Christopher's Mercedes. Nearly all the scurry of boys with caps and jackets in the colours of Aberford School are bigger than him and nobody's taking any notice, as if he and the rest of the Thorntons and their shiny new car are invisible or that other 'in' word; insignificant. But Auntie Ellie's smiling and so is Uncle Christopher. It's all right for them. Grannie Mac isn't smiling.

On the way here Uncle Christopher had asked him if he would like to call him 'father': "You know, after being part of the family here in England for almost four years? But only if you want to, my boy," he'd added.

Thomas knew he meant it. "Yes, I'd like to call you father, uncle," he said, because Uncle Christopher had always been very kind and he knew it would make him happy.

"That's good. From now on you'll have two homes, one in this wonderful old school where I went when I was your age and one in the holidays, back with us."

His new father has parked in the middle of a line of smart looking cars underneath these massive trees right in front of the great big, grey-stone boarding school. On the other side of the trees are the sports fields. A few bigger boys in muddied-up rugby kit are running with a ball, practicing tackling each other. Uncle Christopher who is now his father gets out his trunk; the trunk is black metal with 'Thomas Thornton' painted on it in neat white capitals and '1st Form' in smaller ones, the '1st' being on a stick-on label. Even after all this time you're still not really used to your name being Thomas Thornton instead of John MacRae. He had asked Uncle Christopher, were there any Roman Catholics at this Aberford School. Uncle had coughed a bit, then said he didn't know but it didn't matter anyway. He was making that up. You could tell.

Thomas doesn't want to be a school boarder here in England but he hasn't said so and he isn't going to show them he's frightened. As he gets out of the car he says, "Father, when will they let me join the army cadets you told me about, please?"

Auntie Ellie shakes her head, says, "You'd think he'd have had just about enough of guns, wouldn't you?" but she wasn't being unkind.

Uncle Christopher laughs and pats you on the top of your cap. "Soon enough, my boy, soon enough."

He leans back in and asks Auntie Ellie and Grannie Mac if they're sure they remembered to pack his daddy's poems. Of course he means his real daddy's poems. Grannie is doing her best not to let him see the extra shine in her eyes so he tells her it's all right and she says, "Oh, take no notice of me, little man. It is just some dust, so it is." Then she says, "Yes, of course we packed your daddy's poems for you." Embarrassing him now, she leans across to hug him and goes on, "Your daddy would be proud of you if he was alive still, so he would. And your grandfather too and all those others beneath the ground in the name of the Union; damned Union. Union between the devil and the grave, more like." She's always saying that. She always does when she cries and her voice goes all funny.

He's lying in bed in the new boys' dormitory in the dark listening to the sounds of some of the others trying not to let anyone hear them. There seems to be a lot of crying going on today. He thinks about that time before he and Grannie Mac came to live in England, soon after he had the big fight and everything was still hurting. He remembered the taste of blood and Miss Hunter saying, "Oh yes, you may be but eight years old but you are a good man, Thomas." But it's all right, living here in England. Hardly anybody ever gets killed and people who don't know each other sometimes smile at each other and you don't miss Belfast. Not too much; not any more, anyway.

Lying there in the dark on his first night at Aberford School, feeling sorry for himself, he does miss Grannie Mac and Uncle Christopher and Auntie Ellie but most of all he misses Sheila, his cousin and his very best friend; and her sister Flic, short for Felicity; he misses her as well. Lying there quite still he thinks about that, for some reason not comfortable with the thought that Sheila and Flic must be his sisters, now that their father is his father too.

(Interval 15 months: Saturday March 28th 1976)
Winning ways

This match, the one against Stowe, this has been the best. Aberford a distant second favourite but now winners with thirty points to their eighteen. They're all larking around in the changing rooms, muddy and high on being victorious; himself and Blake and Simon Reeves-Porter and Ridgeon and the rest of the under-fifteens.

Taking part might be good but winning things is much better; whether it's sport like playing Stowe at rugger or winning essay prizes or just beating up Butcher Hammond behind the sight screen for those damned insults with most of the third form watching. Hammond is bigger than him and one form higher but he wasn't so tough, not nearly.

In the changing room Ridgeon notices the sting marks on Freddie Blake and Freddie tells them about how Thomas and himself had found the hornets nest last Sunday. He can't ever keep anything quiet, can he? Freddie says about how the two of them had climbed the willow tree down by the side of the river so they could get a good view of what those two were up to in the long grass and about how the hornets had swarmed out of their nest-hole up there and how the man had heard Freddie's shout and had jumped up with his cock still sticking out and they'd both had to leap out of the tree into the river and swim off to the other side to get away from the man and from the hornets. "It was damn well worth it, though, seeing the lady's thingie and all that," Freddie says.

"You absolute bastards," Simon says, and Freddie says, "It's no good turning away Simon; we can all see you've got a rise on."

Thomas stands up. He knows there would have been trouble if they'd had any clothes on, but they won't touch each other naked. Using his new Aberford English voice he says, "Calm down now, children." He knows they will and not just because he's the team captain. It's because, for some reason, most often they'll do what he does or what he wants them to do.

(Interval two years and four months: July 15th, 1978)
Sheila, lovely Sheila

The two of them are walking along the otherwise empty beach, a soft rain ringing the wet sand. Great big grassy and dunes roll away on their right and nothing but the leaden-grey sea loch to the left. Nothing else; no houses, no trees, no people. Just the two of them and the pair of red setters, little more than puppies still, running up and down the dunes, up and down, up and down. Sheila says she's worried about what Mummy and Flic would have to say when they got back to the car. "You know, about the state the dogs have got into. It's all right for them, waiting in the dry, reading their silly old magazines," she adds. She asks him why he hadn't gone out fishing in the boat with daddy but she knows well enough why not. You can tell that much. Oh, she is pretty, this step-sister. Thomas leads the way, scrambling up the sides of an

5

especially large dune, flopping down on to the wet grass rim of it. The dogs are casting about at all the rabbit scent. He looks up to her, sees the whole new shape of her ... it makes him go dizzy. Literally.

"Oh, why are boys so predictable?" she asks, breathlessly. She does not sit down. "But you like Flic just as much as me, don't you, Thomas?"

He decides to take a big chance. "I do like her, yes," he tells her, "But, Sheila, it's you I think of when I'm away at school. I think of you all the time." He hesitates then out it comes. "After lights out, specially then. I - I think you're lovely." He shivers with the excitement of something yet to happen, feels his cock stiffening against its confinement.

She laughs, pushes a stray lock of hair back under the hood of her Musto. "Oh do come on, Thomas, we're both your sisters, remember?" She laughs again, breathlessly. "We have to get going. They'll be sending out search parties."

"Oh God, Sheila, don't let's go just yet. Sit down here next to me." He wants to reach out to touch her.

"Do stop it, Thomas," she says. But he can see how excited she is. It's in her voice and he can see how her eyes have turned serious and how dark and full are her rained on lips and he's filled with this hammering sweet pain that so easily casts out any restraint.

She says, "Oh all right, but I'm not sitting down and you can't touch me." Then she unzips her coat and does something behind her back and draws up the front of her jersey. She's looking down on him. He cannot stop his eyes from leaving hers, going to the twin breasts with the nipples that had been like his own a little while ago but are now these great, swollen, heart-stopping things.

"I don't think I'm wanted here." The voice filled up with shock is Flic's. She's down there in the hollow of the dune, standing still, staring up. She seems about to burst into tears, but turns and runs instead, the dogs running and barking and bounding up around her.

Sheila calls out, "Come back here, Flic. Come back at once." There's no response. She shouts, "Oh, please." Her brassiere and jumper now back in place, she's looking down on him still sitting there. "See?" she cries, "You've done it now. She'll tell Mummy." Thomas sees the tears in her eyes along with the raindrops on her face.

"What? What will she say, then? She can't say anything, can she? We haven't done anything," he mutters.

You can tell she's frightened now; it's in her voice. And she's ashamed; that's in the colouring of her face. "*You* may not have, Thomas," she says, "But you just made me, didn't you."

He knows it's spoiled and just wants to hide and to stay hidden. But later that day, after the talk with the man he and Sheila and Flic call father, the man he likes very much and who seems to like him and more importantly to know him, he reads it again: his real father's last poem. He reads it slowly. It's the one called 'The Fourth Light'. He's doing his best to understand it all. Yes, he knows this one is better than any of the poems he's yet written himself; the poems he never shows to anybody.

(Interval two years: 28th July 1980)
Tell it to the Marines

The recruiting office sergeant tells him there's no such thing as just 'The Marines.' He says it's actually The *Royal Marine Commando*, originally formed in sixteen sixty four as the Duke of York and Albany's Maritime Regiment of Foot Soldiery.

He says he's interested in applying to enlist in The Royal Marine Commando. The sergeant asks him, why? and why in the ranks? "Why not apply for a commission?" he asks.

"Because I'm against privilege, sir," Thomas says.

The sergeant snorts and says how he would be privileged just to be accepted for the selection course, never mind get selected, never mind complete the training and get the green beret. "Many are called and few are chosen, laddie," he says, and Thomas has to wonder, why have a recruiting office in London then? But he starts with the history, aided and abetted by the old man in the well-worn, well-pressed clothes who's wandered in with his stick and all the medals on his jacket: very special medals according to the sergeant. The old man wears one all right, one of their famous green berets. It seems to be moulded to his head. "It's in me will, son," the old man says, "It's in me will for me to be buried wearing this thing, right?"

"I could go on for ever, talking about history, Mister Thornton," says the sergeant, "But you'll be thinking, shit, this is just history. Well, it isn't. We're not history, history's us, right? For example, you see this?" He points to one of the many pictures on the wall. "That there's a black hole called Gallipoli. See all those men lying on the beach? They aren't there bloody sunbathing. They're just a few of our grateful dead and the bloody dying. Mister Churchill's little fiasco in WW One, that one was, but you'll likely know all about that, being an educated young man.

Unless I'm much mistaken you don't hail from the back streets of Liverpool nor any Comprehensive." They keep on saying that if he can hack the training, and about ninety nine percent haven't got a hope, he'd be best off applying for a commission, specially with his Army Cadet training. "'Ruperts' is what we call our officers. 'Rupert Bear,' get it? But it's not taking the piss, it's just a special relationship between our officers and we in the ranks. Same training. Tougher for the Ruperts if that's possible."

"Are the Royal Marine Commandoes in any way connected to the SAS?" Thomas asks.

The old man, whose name you now know is 'Smithy,' laughs and says, "I should fucking cocoa, son," and the sergeant says, "SAS! Saturdays and Sundays I call 'em. On account of they're always getting themselves in the weekend papers. Ours is better than that. We have the Special Boat Squadron, laddie. SBS and SAS are both what they call Special Forces but SBS is us and its more intelligent. SAS is Army. And no," he says, "Until you've worn this here green beret for a couple of years - which already means you must be one out of a hell of a lot, you can't even apply to join the SBS."

Thomas tells them about how they want him to go up to Oxford but he wants to join the Royal Marine Commando instead. Then the sergeant says something trite about the University of Life and the old Marine stands up, not without difficulty because the sergeant has said privately that he still carries in his leg a present from the Germans, one they gave him at Dieppe, and says, "Good luck then, son. I reckon there'll still be enough wars to go around and still enough real men to fight for the old country. And may God bless you." Thomas realises the old chap is actually saluting him! Embarrassed, not knowing how to respond, he holds out his hand.

*****

He takes the train back from London, reading all the brochures. What's it to be? Back to Aberford for another year, then Oxford University? Or down to Lympstone in Dorset with the Royal Marines? He has to ask his father's opinion, and not just because he'll need his father's signature if he decides to go ahead with the Marines.

Father knows there's something up but he's being patient, gets him into a discussion about this great painting above the fireplace in his office, the one showing the charge of the Light Brigade. But after a little while Thomas says about wanting to join the ranks of the Marines and father just looks at him for a moment, takes a sip from his tumbler of whisky

8

then goes over to the painting. He says it's a copy of the original. "See the cannon there, Thomas?" he says. "Those enemy ones? They were made by my company - our company - and sold to the Russians a hundred and forty years ago. Now look at this officer, this one out here, up with the leader. That's Fazakerley Thornton, son of the founder of Amalgamated and my great great grandfather. Killed of course, as were the vast majority of the Light Horse Brigade that day. Killed by his own weaponry." He looks at Thomas searchingly, his eyes straight and true and caring. "The thing is, Thomas, I had you marked down as my successor." He smiles his understanding. "I suppose you're saying you would rather use our weapons rather than make them?"

Thomas has grown very fond of this second-hand father. He's always been everything he could have been. But he can sense that his father also knows how he still feels about Sheila. Out of courtesy he promises to think it over some more but father gets the message, nods slowly, staring into his almost empty glass. Then although Thomas doesn't like the sea-weed taste or the bite of it, he's happy to accept this first glass of whisky, and drink it with his father before joining the rest of the family for dinner.

When everybody's seated Christopher Thornton stands up at the head of the table. In the new silence he says, "Ladies, I have a toast for you. This is to our son and your brother. I wish him well, as do we all. Thomas Thornton is going off to be a soldier."

They're all looking at him now, astonished, still silent. He feels his cheeks reddening, He looks down, fiddling with his fork. He says, "Actually, to be a Royal Marine Commando, father: That is, if they'll have me and if I'm good enough."

Sheila rushes from the room in tears. Auntie Eleanor looks concerned. Flic is clearly undecided, doesn't know yet how she wants to react. Grannie Mac seems very suddenly to have grown even older. Older and greyer. And she has her eyes shut tight.

(Interval 2 years: 4th June 1982: 01.00 hours)
Staying alive

'Falkland Islands! Well, he thinks, you were the one wanted action. Happy now? Better than Belfast though, or Derry; Londonderry even. No sooner the green beret than out in the land of his fathers with an M16. But this South Atlantic thing - oh yes, this was more like it, more like what he imagined; even pinned down by enemy fire in the pitch dark and the freezing rain halfway up some desolate, stony bloody hill. He's flat down behind a boulder with Backie and Ben Benedict and Corp; Corporal Vandenburgh with his bloody stump of stripped off thigh bone and his other leg not much better, making all those terrible sucking and groaning sounds in spite of the morphine.

The Argies must have a night scope up there but one of them has to make some kind of a move. The corporal's going to cash in his chips if he doesn't get medical assistance and soon it'll be getting light and then it's Goodnight Vienna, one and all. That's what he whispers to them, anyway, and Backie tells him what he already knows; that the Argies are a hundred metres up a thirty degree slope, nice and safe under their rock overhang. "What you want to do, Tommy," he says, "fucking fly up there? One mighty bound, is it, Superman?"

"You stay with Corp, Backie," Thomas whispers. "You can't do too much with guts in the state yours are in. Listen. Ben, I'm going to split off to the right. Chances are they've only the one night-sight. Soon as you see the tracer following me you go wide left and get your arse up there. There's plenty more boulders where this one comes from so I should be OK for cover. You'll see the muzzle flash when you get close enough. For Christ's sake mallet the bastards, will you?"

Baker mutters it'll be for all our sakes, not just Christ's. He's been complaining for hours about his Galtieri's revenge and the smell is appalling. Ben says he'd rather have the Argie's than any more of Baker's shit stink. Thomas take a couple of deep, unpleasant breaths. As he takes off into the nothingness, bent low, Baker shouts, "And may your God go with you." Bullets are whispering and snapping past his head, one in eight of them red incendiary so he could have seen them coming if he'd had time to look. Not that he'd have been able to avoid them. You wouldn't ever see the one that got you; that's what they all said. Anyway he gives it maybe twenty seconds of running and dodging, blind as a bastard in the pitch black, then falls flat on his face over a boulder and scrambles well down behind it. He can't believe they missed him with all that stuff and they haven't, not entirely anyway. Nothing much though, just a nick to the left arm, upper. He's been lucky, so far anyway. But oh how it do sting. Bastards!

Soon enough he realises the Argentinian bullets have stopped chipping away at his rock shelter and there's new shooting going on up there and it's Ben's SLR , definitely. He gets his face out of the muck and the ice and the soaking wet heather, stands up half expecting something then moves off up the hill, fast as he can in as straight a line as he can. He's stumbling, sometimes falling, wondering all the time when he's going to be cut down. But, hell, it's wonderful. He's OK with all of this, somehow. For the first time he's looking for someone to kill.

(Interval 7 months: January 20, 1983: 10.00 hours)
Onwards and upwards.

He likes the feel of his two new stripes and the way the blokes treat him now he has them sewn on. Even the Ruperts treat him differently. Respect. That's what it is.

"How's your arm, Corporal?" the Adjutant asks.

"It's fine sir," he says. He's surprised by the question because it was only a scratch and he's forgotten about it.

Ben, standing to attention alongside him, is similarly asked about his leg. He says, "Yes sir, it's a hundred percent. Have you heard how Corporal Vandenburgh is, sir?"

"The Corporal's fine, Benedict. Home leave now." The adjutant coughs. "Unfortunately he won't be able to dispense with the wheelchair for some time yet."

When the C.O. arrives he asks the Adjutant to read out the citation and when that's finished he pins on Thomas' Conspicuous Gallantry Medal and shakes his hand and then does the same for Ben before stepping back, saluting. He dismisses Ben, asks Thomas to remain. "Tell me, how's your father?2 he asks, and Thomas realises once more how long a reach is that of his stepfather. Everyone in the business of weaponry and war knows, or at least knows of the chairman of Amalgamated Arms and Engineering. "And what about you, yourself, Thornton? Thought any more about applying for a commission?"

"Yes, as a matter of fact I have, sir," he says. "I would like to make such an application when you think it might be advisable." The Colonel nods, waiting for more. "I'd like at the same time to apply for SBS selection if at all possible."

"Yes, I thought you might," says the Colonel. "You know the Special Boat Squadron is now to become the Special Boat Service? Don't ask me the whys and wherefores. But it's still the SBS. Our SBS. Apply for it? Why not, but don't you think you're being just a bit of a glutton for punishment, Thornton? A further year of the toughest and most demanding kind of training and all that?"

Thomas says that he's thought it well through and still wants to go ahead and when the Colonel asks why he'd opted for the ranks in the first place he tells him what he'd told the recruiting office sergeant and all the others, about unearned privilege. The Colonel smiles, says this is all a bit too much on the philosophical side for a simple military chap but that anyway, he'll back you, and good luck. He signals the meeting is at an end. Still standing to attention Thomas hears his commanding officer pause at the door behind him. "Do I take it, then, that you feel you've now earned some of that privilege, Corporal Thornton?"

"Yes, sir," you say, "That's right."

He's strolling along the river bank with Sheila. The setters are in and out of the rushes looking for ducks to flush. They're getting old now. Every time he gets home on leave he notices the changes in them. "So you're not allowed to tell even your little sister where they're sending you, Lieutenant Thornton?" she asks.

"That's correct, young lady." He laughs, squeezing the arm that's crooked through his.

"Not even how long you're going to be away?"

"Nope," he says, and really, he doesn't know. Six months saturation in Arabic, its dialects, Islamic cultures and all that, and then what? Out in the desert with the Arabs? Military attaché somewhere in the Middle East? Christ, he hopes not that. But for how long? "Will you miss me, Sheila?" he asks.

"Oh no, not one little bit, stupid. Why should I miss you when I have my studio and my painting and my lovely Harold."

Harold! He needs not look at her to know the truth.

(Interval 4 years: June 20th 1987)
One thing resolved

At least the beer tastes good back here. But how he misses it all: the Marsh Arab Ma'dan with their great, wallowing buffalo; sound of wind through endless reed-beds; the laughter of the children; the every evening philosophising in the mudhif over thick, strong coffee and the sweetest of dates; the freedom of their - now his clothing, minimal, loose; the touching and the other things of and by the woman, Fa'iqah, in the darkness of the tent. He sighs. Back in this disunited Kingdom, deep undercover in the frenetic north of Ireland, Special Forces Captain Thomas Thornton misses the unhurriedness of his time in the Tigris-Euphrates delta.

Well, any minute now Maloney's going to react. The lovely Caitlin's making sure her boyfriend can see she's giving Thomas the cold shoulder. Whenever Thomas smiles at her he can sense the man's anger. Well, why wouldn't the guy be angry? Once again he wonders whether

12

the bastard's carrying, whether Caitlin Sherry is for that matter. He orders another pint for himself, "And whatever the two of them over there are drinking."

The barman looks at Thomas, saying nothing. Unshaven young men with Jesus Christ non-hairstyles and beards and scrappy blue denim clothes don't impress him. He takes the others their drinks but returns still holding them, plonks them down on the bar. "They don't want any drink off of you, so they don't," he says. "That'll be two pounds sixty. Maybe you'd best be on your way soon, son. We don't want no trouble here." He leans across the bar top. "Listen, you surely don't want none yourself, not with Brendan Maloney. You know? You know Brendan?"

Thomas shrugs, gives the man the money, takes the two glasses over to stand in front of their table. "For fuck's sake what's the matter, man?" he says, "Jesus, I'm just trying to be friendly." But he's making it clear it's the girl: she's the one with whom he wants to be friendly.

Maloney shakes his head and gets up and the other two over there look ready to get to their feet as well. Caitlin's gone quite pale and everyone else in the pub is suddenly deep in their own conversations. Quietly, Maloney says, "You are some stupid prick. You're not from around here, sonny, so you're not."

Thomas looks towards the door, eyebrows raised, says, "No-one calls me stupid, old man." The next bit is predictable and satisfactory. Maloney follows him out, the others following along behind. It's a warm night with a nice bright moon but he can't see Ben. He'll be well down in the car with his H&K good and ready now he's seen what's happening. He bloody well hopes so, anyway; hopes Ben hasn't gone to sleep or anything. Then Maloney's men have him, one to each arm. Maloney comes in with a hard right to the stomach then punches him twice more to the left side of his face. Shit. But nobody sees Ben moving in until he gets real close and then Maloney just says, "What the fuck, " and goes for his weapon and Ben looses a short, well silenced burst that sounds like a small outboard's underwater exhaust. One of the others has his own gun out and pressed into Thomas' back. He's yelling, "Get yoursel' the fock out, ye focking cont, ye." But Ben's next burst goes right past Thomas' ear and hits the man in the face with a noise like smacking a ripe melon with a big stick and then there's the bang and Thomas can feel the bullet that's torn through the lower left hand side of his ribcage. As he bends to pick up the fallen guy's gun it's not hurting much; not just yet, anyway. He straightens up, grinning in the silver light. "Nice going, sergeant," he says.

The last of them is backing off, hands up in the air. "Holy mother of God, ye've murdered the two of them. Oh, Christ... "

Thomas says, "And hello to you too, Ryan; blown up any buses lately? May your God have mercy on the blackness of your soul." This one's going to be for his father - for his real father.

Ben says, "No Tommy. No sir. He's unarmed. Don't make a hero out of the bastard."

Thomas squeezes the trigger once and then again, putting the first into the thick of Ryan's body and the second into his head as he's falling, just to make sure. And now his side really is hurting. Ben supports him, gets him into the car. They swing at high speed out of the pub car park and off to the military hospital, because high speed is the only way Ben knows how to drive. In the side mirror Thomas sees Caitlin Sherry. She's standing just outside the door of the pub, looking down at her friends and then up at her friends' killers' car, fast disappearing.

Thomas says it again. "Nice work, sergeant. At least we won't have any trouble proving self defence, right?"

Ben shakes his head and Thomas tries to laugh, though softly, and even though he now really does hurt like hell he also feels how good it is just for once to resolve something here in this bloody, bloody, lovely old Ireland.

(Interval 14 months: September 10th 1988)
Deep underground

Deep underground is where he's been since he left the Service. Left it, that is, in the eyes of all except the Colonel and a couple of others. Top, top, top security. This 'deep underground' is when they wanted what you did and were good at doing and didn't mind going on paying for it, but didn't need the responsibility of actually owning such a maverick as Captain Thomas Thornton; not any more. Especially not if things were to go pear shaped, right?

Deep underground right now is sitting in the poolside bar of the Sheraton Macuto in La Guaira with Luis Carrapaga, the two of them alone, of course not counting the several smart-suited guns. And deep underground is where Thomas Thornton will most surely be if the guy doesn't believe him, if he doesn't swallow the meticulously created string of untruths carefully put together by experts for the purpose of gaining accreditation, which is step one in the projected damaging or maybe even the demolition of Carrapaga's cocaine to Ireland operations.

But deep underground is also where he's going to end up if the fat man suspects what this visitor might have in mind for his beautiful daughter sitting out by the side of the pool with the rest of the Carrapagas this Sunday afternoon. Christ, it made for great heat just looking out from the air conditioned bar room through the window into the baking sun; just looking at the girl.

Carrapaga is saying, "Words are cheap, Mister Thornton." He taps the rim of his glass, stares at Thomas, reading his mind, says, "But cojones of the quality of your cojones, these are rare and precious things. By killing my friend Maloney and God knows for what other, they tell me you get yourself thrown out of the British Intelligence or Special Forces or by whatever silliness they are named, then in the next thing here you are here in Carrapaga's Venezuela, offering yourself to him for money - and even with eyes for his little Consuela. It is true what they tell me, you are a crazy? You do not look or speak like a crazy, Senor Thornton. You look like a nice boy: in fact you look like the best and the worst and the most dangerous kind of an English boy, I think."

Over his shoulder, through the big window, Thomas can see her. Now and then she's glancing back at him over the top of her sunglasses.

Carravaga goes on, "But I like you. I am going to take a chance, Mister Thornton. You will come to stay awhile at the hacienda and we will talk some more." He nods imperceptably. The one with the Uzzi comes out from the room behind the bar. This is one ugly bastard. Also comes out the barman who goes to unlock the door so that Thomas and his new target can go out into the sunshine, join the family gathering.

(Interval 3 months: 18th January 1989)

Los Alamos

obody sane argues with a silenced Heckler and Koch nine millimetre machine pistol but this Captain Alfonso DiMontenaro, he's pretty drunk. Thomas watches the man's hand inching towards the radio on-off switch so he lets go a burst. A line of holes stitches across the wheelhouse window, right in front of the Captain's face. The hand stops then retreats as a few more shots smack directly into the radio.

"Jesus H Christ," shouts Alfonso.

With the face mask on and the H&K in his hand it is too easy to feel like God. The door opens and Ben Benedict looks in and Thomas tells him that, yes, everything's OK. "No problem. The Captain here thought he'd like to call home but changed his mind."

The Captain says, "Why you guys do this? Why you come up on my ship out the fucking sea? You some kind a fucking pirates or something? And why you make me sailing west? Where the fuck you plan on us going? USA?"

Ignoring him, Thomas asks Ben if everything's ready. Ben says, yes it is, apart from the young girl. Nobody had anticipated that one. "She's locked herself into one of the cabins," Ben says. "Real looker, too. Good bit too classy for the skipper here I should reckon. Says her name's Carravaga, would you believe? Consuela Carravaga." Captain Thomas Thornton's stomach lurches in a way that has nothing to do with the motion of a ship at sea. He's glad of the mask.

"We'll be taking her with us," he says. "So use the needle, OK? We'll need to keep her out till we can get her ashore." He can't read any expression behind Sergeant Ben Benedict's eye-holed balaclava. He thinks the sergeant might want to argue but he won't say anything, surely not in front of this Alphonso.

"Neither of their lifeboats look in any better shape than the damn crew of this tub, not to me, they don't, sir."

"Lifeboats?" says the ship's captain, "What the fuck you mean with life-boats? Listen to me. This old Los Alamos, she is all I have for feed my family, sirs. My family, they are many. Take all the fucking guns, take what you like. You leave me my ship, OK?"

Thomas says, "Please just keep quiet. You should have thought of that before you loaded all that white shit and Carravaga's guns and enough Semtex to blow up half of mother Ireland and England too." He turns to his sergeant. "Let's move it on now, OK? Get the guys organised."

Right, organised; laying their own explosives deep down in this rusty hull. Minimum charges, maximum rate of descent of her and all she carries right to the bottom of the deep Atlantic.

Alphonso is a case, all right. The guy tries bribery next. Thomas knew he would. He's surprised he took this long to get to it.

Seventy minutes later and he's back with Ben and the other two on board Smith-Mandeville's sub. He's waiting and watching through the periscope, sees the flash, immediately followed by the two ends of the Los Alamos rising up as if to say hello to each other before sliding sedately below the waves. There's a boil of escaped air and that's it. "These fertiliser cargoes; so very unstable," Thomas murmurs.

Lieutenant-Commander Smith-Mandeville does not like covert operations. "I don't know about you people," he says, "You seem to think you can break about every rule in the book and get away with it. And just what in hell are you thinking of, Thornton, bringing a sedated female aboard my submarine? This is an operational vessel of the Royal Navy, for God's sake. I've had to mount a guard outside her cabin. Crew are all for queuing up to take a peek at your bloody sleeping beauty."

The Lieutenant-Commander seems more concerned about that, and about Alphonso and his crew of deadbeats last seen adrift in the least rickety of the Los Alamos's lifeboats thirty miles off the South West of Ireland; he seems more concerned with that than the success of the whole operation.

Thomas says, "Not to worry, skipper, the crew will soon be picked up by the air-sea rescue we're about to call in, anonymously of course. As for the girl, she'll soon be off your hands and mine, too, safe and sound in the Republic." Which was where she'd wanted to go anyway, probably looking for me, he might have added.

(Interval one years and 4 months: May 3rd 1990 - 19.00)
A walk in wet woodland.

It's sheeting down, gloomy already with an hour of semi daylight still to go. Great gobs of rainwater shake free from the overhanging beech branches at each new gust of wind. Colonel Grenville answers on the second ring. No name, just, "Yes?" but the voice is pleasing, confident, same as ever.

"Are you selling tea roses — the old fashioned sort?" he asks, then pauses whilst the Colonel switches on his scrambler before answering in the affirmative.

"Nice day for a walk in the woods, Colonel," says Thomas.

"Twenty minutes, Captain."

"Yes, sir." It's only a ten minute drive for him but the Colonel would need time to brief his security. Soaking wet from his trainers up to his baseball cap, Thomas waits patiently, listening to the swish and splatterings of rain from well inside the trees. Hampshire wood; great smell at this time of year. All bluebells and wet earth.

A Range Rover pulls into the otherwise empty car park. He looks at his watch. Twenty one minutes. He sees the tall, grey headed figure putting on his raingear, letting out a black labrador, locking up. He calls his dog to heel and starts out along the darkening track. With the labrador now well under control a slight hand movement sets him free to go hunting. It takes the dog no time at all to find and recognise Thomas; just long enough for Thomas to be sure no-one else is about, no-one following. He steps out on to the track, falling easily into step alongside his commanding officer, Colonel Robert Grenville, MC, DSO and bar.

"Evening, Thornton," he says, "How good to see you."

"Evening, Colonel. Nice new dog."

"Yes. Known as The Black Bastard. That's 'BB' for short. He had a taste for breaking up the happy home before I convinced him he wasn't the alpha male around here. Now he's my friend and my best reason for a walk and a pint in the pub, aren't you boy? Go on then, bugger off." BB lopes back into the trees, wet-shining black in black.

"How's Lady Dee, sir?"

"Very well, Thomas, very well. Sends her love." The Colonel looks sideways at him, straight-eyed from under the dripping peak of his tweed cap. He's old but fit: good face, moustachioed, unworried, unsurprised; who can tell, perhaps even happy to see him? "Yes indeed, it's good of you finally to show up, Captain," he says, then, "What is it, two years, give or take? We'd have thought you were underground in more ways than one had not the money kept emptying itself out of our bank account."

"And into the Corpus Christi Orphanage, yes?"

"Oh yes, I'm sorry. I'd forgotten about that; in Belfast. You have what used to be called 'independent means', and all that."

"I'm now a fully salaried, well incentivised salesman, remember, sir?"

"There was a rumour … I take it you're now most likely going to tell me what you've been up to?"

"How long do you have, Colonel?"

"Did you know this was a medieval cart track? It'll take us all of thirty miles into Southampton if we feel like it. Go ahead."

Thomas says, "After the Service ostensibly dispensed with the services of one Captain Thornton, amazing how quickly the wild men of the north got to know about it, and about my original MacRae connection." It's almost dark. He steps carefully around yet another muddy puddle of rainwater.

"Of course. We didn't exactly send them a letter about it but our people laid a pretty clever trail for them." He tests the ground with his walking stick. "Yes, Thomas, I gathered they'd recruited you, you were re-based in Dublin?"

"Right." Thomas stops, hands over the list of names. The Colonel takes out a pencil torch. In its reflected light there's a frown on his face as he reads the names. He tears the paper into tiny pieces, puts them into a pocket of his Barbour. They walk on, for a while saying nothing. There's a sudden clatter of wings through foliage and an angry cackling as a cock pheasant rises vertically, his long tail feathers shaking in black silhouette as he rockets across their path. The Colonel takes imaginary aim with his walking stick. "So, Captain? You're supposed to eliminate some of these fellows?"

"That's right; all six, actually, over time. Trouble is, I'm pretty sick of this whole double agent thing and I'm sure as hell not cut out for a hardwood salesman. I can't help thinking how come I fought my way through the Royal Marines and Special Forces training, not to mention 14 Intelligence, and end up to all intents and purposes an outcast, living on my own in some Dublin bed-sit, plotting and scheming my way through every living day and with no obvious way back?"

"I can understand that but whatever the world may think, you are on the side of the angels and one day you will indeed find your way back because you are anything but alone. There are people who view very favourably what you've done, and no doubt what you tell us you're going to get up to now. You're seen as being all the more the man of the moment now all hell's breaking out between the madman Hussein and your old Marsh Arab friends. It seems highly likely it's going to end up as a shooting match with us and the Americans very much at the centre." He stops and Thomas stops but Thomas is unable to read the expression on his commanding officer's face. "Meantime, our people appreciate the extreme hazard under which you operate. You will not find them ungrateful." He calls out, "BB!" and the dog quickly materialises at his side. If anything the slant rain is heavier, driven hard before a risen wind. There's the sound of branches bending, the thrashing of foliage. They walk on, for a while in silence, taking a left hand fork that must lead back to the car park. Then Colonel Grenville says, "I shall refrain from asking you about the girl, this Carravaga female. Enough to say we know she's in Dublin, that you have met her at least once and that this truly is the most dangerous of liaisons. I'm only saying, please do be very careful, Thomas. That isn't just your Colonel talking. Lady Dee and I actually do care about what happens to you. We would like you to know that. By the way, how do your family view things now?"

"They're OK," Thomas says. He cannot bring himself to mention the bad vibes when he couldn't fill them in on what was happening with him. He didn't want to say he couldn't expect them actually to welcome back their failed soldier, now the salesman with his pathetic little billet in Ireland.

"Good," says Grenville. "There are times when we all must wonder, well, about the legendary call of duty and all that. But God willing there has to be an end to it, old chap. Let's hope it's to be the right one. Look, we'll be back in the car park in a minute so it's best if we separate here. I take it you don't need a lift anywhere?"

" No, sir. Good of you to ask but no thanks."

In the darkness they shake hands and the Colonel turns away. A blacker form takes up walking station beside him. "The very best of luck to you, Thomas. May your God, as they say, go with you."

Thomas steps off the track, stands under a tree, waiting. He's well trained at being very good at waiting. Soon enough he sees the Range Rover's headlights come on, swing around in a wide arc, making magical the moving shadows and slender threads of golden rain before fading and dying. Thomas Thornton is on his own again.

(Interval a year and 4 months: September 15 1991)
Kerrigan

On the way home from the bar he'd had a sense that he was being followed. Now he's lying on his unmade bed, in the dark, waiting. Finbar Furey's marvellous Roisin Dubh is turning around and around in his head. Now and then the alcoholic darkness dips and turns along with it.

The door isn't locked so this guy's in and has the light on and there's a revolver stuck in his face. It's a big revolver with a bloody great muzzle. A forty five, for Christ's sake, like something from the wild west or the O'Connell Street Post Office! The guy has to be joking, but of course he is in no way joking. Thomas acts out the shock but the man seems not to be unfriendly, asks him to sit up a minute, feels under the pillow, throws it on the floor then tells him to lie down again. He doesn't think the man is as old as the grey hair and the weapon say he might be.

Wonderful. He does as he has been told, having just recognised the man as Michael Kerrigan. Kerrigan's name is high on his list. "Thomas Thornton, by all that's holy." The man speaks in the strangled patois of North Belfast

20

Thomas carries on pretending the shock, using his best Dublin accent. "No, you have the wrong guy, pal, I'm MacRae, Johnny MacRae, OK?" Now he remembers; Brian's Bar, earlier tonight. He should have recognised Kerrigan sitting at the back in the semi dark, all by himself. But he, Thomas, had been right up front; the salesman-poet singing along with all the lovely old songs of pre-EEC Dublin. Kerrigan wants to talk. If he didn't he would have made his move by now and if he had, if he'd done so, if his intended victim had been good enough after the Guinness, he would have made his move, too. Thomas thought, 'He wants you to tell him something, anything to give yourself away, help him make sure he's killing the right guy. That's very bad news for him; he should never have started this without knowing for sure.'

Cheeky sod asks you if you want a cup of tea, goes over and lights up your gas ring, makes sure the kettle has water, puts it on the heat, comes back to stand over you with his revolver hanging loose by his side. He's spotted the pile of your writing by your laptop. Here it comes now. 'Too close, old man,' you want to say, 'much too bloody close.' But of course he doesn't say it.

"Ye're not going to tell me jack fuckin' shit, are ye, Tommy? Well, no matter, what ye're doing here doesn't seem like a whole lot, son, if you don't mind me saying so." He waves his revolver at the laptop set up. "You writing all that poems and stuff about us?" He shrugs and grins. "Fame at fuckin' last, so it is? And the girl, Tommy, what the fuck's with the little Carravaga girl? Our dago friend don't like what you're doing with his little girl; oh no Captain, sir, he sure as shit don't like you no more."

The kettle starts to rumble, begins with its bubbling low down whistle, rising. Thomas rolls over very quickly, taking the knife from its slit in the mattress under his right thigh. He buries the blade of it deep in Kerrigan's side. Easy. He has hold of the man's gun arm but he has good strength, considering. Thomas had never heard a cowboy gun going off anywhere, never mind close by his ear. Deafening, literally: Instant explosive smell. Very bad news for his left elbow. His knife twists free as Kerrigan falls. The kettle's screaming. He gets up off the bed, bends to pick up the revolver and goes over to turn off the gas tap. Holding his limp-bloody arm under the running tap, he hears Kerrigan saying something that he can't make out, not with the roaring still going on in his ears. Now Provo Commander Kerrigan is looking up with lost savagery into the muzzle of his own gun. "Come on then, ye cont, ye," Thomas thinks he might be saying. "What the fock ye waiting for?" Yes, that's probably what he's saying.

21

"Is this the way it always has to end, Kerrigan?" he says, "Just with pain?" His voice seems to come from a long way away across a storm at sea. He uses his thumb to lower the hammer into safe, sticks the gun inside his belt. He looks around; like a knacker's yard in here. Blood alley. No cold blood, though; he'll let this Kerrigan do his dying all by himself. He improvises a tourniquet from a strip that he tears off a pillow case. Lucky the shot was so close. Good clean in and out, blood pulsing from both ends, bits of bone. Fuck. Do it ever hurt. Don't try to bend it.

He puts his papers into a plastic shopping bag, adds the knife and the gun and his laptop, turn out the light, goes out and downstairs and outside into the street, into the rain. The whole house must have heard the shot and half of the street as well but he doesn't think anyone will have reported it. Not here. There aren't even any lights showing. He calls Connie from a telephone kiosk, arranges for her to pack a case, drive over to pick him up at the corner of Phoenix Park, across the river from the railway station. Then he makes a call to the emergency services, tell them no he won't give his name, tells them where to go to find a man with a bad knife wound. He knows that, in making that call, he's finally severing his last connections with Her Majesty's armed services.

He walks slowly in slow rain down empty streets from one light-island of rain-shining yellow to another. In the middle of the bridge over the Liffey he stands for a moment then drops the weapons and the laptop and all his poems into the blackness. He thinks he can hear the splash but cannot be sure. He's feeling really bad now. Bad because of the loss of his blood, bad because of the loss of his poetry; poetry like his father's. Not as good as his, probably, but all gone now for good or for bad.

He had tried; he had … like that other old MacRae, right? The Colonel with the Canadians, the one who'd found his beautiful words in amongst the gas and the stinking unburied multicoloured corpses and the unnatural desolation of Passchendale; the Colonel John MacRae who at the dawning of one day had sat down and thought of the words and had written, *'though poppies blow in Flanders Field.'*

Thomas Thornton, aka John MacRae, collapses on to a bench on the pavement alongside the unseen waters of the Liffey. Only half conscious now … the river … into his mind swirls the line from one of his own, now extinct poems: *Look down into that blackest boil / That flood that eats a blood-beloved island's soil.* But this is not good. His head keeps falling forward and there seems little or nothing to be gained by keeping on trying to raise it so he lies back along the bench. Cold tears from the dark face of heaven fall directly into his eyes. He can feel the tiny impact of each one and the trickling of them down his face. He imagines them gathering into a puddle on the hard paving beneath the seat, the puddle being tinted a deeper, ever more glorious red if only there were light to see ...

Lying there he thinks then about his first - his real father's poem; the one that had been taken away from him and then given back at school after his real father had been killed, the poem he'd carried with him ever since and was now in the wallet that was in his pocket, the one that tells about the fourth-light that will not naturally fade and extinguish itself until after a person dies and that says the fading of it can last for a matter of moments or for a thousand years, or that, shining with such a truth, with such a strength, will not in any way fade so long as foot of Man shall walk upon its mother earth.

And so, which kind of light are you, MacRae?

Men, like poppies, die, so don't ask why | nor is it fair, for who's to care?

It's the end of deep cover. Of everything? Well, everything except Consuela Carravaga? Come on, Connie.

(Interval 2 months: 6th November 1991)

Dismiss

The hall porter comes back into the lounge, empty except for the two of them. "Can I bring you some more coffee?" he asks.

Colonel Grenville says, "No; thank you but no."

He hasn't asked Thomas so Thomas asserts his new independence. "Not for me, either." He can sense his Colonel's surprised relief. Time to go. Maybe today hasn't been so easy for him, either. It's never easy for anyone, firing people.

"Just the check, I think," says Grenville.

When the porter leaves Thomas sums up. "So, as of now I am formally and finally 'off the books,' if I can put it like that, sir? I must be the only twice-discharged officer in the history of the Service." He tries a laugh but there's no warmth to it and no reciprocation. "I can't say it's in any way unexpected and I'd just like to thank you for - well, for securing my gratuity, amongst other things. I was by no means sure about that."

"Yes, Thomas. Off the books and off the hook. Go and make something of yourself. The gratuity? We had a sense the money side would be pretty important to you these days."

"Since my father lost interest, you mean?"

He ignored that. "This isn't the way I hoped it would end for you, Thomas, you know that. This saying your farewells to the Service with just the two of us in some damned hotel lounge. I'm really sorry." He stands up, all six feet three inches of him ramrod straight, feet set apart, hands clasped behind his back, back to the non-existent fire. "Bit like that Greek chappie, you know; flew too near the sun once too often? At one time I had you down as a likely candidate for high office. Higher than mine, most probably."

"You flatter me, sir."

"No, I don't think so. But you're just that bit too much of a risk-taker, Thomas. Stuff of heroes and all that, but a chancer. A bit of a throw-back to Jumbo Courtney, Clogstoun-Wilmott, Stirling and so on. Our great creators. Fellows only really happy amongst the muck and bullets." He shakes his head, bends to pick up his tweed cap and his Financial Times from the coffee table. Thomas has too much respect for the older man to say anything about pots calling kettles black. "Talking of bullets," Grenville goes on, "They seem to have done quite a job on your arm. How is it?"

"It's OK, sir, thank you. Not as good as new, they tell me. But OK."

The porter returns with the check. Grenville hands him the money plus a generous tip. The man's smile switches from habitual to genuine. On the way out of the hotel Grenville murmurs, "So, your arm? how many perforations does that make, all told?"

Thomas says, "Well, the one from East Falkland was just a graze so it doesn't really count, then there's the one in my back - fairly typical for the boyos, that one, being in the back. And now this left elbow, Mister Kerrigan's gift. Nice balance, really."

"And your wife? How is she?"

"Connie's fine, sir. But I forgot to ask, did you find out anything about Kerrigan?"

"I'm not allowed to tell you. However regrettably it seems the man is alive and still kicking, thanks to your telephone call." They're out in the street now. There's a cold wind. Colonel Robert Grenville turns up his camel coat collar. He's rock faced, offers his hand. "You will keep in touch?"

"Yes, sir, I will."

"That's not a politeness, Thomas. I only say it when I mean it, understood?"

"Yes, sir."

"Good luck with your business degree. MBA course at MIT, isn't it?"

"Yes."

"Good choice. I gave them a fine reference, you know. No mention of the last few years, of course. We've been out of touch for a while, yes?"

"Of course. I've had my security cleansing, you know that."

"Yes … well, you'll like it in the USA for a couple of years, away from - from all this with your new wife and all. I expect, after that, you'll be planning to mend fences, join forces with your father at Amalgamated?"

"No sir. I'll do my best with the mending but not with the joining. Thank you for your good wishes though." The Colonel looks as if he wants to say something else but he doesn't, only, "Goodbye then, my boy." They shake hands. The Colonel shakes his head.

Thomas goes back inside, back into the warm. Connie's coming in to join him for lunch, Bradley Scott as well if he can get away. *Captain* Bradley Scott now. He remembers their first meeting, both of them raw recruits waiting for transport at the railway station. It's not been easy, keeping his closest friend in the dark about so much, so much of the time. He checks his watch; another half an hour. He sits up at the otherwise deserted public bar, presses the button for service. When the hall porter appears he gets himself a large Lagavulin with very little water. It's a bit early for the strong stuff but what the hell. When the man's gone back about his business Thomas toasts his own image in the behind-bar mirror, "Here's to freedom, the civilian life and the big wide world," he murmurs. Right now the big wide world seems to be quite a lonely place, Mister Thomas Thornton, he thinks, even more lonely and in some ways even more dangerous than those other ones, gone by.

(Interval 2 years: 7th December 1993)
Bradley, Connie, Rose Feather

Good old Brad. Right on time. By the time Thomas has bought the drinks back to the table he and his Rose are deep in conversation with Connie.

He looks up, having to speak up to make himself heard; "So how's it going, Thomas?"

"Fine," he says, "It's going just fine."

"How's the arm?" Rose asks.

"This? I don't think about it much. Doesn't do much in the way of bending but apart from that ..." He sits down, picks up his pint with his right hand. "So, folks, you're having a good day?" He grins, takes a drink. "See, I've even picked up the language. Everything's always just fine in the USA. Right, Mrs Thornton?" Connie smiles happily, first at him and then at his friends. She looks great in the black trouser suit, shiny black hair halfway down her back; impossibly fresh and young for a mother, really. He says, "We stayed here because we wanted David to see his very first Christmas tree in the UK rather than in Boston. So, how's everything with you two?"

"Big news here," Brad says, "Is that I hung up my Service boots and the Colonel's asked me to work for him. You heard they pensioned him off ? He's now International Trading Group, aka ITG, one of the dreaded arms dealers?"

"Yes, I did hear. Ben Benedict gives me the updates. Ben's based himself down in Portsmouth, got himself a nice little charter fishing business. But the old man seems to be doing pretty well. Mind you, he's picked himself a boom market. Lots of shooting going on all over the place. And according to Ben he's turned his hobby with those roses into a nice little earner, as well. Talk about age shall not weary them!" He smiles at the other rose, the one alongside Brad. The girl woman that some would think even more beautiful than Connie. Honey brown skin, black, cropped close hair. She's wearing a pale blue trouser suit with a high collared white shirt open to show off one of those long, African, incredibly feminine necks. "And you, Rose?" he asks. "How are you?" He takes another swallow of beer.

"Oh, I'm never going to make World Champion but I'm still playing, still winning some of the money some of the time."

"They want her out in the States," Brad says. "Want my girl to go on the pro pool circuit."

"No way," Rose says. "I'm having too much fun here with my snooker and my very own ex-soldier boy."

The hotel music system is primed with Christmas carols to go with the decorations and the splendid tree over in the corner. An office party joins in with *The First Noel*, singing it very badly. Thomas laughs, picks up on the words. "I don't know about, 'when the angels do sing'! But hey, when I finally get my degree I'll be knocking on your door for a job, Mister Scott, sir."

"Don't joke: Why the hell not?"

"We'll see ... Dare I ask what's up with the Service, these days?"

"How's that?"

"Well, Ben tells me the boys seems to be leaving, wholesale."

"There's nothing too dramatic. Bit of confusion I suppose. Nobody ever seems to know if we're going to go on as we are or get merged - 'submerged,' if you listen to the Hereford lot. That means a bit of unrest. And would you believe, British Special Forces bodyguards are the latest celebrity accoutrement, specially in the USA. They all seem to want one. Whether or not they actually need one is quite another matter. SAS preferred, naturally, but SBS is fine if you say it quickly." He smiles that sudden boyish smile of his.

Later on, upstairs in his and Connie's room, lying naked in the dark, hearing the light and even breathing of their baby son, his wife whispers, "You are a hot boy tonight, Mister Thornton. I can feel how hot you are. But I am thinking of the way you look at your friend's girl. You are a stallion to need so many mares, even she of your friend? What is this?"

He says, "Darling girl, don't be a silly. Just concentrate on what we're doing here, OK?"

The fingers of Connie's other hand are playing with the hairs on his chest. "This girl, Rose, she is more interesting in your friend than in all you other men so I am happy," she says. "Now, you have to tell me how much you are loving me, yes? But not the dirty talking, yes? I like good things. I am not a tough player of men's business games, as are some other ladies."

"How good is this then," he says, "And this, for a man with a bad arm? And how is that for saying how much I love you, Consuela Thornton? And how are you with these of yours? I am very happy with them and to love them and just to feel them and sometimes they - you - make me want to die."

"Kiss them, I command you this, sir …yes; oh yes, that. Yes."

As he begins to go to sleep Connie murmurs, "I do not think Rose could do such things, Thomaso. Perhaps the hot blood of Africa has been cooled by your cold and lovely England."

"Yes, perhaps," he says, then, as he says every night, "Sleep in peace; I love you, wife. Tomorrow I shall introduce you and our little David to my family." For some time he lies awake, simulating the breathing of a man asleep, thinking about his sisters and their mother, his auntie but adopted mother, and about her husband, his uncle but adopted father who knows of the Carravagas and who has told him that he would prefer not to meet with his adopted son's new wife.

Pain, so much pain: why is it that Thomas Thornton attracts pain? he wonders. Perhaps just as a magnet attracts shrapnel.

(Interval 2 years and 9 months: 4th September 1996)
Sheikh Abdul-Rahman Bin Sulaiman Al-Sottar

A full moon silvers its shivering pathway across the surface of the water. "You'll take another of those, Thomas?" Abdul-Rahman nods at his bottle of beer.

Thomas shrugs. "Guess one more won't hurt. Thanks very much." It is so pleasant on the beach here at this time of night.

Abdul-Rahman is knocking back the Black Label. "Joey," he shouts, and the diminutive Philipino comes quickly. "More beer for Mister Thomas. And the Black Label here."

The sheikh asks him a few questions more about his time in the States and his business degree. But he doesn't seem too much interested in history, not at all in his two years at Falmouth Maritime or in what went wrong with the steel cans job or selling hardwoods in Ireland. Not even about what he'd been up to before that. Thomas is beginning to wonder whether he's even read the recruitment agency's report. The guy seems OK, though. Very OK, really. Bit overweight but nice looking with his Viva Zapata facial hair. He's bright, for sure, about his own age, dressed western casual in shorts and sandals, T-shirt, baseball cap. Thomas breathes in a lungful of warm, water-logged air with its mixed up scents of tropical flowers, salt sea-weed and something hot and spicy being cooked inside the house. House! More like a mansion really - literally fantastic. Arabic music warbles out at low volume. Best go easy on the beers.

Abdul-Rahman says, "You would like to take a walk along the beach? You will not need your shoes." Thomas takes off his shoes and socks. Replenishments in hand, the two of them stroll down to the edge of the sea, the caked fine sand of the beach still hot, creaking like snow beneath the soles of their feet. Abdul-Rahman stares out across the Arabian Gulf. Or Persian Gulf as it was once known. "Is this not beautiful?" He turns to Thomas, raises his glass. "As you say it: Cheers, Mister Thomas, and welcome to The Kingdom of Saudi Arabia. Your return flight, it is later this week I believe?"

"Thursday night; I'd like to take a look around Al-Khobar whilst I'm here, if that's OK. Of course, irrespective of whether or not I get a job offer."

"Job offer? You are already General Manager of Al-Sottar Marine, Mister Thomas, if such is what you want. I shall cancel the visits of other candidates. Therefore in this way, by accepting, you will have made your first contribution to saving my company's finances." He looks at Thomas, deadpan.

Thomas has to think this all too easy but, whatever a gift horse is, he's not about to look into its mouth. "Thank you," he says. "This is the best interview I remember having. Talking about finance, sheikh, the terms are negotiable I believe?"

"Abdul-Rahman, Thomas. I leave all such matters to Joshi. In the morning Joshi will collect you from your hotel. He will show you around the area and also some choices of accommodations. He will also show you some schools, although as I remember it your son David is now only three years and Paul, not yet two?"

Thomas nods. The man has, after all, done some homework. The two of you are now walking on wet sand inside the tide-line. He says, "You have very good English, Sheikh."

"Abdul-Rahman, please. Newcastle-upon-Tyne. Geordie English, yes? My father sent me to this place in England of which he had not heard. He had heard of nowhere in your country except London and he wished to protect me from trouble of the wine, women and song variety. But your Geordie-land, it was wonderful for a young man." He laughs, makes a crude gesture with his forearm and fist. "I did not much singing, but the wine and the women - like a fish and a rabbit, man! You like girls, my friend?"

Nobody had ever asked Thomas that one before. "In the singular," he replies. "One's enough for me these days." Quick to change the subject, "Tell me, Abdul-Rahman, how do you see the political situation to the north?"

Abdul-Rahman stops walking, takes a big swallow of his whisky. "We do not talk about politics except amongst our friends. But we are now friends, Thomas, I am right?" Thomas nods. Abdul-Rahman goes on. "That conflict, the one they called Desert Storm, it ended five years ago." Thomas nods again. "According to what I have read you were in the British military at that time. You took part in this so-called 'war'?"

Thomas says, "I'm sorry, but as I told your agency people in London I'm still bound by the UK's Official Secrets Act."

Abdul-Rahman sighs. "Of course. Forgive me for asking but it is no matter. Tell me this, you acquired no Arabic language at that time?"

"Unfortunately not, no." He has no trouble with the direct lie. So much practice and the language thing is the business of that other life. Besides, it could become a positive advantage out here, no-one knowing he can understand what's being said.

"You ask about my views as to the political situation." Out in the darkness but close in to shore a fish has double splashed. As they recommence their walk Abdul-Rahman goes on, "It took Arabia one thousand years to rid itself of the Hashemites from the north, my friend. What do your people think is five years to the leadership to the north that is humiliated but intact; unbeaten in its own eyes and the eyes of most Arabs?"

Thomas takes a swallow from his can of beer, saying nothing.

"Enough of such things," says Abdul-Rahman. The guy really does have the greatest smile. "You will come here to Saudi Arabia and make yourself a bright new life with me, and you shall become wealthy if that is what you deserve and what you desire. And when you have succeeded in this you will be able to go home and sit as an equal with your father, the estimable Mister Christopher Thornton, with whom I am told you do not now enjoy the best of relationships. But your can is empty. Therefore, Thomas, let us go back and find you another one."

Oh yes, thinks Thomas, this man knows just what he's doing. But that's OK. He only hopes Connie and the boys are going to like it here.

(Interval a year and 7 months: April 17, 1998)

The beach party

None of the buggers are going to go home in a hurry. He takes a surreptitious look at his watch. One o clock. Connie's going to be bloody furious; he'll definitely have to make a move soon. It's been a good evening but apart from anything else it's quite cold now, sitting outside with all these world class talkers. They'd been using English in polite deference to himself; using the Arabic only for their asides to each other. And Thomas of course had found the asides more interesting than the mainstream conversation.

Mumtaz Kaloumi concludes the point he's been making and the banker, Ali someone, responds with a trite, "Money is like good health, my friend. It is never a problem until you do not have it. But you would rather not have money than not have good health, I think." There is a murmur of general agreement. The man goes on, "But myself, I would like to hear some singing. My friend Abdul-Rahman tells me you have a good voice and a good memory for Frank Sinatra, Thomas. This is so?"

Oh, no. "Thank you for that," he says, "But don't mention me in the same breath as old blue eyes. I would just hate to ruin a pleasant evening."

Abdul-Rahman shouts, "Joey". The Philipino servant appears as if by magic. "Bring Mister Thomas the microphone." He leans forwards. "But before that, let me ask you something else that is serious, my friend. In our lifetime, what have been the two great competing influences in the West? There is capitalism and there is communism, am I right?"

"Yes, I guess so," Thomas says. He wonders where his employer is going with this.

Abdul-Rahman says, "Yet one of these great competing concepts, this - what you call it - this philosophy of communism, where is it right now? Gone, finished, from one day to the next, caputo. Therefore capitalism is the winner?"

"So it would seem," Thomas says, cautiously, "Although politics and philosophy really aren't my subjects."

"That, my friend, is what you would call a cop-out. Listen to me now; this demise of communism, you saw it coming?"

"No of course not, Nobody did. Nobody I know of, anyway."

"Exactly. And you cannot see now the demise of capitalism?"

"Come on, Abdul-Rahman," he says, "You might as well say the demise of everything."

"Exactly, my friend. Every *thing*! But more important for us than *things*, than wealth, is the life of the spirit, of God. This - this is the difference. Our lives here are, let us say, eighty percent spiritual and twenty percent material. You of the west are the other way around." The sheikh looks around at the bearded faces of his big-money friends. "Nothing is forever, we know this to be true. And when capitalism passes away, as did communism, what will be left for you and what for us, Thomas? What will be left for we of ancient, Arab descent who are neither east nor west, we for whom your capitalism is just a temporary tool, we the people from amongst whom God has always chosen his prophets?" There is a silence whilst Joey refills the whiskies and hands you a microphone, its lead trailing across the marble patio floor and back inside the house.

Thomas says, "You talk of the future, Abdul-Rahman, and you may be right. But I would like to propose another toast, gentlemen." He lifts his re-charged tumbler. "Here's to life here and now and to all the good things of this wonderful world." The five Arabs raise their glasses, nodding their approval, murmuring endorsements. Thomas blows experimentally into the microphone, goes into the first lines; ..."Start singing the blues, I'm going today... " He's unsure of the exact words but hell, what does it matter? Soon enough, he passes on the microphone. Most people know some of the song and can even hold the tune a little, but he's trying to overhear what Mumtaz is saying to Abdul-Rahman on the side. He's speaking in Arabic. Mumtaz is saying, "You are sure your Englishman has no Arabic, Abdul-Rahman?"

Abdul-Rahman shakes his head, says something indistinguishable as the big banker, yet another Mohammad some-one, starts out in a big baritone; "New York, New York ..."

"I assume you will not be bringing the girls or any further recreation whilst he is still here?" continues this Mumtaz.

Abdul-Rahman says, "No, of course not. But he will go home soon to his wife, and for that he is lucky for she is a beautiful woman."

Ziad the investor joins in then; "But yes, I like this English. He sings very well and he is a man of intelligence. But he is, I think, a man who it is best not to underestimate."

Thomas wonders about the reference to girls. What happens here after he's left them to it? He takes back the mike, sings, "I'm king of the hill, top of the heap..." Everyone here seems happy. What the hell does it matter?

(Interval a year and 11 months: Thursday 16th March 2000)
Looks Like Trouble

"Oh boy, what a horse! 'Looks like Trouble'? Funny old name but no bloody trouble from where I was standing." Thomas has to half shout above all the craic in the downtown Cheltenham pub.

"Damn silly name for a horse," Kit says. "How much did you make anyway?"

The leader of the Irish brigade whose table they're sharing, this Jack, he says, "God, no. Bad luck to ask your friend **a** question like that." The accent is pure Dublin Irish.

Thomas says, "Quite right." With others listening he can't talk about the old days, the shared times wherever they both were, which was

32

often wherever the shooting was. Just as well, really. He can feel the alcohol and the night yet young. "But plenty enough to cover dinner and drinks tonight. How much did you lose, I might equally ask, my friend, but I won't."

"A bit more than I can afford," Kit says. "Anne's going to be a bit pissed off with me when she gets into our March numbers."

"Anne does Sea Fibres' books? I'm impressed, Kit."

"Sea Fibres? Good God, no. Not that it's a bad idea, another salary coming in and all that. No, I'm talking about our domestics. Anne watches our pennies and ha'pennies like Ebeneezer Scrooge. Unfortunately they do need watching. Nobody's getting rich out of Sea Fibres Limited." He laughs. "They're not bloody going to, either, not at the prices you're forcing me to sell at."

"It's no bad deal and you know it. I only wish I could sell the buggers to the Saudis as easily as Abdul-Rahman likes me to order them. Well, it's his money, plenty more of it where this lot's coming from. Cheers." He raises his pint glass. Kit raises his own and so do the Irish, who've been listening with interest.

"You and your boss are gentlemen and scholars, both. Thanks. Hey! I keep seeing the bottom of this bloody glass. I think it must be leaking. Not bad here, is it? So what you having?

Thomas shouts, "No, my turn. All ready for a refill, gentlemen?" Lovely, the way in which the glasses so rapidly empty. Everyone loves a winner, wants to help him spend his winnings. Assisted by his new friend, the Dubliner, Jack, he pushes way through to the bar carrying the six empties, tries to catch the barmaid's eye. Whilst they're waiting he says, "I'm sorry Jack, but I didn't get all your names?"

Jack says, "The one with the shiny head, he's Paddy, what else would he be, now? The big fella's Michael and the one sitting next to him, the quiet one, that's Rory McMahon. Jesus - the only Irish man in Cheltenham tonight who's admitting to backing a British horse against The Pearl for the Gold Cup, and the bugger only goes and wins on it! I'll stay with you here, for the carrying."

The blonde with the name-tag 'Lucy' pinned to her bosom darts over, raising her eyebrows, pushing a stray lock of hair back in place. Thomas says. "I'll take four pints of the Guinness please, Lucy, and one in the till for yourself."

"Thank you," says Lucy, two fresh glasses already under the taps. She bends for two more.

Jack says, "Pretty girl, so she is. Lucky Lucy. And I think you caught her eye in more ways than just for the Guinness. You've been to Dublin, yourself, I'll be thinking?"

"Oh yes," he says. "Years ago. On business."

"Right. And you used to go to Brian's bar, down there on the Liffey?"

Suddenly he hears the warning bells. Shit. "Just now and then," he says. He takes the top foam from the first of the new pints to hit the bar-top. "That's the only thing about Guinness," he says, trying the deflection. "It takes so long to get it."

Jack says, "You were doing some writing, I think? And singing, you were a damn good singer. It was the singing I remembered. A salesman and writer from the north with the poetry and the songs of the Republic and the voice of Gabriel at the drink. You're not easy to forget. What happened, my friend? I can't remember - you didn't say your names, now?"

"My friend is Kit and I'm Thomas, Tom, Tommy, whatever you like. What happened? Oh, just the usual. Family, career, all that stuff." He hands the notes across the bartop. "Keep what's left of it, Lucy."

"Sure and ye've more English in that voice than the Irish, now. You are a regular here in Cheltenham Spa, Thomas?"

"No, I live in Saudi Arabia. Just here on a business trip." He had almost to shout above the hubbub.

Back at the table Michael lifts his glass in a toast. "Here's to the winner and to Florida Pearl, you beauty. Second home today and no disgrace, but the first horse of Ireland, so ye are."

Jack says, "And to John MacRae here, whose 'Sweet Sixteen' shall bring tears to the eyes of Hard Hearted Hannah herself."

Very sober now, Thomas says, "No, Thornton; Thomas Thornton, Jack. I'm not called MacRae."

Jack puts down his glass, looks up, straight and slow, says, "'The Fields Of Athenry' will it be then, Thomas?"

Later on, in the toilet with Kit, pissing in adjacent stalls, Thomas says, "That was a close one. I could hardly deny about Brian's Bar. But they'll all have forgotten it by tomorrow. Anyway, we're talking ancient history now. We're all of us ancient history, right? My God, Kit," he says, "I can't remember when I had so much fun."

Kit says, "You have to loosen up sometimes, hard man. Bloody glad you still can."

Outside, under the awning of the hotel, he tries the number for the fourth or fifth time. The rain's still sheeting down. England must be floating. He imagines the heat bouncing off the wide roads and the blue swimming pools of Khobar.

"Consuela Thornton." There's loud music behind her voice.

"Connie! Thank God for that. I've been calling, leaving you messages. What's happening?"

"Nothing is happening. Just as always happens," she says. "I not understand this message thing, Thomas."

Calling him Thomas is never a good sign. If she's feeling good in herself or good about him it would be Thomaso, wouldn't it? But she's definitely been drinking. He can hear it in her voice, in the way her English has lapsed a little. There's no warmth and there should be after almost ten days away. He changes tack. "How're the boys?"

"The boys are out around the pool."

"Isn't it a bit late for that, with school tomorrow?"

"They are with their friends," she says, as if that excuses it. He takes a deep breath. "Right. So how are you, Connie?" But her music is too loud. "Please will you turn down the volume a bit?"

"Where you are, Thomas?"

"Me? I'm trying to keep out of the rain, standing outside my hotel in Southampton, missing you and David and Paul, Connie; that's where I am. Tomorrow I finish the business with Sea Fibres and then I take the train up to London. I have a meeting with our Agency people. I'm meeting Brad for a drink in the evening before flying back on the overnight. You have my schedule – "

She interrupts, "And your friend's lady, Rose? She will be there also?" She hasn't responded on turning down the music; something wildly South American.

"I don't know," he says, and that is the truth.

"I do not like this Rose."

"For Christ's sake, Connie, are you pissed or something?" A taxi has pulled in under the awning to discharge its passengers. "Hold on, please," he says, "I can't hear myself think." Alone again he puts the phone back to his ear, says, "It's OK now, they've gone. Please understand Connie, I do love you." He waits for a response but there is only this silence. "Whatever the problems are, the two of us can sort them, OK? We'll have a really good talk when I get back, yes?" More

35

silence. "Connie? Connie? You still there? Connie?" He waits a little longer before switching off the mobile and going back into the hotel lobby.

The hall porter says, "Everything all right, sir? Can I help you?"

"No thanks," he says. He walks to the elevator, murmuring sotto voce, "Not unless your name starts with G and ends in D, you can't help me."

"I'm sorry, sir?"

The guy must have bloody good ears. "Nothing," he says.

(Interval - the next day: Thursday June 21st 2001)
One for the road

Brad says, "You've a bit more time yet. What you going to do, go out by tube?"

"Yes. Heathrow calls," he says, "And if you gotta go you just gotta go."

Right out of the blue Rose says, "Tell me, Thomas, are you and Connie happy living in Saudi Arabia?"

"The job comes first, alongside what's best for the family. But expat life in Saudi is in no way difficult. Not once you get to know the rules of the game. Just the opposite in fact. Nice living quarters, wall to wall sunshine, no taxes, no crime worth speaking of. And there's nothing like the stress levels of an equivalent job here in the UK. All in all, life in The Kingdom has a lot going for it."

Rose smiles at him. "If I were a judge in court I'd say, 'please answer the question,' Mister Thornton, wouldn't I?"

"I thought I had," he says, even though he knows he hasn't. He switches it around. "How about you? How content are you two with Old London Town?" Brad says, "Well, speaking for myself, on the business front everything looks to be set very fair. Colonel Grenville lets me get on with my own thing, lots of opportunities, some of them abroad. Domestically speaking, of course I'm the original happy man. Not that it wouldn't be nicer if my lady would spend less time at the snooker table." He turns to her. "Actually we've offered you a job with us, haven't we dearest?" Rose says, "Yes you have, but I already have a job, dearest. Excuse me, I'm off to find the loo." She stands up, smoothing her skirt, plotting her route. Christ, what a figure, Thomas thinks. "I won't be a minute," she says, going off, smiling to left and right; everyone making way.

Brad says, "Why don't we just have one for the road?"

"To hell with it, why not? I'm driving nowhere." The Fureys are on the pub's music system, turned up high volume: *The Red Rose Café*. The song's all about people drinking in a dockside bar in Amsterdam. Thomas knows all the words to this one.

Now they're alone Brad says, "I won't ask any more about life at home, but I sense all may not be perfect. If you want to talk about anything, fine. You know me - world class listener; excellent doer by special request." The two of them get to their feet, head for the bar.

Finding space at the bar, Thomas says, "I hear you. Maybe we'll speak on the phone in a day or so. But you're a lucky bugger, Bradley Scott." He smacks the bar-top and when the barman looks up he smiles and says, "Two more pints please, whenever you're ready. And a white wine spritzer with lots of ice." Brad had seen it so easily. He says, "I may need a job back here soon, if you should hear of anything going. Things aren't working out quite as I'd hoped on the business front. And yes, you're right, Connie's getting pretty fed up - with Saudi or with me, I don't know which. Hey, how many have we had? It's too much, all this laying bare of one's soul in some strange pub."

"Modern tribality, Thomas, that's what it is. In the English pub I mean. In vino bloody veritas. Everybody talks. Just be here and be happy and you don't even have to look happy. Furthermore you can leave and rejoin the tribe any damn old time you like. Lovely. You don't get too much of that where you're heading, do you?" He punches his friend playfully on the shoulder. Instinctively Thomas turns to shield the bad arm. "Sorry. Myself," Bradley says, "I'm just off for a pee." He pushes his way through the throng just before Rose returns. He hands her the fresh drink.

"What happened to Brad?"

"Off to the gents. Cheers. You know, it's been great, being with you tonight." He hesitates, takes a long swallow of his beer. "I'll miss all this. I'll miss you too, Rose."

"You will? I know. Me too"

"Yes?"

"Of course. But we move on with things, like always. We wouldn't want to change anything, would we." It wasn't a question. She smiles as they clink glasses. He has to avoid her eyes now, has to stop wanting to touch her hair and her face, has to blank off. As soon as his friend returns to the table Thomas drains his pint glass, stands up to say goodbye. There's the strong handshake from Brad and the soft touch of a kiss on the cheek from Rose and there's a final waving of hands as he goes out alone into the small rain; into London's bright-lit night.

More Deaths Than One

Chapter One

He dodged his way through the crowd, looking out for the shortest immigration queue. Fajr prayers were sounding out, the marble floors and high pillared walls of the airport building echoing with the dawn chorus of Islam; half chant, half song, one cohesive whole stepping easily up and down the scales. He imagined the thousands of other Qu'aranic chantings relaying their way across the sun-burned sands of Arabia as the darkness rolled away this one more time.

There were just sixteen lining up ahead of him. Five minutes at the desk for each one if you were lucky, then it's a limo to the compound.

The bigger the beard the more Islamic the wearer, or so they said, and this particular immigration officer's was really impressive, untrimmed in the way of the Wahabbi. The man glanced up at him, jet-stone eyes without expression, then down to his keyboard. He tapped some more into his computer, looked up again. "Your name?" Thomas' passport was on the desk, wide open.

"Thornton: Thomas John Thornton." He tried another smile. No good. The man tapped some more on his keyboard then picked up the telephone, muttering the rhythmic syllables so quietly that Thomas couldn't make out any of the Arabic. Not that he would reveal his knowledge of it; long practice at that. Now the double thump of official stampings and he had once again been permitted to enter into the Kingdom of Saudi Arabia.

His suitcase was already through and off the carousel and he'd picked it up and moved off towards the queue for Customs inspection when the uniformed policeman stopped him in his tracks, gesturing off to one side, the bearded face also without expression. "You come," the man instructed. Some of Thomas' fellow passengers stopped to observe the scenario, brown faces anxious to know as much as possible about a stranger's predicament, especially when the stranger was a Westerner.

"Come? What for?" Thomas asked.

"You will come with me," repeated the policeman.

He shrugged, followed on into an office off the main concourse. Some kind of random check? A green overalled worker had come in, a tiny man but able to pick up his case with surprising ease.

"You will come with me," repeated the policeman, adding, to the worker, "And this other, also."

Thomas handed over his shoulder bag with it's laptop. Alone now, he thought over the possibilities. Something wrong down at the yard? Some irregularity with his visa? He shook his head, took out his mobile, watched as it picked up the familiar Al Jawwad server. He dialled the compound then pressed in his extension number, glanced at his watch: six thirty. The answer message kicked in: 'This is Mrs Consuela Thornton. There's nobody ...' He pressed the off button; Connie would most likely be in the shower and the boys wouldn't hear anything much quieter than a nuclear explosion on a sleep-in Friday.

"Your passport, Mr Thornton?" There were two of them, one standing respectfully just behind the other, both of them wearing pristine white thobes with the familiar, red and white checked, black banded head gutras. The speaker's face was unfurnished by beard, only the mandatory moustache, this one small and neatly tended. Fortyish? Around his own age, anyway; light-skinned, nice looking in that classic, hawk-nosed way.

"My passport? Sure, but can you tell me why?" His questions hung unanswered in the air. The hand was still outstretched. Reluctantly he took out his passport and handed it over, vaguely reassured by the glint of its gold embossed royal coat of arms.

"Thank you Mr Thornton, please sit." He did as he had been told. His mouth had dried up. He knew himself not to be looking his best. Last night's beer in London; red wine and little sleep on the plane.

The lead guy slipped the passport into his breast pocket. "You are Thomas Thornton, resident here at Al-Mhoubi compound, villa two six three?"

Thomas did his best to irrigate his mouth and throat. "Yes, that is correct. Might I ask who you are? And again, why I'm here?"

The second Saudi said, "We are police officers, Mister Thornton. Captain Mohammed Al-Muttawi is a senior police officer."

Ignoring the exchange Al-Muttawi asked, "You are the general manager of the company Al-Sottar Marine?"

"Indeed I am," Thomas said, "So what's the problem? Some kind of an accident?"

"I shall explain, Mr Thornton. But first you will understand that I have to be sure of the information in my possession. We have noted

40

your degree in business studies and prior to that your career with the British Military. This is correct?"

"My ... ? Well yes; but so what?" What the hell was all this about - all this ancient history? Al-Muttawi waited in silence. Thomas went on, "You will probably understand, Captain, that I cannot comment on my military background; especially as I haven't had any contact with it for the past seven years." It was becoming ever more difficult to keep traces of sarcasm and anger out of his voice.

The desk telephone rang. Al-Muttawi picked up, listened intently, saying nothing until the murmured "Shukhran" and the replacement of the instrument. He stood. "I think it would be more comfortable, Captain Thornton, to pursue our discussions elsewhere. Please come with me. We shall bring your baggage." The original uniformed policeman had returned, had taken up station by Thomas's side.

Coming from nowhere it was there, in his head; training manual, Code X -010; *Display no fear but do not denigrate nor attempt in any way to dominate your temporarily more powerful adversary,* the book had instructed.

He said, "Look, before I go anywhere I need to call my wife, is that OK?" He took out his mobile. "I'm also going to speak with my sponsor." Pressing in the auto key for his home he murmured, "You will know of Sheikh Abdul-Rahman Al-Sottar?" He glanced up. Nothing, no reaction. This was wrong; 'Emergency call only' had appeared in the mobile's window. He tried once more with the same result. A coldness had enveloped him. He cleared his throat. "My mobile seems to be out of order. May I please use your telephone?"

The flat denial. "No, Mister Thornton, you may not."

Inside the down town police station they walked in single file to a room with an Arabic language 'Interrogation' plaque on its door. The room was badly furnished with worn leather armchairs, ancient carpets, the inevitable out of date portraits of the ruling triumvirate. There was a background whiff of spiced foods and bad sewerage, familiar to those who knew this, oldest part of the city. A wall mounted air conditioning unit creaked, clattered and moaned. Two more uniformed men had joined the party. God, but he was so tired of all this; a dishevelled British so-called businessman; and alien in every sense.

From behind the desk the senior man said, "You are aware that I am Police Captain Mohammed Al-Muttawi. How do you wish me to address you, Captain?" The emphasis was very much on the last word.

It occurred to Thomas that the proceedings were being recorded. "Mister. *Mister* Thornton will do well enough for me, Captain Al-Muttawi." He tried to lighten things. "Perhaps it will save confusion, yes?" Nothing. No reaction. "As I think I said, my service career is an irrelevant piece of history."

Al-Muttawi gestured around the room. "We are here to conduct an investigation into certain allegations concerning your importation into the Kingdom of prohibited substances." The air conditioning had clanked to a temporary halt and now the silence was absolute. Thomas looked at the policeman, conscious that he'd opened his mouth but having not the words. What materials? Who the hell had 'informed' them about exactly what? He shook his head. "I do not know what on earth you're talking about but I do think we had better get in touch with my sponsor, and right now."

"No, Mister Thornton, you may think this but I do not. Sheikh Abdul-Rahman is aware of these proceedings. You will please tell me how must we interpret your lack of response to the stated allegations." He glanced up at the ceiling. Thomas followed his eyes, noticed the CCTV camera.

"As a total denial, Captain. You can interpret it as a total denial. I have done no such thing and I must formally demand to see the British Consul. I ask you again, may I please use your telephone?" Prohibited substances? Drugs? He remembered the line of red italics across the top of the landing card; 'Death to drugs dealers'; plain and simple.

"And I have told you once; you may ask or demand nothing," Al-Muttawi's voice may have risen an octave. "You may make requests only after you have been charged. You are not yet charged." Unexpectedly the perfect lips below the perfect moustache twitched. "But we might find it not easy to locate anybody to talk with at your British Embassy. No doubt, this being the day to rest, those in your Embassy who have left the comfort of their beds will at this hour be nursing their - what you say, their hangovers? But I am still wondering, Mister Thornton, why do you not ask me something of the stated allegations? This we must find surprising."

Thomas felt the prickly break out of sweat from his forehead. More of it was trickling down his chest, down his sides. The air conditioning clanked and roared into a new bout of ineffectual action. He cleared his throat, "Because the allegations are absurd, officer. You are making a very serious mistake here." The voice was not quite his own. "Might I please have some water?"

42

"Later." Al Muttawi sighed heavily, consulted his notes, looked up again. "The allegations I have referred to are that you have arranged with your European business contacts for the illegal importation into the Kingdom of Saudi Arabia of substantial quantities of a prohibited substance, and that you have been selling this substance to citizens of the Kingdom of Saudi Arabia for personal gain."

Thomas stood up quickly, five of them at once following suit, only Al-Muttawi remaining seated. He spoke more loudly than he had intended. "This is absolutely ridiculous. Look, I am a businessman with no record, here or anywhere else, of anything such as you have indicated. I came to this country five years ago, contracted as General Manager of Al-Sottar Marine. Actually I can say that I detest drugs - prohibited substances as you call them. I'm well aware of just what they can do to some people, Captain."

"Kindly be seated, Mister Thornton. My colleagues might interpret your attitude as threatening." The policeman sat forward. "I believe your wife's family name was Carravaga, was it not?"

"Yes. So what?"

"So the connection between the family Carravaga and the drug, cocaine is evident to all the policemen of the world, Mister Thornton. You think us ignorant?" He looked and sounded almost pleased, nodded to the side. One of the five men carefully placed a clear plastic bag on the desk, visible inside, a familiar brand of talcum powder. "This, I believe, belongs to you." He looked up at the camera, speaking in Arabic now. "This item which is one plastic container of perfumed talcum powder was removed from Mister Thornton's baggage, as signed and witnessed."

Even after all this time out here Thomas remembered just in time: no Arabic. He shrugged. The talc was his brand for sure. Rivers of sweat had dried cold on his skin. He said, "It could be mine, I guess. But once again I have to ask you, Captain, so what?"

Al-Muttawi put on a pair of surgical gloves. "We must of course leave undisturbed your fingerprints." Opening the bag and removing the protective cap he unscrewed the sprinkle top and then inserted his forefinger inside the container. Carefully he pulled out a small square of tape that seemed to have been used to affix a cotton thread inside the neck. The thread now hung suspended from between his finger and thumb, at its end a bulbous screw of talc dusted plastic film. "Enough for several of what I think you would call 'lines', Mister Thornton, yes? A small sample, no doubt. Enough for your personal use and of course completely invisible to our X-rays; also undetectable by European sniffer dogs behind the perfume. Very smart, but not very original, I am afraid."

Thomas shook his head. "Look, this is some kind of a nightmare. If what you say is true then I've been well and truly set up. I know absolutely nothing about any of it."

Al-Muttawi stood up. "You please rise."

Thomas got to his feet, the fear and the anger now balled up in his stomach, his mind bursting with unanswerable questions.

"Mister Thomas Thornton I am now formally arresting you. In accordance with the law you will be held pending the completion of my investigations. Materials will be provided for you to write a statement responding to the allegations that have been made." Thomas sensed the satisfaction of the silent group of watchers. "In your statement, if you are going to confess to the charge. In the circumstances you would be advised. You will find it to your benefit to name your accomplices; also those you sold the prohibited material." He turned and made to leave the room. "That is all for this time."

Desperately, Thomas said, "I need to call my wife and my sponsor and they will need to get me a lawyer. Right now, please."

Al-Muttawi turned back to face him. "No Mr Thornton, this is not permitted. This, as a resident in The Kingdom I am sure you know." He spoke now with a kind of weary patience. "The law is that you will be allowed no outside contact until our investigation, it is finish. None at all may you talk with. Not any family or friend or employer and no consul. No lawyer. To an intelligent man the logic of this is surely clear. 'Covering your tracks'. Is this not your expression? Of course I have taken the action to disconnect your mobile telephone service."

Thomas said, "My God. And how long is this investigation of yours going to take?"

"I do not think very long. Already I have worked on your case for more than one week." He shook his head. "Mister Thornton, also please know that it may be usual in your country, but we here in The Kingdom find blasphemy greatly of offence. That is all."

The five guards with him in the van were totally uncommunicative; They moved slowly through downtown streets already crowded with cars ancient and modern, slow moving and double parked, and with men in Saudi thobes, white ranging through downright filthy, or with smaller men in all the colourful dresses of the sub-continent, milling round, overflowing the pavements on this Friday, their Holy day and therefore free of work. The police van inched along its way, its horn adding to the general cacophony. Near the Corniche the crowd had thickened. People completely blocked the roadway. The police van needed to barge its way through before coming to a full stop, becoming a part of the now still and silent throng surrounding a space kept open and clear by uniformed policemen. Standing alone in the space was just this one black-African Saudi. Thomas knew at once what this was. The driver switched off his engine, rolled down the windows, letting in a billow of superheated, super-humid, drainpipe air. Thomas was aware of the faces, their excitement. But then … Hector? Hector Comancho? The little Philipino foreman, shackled and held between two policemen, stared up at him through the van window, his face a tragedy of pale and helpless desperation. Still not properly able to accept what he was seeing, Thomas could only watch as Hector was led out towards the man with the curved sword, point down on the paving.

Tears now mixed with the beaded sweat that coursed down Hector's face. For a moment forgetting everything except this, Thomas shouted to no-one and to everyone, "What the hell's going on here?" but he knew now, full well he knew. "What the hell do you think you're doing?" His shout reverberated as an obscenity within a silence disturbed only by the blaring of distant motor horns.

Those who had turned to look at the shouter returned quickly to their observation of the tableau in the square, anxious to miss nothing. In truth there was not much to see, not much to miss. Hector was forced down to kneel in front of his executioner. Just for a moment he looked again directly at Thomas, his face a mask with such a depth of hopelessness, and then a policeman's stick between the shoulder blades had encouraged him to bend low and the expressionless black faced Saudi was a whirling blur, so graceful for a man of his size. His sword was a flash parabola and Hector's head was gone. Gone, just gone, hitting the concrete open mouthed, terrified, rolling. The slight body had fallen forward, hinged at the knees. Then came the pulsing evacuation of its blood, a bright red pool gathering, spreading, dulled quickly by its eating up of sand and dust.

The guards inside the van were taking a more direct interest, seemed eager to observe Thomas' reactions. He told himself, don't lose it; if you lose it, Thornton, you lose yourself. But some of them had begun to giggle … For a moment he was immobile, paralysed by what had happened, by what would happen, by an upwelling fury, a spinning out of control. He stood up in the van. His fists, linked together by bright metal, closed up hard and tight

Chapter 2

The hook-nosed, well bearded guard, probably Pakistani, grinned
through the wire mesh, speaking loudly in Arabic. "All you Western
people are shit and you are shit and your mother is shit." The nearest
of the inmates turned to look.

Thomas shook his head to convey his false lack of understanding.
"Mafi Arabi, my friend," he tried to indicate the shoulder bars of a
senior policeman. "I have to speak to the Head Warden, OK?" It was
necessary to shout if you were going to be heard over the babble.
Visitors one side, inmates the other, two metres of well marked space
and this bloody wire between them.

The guard said, "Mafi Inglezi," meaning he had no English and
then, with clear satisfaction, "Go fuck yourself a camel, camel shit."
He turned away, still grinning.

Thomas made his way back to cell nine. This was one of the worst
of the worlds he had known in his life or had been told about. Cell
nine was in cell-block three. Cell-block three was a prison within Al-
Mahli prison within the highly secured Kingdom of Saudi Arabia.
From the first, when he'd been led here with his wrists and ankles
manacled after the affair with the police he'd been a man marked out
by the prison guards for special attention. Three days gone now, and
still his knuckles bore the marks of the fighting in the van with all the
small brown faces crowding excitedly outside, up against the windows.
What a bonus! Hector's blood already clotting in the heat, his head in
a plastic bag and now this crazy Englishman fighting with policemen.
Three days and still Thomas carried the pain of what had happened
and of what had happened afterwards. But now his bad eye had re-
opened and the truncheon split across his right cheekbone was
mending itself and the ache in his balls had almost gone.

But there was a kind of satisfaction in the knowledge of the
cowardice inside them, for he had seen in their eyes their fear of the
man who shows no fear of the gun. That much he had brought with
him down the years. The manual again; 'Respect the gun and the holder of it
but demonstrate no fear for either. If he is considering whether or not to kill you,
your fear will not go in your favour. Remember you are looking only for time and
the opportunity to redress the balance.'

Cell nine in cell block three measured three metres across by two
metres long. Narrow, three-tiered wooden bunks ran down both sides

of the cell but nine men were living in here. Three of them needed to occupy the floor space and if you were forced to take a pee in the night you could not avoid waking them on your way out. All eight of the Westerners presently in Al-Mahli jail were here in cell nine, plus the big Sudanese, Saeed. Thomas had learned that, inside the block itself the authorities were content to let the prisoners rule, and that the occupants of this row of cells were the ruling ones over all. The other three quarters of the inmates, the ones who couldn't find, or fight and win, or buy a place in one of the actual cells spent their days and their nights on the floor out in the main hall.

In cell nine you as the newcomer slept on the floor and would continue there until by force or by bribery or through the release of a bunk holder you were allowed the upwards promotion that still did not save you from the attentions of the cockroaches and the bugs against which you needed to wage a daily and a nightly battle. Still, there was a small, heavily barred window high up on the end wall so that a man as tall as he, and the men on the top bunks, could admire the view of the back of the cookhouse with its overflowing garbage bins and its permanent clouds of flies. He thanked God for the fine wire mesh that served instead of glass. Through this window he could at least see the daytime sky of an almost perpetual cobalt blue or, at night, an increasingly familiar group of stars.

Neither boarding school nor the military nor any other life-change experience had come close to this level of subjugation. He'd stood there and looked with his one good eye down the length of the high ceilinged hall. All of Asia and Africa seemed represented here. Himself the focus for so many eyes, he'd been almost physically assaulted by the stink of over-crowded, over-heated humanity, of its festering ordure. And the constant bloody shouting! What in hell was there to talk about in here, never mind shout about? *Hell* was about right. This place was some kind of awful, Hieronymus Bosch-like dream of hell. He had wanted to turn his back on them all, tearing with his hands at the wire, screaming out his innocence.

The squat figure of a white man in jeans and dirty sweat shirt had shouldered through and had held out his hand. The guy had the marked-up face and the flat blue eyes of a fighter. "Hey buddy, I'm George Schwartz," he'd yelled. The accent was very New York. Shaking hands in there had seemed an embarrassing irrelevance.

"Thomas Thornton," he'd shouted back, "Pleased to meet you."

"I don't fucking think so. You look like shit, baby. What the fuck they do with you?" He'd grinned. "You from England?"

"Right."

"Come on and meet the guys."

Once inside cell nine with the door closed it was possible to talk less loudly. The residents, as they called themselves, were sitting or lying along each bunk. "Meet some more Brits and some lesser guys like me," George had said, laughing.

Jimmy Bellingham and Darren Dicks were younger than himself, late twenties maybe. Jimmy was from Durham and Darren was a Manchester man, a shaven headed, sharp faced Manchester United football man in fact. He wore the faded red shirt with its proud MUFC badge and had one of the guards primed and bribed to bring him the UK Premiership results from the BBC World Service each late Saturday night. "Play the game yourself?" Thomas had asked him.

"Used to be a decent midfielder. Had a trial for Halifax Town, once over."

"Well, I'm impressed, Darren. Do we ever get to play football out in the yard?"

Darren had snorted. "You must be joking. You don't even get out for any exercise 'till you've been in here a twelvemonth. After that it's Cell Bock one and a bloody sight better than this. That's if you've got a clean sheet to your name and if they remember to move you. The cell block one guys get let outside for fifteen minutes a day." He'd gone on to volunteer how he and his mate Jimmy'd been caught drunk driving almost a year ago.

The Dutchman, Henk Strikkers, had acknowledged his introduction with a barely perceptible nod. Big, bald, sixtyish, Henk was a relative newcomer. George told him he'd spoken very little over the month he'd been here. No-one knew why he was in here, just that the poor bastard had only been in the country on a visit.

Then there were Virgil and Johnson, both of them black Americans. "These guys were expats with me at Aramco," George said as he introduced them. Thomas had asked about how come they were here but understood at once that it was OK to be told but not OK to ask. Later on George did tell him how the pair of them had been found one evening in their car in a far corner of the Giant Store car park, fucking with a couple of Saudi girls. They hadn't even been charged yet. "They'd definitely be for the chop if they were anything but American but for American guys from Aramco? Well, my guess and their hope is, they'll be taken out of here one night and wake up Stateside, the lucky bastards. And me?" he'd added, "In case you're wondering I'm in here for alcohol. You know, trading it and making it.

48

Making big bucks too, 'til some bastard ran into my pick-up. Bottles of my best stuff rolling and broke all over the fucking highway. But, I'll have a fair old shit-load of the greenstuff back home if the bastards ever let me get at it and if my girl hasn't fucked off with it." He grinned. "Shee-it, guess that could be two 'ifs' too many."

Finally there was Maurice, the permanently frightened, pale, pretty young Frenchman. In a land where homosexuality was illegal, if as commonplace as everywhere else, Thomas had not long needed to wonder what offence had resulted in that quiet young foreigner being incarcerated in Al-Mahli.

Now it was the middle of the night and they were all sleeping. He lay on his thin foam mattress on the concrete floor, his hands behind his head, looking up at the light bulb within its metal grill. No light in here was ever dimmed or ever turned off. The same old questions marched across his mind. Where the hell was Connie? What about the boys? Why hadn't Abdul-Rahman put in any kind of appearance? He'd always been happy enough to perform his sponsorship role and for sure the guy would know by now what had happened. And what exactly had Hector been up to? Was it Hector who'd set him up? It was difficult, verging on impossible to believe.

Christ, it was this not being able to communicate, that and the helplessness of it. That was the hardest part. Well, the second hardest, because the hardest part had to be knowing that someone had done this to him, for whatever reason. And why? Why? Why?

He was hungry but already he'd become used to that. He couldn't eat much of the prison issue stuff. They'd told him about how he'd soon forget to worry about the food or to notice the stink and the noise and being forced to bear in respectful fortitude the five times a day rousting out to the back of the hall for the non-Muslims, whilst the rows of believers in front of them chanted their responses. Well, you boys can accept what the hell you want, he thought. But me, no. One way or the other I'm leaving, and I'm leaving soon. All the old anger bubbled up; Thomas Thornton felt the hardening of the muscles around his shoulders and his neck, felt the resurgence of that long disused violence.

What was happening to Connie and the boys? What had they been told and by whom? And why wouldn't the police just charge him, then he might at least be able to talk to someone, get some answers? They had the evidence of the talc and God only knows what else someone had planted. On day one he had demanded and been granted materials and had carefully re-written his statement of respectful innocence, pushed it out through the wire to a guard, but George had told him to forget it because it would probably have been filed or destroyed as soon as they'd understood it contained no element of a confession.

Thomas turned over, the better to get some kind of comfort from the skinny mattress. How about the Embassy? No doubt the diplomatic lines had been abuzz with the name Thornton; just as all their going through the motions would amount to nothing whatsoever. Thomas Thornton versus the big aerospace contracts? No contest.

Always his thoughts turned back to that can of talc and to Hector's beheading. None of it made any sense. And the boats? All of them had come from Sea Fibres, the firm that made them in Portsmouth, in the UK. He thought about the day out he'd had at Cheltenham races with their managing director Kit Mahon, another of what they'd jokingly called 'the X-SBS Brigade.'

Maurice climbed out of his bunk, trying to step quietly around the three on the floor. Noticing Thomas's open eyes, the boy smiled shyly, surely a natural target for the lip lickers and thobe twitchers out there.

Looking up, he saw Saeed peering over the edge of his bunk. He liked the humour of the massive man in the top bunk, the man most often deep into his one and only book, head supported on one huge hand, elbow bent. He must have known that book word for word. Thomas had asked him if he'd been here long.

"No sir. Not long. I should have been out by now; out and up," he'd pointed skywards, "Maybe out and down where bad boys go. Or maybe this fuzzy wuzzy head upstairs, the rest of him gone down." He'd roared with laughter, the white of his teeth and the ivory of his eyes outstanding in the shine of his face.

George had said, "Take no notice, Tommy. The guy's a fucking accountant. An Islamic fucking accountant. How nutty is that? Like, in a place where money earns you no fucking interest? Where most of the businesses make no dough anyway? On his way back to the bank with cash this Yemeni goes for him with a knife. Goes for our old Saeed? Guy had to be on something or sick in the head. So what does our man do?"

"I am not proud of taking a man's life, Mister George," Saeed had interrupted, quietly, "Although it is a common enough thing. As I grow up there are men killing men, and my father and my mother, for war or sometimes merely for fun." He'd shaken his head. "War and killing does not end."

50

"Guess you know murder doesn't need to be a problem here if you have the dough, Tommy?" George had said.

Thomas had nodded. Murder in Saudi was a crime against the person, redeemable by the payment of money to the relatives of the deceased. It wasn't a crime against the State. Not serious stuff, not like drug dealing for instance. He had a vision of a whirling thobe and a flying ghafia and a wide glimmer of steel in the sunlight. He'd asked what was the going rate for blood money and Saeed had laughed. "That depends on if the one who is dead was a believer; you know, a brother Muslim like myself? The rate for killing a Christian is one half of that. But it is much better to kill a lady. Your family gets away with half price for a lady, Mister Thomas. So if you plan to murder someone in this Kingdom you must make sure it is a Christian lady, OK?"

Thomas had felt he ought to change the subject. He picked up Saeed's tattered book, read out loud its title: "Winston Churchill; *The River War.*"

"Yes, The River War. You know of this?"

"Yes, of course."

"My great great grandaddy was a sergeant in the ninth Sudanese, with your Brigadier MacDonald at Omdurman."

"That's incredible," Thomas had said. "One of my own family was at Omdurman. Gedid as well. My god, Saeed, they might actually have fought side by side! Eighteen ninety seven, wasn't it?"

George had interrupted, "Eighteen ninety seven! Holy shit, you guys have to be kidding."

Saeed had come down to the floor at that, had shaken his hand. "Yes, Mister Thomas, year of eighteen ninety seven. You are even more very welcome, and it is even more very nice to meet you."

"Maybe 'nice' isn't the best word for meeting this Englishman," he'd said. He hadn't undressed in the four days since he'd left England apart from when taking his soap-less shower each morning.

After mid-day prayers a man came to tell him his name was being called. George said, "Right on. Go get 'em, man." Saeed looked up from his book. "Remember, Mister Thomas. Live like a monk and don't be getting drunk." His laughter came rumbling. "Allah Akhbar; God is great, you know."

"Right. I'll see you soon, guys," he said, but he hoped he wouldn't see them soon or ever again and he also knew that they knew this, and that they understood what lay behind such a hope.

With ankles and wrists chained he was escorted by two guards out through the gate in the wire of cell block three and across the square and up the stairs into the Warden's office. This was that other world of carpeted quietness and dark hardwood and old leather furniture. Standing there for a while, being ignored, a silent guard to each side, he was very conscious of his chains and of his four day stubble and of the state of his jeans and his not now so crease-resistent Ben Sherman shirt. He was especially conscious of this because the British Vice Consul, the immaculate Jeremy Ferris-Bartholomew was also present, seated to the left of the Warden's desk. Thomas remembered meeting him a time or two at the Embassy's business functions. Police Captain Al-Muttawi made up the tryptich, expressionless in the armchair to the right, also facing him. After a moment of uncertainty Ferris-Bartholemew got up and came across, holding out his hand. He said, "Thomas old boy, I shall refrain from asking you how you are." He was wearing the smallest of his standard smiles. "I think I know your answer."

Thomas said nothing, merely glancing down at his manacled hands. Ferris-Bartholomew returned to his seat. The words again, the manual; *'Don't ask questions unless (a) it is essential for you in the interests of escape to have the answers and (b) you are reasonably sure that they will know the answers and therefore you will not embarrass them and (c) they will be prepared to tell you what you need to know'*. He waited, saying nothing. Ferris-Bartholomew said, "Captain Al-Muttawi has been kind enough to waive the rules, old chap. He is actually trying to help you by allowing me to see you. You have of course met Mr Abdullah Al-Khomein." He indicated the unsmiling Head Warden.

Thomas said, "No, Jeremy, until now I have not been afforded that pleasure. Look, is there any chance of getting rid of these damn chains?"

Her Majesty's Vice-Consul coughed politely. "Yes, well, as I recall there was some kind of trouble with your, er, incarceration?" The Head Warden motioned to one of the guards, who unlocked and removed the manacles. "Thank you for that, sir," said Ferris-Bartholemew.

Al-Khomein nodded, saying nothing.

Thomas said, "Look, Jeremy, the police forced me to watch my foreman being beheaded. Something of an unpleasant surprise, which seemed to amuse them. Not satisfied with the entertainment value in that these Neanderthals thought it a good time to play tunes on me with their bloody truncheons."

"Be that as it may, you have been arrested but not yet charged with any offence. Therefore you should understand at once that I am not in a position to discuss any aspect of the case against you." He straightened his tie and Thomas wondered which one it was, Eton or Harrow; it could hardly be one of the lesser schools. "Any aspect of the case whatsoever," the man repeated. "I can answer any question you may have other than those on matters related to the case. But there is this one exception. I am led to understand that you have so far refused to make a statement to the police, and I am permitted to advise you that without a statement from you the police will be reluctant to lay their charges. Of course it is only after the charges are laid that you will be allowed to receive visitors or become able to secure proper legal representation." The warden sat forward, expressionless, his elbows on the desk, fingers steepled in front of the beard. Al-Muttawi sat motionless.

Thomas said, "But I wrote out my statement and delivered it to one of the guards as soon as they put me here. What's going on?"

Once more the Ferris-Bartholomew smile. "Be that as it may, Thomas, clearly the police have their reasons. My advice to you is to write out the fullest and most carefully considered and of course the most truthful statement in response to the charges. The Saudi Arabian police have no interest in malicious prosecution or the harassment of British nationals over and above the law of the land."

"Is that so? How do they feel about Philipinos?" Thomas asked.

"I beg your pardon?"

"My foreman, Hector Comancho? Last seen with his head rolling around all by itself?"

The Vice Consul coughed quietly, ignored the question, "Is there anything I can organise for you whilst you're here?"

"Are you able to mention what is happening with my family? I mean, for instance does Connie know where I am?"

"Ah yes, I was coming to that," he moved uncomfortably. "I can certainly confirm that they are quite all right and that they are aware of this unfortunate … Yes, I understand that your wife elected to return pro tem to her family. In Venezuela, I believe? And as I have it, in all the circumstances she felt it best for your sons to go for the time being into the care of your sister in England."

"But I find that unbelievable, Jeremy. Not that the boys have gone to Sheila. I'm happy enough they'll be OK there for a while. But Connie hasn't so much as spoken to her family since before we were married. Why would she want to go to them now?" In the ensuing silence he realised with total certainty that, so far as these three were concerned he was simply a temporary embarrassment, a dead man walking. "Oh, right, thanks for telling me, Jeremy," he said. "I might have worried." That bloody dryness in his mouth again.

The Vice Consul stood up, seemingly unable to prevent the momentary twitching of his nostrils. "How about food?" he asked. "The Warden here has no objection to our sending in a daily parcel for you." He picked up his papers, returned them to his briefcase. "And perhaps some fresh clothing?"

Warden Al-Khomein spoke for the first time, albeit without eye contact. "We are holding Mr Thornton's baggage. It is now inspected and cleared and therefore he may have that in his cell. There are adequate toilet facilities. Quite adequate," he repeated, pleased with his use of the word. "We are not savages."

Thomas nodded. "Thank you for that," he said. He thought of the warm water trickle from the four taps in the room that doubled up as open latrine cum shower room and as the laundry where prisoners literally beat the shit out of their thobes and baggy underwear. "I think I would like to make a statement now." Hope rapidly disappearing, it was very important that he be charged because this was the only way he could expect to change the status quo, receive visitors, establish some kind of link with the outside; the only way to get some kind of control back into his life. He had to gamble that, for a foreigner of some standing, there would be no immediate sentencing nor any precipitate expedition of the sentence such as that with Hector Comancho.

Ferris-Bartholemew re-seated himself, clearly surprised. "Well done old chap," he said. "In my experience it's always best to get things off one's chest, start from a clean sheet, you know."

A clerk having been summoned to write the statement, for ten minutes Thomas related everything that he judged they would want to hear. Al-Muttawi said little apart from asking a few seemingly trivial questions. Alone amongst them he seemed unimpressed. Thomas knew the policeman would have access to facts about his supposed importation of cocaine, in the boats, that could not possibly coincide with this account of his, as vague as he had tried to make it. When it was finished Thomas initialled each of the English language pages, ignoring the Arabic translations, then signed at the end. The Warden's signature was a great, grandiloquent flourish over the Al-Mahli prison seal.

54

Al-Khomein said, "Kindly remain seated Mr Thornton. We have further discussion. I am sure the British Vice Consul and Captain Al-Mutawi have much of importance so we need not keep them here."

"Might I enquire as to what happens now?" Thomas asked the police officer.

"No," replied Al-Khomein.

The British Vice Consul clearly could not remove himself fast enough. The handshake was soft, the eyes travelling here, there and everywhere except to Thomas's. "Leave it to me to see about an issue of food whilst you're here, old chap."

'Whilst you're here!' Jesus, what did that one mean? How bloody ominous was that?

With the others gone, the manacles replaced and the guards once more to each side of him, the Warden shuffled papers into a neat pile central to his blotter. Finally looking up he said, "Mister Thornton, you have inflicted much harm on the policemen as you are being transported to this prison." He held up his hand for silence. "This is not a matter for reply or discussion. It is my duty to punish for this. We are peaceful people and here, violence will not be tolerated. We have none of your, what you call them - your hooligans - in Kingdom of Saudi Arabia." He seemed satisfied with the point. "You are quite new to our ways and for this I shall punish you only with twenty strokes of the cane. This is public." Addressing the newly returned guards, "Immediate."

In the centre of the courtyard stood four iron pillars. He was instructed to remove his shirt and to lie face down. *'The anticipation and the humiliation of pain will do more damage to your morale than the pain itself,'* had said the book, *'unless you are well prepared mentally.'* Well, was that right? How bloody wonderful. His wrists and ankles were secured to the pillars. His bad arm was hurting and he could hear and feel the thump of his heart against hot concrete. The guards were ushering out the human contents of cell block three, the usual shouting and jostling dying down as they crowded in as close as was permissible around the pillars.

With his head tilted up to one side, keeping it as far away as possible from the heat, he could see that George and Saeed and the rest of cell nine were now front row spectators. George returned his wink. After the first of the blows had cut across his shoulder blades Thomas called out, "one," and then, again out aloud, "two," and after his "three" George and Saeed took up the cry and by the time number fifteen came they had all joined in and soon enough came the great triumphant roar, "twenty!" in so many of the languages of the world. Only the pain was left within the new silence but still he smiled. He remembered the camp in Dorset and more of the counter interrogation training. *'Think about each blow as if it is a precious thing, a museum piece, there for your most attentive consideration. Examine it and grade it for its quality and its meaning. This will help you to achieve the essential objectivity and to overcome.'*

Finally unshackled, he got to his feet, staggered, his back a screaming riot, but still he smiled. And then Al-Khomein, his voice high pitched, "You find funny, English? Maybe you too much enjoy?" He nodded. "Yes, I think soon we will show you our special down the stairs. I shall find this funny, you shall not."

He had heard all about this 'downstairs' of theirs and had no wish to find out for himself. But now, suddenly, he recalled one of the few literary quotations in Code X-010; *'Man can be destroyed but not defeated,'* had said the book. No more compromise and no need for loudness in the waiting silence; "Go fuck yourself a camel, camel shit," he said, speaking the words in English then in deliberately, haltingly bad Arabic. In the silence someone laughed nervously and then another and soon the great wall of it had been built. Al-Khomein glanced from side to side as if to make sure this madman was well held. "Repeat," he shouted to the guards, and then in Arabic, "repeat the sentence. Now."

And this time Thomas kept silent, his head turned away from the other cell nine guys, as he received this second caning, in case they saw anything in his face that he did not want them to see. But this second batch of cuts seemed if anything easier than the first.

Afterwards two of the guards attempted to help him to his feet but he shook them off and they kept him standing, chained to one of the pillars by his bad left arm, his eyes narrowed against the sun with the blood drying down his back, his flanks and the backs of his legs. Left by himself all afternoon, he stayed within the meagre shade of the pillar so as to minimise the sun-burn. He had all his thoughts, through which to rise above the conflagration that was the back of his body. He thought much about Connie and about serious, beautiful David and mad-cap Paul and what would Sheila be thinking and saying to them as she tucked them up in bed? And Connie? Oh Jesus, and Connie...

As the sun finally dipped below the heights of the prison wall, before maghreb prayers, the guards returned. They unchained him, took him from the courtyard into cell block three then released him to enter through the gate in the wire mesh, and he realised that he was not being treated with the customary unkindness. The babble faded. All eyes turned on him and men made way as he shambled across the hall. Halfway across, this ancient Saudi Arabian barred his way, looking up. The old man's eyes were very dark, his nose especially well hooked. This was the deep lined, grey-stubbled, weathered mahogany face of a man of the Arabian desert. In the language and the dialect that Thomas now knew so well but could not acknowledge the old man said, "You are welcome here," he said. "You are truly a man, English. I wish to take tea with you when you are rested."

Thomas shrugged and smiled and nodded. "Mafi Arabi, old man, I have no Arabic. But shukran anyway."

Inside the cell he found his blue mattress now on the top right hand bunk. Saeed said, "You the man now, Mister Thomas. The Man has to have the right place, OK? Just watch out for camel shit, yes." Then that great basso profundo laugh.

Later on he went back through the hall to the latrine, crouching over the hole in the floor to defecate without noticing or caring about any of the dead or alive abominations that had up to now so sickened him. It was not his rota for the shower but the ones waiting grinned, encouraging him to the front of the queue, and soon he stood naked under the warm cascade of mustily desalinated water, his head down, fists clenched against the pain, watching the lazy, blood-pink swirl of water around his feet.

The Sudanese's whisper was a low rumble. "They can plant no bug in here with the water noise. Mister Thomas." He realised that Saeed had arrived, was standing under the shower in the next cubicle. "Listen, I'm telling you … I'm going out of this place. You want out? Tomorrow I tell you the plan, my man, OK? Like your Mister Shakespeare… 'Tomorrow and tomorrow creeps in this place from day to day. Yes?'"

Thomas picked up on the Macbeth, whispered back, "Then something about lighting fools the way to dusty death? Not too great in all the circs. Anyway, nice one, black man. And the answer is yes, OK, let's bring it on."

"You have seen much pain, white man, and you are no stranger to the nearness of death. The shape of your arm and the scars of three bullets, not of the same, they tell me this. And I believe you have only as much of fear as any truly intelligent man must have. I would count it an honour for you to join with me in this escape thing, Mister Thomas."

Now he lay on his chest to minimise the pain, looking through the window grill at the night sky and the flood-lit cookhouse and the prison wall. The burning of his back was a constant thing and therefore more easily handled than something that hits you in fits and starts, something for instance like the on-going aftermath of a close range, thirty eight calibre, nickel plated bullet that ricoceting around in the bone and the sinew of your left elbow.

The last chants of *isha* prayers were still echoing from mosques close by and far away, blending each with the others and into the stillness of the Arabian night. Looking up at the light he wondered if that which they had told him was true? Whether there, within the wire grill they had secreted a CCTV camera? Whatever, irrespective of the plan that Saeed had in mind it was certain to be bloody dangerous. And even if they did succeed in getting out and then right out of the country, what comes next? What kind of a fugitive future for an escaped drug dealer, whether real or simply supposed?

Half asleep now, he thought about Abdul-Rahman Al-Sottar and about how the guy had attempted once to put things into perspective for him. The two of them had been sitting with Connie outside the house that was more like a palace right on the beach. Connie was only invited when Abdul-Rahman had no other guests than them. It had been a night like this, hot and humid. He and his sponsor had been in T-shirts and baseball caps and had their cut glass tumblers of Black Label whisky, illegal for the masses but quietly OK for the leaders. What was it Abdul-Rahman told him? Yes… "You must remember, Thomas," he'd said, his tone that of the teacher to the pupil, "We of Saudi Arabia are the product of thousands of years of slave-owning, you know." Abdul-Rahman had been observing him closely, looking for understanding, ignoring Connie. "We have always called upon Africa and the East for our labourers and more recently to the West for your technology and your so very honest work ethic." Sitting back, the man had taken himself a good draft of the stuff of Scotland. "We are God's chosen, Thomas. The ones to whom Allah, may peace be upon him, gave the gift of oil and therefore of power and of money, which are not the same things even though you, as all Westerners, will think it is."

"The meek shall inherit the earth, that sort of thing?" Thomas had asked, but his quotation had not been appreciated and Connie had shaken her head at him.

58

Here in his stinking hot, overcrowded cell he smiled, thinking about his wife and before that about the military and before that his school and the man and the girl by the river. He often thought about that girl and the hornets.

They are going to kill you, Thomas Thornton, he told himself. They have taken away from you your good name and your wife and your beautiful sons and soon enough they will take the head from your shoulders as they have taken the head from the shoulders of Hector Comancho. And you, Captain or Mister Thornton, unless you find a way to get yourself out of this place you will never know why someone wishes to do you so much harm. So bloody well get the hell on with it; get the hell out!

Chapter 3

This time, when he slept, he had dreamed of the time he had been with David and Paul when his boys were very little and it was to do with that time he'd taken them out in a dinghy. They'd been fishing a sea loch in Wester-Ross, in Scotland, and had caught this huge, slippery codfish; he could see its mottled green-brown back and flanks and the dirty cream belly of it. He could hear its great spade of a tail thumping out the last of its life down in the bilges, he could smell the clean, fresh, almost chemical smell of it. And there was this excitement that he recognized as the excitement of the hunter in the sea-sprayed faces of his sons. But at another time in the night he had also dreamed of the sexuality of his wife and of the saying of her name, 'Consuela,' and of the woman's facial beauty and that of her body, naked and shining and the cause of his arousal this time and always. How difficult it was to come awake after this sixteenth night in Al-Mahli jail.

"Good morning, Mister Thomas," Saeed said, "You was having such a time." The others joined in his laughter. "Listen to me, man," Saeed said, "You could sell that movie for millions." But soon afterwards Saeed passed him a scrap of paper, tight-folded, shaking his head for serious caution. Thomas read in secrecy what Saeed had written, 'It is time for me to get out of here, if Allah wills. Will you come with me?' He scribbled his response, 'Yes. What plan?' There was always the fear of being observed or listened to or even betrayed by someone so they continued to use surreptitious scraps of toilet paper for their communications. 'We hide in the garbage bins and get taken out to the dump', wrote Saeed, 'OK?'. Thomas licked the point of the stub of pencil, wrote, 'Not OK, its too old a trick.' That would be as good a way of committing suicide as any, through disease if not by getting themselves shot or by being horribly crushed. 'Let's think some more,' he wrote.

George Schwartz was first to notice the exchange of messages, then Darren and Jimmy cottoned on to this strange new paper chewing habit. Realising the impossibility of further concealment here in cell nine, Thomas issued to each of them a closely-written invitation to join in on the making of an escape plan. All of them said yes, even the massive, still silent Henk Strikkers and the French boy, Maurice.

It rapidly became clear that escape theory was not new to anyone although none of it seemed to Thomas to weigh favourably on the scales of risk and reward. Most ideas were simple daydreams. So far, as George pointed out in one of his messages, there had never been a successful escape from Al-Mahli jail. And getting out would be hard enough but staying out would be still harder; and then getting out of the country? That would present the escapee with a wholly different and just as severe a degree of difficulty.

Later that morning the police came for him. He'd been expecting them. Everyone knew it was a part of the Sharia ritual to take the accused to the scene of a crime, there to have him enact his confession. So now they chained up his wrists and put him into a prison van with five uniformed guards and with Captain Al-Muttawi himself, as uncommunicative as always, sitting up front alongside the driver.

He raised his manacled hands to scratch at his chin through its new-sprouted beard and the closest of the guards shifted away, disgustedly grunting something in the accents of the deserts to the south about this prisoner being a big white pig. Thomas grinned at him to reinforce his lack of the language, no longer especially uncomfortable with his own body odour. But he was enjoying the ride through the traffic. He turned his head to look up out of the window, observing a military jet crawling across the powder blue sky, its contrail pointing the way north to Iraq. From up there its pilot would be looking down on the Dammam, Dharan, Al-Khobar conurbation with its web of highways. He would be able to see the coastline and the wide curve of the highway across the causeway to and from Bahrain. Thomas shivered, feeling the renewed upwelling of his longing to be free. Bahrain would represent freedom, but even if he managed somehow to get there … Could there be anywhere in this world receptive to an accused dealer in drugs? Even a self-professedly innocent one? Again and again the same questions; little comfort in any of the answers.

A policeman was stationed at the main entrance to Al-Sottar Marine in place of the old gateman, Mohammad. No sign of any of the other workers inside the yard. He could see the chandlery shop was closed. They'd had all the new boats lifted out of the water, sitting now on wooden stocks like a row of great white sharks beached beyond their natural domain. The boats spoke of a power and a grace and of a freedom, albeit one that they would never find in the close confines of this ultra-guarded coastline. Untroubled waters mirrored the Marina pontoon walkways and the big, sun-decked, rich men's toys floating alongside them. Once outside the van he caught all the familiar smells: new fibreglass resin, teak dust, warm oil, steel-work super-heated by the sun. He turned to the waiting Al-Muttawi. "So, are you going to tell me what you've done with my people, Captain?"

Al-Muttawi made no reply until they'd reached the office; Thomas's office, where the policeman sat down behind the desk; Thomas' desk. He looked up, said, "On our advice Mister Abdul-Rahman Al-Sottar has closed his yard. Of course it is temporary. To you the reasons should be obvious."

Thomas repeated his question. "So? What have you done with my people?"

"We are here only to test your statement and in this way to complete our investigations." There was this boredom, this contempt in the way the man spoke. "No other matters may be discussed. You shall show us where on the boats the illegal substances were concealed as indicated in your signed and attested statement." He adjusted the precise lay of his ghafia, flicking the red checkered material back around the sides of his head and shoulders then using two fingers and a thumb to adjust its frontal creases into a perfect symmetry. "Please understand, your actions will be video recorded. Do not make any mistake, Mister Thornton, it will not go well for you if you continue to attempt to - to muddy the waters, I think this is what you would say."

"But Hector must have told you all that, where the stuff was hidden and so on? You know, before you killed the poor little bugger?"

"I am now investigating the case against only you, Mister - or Captain - Thomas Thornton. As you correctly point out, the case against the Philipino is finished and is therefore, as with all things, in the hands of Allah, may He be praised." Abruptly Al-Muttawi stood to lead the procession out into the brute heat of the yard. He pointed to an SF 40 up on the dock. The most recent import, she was still undergoing her final fitting out. The name newly painted on her stylish bows in Arabic script translated into, Distant Waters. Bloody silly name for a boat that wouldn't be allowed more than six miles off-shore or a few dozen miles along it either way; not without her owner knowing someone very highly placed and even then not without filling in and submitting all the documentation, so carefully designed to keep the Saudi cage door firmly closed to all but the rulers. The Captain of Police spoke with a weary theatricality, "Mr Thomas Thornton, you will now show us where from was retrieved the substance that your accomplice in England hided away on this craft."

There were a hundred places where packages of something could be concealed on a forty foot part finished glass fibre motor yacht. Thomas had thought up the most likely and the least likely ones, always aware of the worst possible scenario which was that he would unknowingly indicate the right place, thus inadvertently proving his guilt. But above all else he had to get himself charged and thus gain access to visitors from outside Al-Mahli jail. He climbed the ladder to board the boat, the ascent made awkward by his manacled wrists, then descended the companionway into the main cabin. The entourage followed him. It was very crowded; extremely hot in here. He turned to Al-Muttawi. "You'll need to get these floorboards up, Captain."

"I do not think so, Captain Thornton. No, I think we have already wasted enough of time on your games, do not you?" The mask had slipped a little now. "Your man, Comancho, he was much more co-operative. I take it that, in the same way, you will continue to refuse to tell us the true names of your collaborators in England? Or perhaps you will nominate your Prince Charles?" He tried on a smile, however bleak, at his own attempt at a joke. "But, Captain, you should know that English policemen are for once taking an interest in our primitive investigations. Nobody knows better than you, *Captain*, that the narcotics industry is truly international. In fact already they have made several arrests at the factory of this boat."

"Is that so?" Thomas' mind raced ahead. Which of the boys in Portsmouth would have had the sky fall in on them? Just who had they been working with, here in The Kingdom? Hector? Never, Hector couldn't possibly have handled all the necessary communications, never mind the local organisation. He shook his head. "I thought you told me all this was only about my own statement, officer?"

Al-Muttawi ignored that. "I should also say it may not please you to know that your Island of Jersey bank account has been frozen, and therefore that neither you nor any member of your family will be able to obtain this filthy, contaminated money."

64

Thomas shook his head in disbelief. "For eight thousand nine hundred and fifty six pounds sterling, much good will it do anyone. That's all I had in my bank, last seen."

"I believe the sum mentioned was a little over two hundred thousand pounds sterling. And naturally, the authorities are looking for your other bank accounts."

"What? That's bloody ridiculous." Astonished, he leaned in towards the policeman then one of the others must have hit him on the back of the head. He knew only that he was down, was barely conscious of being pulled up the cabin stairs and lowered down the outside ladder, trying to prevent the bumping of his head on each of the rungs.

They took him to the police station rather than back to Al-Mahli. At the police station he was led, stumbling, down to the cells, his hands still manacled and his forehead bleeding. This time it was a communal cell with standing room only amongst a throng mainly of Pakistanis, their dirty, long tailed shirts worn over baggy trousers. He at once became an object of special curiosity. Looking down, he seemed to be standing in urine.

It was some while before his name was shouted out. Through the grill in the door was a face speaking in another Arabic dialect new to Thomas. "You are a piece of dog-shit," said the grinning face. "They want you upstairs but I was hoping they had fucked you dead in there, English." A gob of spittle smacked into Thomas' left cheek before the jailer retreated to insert his key and open the door. With a calmness born of recent experience, still desperate not to reveal any knowledge of the language, he wiped away the spittle with the ragged sleeve of his Ben Sherman shirt. Then, in a new silence, he stood quite still as the man outside physically recoiled from the murder that must have been in his eyes.

Upstairs in the interview room a senior policeman identified with the Arabic desk plate 'Colonel Ziad Al-Shurais' looked up from his papers, seeming to find their contents and these whole proceedings and Thomas's appearance boring and distasteful in equal measure. Captain Mohammed Al-Muttawi stood alongside the seated Colonel. In his very passable English Al-Muttawi said, "Mister Thornton, you will now be charged formally with the offences that in your statement you have confessed. The charges will be in Arabic and translated into English by this person for your benefit." He indicated an Indian clerk with pen and notepad poised.

The Colonel turned to Al-Muttawi, speaking in Arabic. "This man has been roughly treated, Captain? He does not look so good." He seemed in no way troubled by the observation.

"As you are aware, Colonel, Thornton has always resisted custody." Al-Muttawi glanced at Thomas for any possible sign of understanding then proceeded, reassured, his voice the voice of quiet reason, "In fact two of my officers are still on sick leave, sir. This is a very dangerous man, a very highly trained man. But as I have reported, his statement was corroborated during the on-site demonstration and his present appearance is due to the fact that he fell down some steps on board the boat."

"This is all recorded for the Court?"

"Not in whole. Unfortunately there was not enough light or space inside the boat to tape record all of his corroborative actions. May I remind the Colonel that I have reported our need for a more up to date VHS recorder?" Point made, he went on, "But he did indicate the engine compartment, and in front of myself and other witnesses. The Colonel will recollect that the one hundred and fifty kilos of cocaine were concealed beneath the bed of the engine? You will remember it was revealed to us by Thornton's man, the executed Philipino?" He shrugged his shoulders; contemptuous, dismissive. "Of course this will not prevent this accused from trying to deny his confession, especially since, now that he has been charged, he will be able to take advantage of the *advice* of the British Embassy." He smiled at the cleverness of his own joke.

The Colonel said, in English, "Captain Thornton, you will now sign here to testify that you have received and have understood the charges made against you by the Kingdom State of Saudi Arabia."

A hundred and fifty kilos! Christ, Hector must have needed to lift the engine to get at the stuff! But who the hell had put it in there? He stepped forward, bent over the desk. Taking up the pen he pretended to read through the English version of the document but he was listening as the Colonel spoke to Al-Muttawi, having reverted once more into the Arabic. "Captain, I do not think the prisoner's Embassy will be to him of any help even if they were willing to try to interfere with the process of our Law. He will not receive sympathy from the general public of his country and therefore would expect very little from their politicians." The well manicured nails of his left hand beat a tattoo on the desk top. "As usual the politicians will be more worried about their news media." He shook his head. "It would always seem that these Westerners - Presidents, Prime Ministers, even Kings - they

66

are the prisoners of what they are pleased to call their free press. Very strange."

Thomas put down the pen and stood consciously to filthy attention. "Colonel, I would request that you put it on record that I am signing this document under duress, that I am renouncing my statement that was also made under duress and that I am protesting against the physical abuse to which I have been subjected." But even as he spoke he recognised the uselessness of his words. Here in this temporary silence, within the aura of the Colonel's heavy perfume and the alien drone of the air conditioning he felt himself abandoned, without meaning, without reason, beyond help.

The Colonel had already returned his attention to the dossier on his desk. "You will be returned to prison to be held there until your trial. Some limited access by visitors is now permitted following the charges against you and signed by you today. According to custom your Embassy and your sponsor will be informed." Now, with a small motion of the back of his hand he signalled the end of proceedings, the removal of the prisoner and the total non-existence of the prisoner's remarks.

Thomas Thornton did not know why, but he felt better as soon as Al-Mahli's steel framed wire mesh gates had crashed shut behind him and the keys had turned, grating in their locks, and the electronic double locks had been clicked into activation. He had once more become a resident of Saudi Babylonia, and once again the mad little old Bedouin was there, standing in front of him as he had stood before, speaking in Arabic as quietly as was permitted in the general din. "So, they have sent you back amongst us, my son. You are welcome." He nodded gravely. There was a twinkle in the rheumy black eyes. "I see you have been treated still with disrespect. But know that I have seen by the light in your face that you do understand my language, which is the language of God." Startled, Thomas shrugged, "Mafi Arabi." He made to move on but the old man held up his hands, palms outwards. "No, there need be no secrets between us. I mean you no harm and I have something you should know. My name is Mubarak Al-Jidha." The old man had seen the approach of George Schwartz. "When all is quiet, before first prayers, go to the latrine, Mister Thomas. I shall see you and follow and you shall know all that I know." His voice dropped. "It is of your wife."

George shouted out, "Still got your head on, buddy? Oh, shee-it, looks like you been getting yourself in more fucking trouble.

Bastards." He noticed the old Bedouin. "Hi there, Grandpa, how you doin'?"

The Arab said, "Put not your trust in any man, Mister Thomas. Trust only in God."

George grinned. "Wonder what the hell the old guy's saying? Crazy. Like he thinks you understand him, Tommy."

Thomas shrugged.

In cell nine the two Brits, the French lad and the two black Americans had a game of cards going on the floor. They suspended things on his arrival. Saeed got to his feet, grinning his grin, hand extended, and there might even have been some kind of a welcome on the usually impassive face of the huge Dutchman, lying full length on his bunk with his hands behind his head.

Virgil said, "So where you hide the file, Tommy? Christ no, don't fuckin' tell me."

"Good to see you, too, Virg," he said. "What file's that, then?"

"The one you're going to get us through those fuckin' window bars with." He looked straight up at the caged light. He was the only one laughing. "The one you got stuffed up your arse, my man." He shouted at the ceiling, "You listening to me, raghead?"

George said, "If they're watching your shit, they won't find that funny, Virg. Tommy don't, either. They've not been fucking joking around with him, OK? You can see that."

Virgil unfolded himself from his bunk, towering over his fellow American, full of sudden menace. "Don't need no crap out of you, Georgie, OK?" He nodded over George's head at Thomas, "This guy's the officer i/c. What he says goes, far as I'm concerned, but you ain't no fucking officer nor never will be."

George said, "You surely are some kind of a cunt, Virgil," then moved his head very quickly to avoid the punch, at the same time bringing up his knee to try for the groin. Then Saeed was holding them apart and the Dutchman was on his feet, looking quite happy to lay into all within reach. Quickly, Thomas climbed up to his bunk, inserted two fingers into his mouth. Thinking of the effect on any electronic eavesdropper he gave out with the loudest, longest whistle he could muster and, as suddenly as it had started, the fighting stopped. "Come on, children," he said, quietly. "Let's take a time out, shall we? We're all in the A team, here, remember? Save this stuff for the opposition?"

George tested his left cheekbone, already showing signs of damage. "Yeah, you're right." He raised his hand above his head, facing his adversary with open palm. Virgil shrugged and high fived, the light of battle dying from his eyes.

George said, "Hey, Tommy, you missed your food box. Goddam rag-heads must have had the whole fucking lot. Here, I saved some of mine for you."

Thomas drank the carton of milk, ate the apple and something cold and meaty wrapped in Arabic bread. His case had been returned. Sitting on his bunk, he opened it up. They'd left him the business folder with its notepad and ball point pen inscribed with the Sea Fibres logo. They had not stolen too much of his clothing, maybe because it was too big for them or maybe because most of it was ready for the washer after his ten day trip. Either way, it made for him a kind of pillow. He still had his wash bag as well, with only the talc missing inside it. All the presents had disappeared: David's *Big Game Fishing of the World* and Paul's *Action Man* and, naturally, Connie's black silk negligee in its Harrods green and gold gift-wrap.

Opening the business folder he ran his fingertips across its calf-hide inner cover. Amazingly, he could feel the slight bulge. Lying on his side, facing the wall for maximum secrecy, he took out what was still there; the ten one hundred dollar bills and the spare Amex gold card and the tattered piece of paper he always carried with him, the one bearing his natural father's poetic legacy. Carefully he returned it all to where it had been hidden.

The card school had re-started. He knew they were all waiting on his lead but in here there was never any hurry. There, he knew, lay the danger. There was always tomorrow but, for some of them, tomorrow would fail to arrive. He returned the folder to his case, rolled over on to his back. "Keep it quiet, lads," he murmured, "I might look like I'm asleep but I'm going to be doing some thinking."

He touched his fingers to his forehead. The blood had dried. He remembered the fight in the Belfast school yard. Saeed said, "I'll see your cards for five lovely little pieces of biscuit, Virgil."

"That's tough, black man," said Virgil. "Two deuces plus three of the big ones, OK?"

"Not OK, but you win," said Saeed. "So eat my biscuits."

Thomas was remembering how he'd told Miss Hunter about his father being a good man. 'I can tell from that poem; a good man. And so are you,' she'd told him. Here in Al-Mahli jail, a place redolent of the worse than animal smells of unwashed humanity, his eyes closed and near to sleep, Thomas remembered the lady's silver curls stiff and unmoving and the perfumed smell of her and how he'd thought the head of school was quite a lovely old lady when she smiled. 'Listen, come over here and shake hands with me now like a good man, Thomas Thornton,' she'd said. He knew his real father's poem by heart. Perhaps he might now be sleeping as he spoke the words to himself. How many of them would have the courage to go with him when it got right down to it, he wondered. He could be sure only of Saeed, and maybe George given any kind of a realistic plan. Possibly the Dutchman. Most of the others were going through the escape motions for interest only, pending what they expected would be their release. But for those who would try, just getting themselves clear of cell block three would be the main problem, never mind breaking out of Al-Mahli. For some time now he had thought there was only one way to get out of here and it would have to be the one that involved main force and almost certainly a good deal of blood. But the really essential need was for active outside support. Neither he nor anyone in here had any of that - at least, none that might conceivably be able or willing to go out on the kind of a terminal limb he now had in mind. The manual's words again came back ... *When, as a prisoner of the enemy, you plan your escape, you must think of logic, of time, and you must be patient. Assess the odds against success and balance this against the risk. Remember the Count of Monte Christo. If you do not know it or cannot remember that book, then read it.* He had read it with great care even though he had already known the book quite well. The Count had made a beautifully contrived escape.

It was around four in the morning as he picked his way through the sleepers and down the corridor and through a hall now resonant with the whimpering, grunting sounds of sleep. Out in the latrine the cockroaches swarmed away from his advance. Dropping his jeans he placed his shoes into the filthy, cracked earthenware footholds then crouched, leaning well forward as he had learned how to do it. He remembered what George had told him about how quickly he would become inured to everything; George had been right.

Mubarak Al-Jidha arrived very soon. Gathering up his dirty grey thobe, tucking it into the small of his back the old man crouched over the adjacent hole. "This is a good morning, my son," he whispered.

Without really knowing why, Thomas had decided on a policy of trust. He replied in Arabic. "Good morning, father. So, it shall be a fine day?"

"Insh'allah." The old fellow grinned his bad-toothed grin. "Your tongue is good but not so good as are your ears."

70

"I would respectfully request that you do not reveal this knowledge to anyone else. Do you agree?"

"I agree and yes, I was right. Listen to me. I was in the police cells when your man, the Philipino was brought in. They kept him on his own until he was taken for his death. But before they took him away he was able to speak to me." He waved away Thomas's question. "It matters not how we accomplished this. He told me that he was guilty of the crime with which he had been charged and that now he looked forward to his death. He had been tempted, as many men are tempted. He told me that he was sorry, not only for selling that forbidden thing but also he was sorry for stealing it from yourself, a man for whom he had much respect."

Thomas interjected, "That is not true, father. The Philipino Hector Comancho was mistaken, for I had none of that for him to steal nor any knowledge of it."

Al-Jidha shrugged and waved away the protest. "And I have little interest. As I say, the Philipino was prepared for his death according to the Law. This is not what I have to tell you. If you know not already, I have to tell you that your wife is still in my country. She is with Sheikh Abdul-Rahman Al-Sottar. Only your sons were sent away, by themselves, after you were caught." His function completed, he stood up, letting the thobe fall back around his ankles. "Listen to me some more, my English friend, Sheikh Abdul-Rahman Al-Sottar is a very dangerous man. This, everybody knows." He went to the basin to begin with water on his hands and his face and up and around his arms. "But God is great. He will help even you, an infidel, although perhaps a good one, as the Philipino has said to me." The first wild notes of the first of the day's calls to prayer had begun, their passionate appeal self-evident. "Go now, the fajr begins to call the faithful."

His mind bombarding itself with questions Thomas made his way to a corner at the rear of the hall, there to stand up against the wire, flanked by the other awakened residents of cell nine. In front of them the rows of kneeling prisoners murmured their responses to the caller's entreaties, their backs rising and falling in rough unison for their foreheads to touch the floor, seemingly at one with each other and with the rhythmic flow of all things. Perhaps people in so hard an environment as this of the desert really did have a crucial need for so absolute a belief in their destiny; in another and a better place. Turning to look behind him through the wire he could see the few guards on duty at this time were also on their knees, temporarily equal, he supposed, as must be every man before his God. Their weapons were stacked up against the wall. Allah was Great. They had no need for such as weaponry when they came to address Him. Was He not the one true God of peace?

Thomas thought about his wife and about what she might have done and why she might have done it, or perhaps she had not acted of her own free will? Could it really be that she was some kind of enforced captive? But in whichever direction his thoughts ran he had no doubt about the truth of that which the old man, Al-Jidha, had told him, and his thoughts always ended with his employer, his sponsor and his erstwhile friend Sheikh Abdul-Rahman Bin Sulaiman Al-Sottar. His suspicions had been growing and now he was as sure as he could be without access to proof positive. Yes, Al-Sottar was the one who had had him set up. But Connie? Oh, Connie! And David? And Paul? What of them? He shook his head, angered further by the blurring of his eyes. Well, they'd be all right. They'd be all right with Sheila.

He remembered how, in his own bedroom late in the day, the day when Flic had reported them, he'd retrieved that shiny, well thumbed magazine from its hiding place and, in the middle of the night, he'd crept quietly downstairs to the boiler room and fed the shameful pages, one by one, into the furnace.

Chapter Four

The Vice-Consul looked exceptionally well cared for; slightly overlong, fair hair exactly parted, small moustache neatly trimmed, white teeth agleam within the practiced smile. The diplomat leaned forward conspiratorially. "Bit of a privilege you know, being allowed to meet in here. Anyway, everything all right for you, Thomas?" The Head Warden's office smelled of furniture polish, well-spiced Arabic food, male body perfume.

"No, but thanks for the food parcels. Much appreciated." Thomas glanced at Al-Khomein but the Head Warden was busying himself with his paperwork, apparently uninterested. "While we talk can you get them to take off these bloody handcuffs? Just what do they think I'm going to do?"

"Can do, Head Warden?" Ferris-Bartholomew enquired.

Al-Khomein shook his head without looking up.

Ferris-Bartholomew endorsed the shake of the head, shrugged as if in apology. The smile disappeared. "We received formal notice of your charges. I don't have to tell you how very serious is the situation." He flicked a speck of something off his sleeve. "His Excellency wonders whether you might need any help in organising the defence?"

"Look, I'm charged with a capital crime of which I have no knowledge whatsoever, my sons have been sent back without reference to the UK, my wife is God only knows where or why and, oh yes, I'm informed my bank account in Jersey has been inflated out of sight apparently by deposits the origin of which is a total mystery to me. And I am still being held here in conditions that would have been shameful in the bloody seventeenth century. OK? Do I need any help, you ask!" He'd ticked off the facts on his fingers. Al-Khomein had looked up.

Ferris-Bartholemew took out a gold cigarette case, extracted a cigarette, snapped a flame from its in-built lighter.

"Oh yes", Thomas went on, "And there's more, as they say. I've had neither sight nor sound of my bloody so-called sponsor so have no idea whether I'm still getting paid by the man. And just by way of the starter that I almost forgot, this person," he indicated Al-Khomein, "this *bloody* person has had me flogged in public for daring to react after being set upon by men in uniforms after they so kindly allowed me to watch my poor bastard of a foreman's head hitting the deck."

"Yes, all very unfortunate." Ferris-Bartholemew coughed. "But we who choose to come here - or anywhere where we are not native - we must know and must respect the law as well as the customs of our host country. I'm sure you'll not disagree with me on that, Thomas?"

Al-Khomein shuffled his papers, glanced at his watch. Thomas had noticed the similarity of the warden's watch to the one that had been his own. "Five minutes," the man called out. "This visit must finish after five more minutes."

Thomas said, "I've made a short list of things. Can I run them by you, Jeremy?" He didn't wait for an answer. "Starting with my wife. As I have already told you, I have no idea why she would need to go to her family in Venezuela, if indeed she has gone there. I'm very confused about this. Can you not find out her contact details for me?"

Ferris-Bartholomew looked doubtful. "I'll do my best, old son, but I don't think my people will wear the cost of me going through channels on such a personal issue. Perhaps Sheikh Al-Sottar has some ideas. He is, or at least he certainly was sponsor to all your family, not just to you yourself, you know."

"Yes, is that right? Jeremy, you're kidding me. I've told you, I've had neither sight nor sound of that bugger."

Ferris-Bartholomew simply shrugged, his smile beginning to dismember under the unaccustomed barrage.

Wearily Thomas said, "OK, I get it. So how about a lawyer then?"

"A recommendation and initial contact on your behalf is no problem. But you'll need to sort out the financial side for yourself. I'm afraid we can't help in monetary terms. Too close to aiding and abetting ... things. I'm sure you see what I mean." Light blue smoke trickled simultaneously from the elegant diplomat's nose and mouth. "Lawyers here tend to price themselves according to the practice in their client's homeland. Now, is there anything else, Thornton?" No cosy first names any more. The man couldn't wait to get the hell out of here.

74

"Have you any idea when they plan to send me for trial?"

Ferris-Bartholomew shook his head. "No idea at all, unfortunately. If precedent is anything to go by it should be soon but there's no statute of limitations here in that respect, at least so far as I am personally aware."

The warden's office had been built over the main entry gates. Outside in the street two car horns vied with each other, their drivers shouting an enraged accompaniment. Ferris-Bartholomew continued: "For instance your man was arrested on a Saturday. As I understand it he was charged and tried and found guilty almost immediately." He blinked away the smoke, discreetly annoyed about allowing himself to be led down that particular pathway. "I understand that the execution of his sentence took place on the following Friday after having been duly authorised by the Crown."

"OK, or actually not OK," Thomas said, "But what about my money? The police told me my Jersey account has been 'frozen,' whatever that entails. I'm going to need to access some funding for my defence."

"Yes." The Vice-Consul coughed again, politely, into his closed fist. "I have to tell you that your account was frozen by the UK police authorities." Half of his cigarette remained but he was extinguishing it anyway, tapping it carefully in the base of the glass ash tray as if to save it for later. He bent forward to lift his briefcase, clicked it open, extracted a windowed white envelope. "I have here your bank's statement of account."

"Where the devil did you get this?"

"I'm afraid I'm unable to tell you that."

Thomas ripped open the envelope, unfolded the two sheets of paper, went straight to the bottom line. Two hundred and seven thousand pounds and eighty five pence. The big money had arrived in one hit a little over a month ago, just as he'd been setting off on his trip. It had come from an unstated source at Banco Commerciale de Geneve. He re-folded the statement, put it into his shirt pocket.

Ferris-Bartholomew coughed, made to stand. "On the back of the statement are the terms and conditions. I suggest you study them most carefully at the soonest opportunity. They're highly relevant to the present situation. If that's it we should close now. Wouldn't wish to outstay the old welcome, eh?"

Thomas frowned. 'Terms and conditions'? Was the man trying to be funny? What the hell was he talking about? But, "Just one more thing," he said, "And, please, this is very important to me. To give myself any chance at all I must have some telephone access. Would it be possible for you to arrange something now that I've been charged? My mobile is still in my case but they cut off the server."

Abdullah Al-Khomein provided the Vice-Consul with the reply. "No telephone. The rule is for prisoners to have only visits which will be between afternoon and sunset prayer times on Wednesdays and Thursdays, and shall be conducted through the wire as with all other prisoners. However, more access is allowed to lawyers authorised by myself and for that there is use of private room. We are fair, but no active telephone in cell. No." He rose to his feet.

Ferris-Bartholomew shrugged, said nothing, followed suit.

Thomas said, still seated, "How about my Walkman? They have that too. I find not having any music here almost as much of a bastard as anything else."

The Head Warden shouted out for the guards, his contempt now fully on display. "No music. This is punishment. It is not what you call holiday hotel or some entertainment."

Smoothly, the Vice-Consul intervened. "Yes, of course, we do take your point, Head Warden, and we accept what you say. Nevertheless perhaps we should note that Mr Thornton is not being punished. He has not actually been found guilty of anything as yet, what?" The frozen, one official to another smile was nicely back in place.

On his way back to cell nine, shouldering through the throng in the hall of cell block three Thomas paused to shake old Mubarak's hand and those of a number of others who'd crowded around him. Back in cell nine, lying atop his bunk, he realised how easy it would be to relax and let things happen. A few temporary friends here and the endless escape speculation and the odd flare-up just to add a little zest. Bearable, yes, but only until they come one Friday to inject you with a little something against any unseemly resistance, take you out to the public square, kneel you down in front of the silent crowd and then gone, all gone and soon forgotten by all except perhaps by two small boys growing up fatherless, wondering. He realised that his fists were clenching and unclenching. The old aggression. He welcomed it back as an old friend. Focus, it gave him focus.

Abdul-Rahman Al-Sottar, he had to be the key. The only one with the knowledge, the opportunity, the essential police contacts and the motivation. And Connie. No reason to doubt it. He turned over on to his stomach, his eyes to the wall. The whole deal must have been planned way before he'd set off on the trip. Had she even then been in on it all? The talc, the money? Hector, the original sacrificial lamb? A fat, reddish brown bug scuttled along the wall, quick but not quick enough. The side of his fist smashed its carapace, however hard, to pulp. Hot, hot, hot. It must be over fifty degrees of heat in here right now.

Again he looked at the bank statement with its familiar withdrawals and deposits and the one enormous, unfamiliar deposit. Remembering Ferris-Bartholomew's enigmatic reference he turned it over, started to read the tiny print on the back, sat up as soon as he started on point three. Someone - he assumed Jeremy - using exactly the same minute typescript had written, 'T.T. Please destroy this having read it. We suspect … has been using you and the Marina to import C. Your Philipino found out and tried to get in on the act, believing the operation was yours. He was discovered. Now you are taking the fall. No proof and even if we had proof we could not overtly use it. We have done everything possible to delay things and will try to go on doing so, but …' (in case this was read by the wrong person the diplomat left out the name Al-Sottar)… is highly connected and probably has some of the authorities in tow. C is still in the Kingdom, safe but sorry to say on the other side. Bear up, Thomas! We are trying.'

Slowly, still facing the wall for what small privacy there was, he tore the statement into small pieces ready for depositing, later, down the latrine drain. For the first time since the plane had touched down he felt himself other than completely on his own. And now it was as if his mind had reached out and had found the old, cold focus. So you lie here until it happens or you make a move to get the hell out. What do you want to do?

He tried to round up the Magic Circle escape thinking to date. But all of that was just so much bollocks.

Maurice and Henk had been summoned by the head Warden and told they were to be released. Now they were back, packing up their small possessions. According to the Dutchman, now almost loquacious, no reason had been given. "They just say to us, you are go out. Nobody tell me why. Maybe they know the guys who get me in here - bastards OK to bottom of Zuider Zee pretty soon, huh?"

Thomas scribbled on a scrap of paper, 'Bradley Scott - 0044 02717 8888'. He spoke quietly with Henk. "If you can, will you remember to call that number in England?" Henk nodded and tucked the note into the breast pocket of his shirt. "Soon as you can please, Henk,"

Thomas urged, "I might not have too much time. Brad's an old pal. Tell him where I am and why…" he hesitated, then, "Tell him from me I've been well and truly stitched up. 'Stitched up,' got it? Tell him I need his help, big time and fast. Will you do that for me?"

The Dutchman nodded. "OK, Mister Thomas, 'stitched up'; what you want I should tell this guy to do?"

"Don't worry about that, he'll know what to do." He grinned. "Don't forget, call him before you get too pissed up back in Rotterdam, OK Henk? And for Christ's sake try to stay out of any more jails, will you?"

The giant Dutchman offered him a sweaty palm and a bunch of hard banana fingers. "Yes sir. You keep these guys not go crazy." To the others, "Auf weidersein, you guys. Come, Maurice, my friend, let's go the fuck out of here."

Saeed said, "Dutchman, go have yourself a pint of the black stuff for the black man, OK?" Once more the huge grin.

But the place now had filled with a very strange kind of sadness.

For prisoners meeting their legal representation there was this white washed room without a window situated close by the gate house, and beneath Al-Khomein's office. Doctor Abdullah Al-Ashalli was a slightly built lawyer wearing a startlingly white thobe and gutra and expensive, well polished black sandals. He had been approached and briefed by the British Embassy, he said, adding quickly that of course the matter of his fee was of no concern to them. The air conditioning in the interview room struggled to counter the heat, which had risen to levels exceptional even by Middle East standards. Their first meeting didn't last long, just long enough to establish costs and agree on how he would be paying them. He should be able to cover things from his local account if he could rely on Sheila to take care of the boys' school fees for a while.

On the first Thursday after the lawyer's initial visit Dave and Brian came to call. They were - had been - his neighbours in the compound. Visits like this had to be conducted through the wire, the visitors restricted by a yellow tape laid out across the floor two metres behind the mesh. No touching or passing of anything except words, shouted rather than spoken for always there were more visitors than shoulder space, and more inmates trying to address them. Together with the incredible heat and humidity this led to considerable bad-tempered jostling for position, to imprecations and threats from the guards and to visits of often embarrassingly short duration.

"How you doin' Thomas?" Dave shouted, "Christ, it's like bloody Arsenal - Man U in here."

Thomas shook his head, projecting his elbow into an over-persistent set of ribs. "You can get used to it. How's Marie?" He accepted that the two of them would have been sent as emissaries and as observers to fuel the fires of gossip that always flared and raged around the Compound, even more so now. The wives and all the other families would be waiting their report.

"Marie's great. Sends her love."

"Yes, thanks. Hey, it's good of you to come." Conscious of his six weeks old beard and the general dilapidation of his appearance, he couldn't for the life of him think of anything much more to say, much less to shout.

"Anything you need, Thomas?" Dave shouted.

"How about a girl?" he shouted back, and his grin was dutifully returned. "Or maybe a pair of wings?" then, more seriously, "Books? Biography if possible. Military." That brought some relief but neither of them mentioned his arrest nor asked him, for what had he been arrested. Certainly not for his views on the possibility and type of his impending punishment. They would know all about those issues. Their visit did not last long.

On the evening of that same day he was rousted out and informed by Doctor Al-Ashali that his trial had been set for August 28th. After the trial he would be moved from Al-Mahli into a new jail - that was, of course, if he'd been found guilty. They both knew without saying what kind of a jail that was and where it was and what happened after that in the square that it overlooked.

Another day, another visitor, but this time the one he'd been hoping and praying for, had he the religion. Fighting his way through the scrummage and up to the wire he picked out Bradley Scott standing on the end of the line, apparently trying out some comment on an obviously bemused guard; the mother-shit bastard. Brad looked as cool, as comfortable and confident as always, his film star good looks commanding attention even in here. As soon as he saw Thomas he stepped straight across the tape, grinning, coming right up to the wire for Thomas to shake the three fingers that were all he could fit through the mesh. The guard screamed out a warning, his scrawny face dark with the potential for official violence. Brad turned and smiled at the man in apology. "Just testing," he muttered, raising both hands and retreated backwards over the floor tape. In the new comparative silence Thomas heard him tell the man, "Sorry, I am really sorry my stupid little prick friend," still smiling, watching for understanding. Receiving none he added, the smile increasing into a grin, "Why don't you take a running fuck at a rolling doughnut or something?"

Thomas said, "That's it, Brad, try it in Gaelic, why don't you?" The unholy din was starting up again, the incident forgotten in the general effort to deliver and receive messages of love, desire, regret and / or any other human condition or emotion that could be communicated in these circumstances and in any of the languages here in use.

Brad shouted, "What a bloody memory you have Mister Thornton! My name's Simon; Simon McAllister, remember?"

Thomas caught on quickly. He nodded. "Sorry, Simon."

"I got your Dutchman's message, old son. We knew all about it anyway. And the old man gave me a call. Got me the necessary paperwork. Benefits of having been in the business, right?"

Thomas shouted back, "The Colonel? You're working for him?"

"Yes, I told you in London, right? When do they hear your case?"

"Twenty eighth."

"What d'you reckon?"

"The bastards have me laid out and all stitched up. No chance."

"No plans?"

"Some. Nothing really feasible."

"So you'll be taking the level ten then, right?" Escape level ten? Yes: *When all else has failed and your permanent incapacitation or death is inevitable it is imperative to attempt a full frontal assault on your captors, whatever the odds against. A surprise attack from a totally defensive position can sometimes succeed. However if things have reached this stage your main hope may only be to destroy or disable as much as possible of the enemy force.*

"Right. I need to talk to you," he shouted. "I have my eighty two ten, yes? You have the same. You have it on you?"

For a moment Brad looked puzzled then he nodded, casually putting his hand in his trouser pocket to indicate his Nokia 8210 mobile phone.

"How about some fish and chips?"Thomas shouted.

"You have the batter?" Brad's hand moved. His fingers would be slotting off the battery, extracting the mobile phone's chip.

Thomas nodded. "I have about thirty minutes batter, max."

Brad said, "OK get ready. Let's just hope that guy doesn't have any lead in his pencil." He stepped quickly up to the wire again and their fingers touched and then he had it, he had the microchip, but the

80

mother-shit guard's automatic was unholstered and those who saw it panicked, scrambling and falling over each other to get out of the firing line. For the second time Brad put his hands up in mock surrender, moving back over the line. "Sorry, sorry," he said, "I do hope your brother makes you a gift of his syphilis." He smiled winningly. The scowling guard slowly re-holstered his weapon, the crowd re-formed and the tumult re-started.

"Nice one, Simon," Thomas called, "Simon, that's good. Where's the amazing dancing bear then?"

Brad said, "Very funny. Remember this number: It's UK." He spoke it slowly. "Nineteen sixty two. Eight thousand and twenty. You got that?" The level of his voice had been forced to rise along with the re-asserting sounds of Bedlam.

Tom nodded. "Nineteen sixty two, eight thousand and twenty. The Colonel?"

Brad nodded.

"Got you. You best get going. Where will you be?" It was like shouting through a super heated, Bedlamic mist in here.

"Gulf Meridien," Brad shouted back. "Just stay out of trouble. Stupid of me to say it to you, pal, but still…" He winked, saluted Thomas, waved to mother-shit, forced his way out through the throng.

Very early morning, out in the shit-house Thomas dialled the number. The Colonel must have been expecting the call. Must have stayed up for that purpose. He said, "Good to hear from you, Thomas, I understand we must keep it short." He hesitated. "You're outside? It's raining there?"

"No, sir, I'm standing under a shower. It doesn't rain where I am."

"Well, everyone to their own I suppose. The number you need is nineteen seventy eight then seven hundred and sixty seven and forty six."

Quickly, he entered the number into his phone's memory. "Thank you, sir. That's Brad's new number?"

"Yes. Two quick things though. Firstly, I may take it that your situation is absolutely clean? I would like to hear you tell me as much, if correct."

"Yes sir, correct it is. Clean as a whistle." He spoke quietly, disappointed about the question, then turned it into a joke. "I'm standing in the shower, so it damn well should be."

"You will appreciate that I had to ask you that," the Colonel said. "Number two: I don't want you to worry about your sons. I'm in touch with your sister. I shall see to it that your boys will be all right. And I mean, whatever happens next. Finance included but not exclusive. Is that understood?"

"Understood," he said, "And I think you'll know how relieved I am to hear it. I can only say thank you for that, Colonel. So, I'll be seeing you. I mean, I hope so anyway."

"Pretty well definitely, I'd say. As I recall it you are a most, ah, a most resourceful young man. Good luck to you."

"Not so young any more but thank you anyway, Colonel." He disconnected quickly to save the battery, taking care to keep the phone within the protection of its plastic bag. The warm water that was supposed to be cold trickled through his hair and down his face. He pressed 'send.' The connection was made instantly. Brad's voice; "Simon."

"Evening, Simon. Not much battery. Listen, all the signs are I don't have that much time before the chop. We're going for it tomorrow, soon after dhur salah; sorry, I mean around thirteen hundred. That's my plan anyway. Can you go to the airport and rent a car from Budget? Take it for a week. White Toyota Cressida. If they haven't got that one then anything small and white, so long as it has the Budget sticker in its rear window and the green Arab News draped over the steering wheel. Opposite the main gate there's a side road. Park the car not less than thirty and not more than one hundred metres along there. Leave the keys taped at position eleven o clock under the front right wheel arch then bugger off. I mean get the hell out of the country, fast as you can. Just up the side road there's a supermarket. You'll be able to pick up a taxi to get back to wherever you've left the motor you've come across with. Got it?"

There was a slight pause as Brad finished his notes, then, "Roger: You said 'we', 'we're going for it; can I ask who's the 'we?'"

"A Yank, a Sudanese guy and probably a couple of Brits. Maybe two more Americans but I don't think so."

"Jesus. The Great Escape, yet. Sounds a likely bunch. They're not too, too dangerous or anything? No mass murderers to entertain? And what happens after you go for the car ride?"

"For you, nothing. You'll be well out of it. I plan for us to hide up here in KSA for almost a week. I've thought of a secure bolt-hole. We'll let the heat die down then we'll be crossing to Bahrain in inflatables. No moon on the twenty ninth. I'll have battery charging available so I'll be able to reach you, wherever. Thanks again. 'Bye now." He clicked off.

82

A week: Enough time to find her if she was indeed still here. But then what? Above the faint hiss of the shower head he heard the door opening, turned his back to hide the mobile phone in its plastic bag from the eyes of the incomer.

The old Bedouin spoke the Arabic in his own curiously archaic dialect. "Good morning, my son. There is no need to turn your back for you have nothing to fear if I have nothing to fear." The brown-stained teeth showed in a quick grin, the brown face well channelled, well chiselled by time and by sun.

Thomas laughed, stepped out of the shower stall. He stowed the wrapped mobile within his wash kit. There were no towels but even now, before dawn, the body soon dried itself. He said, "What you see is what there is and what there is, is what God made." The Arabic still came easily to him.

"God did not make your arm like that. A man made the bullet that made your arm like that. You were trying without success to catch this man-made bullet, my son?"

"No, old father. It was an accident of many years ago."

"This man with the bullet and with the accident, he was your friend? I do not think so."

Whilst he dressed himself and then for the time that remained before the prisoners started to arrive for their pre-Fajr cleansing they spoke comfortably together. It was the inconsequential talk of men who like and respect each other and at the end the old man said, "I feel you will not be long in here. I understand many of the ways of men, even of infidels. When you go from here I should wish to accompany you if this is acceptable? And perhaps I may be of help?"

Hearing the approach of another, Thomas said, "Such talk is dangerous, father. Can it not be true that wherever we go, in our hearts we will go together? Is this not enough?" Now that he had a purpose he felt himself cleaner, strong again,.

The old man nodded gravely. "It is enough, yet not enough, this I know," he said. "But you yourself must go from here quickly. For if you should remain here in this place, too soon shall the sword descend. This Mister Thomas, so much still a warrior, will not easily accept such a thing, I think."

'So much still a warrior'? Lying on his bunk, staring at the fly specked ceiling so close to his face, he listened to the other world voices calling their messages of peace and faith from all the minarets of downtown

Al-Khobar. But for Thomas Thornton it was not the time for peace. It was the time for more, again, of the violence.

Chapter Five

Thomas headed the sheet of tissue '05.30: Escape'. He wrote: 'I am going to try for out today. There is big danger in the attempt. Who comes with me & needs to know the plan? All reply by 0900 latest.'

By seven o clock the paper had been around and was back with him ...

06.00 – 3 (George) 'Let's go, OK!'

07.00 – 5 (Jimmy) 'Yes.'

07.05 – 6 (Darren) 'Yes.'

07.30 – 8 (Virgil) 'Sorry pal count me out. I'm going out the easy way and soon thanks very much good old USA.'

07.50 – 9 (Johnson) 'I'm with Virg. All the luck chief.'

07.55 – 1 (Saeed) 'Let's go Geronimo!'

He was getting used to the taste of toilet paper and ball point ink. Outside the window there was no sun for a nice change and a low haze. Wind gusting maybe fifteen knots. A whirling eddy picked up dust, swayed, tottered to the base of the wall. The plastic bag it carried hesitated, spun around and flapped off, disappearing from sight somewhere below the guard tower. He swallowed the message, tore off another sheet, took the presention folder out of his case. With his back to the light fixture he laid it on his folder, scribbled, 'I plan to get myself taken out through the wire then pick a fight with one of the guards. Am hoping they take me outside for a flogging. If they do, when my cuffs are being transferred I plan to take Al-Khomein as hostage and force an exit relying on (a) enough turmoil and confusion and (b) the ground level guards not having any real bullets in their pistols and (c) the south tower guard not disliking Al-Khomein enough to get him killed! And (d) you guys doing exactly as I tell you throughout the action. <u>If you're still in you look to me and only me.</u> Understood? OK? Answer Yes/no.'

Having passed the thing to Saeed for circulation he carefully peeled back the taped leather lining of his business folder, removed the dollar bills and the credit card and the tattered paper with his father's poem, stowed them away in the pocket of his undershorts. He put on his most recently washed shirt and a pair of light beige trousers, replaced the sandals on his feet then lay back, fingers linked behind his head.

George, Darren, Jimmy and Saeed all came back, 'yes,' He thought Saeed's suggested modification made good sense... 'I am with you but you and me should fight, not you with guard. You get yourself killed so where is our leader!'

It didn't take long. He began the argument out in the hall, close up to the wire. "Hey, fuzzy-wuzz, why don't you climb the fuck back up your tree?" he yelled, and Saeed roared out his Arabic threats. Thomas laughed, pretending not to understand the words, just their meaning. He taunted the bigger man and laughed again when the first blow brushed by his ear. But when the fist fight proper started with inmates crowding around, not all of the punches were pulled efficiently enough. He felt the pain of one especially real-world blow to the solar plexus and made a grab for his fake opponent. "Sorry," Saeed whispered. They toppled and rolled in a writhing, straining heap. When Saeed's knee stopped an undetectable fraction short of his groin Thomas gasped out in make believe pain and the crowd screamed and clapped and cheered more loudly then suddenly lapsed into silence. He realised Saeed had relaxed his grip and he was looking up through the wire into the muzzle of a guard's pistol. Thomas staggered upright, holding his crutch as the guard screamed out his excited instructions. The bleeding cut above the black man's eye was real. It looked quite bad.

Warden Al-Khomein seemed not at all disturbed. Not for the first time Thomas wondered whether the guy was psychotic, whether he might physically enjoy the pain of others. Pain there had to be, for Saeed was to receive fifteen strokes of the cane and himself thirty. After the sentencing they were taken out to the yard and chained up, each to a separate post, there to be subjected to a screamed out lecture on the futility of violence. The lecture reinforced by having their toes trodden and their legs kicked at repeated intervals.

After dhur prayers had been called the two of them were left temporarily with a minimum guard. Thomas turned his back to the flurries of wind, slitting his eyes against the swirling dust whilst the guard sheltered in the lee of the guardhouse. Speaking for the first time to Saeed in the Arabic he said, "You are all right, my friend? I am sorry about the eye."

86

The blood from the black man's split eyebrow had congealed in the stubble on his chin. He looked puzzled then grinned widely, whispered back. "Allah! You have the Arabic, Mister Thomas! This is really something of wonder. What other of Mister Thomas that I do not know? But I am fine. And you? I hope I did not really hurt you?"

"Only when I laugh, as they say. We'll need to do less damage than this when they sign us up for the movie stunts."

"Why is it that you pretend no Arabic, Mister Thomas?" Saeed whispered.

"It was in another life that I was taught it, Saeed. It was a part of the training and my work involved the people of the marshes to the north from here. For me, here, it has always been an advantage to understand what was being said without people realising." The chains rattled as he raised his hands to wipe the dust from his eyes. "Listen to me, Saeed. After salah they'll turn out the whole block." He reverted to English. "When they're all assembled, if they follow their usual procedure they'll release us from the chains, probably one at a time. They'll make us lie down then re-fasten us to the posts. They'll probably pick me first. Listen. In the very small window of time when I'm unchained, that's when I go for Al-Khomein." He hoped the pretence in his grin was not too obvious. "At least if they stop me I'll probably have got to hurt the bastard. You need to watch what I do and maybe neutralise the nearest guard, but you'll judge for yourself what's best to support me, OK? I've been told those guns of theirs aren't loaded but whatever happens, as I say, just watch and follow my lead and your instincts. It has to happen fast, bloody fast, but there's no way it can be orchestrated or stopped without blood once it's started. Are you still OK with all that?"

Saeed said, "You prefer reaction to orchestration, Mister Thomas, this I know. Like your soldiers at Obdurman, yes?" He paused, listening to the ending of the song of prayer. "Yes. So here now they come … Mister Thomas? Just one thing. It has been good … you know? It has been very good to meet you…"

"Yes, my friend, I do know; and I feel the same. I know a good man when I meet one." Thomas took a deep breath of the familiar rotting smell of downtown Al-Khobar. He felt loose now, calmed by a sick-making rush of adrenalin. The normal sounds of traffic passing outside the prison walls linked him to the world of which, he knew, he might never again be a part. But this was OK. He remembered: *In a level ten escape attempt almost any major action is better than any more minor one. In fact if your captors momentarily believe you have gone insane then so much the better, you are that much more likely to succeed. For a very short time you must rely on your training to act with total violence, without rational thought or restraint but only and always towards objective one.*

It took them ten minutes to get all the cell block three prisoners out into the yard and standing shoulder to shoulder close in around the flogging posts. As usual the Westerners were obliged to stand in the front rank. He caught George's wink, the fighter's face betraying no special concern. Jimmy Bellingham had adopted an excessively casual look of disinterest. Darren just looked sick. Ten or more of the guards had taken up their positions around the outside of the crowd and there were three more inside the ring with Saeed and himself. Glancing up he could see the guard in one of the towers leaning on his parapet, the better to observe the action, his machine gun on its swivel-post behind him tilted skywards. Finally there was more pushing and shoving as the crowd made way for Al-Khomein and his escorts. Five guards were now inside the circle. Six including the head warden.

Thomas had a quick sense of the terribly bad odds as Al-Khomein's red-chequered gutra fluttered across his face. The Head Warden pinioned it with one hand, and actually licked his lips before nodding to the guard carrying the post chains. The man stepped forward to release Saeed, ordered him to get down on the ground. 'Me first,' Thomas wanted to scream. He had known how easily this could all go wrong He was going to be left here, helpless and still manacled whilst they flogged the Sudanese. But then the guard with the chains went flying and Saeed was howling as he leaped to clamp an arm around Al-Khomein's throat, groping for his holstered pistol. George and Jimmy and Darren were for one instant of time the only moving part of the scene and then the guards had drawn their guns and a single shot sounded, deafeningly close, and Darren was looking puzzled, clutching at his abdomen, his knees flexing, straightening, collapsing, toppling forwards, rolling to lie face up, lips moving without audible sound.

In all the instant of stillness there was this one movement. The old man Mubarak Al-Jidha came seemingly without haste out of the crowd and stepped up to the guard who had shot Darren, shaking his head. "And may God have mercy on him, officer, and on that one there." He was pointing at Thomas and as the guard followed his arm the old man's hand with the steel had appeared from inside his thobe and he had turned with his grey beard close up to the guard's face, seemingly to whisper something highly confidential. Thomas watched the knife

88

slide up and into the guard's belly. The man sat heavily on the concrete. Al-Jidha removed the guard's pistol and tossed it to Thomas but, encumbered by his chains, he failed to catch the thing.

Everything went crazy. He could see George wrestling the keys from a guard with a very bloody head who seemed now to be trying to crawl away through a storm of kicks. "So let's fucking go," screamed George as he freed Thomas from his shackles.

The rest seemed very easy, perfectly natural. He retrieved the guard's pistol, checked that it was loaded - another wrong guess - then took aim and shot to miss the tower guard who he had seen swivelling his machine gun down and towards them. The man at once dropped down below the parapet, leaving his weapon to look after itself.

It was the guards rather than the prisoners who were now trying to escape but more of them went down as the mob of prisoners surged towards the main gates. Saeed still had the fat Head Warden's throat in the crook of his arm. "What you want me to do with this carrion, Mister Thomas?" he bellowed.

"Just keep hold of him," Thomas shouted back, "he's our insurance." He brushed away an unfamiliar, well-bearded Arabian face that seemed to be trying, malodorously, to kiss him. "George, pick up some of the guns. Let's get the hell out of here."

The gatehouse guard had locked himself inside but the mass of prisoners easily broke down the door and dragged him out to open the massive portals on to the street. Thomas fired one shot into the air and all went quiet as the sea of faces turned towards him. He lowered his arm and spoke quietly, in English. "Tell them, no more killing, Saeed. Tell them to go in peace and in the love of God. May He keep them safe from harm but only for so long as they do no harm."

Saeed quickly translated and the prisoners yelled and waved and suddenly it was a river that had burst its dam. Thomas held back his own group until the bulk of them had swarmed out into the road. George was trying to fit several pistols into his pockets. Saeed still held the Warden in an iron grip. He realised Al-Jidha was going to stick with him. No point in arguing that or rushing things now. He looked back in to the prison yard. A few dozen undecided prisoners milled around, studiously avoiding the several uniformed figures sprawled on the ground along with a solitary bundle of multi-coloured rags that might have been an Afghan. But there was this one figure in T-shirt and jeans, sitting with his friend's head in his lap. Jimmy looked up, shouted, "Go on, Tommy, for Christ's sake. I have to stay." Of Virgil and Johnson there was no sign.

The whole thing couldn't have taken more than a couple of minutes. Thomas looked up at the tower, fifty metres away. He took careful aim and fired. A piece of plaster flew off the parapet behind which the guard was still hiding. Prisoners were streaming away in all directions. With his small group tightly bunched he crossed the road and made off up the side street, hurrying now, finding the white Cressida with a Budget sticker in its rear window. He felt for and found the keys, unlocked the car, picked up the square of folded notepaper on the driver's seat.

George jumped into the passenger side, laughing wildly. "Hey man, let's get the fuck out of it. Jesus H Christ, I seen nothing like that."

Thomas nodded to Saeed. He had the pistol thrust into Al-Khomein's stomach, addressed the trembling, grey-faced Head Warden as Saeed released him. "Now, perhaps you would be so good as to return my watch?" The Warden scrambled to get if off and hand it over. "And I need your gutra, your igal and your ghafia," he said. He saw the defiance beginning to build, moved the muzzle up to point into the man's right eye. "I need them now, right now." He didn't have to decide on his action if faced by the negative. Al-Khomein tore off his head covering and threw it down to the pavement. Thin wisps of dyed black hair were an embarrassing attempt to hide his baldness. "You are so stupid, Thornton," the man said, fear and attempted defiance congealing in his voice. "And you are a dead man, English, do not you know this?"

"Pick that up and hand it to me," Thomas said quietly. "And now your thobe please."

George yelled, "For Christ's sake, Tommy! Come on. Let's get the fuck out of here." Mubarak Al-Jidha was standing by, a slow smile spreading over his ancient gap-toothed face.

"Your thobe," repeated Thomas. He moved the point of his aim a fraction and sent a bullet past Al-Khomein's ear. The warden's trembling fingers unbuttoned the wrists and the neck, pulled the garment over his head. Thomas took it and tossed it and the head-dress on to George's lap, ran around to the driver's door leaving the head warden transfixed, comical in his voluminous undershorts and undershirt, black shoes and socks, eyes filling with the silent tears of impotence.

The old Bedouin stood there alongside Al-Khomein, asking for nothing, the first guard's blood stiffening across the midriff of his dirty thobe. In Arabic Thomas said, "Father, will you please do me the honour of getting into this car with us?"

George said, wonderingly, "Holy shit, the man has the fucking Arabic now! What the hell's going on here?"

Calm and unmoving the old man said, "You have need of me, my son?"

"Yes, I do have need of you. Please get in. We need you to come with us." He looked at the scrap of paper: *'Dead ahead five blocks. Farm 15 Supermarket. ATM. Red Merc. Hertz. (Figured you'll need to switch.) Same key place. Luck.'*

Mubarak shrugged and got into the back of the car alongside Saeed. George shook his head then addressed the rear view mirror. "Hiya buddy," he said, "welcome aboard." And then more quietly to Thomas' "Are you crazy? We gonna trust this rag-head?"

Firing the engine and pulling away Thomas said, "There's no problem: George Schwartz, meet Mubarak Al-Jidha."

"Yeah yeah, we were introduced, remember?"

"We need him George," Thomas said, quietly, "And I don't know if you noticed but he just killed a guy for us in there. We wouldn't have made it otherwise." He looked in the rear view mirror. The Head Warden stood unmoving on the pavement. "How many guns we have?" he asked.

George said, "Four plus yours. Christ, I thought you'd blown the warden's fucking head off back there. Shee-it, they still do hanging, drawing and quartering around here? This fucking better be the last we see of Al-Mahli jail, my crazy friend." He shook his head, laughing wildly, Saeed joining in as they pulled into the Farm 15 car park. A kind of euphoria. In the mirror he could see old Mubarak frowning, clearly much puzzled.

Thomas drove once by the red Mercedes then parked fifty metres away. One at a time they transferred, Saeed first with key finding instructions, Mubarak next, carrying the small bundle of Al-Khomein's clothes to hide the blood, then George and himself last. He locked up and strolled into the store then out again to the Merc, patting his pockets in annoyance as if he'd forgotten something.

Saeed took the wheel to exit the supermarket, the big car's engine almost inaudible. Thomas realised he'd been holding his breath, listening for the shouts and the sirens. Nothing. Ten minutes plus and still nothing.

Saeed said, "There is another note around the key, Mister Thomas. You have very good friends." It read, 'Up and out by time you get this. Five o clock high' Brad must be in the air heading south south east. That must mean Dubai then, probably for the switch of passports before back to England. If you read me I guess you've had all the good luck but HAVE SOME MORE anyway. In the trunk - Food for six for a few days. Clothes in case needed. In the glove compartment, few travel bits.' Thomas opened the glove box. In it there was water, soft drinks, boiled sweets, cigarettes and matches.

Saeed glanced across. "Yes," he repeated, "You have good friends, boss, Too much good for the nerves, I think."

He turned west, out on to the main highway. The sign said 400 km to Riyadh. He could see the speck of a plane climbing out of Dammam, heading south south east and merging now with the cloud base. He thought, 'Be on that, Bradley, my friend. Just be on that and be very lucky yourself.'

George said, "Well, I gotta hand it you, buddy. I don't know how you were to the enemy but you sure the fuck impress me. You going to tell us where we're headed now?" The first of a line of police cars was rocketing by in the opposite lane, heading into the city, sirens blaring, blue lights flashing. The car in front had wandered into their lane, its driver concentrating on his rear view mirror, looking for the cause of all the fuss.

Thomas said, "Our situation is this: There's road blocks being set up all over Khobar and Dammam by now, or there very soon will be. For sure they'll be searching every car doing the Bahrain Causeway but I doubt they'll be paying the same kind of attention to traffic moving in this direction, west, inland. Remember they'll be looking for a white Cressida and there must be thousands of those around here. Anyway I plan for us to be back in Khobar soon after dark tonight. I'll explain why later. Until then we'll have to find somewhere to rest up. Saeed, I want you to put on Al-Khomein's kit. You'll carry on with the driving. I'll be the boss in the back and George, you'll be hunkered there with Mr Al-Jidha as near invisible as possible." Saeed had already begun to change into the warden's clothing. He repeated himself in Arabic, glancing in the mirror to be sure of Mubarak's understanding.

The old man's expression did not change as he leaned forwards. He said "There is a place, a little further on if you turn off this highway towards Hofuf. There is a track used by my people who are not there now. Along there we and this red car can be hidden from above and from the ground."

"My thanks to you, Mr Mubarak." To Saeed he said, in English, "You got that, Saeed? Take the track when he indicates, OK."

George said, "You serious? How the hell do we know we won't get bogged down in there?" He swung his head around the horizon of red-beige sand hills.

"No worries, George. If we were in downtown Brooklyn right now I'd trust you, wouldn't I? We're not in Brooklyn, we're in the bloody desert and in the desert we trust our friend Mubarak Al-Jidha."

The track wound its way on through the dunes. Several times he wondered if George could be right about the risk of getting bogged down. He also worried about the dust-cloud, so easy to spot from any searching helicopter. But at last Saeed pulled up beside a group of tattered canvas awnings. Sand-drifted tyre tracks were everywhere in evidence and the wheel-less wreck of a Toyota pickup seemed to have been built into a nearby dune. Mubarak indicated for Saeed to drive the Mercedes under one of the awnings, taking care to avoid its pegged out ropes.

The engine switched off and in the new silence the old man said, "Yes, this is good, and soon it will be time for asir salah."

"Mid-afternoon prayers," Thomas translated. "Everything stops for them".

Saeed nodded. "Yes, this is very good. Mister Thomas, you are hungry? I am very hungry. Perhaps before salah we may see what your friend has placed for us into the trunk of the car?"

They sat in the shade of the awning alongside the dusty red Mercedes, eating and drinking and talking of what had happened and what might be happening to the hundreds of escapees. George wondered whether Darren was still alive but they all knew he was probably not. The vast majority of close range belly shots were fatal. And the guard? And Jimmy, Virgil, Johnson? But finally the concentrated action, and their nervous exhaustion and the heat had overcome each of them except Mubarak, who had climbed the nearest major sand dune in order to keep watch. George and Saeed stretched out on the sand and went to sleep and finally Thomas leaned back against the front wheel of the car, closed his eyes. George and Saeed would be great assets; strong, determined and resourceful, each in their own way. But he worried about the role and the future of the old desert Arab.

When he woke the clouds had gone and the wind had dropped and the sun was low in the sky. The deserted encampment was now in shadow. He stood up, stretched and yawned, decided to follow the old Saudi's tracks up the steep bank of shifting, sliding sand. Mubarak was sitting cross-legged, facing west. He nodded gravely as Thomas sat down alongside him.

From here you could see for a good long way, even though the perspective and distance tended to become confused by the abstraction of a myriad sharply shadowed dunes. He and Mubarak talked together for a while. The talk was of the comfortable, sporadic, inconsequential kind; talk of how it was with the cold silence of the desert by night, the silence in which, if you had the ears for it you could hear the music of the universe. They spoke of how it was with the mumbling of the camels as you rode, in line astern, across the vastness, following the ways of your forefathers, and about the hunting especially that with the hawk which you had trained to drop out of the sun into the eyes of the fleeing gazelle, thus blinding him against the mercy of your knife.

For no reason obvious to himself Thomas took out from the plastic Amex envelope the poem of his father, the one about the Fourth-light. He explained about the writing and the sending to him of the poem, when he had been eight years old, and about how he had received it, and the knowledge of his father's death on that same day. He read the poem through now, out aloud, translating the words as best he was able. The fierce old face was cut by the fast gathering darkness.

When it was finished Mubarak stayed silent for a while then murmured, "Yes. Your father was a man."

Thomas said, "This I know." He could hear the voices of George and Saeed now, slip-stepping up the dune in the last of the light. It was time for sunset salah and the old man knelt, facing westwards to Mecca.

"Mind if we join you folks?" George sat down, breathless. "Wow, that sure is one sight to remember." Thomas put his finger to his lips, indicating Mubarak. Saeed nodded, knelt alongside him. In front of them the sky was of indigo pricked by stars, washed in the west by streaks of pinks and reds and purples. Turning to look behind, in the distant darkness he could see the headlights on the Hofuf road and, far beyond that, the sky-glow of Al-Khobar and Dammam. Seated, silent and unmoving, he felt strangely a part but not a part of any of this.

Afterwards, in the semi-darkness Thomas told them about how he planned for them to drive back to Al-Sottar Marine. He knew a way into the boat yard. Once in there he would get them on board the Prince's motor yacht Jazeera. He told them she'd lain there all summer long whilst her owner indulged himself on Spain's Costa del Sol. There

94

would in the normal way be a watchman making occasional rounds but with the place closed down who could know? In any case the watchman could be avoided or perhaps even bribed. They would play it by ear. They would take care to leave no trace of their presence and on the night of the twenty ninth when there was no moon they would be heading out and away across the straits, making for Bahrain. He would take a rubber boat from the store-room behind the Marina shop. He knew people in Bahrain, people they could rely on for safe shelter. After that, well, he had some ideas for getting them out of Bahrain and into Europe. Of course each of them would need to decide exactly where they wanted to go, but they would have plenty of time to talk through all that once they were safely on board *Jazeera*. He stood up, said, "Everyone OK with this?"

George said, "Tommy, why wait? Why don't we just get the fuck out, fast across to Bahrain on this motor yacht of yours?"

"Not mine, George, and no way. We wouldn't get a mile out in that before they get us on radar and send in the gunboats. Those buggers do forty five knots. End of story." Thomas was speaking in English, his voice subdued.

Saeed murmured, "I understand, but Mister Thomas, I am sorry; it will not work for me. This of the small rubber boat. I am truly sorry. You should know that I cannot swim."

"What's swimming got to do with it, Saeed?" Thomas tried not to smile. "I don't suppose any of us would like to try swimming it. It's twentyfive klix across there, and a hell of a lot more with the tide drift. Listen, you'll just be sitting in a boat with the rest of us, safe and dry, OK? So don't worry about it."

He translated what he had said for the sake of Mubarak. The old man nodded, said, "You will understand that I shall of course not go with you, Mister Thomas, although surely I shall be with you." By the glimmer of the rising half-moon he raised his hands against the protest. "Here, where we are, this is my home. When all is safe I shall find my people. Or they shall find me if Allah wills it."

George said, in the silence, "What's the old guy saying? Anyone going to let me in on it?"

Thomas said, "He says he's staying here, George. His home is here in the desert." Reverting to the Arabic he said, "We understand you, father. And may Allah, peace be upon Him, may He be with you. But will you not come back with us to somewhere safe within the city?"

"No, why do I need the city? I am contented here. Here there is the peace of God and I shall not be found other than by my own people.

Perhaps you can leave me some water and just a little of this strange food of yours?" The old man chuckled.

They got to their feet, ready to go, and the others shook Mubarak by the hand. Thomas embraced the scrawny old figure. "I know not what to say to you, father, except goodbye, and that I go in peace. I shall not forget Mubarak Al-Jidha."

"Thomas Thornton, be kind to yourself. Do not waste yourself on those who offend you and offend themselves and who are an offence to Allah, yes, may peace be upon Him. And remember that a man is not a plant to be plucked from its place in the ground and put down anywhere at will." He patted Thomas's back. "Now go. I shall sit. I shall watch your car lights until they reach the highway and after that, as you once said to me, my son, I shall be with you if only in my thoughts."

Thomas turned away, "Later I shall return," he said. "This I am planning. None shall know of this but you and I and none but you and I can know the reason for it. The reason is that which you have told to me about my wife, old father."

"Yes," said Mubarak Al-Jidha. "This, also, I understand. And you shall know where I am when that time comes, insh'allah. I have said within that house of Al-Sottar there is a man that is to be trusted. He is a man of a foreign place and his name is Joey."

"Yes. I know of this man, Joey," said Thomas, momentarily seeing the beach house and the small, courteous Philipino bringing out the drinks and the food to those seated around Abdul-Rahman's table. Halfway down the dune he stopped, turned to look back. The old tribesman, his hand raised in farewell, was once more seated on the massive but moveable castle of sand, sculpted so beautifully at the hand of his God.

When they had driven as far as the road George broke the silence. "That," he said, "was some Arab, some great old fucking Arab. And I never even got to know how come he was in jail."

Saeed hunched forward over the steering wheel to see past a pair of oncoming headlights. "For not too much, he was in jail," he murmured. "As I heard, he was breaking into the house of some Saudi sheikh. It seems Mubarak's daughter was in much trouble there. They say Mubarak was trying to break her out and I do not know how, but he is said to have hurt some people." He turned on to the Highway, heading back towards the city. "But yet I am with you, George, for that was indeed some great old Arab." He shook his head admiringly.

"Never did I see such knife-work." He glanced across at Thomas. "And he is as a father to you, is he not?"

Thomas said, "That's right, Saeed." I am lucky, he thought; I am lucky to have had three such fathers in my life.

Chapter Six

He gave it ten minutes, sitting in the darkness watching for signs of life in the boatyard.

Tonight downtown Al-Khobar had been a hive of police sirens, dozens of them, and of clattering helicopters and of crowds of people out on the streets, probably quite thrilled by this rare, not entirely unwelcome discomfiture of the authorities, spread by word of mouth rather than any media.

Saeed had been marvellous. On two occasions his understanding of the traffic flows around and about in the city's side streets had saved them from the road blocks and the identity checks that, paperless, they could never have survived. For the past two hours they'd stayed, crouched well down in their seats, in the Gulf hotel car park, speaking only in whispers, waiting for things to quieten down. He recalled the book... *When you are out of cover and being hunted consider the hare. When he knows the dogs are around his first instinct is to lie low. Any movement will give the advantage to the hunter. You should move only as a last resort. When it is absolutely necessary to make a move whilst still in the vicinity of an observant enemy you must act fast and in a pre-meditated direction. As with the hare, the shock of your breaking cover will give you an advantage, however temporary.*

There had been no need for such a breaking of cover. They'd slipped quietly away from the hotel car park, threaded though the streets to the industrial docks area and stopped opposite their destination. Al-Sottar Marine was in moonlit darkness, the name-sign switched off, no lights in the gatehouse nor in the offices nor the chandlery store windows. But there was almost certain to be a night watchman or police guard, probably asleep in the gatehouse by now.

Thomas murmured, "Take the car around the corner out of sight of the gatehouse, Saeed. Stay with it. You too, George. If anyone comes by just make sure you're well down out of sight. I won't be long." He closed the door quietly behind him and walked alongside the wire topped marina wall until it took a right angled turn towards the tide-line. He negotiated the sandy wasteland with its discarded bottles and cans and piles of dumped-out builders' spoil, eventually reaching the place where the wall gave way to spiked iron railings extending out into the water. The moonlight was bright, the night ominously still. Motionless, he stood in the shadow of the wall, listening. From somewhere out amongst the tethered boats came a splatter of fish fry, the surface tail-slap of a bigger fish in pursuit. Nothing else close by. He could see the greyhound silhouette of the multi-million dollar *Jazeera* in her customary pride of place along the pontoon walkway.

He'd been meaning to get the railings repaired after that Pakistani had been found trapped in the razor wire that he presumed still lay there, coiled beneath the surface of the water. Feeling a touch of the fellow sufferer's sympathy, he remembered the vehemence and with what tearfulness the poor little guy with the bleeding legs had tried to deny his obvious, failed attempt at a break-in. He could see that nobody had yet got around to fixing it. He forced open the gap, pulled himself through, moved across the yard between the ramped up vessels. *Distant Waters* was still with the others up on the stocks where she'd been on the day of his pretended re-enaction.

The reserve set of office keys were still in their hiding place. He let himself in through the rear door, keyed off the alarm, felt his way into the back of the store to locate the rack of torches, lights and battery packs. By touch he selected a variable intensity torch, loaded it with batteries, switched it on and dimmed it right down. Inside his office - *his* office - he opened the security keys cupboard and found the set labelled *Jazeera*. He waited a good two minutes by the rear door, watching out through the window and listening. Still nothing so he slipped out and down the pontoon, taking care to avoid the boats' mooring lines.

Jazeera lay like the seventy four foot queen of the Marina that she was. Even now he couldn't help admiring the beauty of her. He stepped aboard, used the key to turn off security. Waiting out the necessary twenty seconds he opened the door then made his way through to the twin level saloon, using the torch on its dimmest setting to open the safe. Bingo, the owner's keys were still in place. Pocketing them, he retraced his steps, closing everything up behind him and replacing in sequence the torch, the yard's set of *Jazeera* keys and the office keys. He moved slowly, with extreme care: *So long as you remain undiscovered and on the run, cover up all visible traces of your presence. But remember your scent cannot be covered completely other than by fire. It may be obscured to varying degrees by water or by a stronger scent but it cannot be eliminated.*

He approached the Mercedes from behind, knocked on the window. George jumped up, wide-eyed, "Jesus H, Tommy, do not do that again," he murmured, "Fucking nerves bad enough without that."

"Sorry, pal, but anyway everything's OK. Let's get the stuff out of the boot."

Saeed said, "I hope you're going to accommodate us in the style to which I wish to become accustomed, Mister Thomas. We are no damn ordinary run of the mill jailbirds, you know." He stifled the laugh, loaded himself up with bags.

"Well, I think you might just like this next bit, black man." Thomas said.

The moonlight made the going easy but the procession would be very visible should anyone be around. He led them across the waste land, this time keeping to a route well clear of the wall so as not to create too obvious a track, then turned left to walk within the tide line up to the broken railings. Later he would have to see if their tracks were too obvious. If so he would have to find a way to obscure them. Once inside the yard, wordlessly he pointed out the hazardous mooring lines and standing bollards as they moved slowly and in extreme silence in single file along the walkway.

Inside the boat, even by such moonlight as could penetrate her eye-shaped windows *Jazeera*'s master saloon was wonderfully impressive. "Man," whispered George, "If this ain't just like home: just like home fucking ought to be, anyways." He was moving around the eighteen foot wide, split level saloon, moving soundlessly on the thick pile carpets, touching the contoured, brushed leather seating, the great mahogany dining table.

"Already I am feeling sea-sick," whispered Saeed.

"I hope you're joking," Thomas said. "But listen up. The A.C. in this boat comes on automatically whether she's occupied or not. It's run off an external power line so long as the boat's moored up. She's very well sound proofed but please don't go turning on the hi-fi or anything. We've got the master bedroom up forward and three more double bed cabins besides the crew's accommodation aft."

Wonderingly, George said, "You could fit half of cell block three in here. This is awesome."

Thomas went to the engine room to look for and find two more torches. He tested them for battery life then went back to hand one to each of them. "We use these only when necessary," he said. "They won't help your night vision so keep the dimmer well down and never on any account show a light that can be seen through the windows. In the morning I'll show you around but remember, all the time we're here it's a case of minimum movement, minimum sound, minimum artificial lights. And no cooking equals no smells so we must use the stove only to boil water. All garbage - and I mean all of it, to be bagged and stored with our goodies - I'll show you where. It has to be taken off each night." He tried to read their expressions, lightened it all up. "Tea, coffee anyone? Yes, we do have the stronger stuff but we're not going to touch it; are we, George?"

George whispered, "Roger and out. Shit, this is unreal. When they going to come and wake me up? Yeah, I'll take a cup of coffee with you, skip."

"Let's all just relax. You can sleep for as long as you like, except for the six hours a day when you'll be on watch. We'll do shifts. Six in the morning to twelve, twelve to six, six to midnight and midnight to six. But right now I have to go back to move the car. It's just too obvious where it is."

"Inshallah. But, boss, you must risk going back to the car?"

"Do me a small favour, Saeed? Please don't call me that. But yes. I want us to leave zero pointers for them; zero, understand? No strange car parked outside, no crumbs, no dirty dishes in the sink, no drops of water on the bathtub, nothing. And not just while we're here. Even after we've gone I want nobody to know anyone was here." He sensed rather than saw their puzzlement. "There's a special reason for this. I'll be telling you about that later on. But about the car; I plan on calling Hertz once we're up and away. Its cost is taken care of for a week."

George said, "Hey, this is incredible. There's dead and damaged guys laid out everywhere, we've got half Al-Khobar after us with long fucking swords and you worry about Mister Hertz's dough?"

"No tracks, George; no tracks, OK?"

"You're the boss."

Saeed said, "It should be me that takes to hide the Mercedes. I am less likely to be picked up. Nobody here will notice a black man in a thobe." As if by way of emphasis came the middle distance rise and fall of a police car siren.

Thomas thought about it for a moment, then, "I think maybe you're right. OK"

George muttered, "They probably have Al Khomein locked up in cell nine with Virg and Johnson. Fucking hope so anyway. But I wish Darren had made it, poor bastard. One of these days I'm going to get to that town of his. What was it, Manchester? See what this soccer of his is all about."

"We have a saying in Sudan, Mister George," said Saeed. "Speak not of a future sunrise for only God can be sure about such a thing."

They stowed their provisions away in a locked cupboard in the galley, made themselves coffee, ate some biscuits and fruit. The master bathroom was that of a four star hotel. Thomas had been looking forward to this as much as to anything. He filled the giant triangular bathtub, climbed down into the hot water, lay back and closed his eyes, his mind racing over what had been and what would be. Taking care to avoid getting the mobile wet he called the number given him by the Colonel. Brad answered on the second ring. Wherever he was he seemed to be part of a group, for Thomas could hear his friend excusing himself.

After a moment, "Hi there, wanderer. You OK?" Brad said.

"Oh sure, but I'm watching words. Very little left in the battery. May cut off but later on I can top up where I am. I have two men with me. Thanks for the all the stuff. I owe you, pal. Plan A's still in place for around the twenty ninth."

"Great. I do believe you left a fair amount of mayhem behind you."

"Guess so. Don't tell me they've woken up to the media?"

"Wouldn't go that far. Channels, my friend, channels. Word is there's been a big riot. Seems your lot hit the streets then someone let out the other cell blocks. But most of those are still holed up inside. There's shit and bullets everywhere. By all accounts the inmates have the Governor or whoever, and they've been giving him more than a bit of the old stick. Anyway, lots of cold ones down Al-Mahli way ..."

The mobile announced it's need for power and promptly died in Thomas' hand. He lay back, tried to weigh up the implications in what had been said. 'Lots of cold ones' and no doubt more to die. And yet, 'was it worth it' was not a question to be pondered. Worth what? How about what the Government had been doing in Ireland with his keen and eager help and the help of so many others like himself? Had that all been 'worth it'?

He dressed in some of the clean clothing. Taking Saeed with him and leaving George stretched out on one of the settees the two of them made their silent way back to the car. Saeed was still in the Warden's Saudi headgear and thobe. There seemed to be an accumulation of helicopters over in the direction of Dammam and the airport but no sign of activity outside or inside the boat yard. Thomas whispered, "It'll be OK just to leave the car in one of the big town centre car parks. It won't get noticed for a few days."

"Yes, I see the choppers, Mister Thomas. I shall walk back to here pretty damn quick, no problem."

"Try to make sure there's no-one about when you come back across the waste-ground, OK? Keep to the shadow of the wall and watch the gatehouse. There has to be a guard in there, probably asleep but you never know. If you see any movement stay clear until the guy goes back to bed. Good luck, my friend. Give me a couple of minutes before you start her up."

"You have it, boss." The big teeth gleamed in the darkness. "We do good work today, right, Mister Tom? They going to have something to talk about, I think."

Thomas said, "Let's just make sure our own story has a happy ending."

Just as he was stepping aboard the boat he saw lights closing in on the marina from seawards, even now beginning the swing around the end of the harbour wall. Inside the saloon George was lying stretched out along half the length of the settee beneath the window that looked out on to the pontoon, oblivious to the danger. "Hi, welcome aboard, skip. Everything OK?"

Thomas locked the door behind him. "Not necessarily. Keep well clear of the windows, George, we have company." He grinned into the gloom. "Funny, I always wanted to say that." From well back inside the stateroom they watched the slowly moving police boat's spotlight playing around the lines of tethered yachts. She crept by, not twenty metres away. He remembered the security meetings with the local and marine police. "I think this is just a routine patrol, except they'll be on special alert for jailbirds tonight," he whispered. Thanks to the sound-proofing they couldn't hear the play of the launch's engines nor the slap of her wash on boats and pontoons. *Jazeera* shifted restlessly. He began to worry that he might have left his wet footprints along the pontoon walkway. The police boat reached the inshore end of the line, turned, reversed and ran forward again, heading back towards them, but instead of proceeding back out to the open sea she cut her speed still further, nosed into a gap a few boats away, ran up alongside the pontoon and stopped. The spotlight extinguished itself.

Thomas said, "Shit. We could have problems now." A dark figure appeared on her forward deck, jumped with mooring line in hand on to the pontoon, expertly swinging a hitch turn around a bollard.

104

"What the fuck we do now?" George asked. An automatic pistol had appeared in his hand.

Thomas felt the comfort of his own weapon inside his belt. "Nothing," he said. "We do nothing except watch and wait and hope to Christ these boys are long gone by the time Saeed comes back."

"OK. So what's plan B, Tommy?" George muttered, "What the fuck we do if our African friend comes marching along, bumps straight into the bastards?"

"I'm hoping he'll notice their lights in time. But if all else fails there's usually three of them on board. If they jump Saeed they won't be expecting us to come at them from the seawards side. Just have to play it by ear after that. I don't know, maybe make a run for it in their boat. We'll have to wait and see." He groaned softly as one of the launch's uniformed occupants jumped down on to the pontoon then began to stroll shore-wards, losing himself behind the line of boats. A light had come on in the guardhouse. They could see someone coming down to the pontoons, torchlight weaving around. "It's the boatyard guard. Probably routine for him to meet up with them."

"They'll never take me alive," George murmured, "And that's one *I* always wanted to say." Thomas checked on the time: 01.00. Very faintly he could hear a short, staccato burst of voice from the police boat's radio. By 01.30 there was still no sign of Saeed and the patroller had re-boarded the police launch. The guardian of the yard disembarked and shouted out his goodnights, waved once and walked back up the walkway. The launch's mooring lines were released, then came the reverse burst of power and the forward swing out into the channel. Her spotlight came back on, picked up and played around *Jazeera* and the other craft then gathered speed, the boat's stern settling down and her bows lifting as she was gunned up to churn her way out into the open sea, a greyhound from the traps.

"Thank you, Lord, for that," said George as she disappeared around the harbour wall.

Thomas saw the light in the gatehouse window go off, then came a tap-tapping on the stateroom door. It was his turn to jump. Saeed stood outside, stark naked and dripping wet but grinning his most gigantic grin. "Mister Thomas, just let me in here," he said.

"My God, Saeed, welcome home. You had us worried. What the hell's with the nudist thing?"

"Boss, I am changed into some kind of a fish. I saw the lights only when I got halfway back along the pontoon and then there was the man. So I slipped into the water, and took off my clothes holding on underneath. Black man in black water. Great, yes? But this water thing I did not like."

"We know how much you think about the wet stuff."

"What is that you English say? 'Needs must when the devil drives.' Yes." The massive chest shook silently. "Only problem was, the man took it into his Saudi head to take a piss. I think maybe that should be 'into his hand' to take a piss - my head was what it was all over. The man is splashing the planks and humming his love song while I'm down there in the water taking a hot shower. Then the other guy comes up and they start with talking."

When they'd finished laughing Thomas found him some Arabic clothing and a sheet in the linen cupboard for their use as a table cloth. They moved around the galley and saloon with the aid of the faint moonlight and their dimmed down torches. George opened some of the cans and a few of the plastic bags of fruit, found plates and dishes and cutlery and a knife to cut slices of bread which he coated thickly with jam. Sitting around the great table, Thomas raised his carton of juice. "OK now," he said, "I'm not going to make a speech but I just wanted to say thanks. I mean, to you two guys. And hey, here's to all the others who helped." He took a long drink.

George said, "Yeah, all two hundred of 'em and specially your great little old Mubarak Al-Jidha, wherever he be right now." As they ate they talked about the escape, theorising about whether any more of the guards had been killed, what horrendous punishments were being meted out to re-captured prisoners. Saeed shook his ebony head; "The Saudi, he does not like to have people see him brought down. It is this thing of dignity and of respect." He hesitated, chewing his sandwich. "But I hope they are treating Darren right."

Thomas said, "Yes, so must we all, but at least it might wake up our damned Embassy. They'll have to get up off their arses now. If Darren was killed they have to get his body back to England and I wouldn't be surprised if the Saudis don't take the opportunity to get rid of Jimmy at the same time. You know, just let him go. He didn't do anything for the escape, did he?" He took a great bite of bread and jam, then, "Time to lay down the markers, boys. I'll tell you straight out, one way or the other I'm out of this country. For me it's kill or be killed time. Has been since you laid hands on the Warden, Saeed." He looked from one to the other in the virtual darkness, trying to read their expressions. "I'd rather be the one doing the killing," he added. "Anyone have a problem with that?"

George said, "Life's a war, man. Life's a war. Almost killed a guy in the ring once. Rated a good fighter, too. I was nineteen. So was he. Guess the poor bastard's going to be nineteen till the day he dies. Didn't like that at the time and I don't fucking like it now. Shit, when I go I want it quick and I want it clean. If it's right here then you can count on it, partners, I'll be taking a few of the motherfuckers with me." With real affection he patted the automatic that lay before him on the improvised table cloth. "I got as much fucking respect for them as they have for me - which is some place between nothing and zero, right?" For a moment he lapsed in to silence then, then, as if only to himself, "Jesus, him and me, I wouldn't care but we was only amateurs, fighting for fun and for bets, that's all."

"As for me, Mister Thomas, I shall do as I have to do," Saeed said, "You shall not find me wanting." Thomas noticed how every now and then the Sudanese slipped into the antiquated, long-hand English of The River War. "I am tired now," Saeed announced. The great frame rose and stretched, one clenched fist audibly brushing against the fixed chandelier.

Thomas was having to concentrate now, just to keep his eyes open. "Right you are." He finished up the juice and pushed his apple core into the empty carton. "As I said, we'll be here for the next few nights depending on the weather. On the twenty ninth there'll be no moon and that's when we'll be away across the ocean waves." He grinned, thinking what Saeed would be thinking. "No worries, Saeed, if there are any ocean waves we won't be crossing till they've gone back to just little ripples. And remember, in between now and then we clean up behind us; every wrinkle and every crumb, right? And we all keep a sharp lookout for any trouble. I'll see to getting our inflatable. We'll need just the one small one now there's only the three of us. Smaller the better to avoid the radar. Get yourselves some sleep. I'll take the first watch. Then you this afternoon, Saeed. George, you take the evenings."

Up forwards, behind the ship's wheel was the best of observation points. The captain's chair was built to swivel through three hundred and sixty degrees, ideal for outside observation and with no chance of being seen through the dark plexiglass. He knew this boat almost as well as he'd known his own home, having helped specify her final fitting out for the old Prince. He'd already decided they could retreat into the chain locker behind the engine room if anyone should come aboard. As safe a haven as anywhere, short of a specific ship-board search. If anyone was trapped up here in the cockpit they'd just have to get into the chart-room and hope for the best.

Down in the engine room George had gone into rhapsodies over the twin, shaft-driven MAN diesels. "Jesus, these beauties are something else," he breathed. He looked at Thomas. "What kind of performance she got?"

"With this pair of thirteen hundreds, maybe four hundred miles at twenty eight knots. Top speed in a flat calm, thirty three knots." He grinned. "Forget what you're thinking George," he said, "She can't outrun a bloody F16 or a sixteen millimetre cannon."

At seven o clock the police guard was up and about. Thomas called in the others to observe. First the man walked up and down the pontoons, smoking his cigarettes, seeming to be looking at nothing in particular. Fascinated, they watched him stop when he got to *Jazeera*, admiring his reflection in her dark, one-way windows, straightening his uniform and cap, assuming a look of serious importance. No cloud nor any wind today; just another cobalt blue sky and the settling of the heat. A hundred metres away, past office and shop, the front gates had opened a few times during the morning for cars to drive in and out. He had watched the policeman checking their drivers' identifications. None of the workmen had appeared. Normal business was obviously still suspended but customers had to be given access to their boats. On two occasions boats were started up and taken out into the open sea but neither one stayed out for long. The heat was difficult enough on shore but at sea, at this time of the year there would be little pleasure in boating, still less in fishing. At mid-day when he was replaced on watch by Saeed, Jazeera's thermometer told them it had reached an impressive forty seven C out there.

George was asleep on one of the semi-circular settees when Thomas went through, leaving Saeed on watch. He took a piss into a plastic bag, secured it tightly, locked it away with the other stuff for disposal then selected a book from the pristine, mostly Arabic library. Fishes of the Arabian Gulf proved a beautiful book and a sleep-inducing one. It seemed in no time at all that Saeed was shaking his shoulder. "Big white chief coming here," he whispered, "I thought you better take a look what's happening."

A group of three white police vans had parked up inside the gates. Abdul-Rahman Al-Sottar stood in front of them looking out on the yard and at the lines of boats. Thomas snatched up the binoculars. Abdul-Rahman wore his special brown thobe, the one with the gold-braided edging. With him was the smartly uniformed Captain

Muhammed Al-Muttawi and behind them stood the usual retinue; the driver called Sammy and the Jordanian aide de camp, Ali Al-Tigari. Abdul-Rahman said something, sweeping his arm impatiently wide to encompass the scene. Thomas focussed close up on the light skinned face, the neat black moustache, the eyes, for once unsmiling. He said something of an imperative to Al-Muttawi who immediately turned and beckoned. A dozen or more policemen emerged from the vans. Thomas loosened the gun in his belt. Saeed looked at him, shrugged his shoulders. "Insh'allah, Mister Thomas," he murmured. "Insh'allah. We shall be calm."

"I think they're getting ready to search the boats. You'd better go and wake up George and get yourselves down to where I showed you; chain locker, right? Take the gash bags and all the foodstuff with you and make it fast. I mean take everything. Be very certain there are no traces of us anywhere, my friend." He realised he was speaking in Arabic and for some reason reverted to English. "I'm going to stay here. There's room for one under the chart table if they do decide to come aboard. I have to be in a position to know what's going on. Stay hidden till you hear from me or from this." he pulled out his automatic, grinned his pretended assurance. "All understood? Then go, go: and good luck, OK?"

"Inshallah," whispered Saeed.

Just as Thomas had known they would, Al-Sottar and the captain of police chose Jazeera from which to watch over the progress of the boat search. And, naturally, they would have to observe matters from up in her cockpit. But it was not too uncomfortable in the darkness and through the ventilation grill in the chartroom door Thomas could hear their movements and their discussions just a few metres away. He'd gambled on them looking for signs of disturbance or occupancy rather than searching every nook and cranny in this or any of the other boats. He fingered the smooth cool steel of the pistol, wondering how many there might now be on board, whether those now searching the other boats might hear the shots, if and when they had to come..

Al-Muttawi said, "Abdul-Rahman, don't worry, if they are here or wherever they might be we will find them."

Al-Sottar replied without warmth, "Yes? Is that so? A hundred and how many of your prisoners are still missing?" Thomas thought he could smell the guy's body perfume. There was no response from the policeman. Al-Sottar said, "Why you cannot use sniffer dogs like other police forces I do not know. Unclean or not, those animals do the job." Still no response and Thomas thought he could hear the sound of liquid over tinkling ice. "But yes, this is good. The Prince keeps good stuff. I should myself try some crates of this, what is it? This Lagavulin. Your good health, finally, Captain."

Al-Muttawi reverted to English. "Cheers," then back to the Arabic, "When comes the Irishman?"

"Tonight, but with all that is going on I have now told him not to come. We do not need any more problems with Thornton running around loose. Especially now the police in England have arrested the Irishman's two guys in the boatyard. Listen to me; this man Thornton, he is clearly very dangerous. We will not operate until he is found and after that there will be no more mistakes." His voice rose. "Why you could not take off his head quickly as with the Philipino? Stupid, stupid, stupid. You guys risk it all for stupid politics. I told you and I told them all, no politician cares about a dealer in drugs because no western newspaper gives a shit about any dealer in drugs."

Thomas realised he was cramping up. He took in several deep breaths then inched out from under the table and stood up very slowly. The only light came from the slatted door ventilation in front of him. He leaned forward, up close to it, bending down. He could see Al-Sottar's back and the arm that rested on the arm of the captain's chair. In his hand, in the sunshine, the cut-glass tumbler of scotch and ice shot through with amber sunlight.

Al-Muttawi said, quietly, his worry not so well restrained, "But it was perhaps not so wise, that with the girl?"

Thomas noticed how they spoke in English whenever they felt the need to swear. "What the fuck does she have to do with it?" Al-Sottar said, coldly. "He knows not of her. If he did know, how it make some difference?" The glass in hand moved up, the stark white gutra rippled. "The woman is mine by her own desire," he said, and the tone of his voice had softened, its decibel level lowering. "How long your men are going to take here, Captain? Maybe they too much like this boat, I think." He laughed softly, at his ease again. The chartroom seemed to have grown unbearably hot, the smell of teak oil overpowering. Thomas swayed on his feet, the hand with the gun hanging by his side.

Al-Muttawi laughed. "With respect," he said, "I just hope the girl, she is worth all the additional risk."

"Like a rabbit," Al-Sottar said, speaking with soft-abstracted meaning. "Like a hundred fucking rabbits." Thomas locked himself erect, inhaling deeply, trying to banish from inside his head all the stupefying shit of dying and of death but he wanted to move his gun arm forwards, maybe just six inches forwards, knock it against the

110

door so that when they opened it they would find him standing there and Al-Muttawi would go for his weapon and he would kill him with some limited pleasure then turn to Abdul-Rahman Al-Sottar. And he would definitely see and would enjoy the fear in the man's eyes as he saw the reflection of his own upcoming agony and his certain death. It would not be so easy as that, for him. He would do what the boys in Belfast used to like to do, with the knee-caps first and yet not last.

But what then of Saeed and George who trusted him and what of those two little boys in England who loved him? And what of Bradley and the Colonel who had done their best for him? What of all of these? Always it was there, always the memory of Ireland after Kerrigan, of Tralee and the Magharee islands, of the Venezuelan girl who would become his lover and his wife; of her lying back on crushed wet grass. He had inhaled the scent of her and had seen that other redness, that of her lips, and that excitement in the eyes that seemed always to be calculating the effect she was creating.

He lifted up and observed now the hand that held the gun, the hand that had, then and so often since then, possessed her breast, its swollen crest steepling up between his careful fingers and his encircling thumb like some volcanic island just escaped the sea. And he knew again a respite from pain. And what it was to, silent, cry.

He was still there for some time after the sounds of their departure had faded away, still there and calm again by the time George opened the chartroom door. George said, "Jesus Christ almighty, man, you had us going there. Why the fuck you didn't give us an answer? We thought they must have taken you."

Thomas re-inserted the barrel of the gun between his shirt and belt, lodging it firmly in place. He shook his head. "I'm sorry. Didn't mean to scare you. Let's find Saeed. I've just been thinking about what happens next. You know, after we leave this lovely part of the world?"

"What the fuck you mean? We just get the fuck out, don't we?"

"Yes. And then we come back," he said, "Or at least I do. And if you want to get some compensation for all this you'll come back with me."

"Oh yeah? On your own, Mister! You gotta be crazy."

"No, George, I don't think so." He spoke calmly, quietly. "It's just, sometimes the best way forward is all balls out, straight for the throat. Do the unexpected. After we've got ourselves across the water I'll tell you all about it. You'll make up your own mind. Me, I'm going to take it out of that bastard's hide and his bank, in reverse order."

111

George looked at him for a moment then spoke, this time more softly. "Take it easy there, Skip. What the hell; guess you're going to need someone to watch your goddam back."

Chapter Seven

"I'm not in the business of selling you fellows a single damn thing. What I'm going to do is strictly for me, OK?" In Jazeera's moonlit wheelhouse George's face was a pale disc seen through mist, Saeed's all but invisible. He went on, "Listen, the plan isn't formed in any great detail and when it is it may not appeal to either of you. But, assuming we make it out of here I 'm going to come back. Obviously it would be great if I had my A Team with me; we all know the three of us work well."

George said, "Right on. I liked the bit about getting some fucking compensation for all this shit. Up to date I've had nearly a year in goddam hell hole nine and what for? For making people a bit happier, producing a little booze; that's what the fuck for. Any place else and that makes you the businessman with the great big house on the hill and the chair on the Church Committee. Not here, baby." The width of the sudden grin was seeable even in the half dark. "Hey, I don't want to think about what the bastards would do with me now, not after this. The five stretch they give me won't get nowhere fucking close."

"Come into my parlour, said the spider to the fly." Saeed's deep voice seemed to fill the cockpit space, his laugh was like the low grumblings of a reawakening volcano. "You can tell us some more about this, what you say, this compensation plan, Mister Thomas?" It was Saeed's watch so he occupied the captain's chair. He leaned forward for a different line of sight around the marina.

Thomas could see that the gatehouse lights were still on. With the night had come a bit of wind off-shore from the west. Jazeera stirred as if in sympathy. "How old are you, Saeed?"

"I am thirty two years, or something." Again he laughed. "There is not too much government paper seven hundred kilometres west of the White Nile, Mister Thomas. What do you call them, Certificates of

Birth? Most would be destroyed anyway. There, a child may not live too long. My age, this is important?"

"Let's assume we make it to Bahrain. What then for you?"

"Back to the Sudan. Somehow. Town called Nyala. There is my wife I have not seen for five years. There is my five years old Ahmed and my six years old little Bint Nair." He sighed. "Since they put me in Al-Mahli there has been no money going to them. They have no way of knowing. I have to get word back to them, Mister Thomas. I wish to get myself back to them soon, insh'allah."

"You were in Al-Mahli what, three months? Say, another couple for this return operation. How much do you need to cover your family for five months, Saeed?"

"Two hundred seventy five dollars U.S.," Saeed replied, "I have been sending them fifty five U.S. a month from my fifteen hundred riyals each month."

"They weren't overpaying you, my friend," Thomas said, "My God but they were not. Two hundred and seventy pounds, say four hundred dollars U.S.? That's just crazy." He went on, "What if I can cover you and your family costs for the whole five months when we get to Bahrain?"

"Well, Mister Thomas, then I'm with you." Thomas could see the teeth behind the smile in the darkness. "You a good man. Good man gets things done right."

"Yeah, I'll go with that." George said, "But I start from wanting to keep my head right here on my fucking shoulders. It might not be much of a head and it might not be very far up off the deck but it's the only one I got." He paused as if to think about that, went on, "But it could sure be bad luck to start planning to come back before we've even got the fuck out of the place." He reached for the binoculars, focussed in on some distant lights out at sea. "Me," he muttered, "I'm just a simple guy, I just want out of this place first." He lowered the glasses. "I want the feel of a good woman without no fucking clothes and a bottle of Jack Daniels beside a soft bed. And before you ask me, Tommy, number one: I'm a couple years ahead of Saeed, and two: My daddy is my only relation when you don't count my ex's. That tough old bastard's holed up in some log cabin out in Oregon, last I hear of him." He laughed. "And three, I don't have no pension plan, full stop. Oh, shit, like I told you, count me in, why not?"

Thomas said, "Right. Thank you, guys, both of you. And I think you're right, George. No detail on plan B 'til we clear this place." He paused for a moment, then decided to divert the discussion. "See that

114

boat out there? He's maybe a kilometre out. That's the Saudi coastguard, right George?"

George nodded. "Clear as a bell through these." He handed the glasses on to Saeed, who took a look for himself.

Thomas said, "Let's keep a log on them, shall we? We need to know if the patrols happen to a time plan or not, and if they do, with what kind of frequency. It won't be long before we're out there in a tiny little rubber boat doing our best to avoid them. OK, its time for your shift, Saeed. George, why don't we watch some TV, but we'll have to keep the sound right down and drop the window blinds." Shards of moonlight played around Abdul-Rahman's empty whisky glass. "Leave the glass just where it is. Leave everything exactly as it was when they left the boat."

"How long you reckon it takes us to Bahrain, Mister Thomas?" asked Saeed, with pretended casuality.

"Depends on wind speed and direction. Ideally we need a breeze around maybe five or ten knots out of the west or south west. Bit of a chop but not too much. The closer the coastguard boat and the smoother the surface the more likely they are to pick us up on their electronics. Ten knots of wind might not be too comfortable in an inflatable, but at least we'll begin to get lost in the clutter; just be another blip on the screen. So, with three of us in a Zodiac and some strong rowing? We should make it in maybe four or five hours, perhaps a bit less."

George said, "Don't worry, man, the goddam sea's no problem. It's just the bastards motoring around on top of it." He got up and stretched. "Yep. I'm going to catch some TV. The guy that owns it, this boat; when do you reckon he's likely to come back for it?"

"Usually around the middle of September, give or take a couple of weeks. I suppose it depends on when things in Spain begin to get cooler or more boring."

Saeed said, "George, you think I am frightened by the water? Yes, I have some fear. Nyala is in the middle of Africa. I have never seen any sea till I was more than twenty years. I had of course heard of that great river, what you call the Nile, but even the river … When you're a kid growing up in Nyala what you know about is Allah, may God preserve Him, and then about guns and then about how to get something to eat and to drink today."

George said, "Have no fear, good buddy. They say we're all waterproof and we all do float, right?"

The light in the gatehouse had gone out. Thomas said, "OK Saeed, just sit tight on this watch and don't forget the log. You'll find plenty of writing materials in the chart room. George, before we get into any TV why don't you and me go and sort out our transport?"

There were three of the Zodiac Cadet 260S inflatables on their rack inside the chandlery. Thomas thought about opening up the computer to make a bogus sales entry that would explain the one he was about to take but decided it was too messy. He also thought about removing the boat from its bag and re-stuffing the bag with rubbish, but what for? Most likely it wouldn't be missed, not until the new year audit, and even then the loss would simply be covered up, put down to erroneous book keeping.

Next they visited the glass topped knife cabinet; everything there from pen knives through cork-handled yachtsman's knives right up to huge kukhris. George selected a thin-bladed Norwegian fish gutter's knife in a strong leather belt scabbard, which Thomas replaced in the display with one from the drawer below and took from there a second one. "For Saeed. And that's a total one thousand two hundred and fifty riyals off what the bastard owes me, plus a couple hundred more for this." He took down a pocket sized, hand-held compass.

"That's good thinking, boss. Wouldn't want for us to get lost at sea, would we?" George whispered. He set off, back to the boat. Thomas waited outside, just able to see the squat figure with the bulky bag slung low from one wide shoulder moving cat-like up the walkway, stepping around the mooring lines. It was still stiflingly hot. The breeze had brought some cloud in with it and the cloud had darkened up the night. He went back inside the office, locking the door behind him. Sitting in darkness behind the desk, *his* desk, he thought of all the days and weeks and months and extracurricular hours when he'd been in here, doing his best to make a success of the business and to carve out a new way of life. It had been a good life: the early morning runs around a still-sleeping compound, on his return sometimes making love with Connie in the shower, helping her get the boys ready for school, making the car ride in to work, the cheerful good mornings here at the Marina and the coffee that appeared on the boss' desk at comfortable intervals. And the highs when an order finally got confirmed! Brilliant. Especially the orders that would sometimes come at you from right out of the blue. 'That one,' he recalled the Prince's man saying. He'd indicated the Sunseeker's brochure which was opened at the page with the Manhatten seventy four, "The Prince

116

would like it to be delivered to Marbella. You will have the boat named *Jazeera*. Send to me your account." The man hadn't asked about the price.

And sitting here now behind his desk, the darkness near absolute, he remembered the rides home after the working day had ended and the evenings around the floodlit pool and helping the boys with their homework and, later, Connie coming in from the bathroom and the making of love under the whish and the hum of the villa's air conditioning.

He remembered the smell and the taste of his wife and now, also, he remembered the ways in which other men had sought his wife's attention.

The family pictures in their silver frames had been removed from the desk top. On a whim he opened the top left hand drawer of his desk. In the dimness of his dimmest torchlight he could see them now, smiling up at him. David last year on his seventh birthday in his multi-coloured, white collared Barbarians shirt, his old-Beckham style flop-hair centre parted. He picked up the photo of five years old Paul so as better to see the dark-haired beauty of the mother so fixed in this boy's face, the characteristic upwards and sideways look, the slightest and shyest of smiles. From the very bottom of the drawer the studio portrait of Connie looked up at him. God, how he'd loved this woman, still did, except now he wanted to smash the glass and the frame and the photograph with his fist, to see them splintered and torn.

But a light that had nothing to do with him had begun a traverse of the office wall. In a single movement he grabbed the gun, switched off the torch and dropped down on to all fours behind the desk, heart pounding. How bloody absurd! He felt light-headed, wanted to laugh at himself. He heard the door handle being tested and then nothing. After an interval he stood up and went over to the window and from there he watched the pinprick glow of the guard's cigarette end, appearing and disappearing as he walked the pontoons behind the boats, the beam of his torch lighting his way.

It took twenty minutes for the guard to finish his third cigarette, stamp it out in a shower of sparks, walk back past the corner of the office to the gatehouse. Thomas went over everything to ensure he'd left no trace of his presence then, with ultimate care and quietness, let himself out, locked up behind him, proceeded back to base.

The first of the day patrols came right after dawn salah. From Jazeera's wheelhouse he watched the man going through the motions, his sleep-pinched face unshaven, the front of his uniform not properly buttoned up. As the day developed there wasn't much happening out there. Just a few more visitors, mainly police or boat owners. In the skies over the city, helicopter activity seemed to have subsided. George and Saeed reported that there had been no mention at all of the Al-Mahli event on the BBC World Service radio channel. How much in this world, Thomas wondered, goes on out of range or sight of the West's supposedly all-knowing media.

He had barely noticed the insidious slide downhill of his general appearance inside cell block three. He'd had only one blade in his wash-kit when they'd taken him in. When that had become too painful to use he'd made the conscious decision not to barter for a new one, instead just to let his beard grow. Now it was about twenty centimetres long, the grey-blonde of old corn stubble. He decided it would be best to trim everything on his head and face to the same fashionable number two cut and had George make use of a pair of scissors, selected from a miscellany of kitchen implements. At least the time in jail had slimmed him down to fighting weight. All in all he wouldn't look too out of place in the Clipper Bar at the Intercon.

They decided Saeed should stay in Arabic clothing and the bigger the better so far as his beard was concerned. George shaved his own head 'as bald as a bald eagle which isn't fucking bald anyway,' as he put it. He'd also given himself a Van Dyke moustache and beard. Saeed said he looked like a nice enough boy but he meant it well, and as a joke.

Police patrol boats seemed to pass by a good distance out to sea and at about three hour intervals after dark, much less although more at random during daylight hours. There was very little other sea-traffic.

As the days passed, Thomas handled the rubbish disposal, doing it at night and varying the time depending on the state of the light, the perceived guard activity and his own shifts. He carefully segregated the bags into soluble and non-soluble. The soluble, liquid or solid, together with the contents of the shit bucket he lowered into the sea off the end of the pontoon walkway. The solid waste, he carried to the lever-lid garbage bin outside the office, there to insert the bags of cans and bottles beneath a covering layer of normal office and marina waste. The bin could not have been emptied since the closure and there must have been waste foodstuffs in it. The flies, probably many generations of them by now, had found their own Valhalla.

That Wednesday was their last day aboard Jazeera. They spent it in getting everything ready for the trip and listening to the weather forecasts. Eight knots from the south west rising twelve to fifteen later, visibility fair. Thomas pronounced it to be bearable. George nodded thoughtfully. Saeed stayed silent.

Jazeera was equipped with the latest Admiralty Charts. He made a careful sketch of the relevant bits of the Gulf, especially the Bahrain coastal areas, enclosed the sketch in a clear plastic folder and taped the folder against any possible ingress of water. As an afterthought he re-opened it, inserted the five one hundred dollar bills, the credit card and the piece of paper with his father's poem, re-sealed it.

After dark, using the wheelhouse so as not to lose continuity with the watch they pumped up the inflatable and inserted its wooden slat-flooring and the pair of oars, held neatly in clips along the tops of the side tubes. There was a single, wooden rowing seat half way along the two and a half metres length of her. He showed them how to develop a rowing rhythm using back and legs equally so as to limit the strain on either. George pronounced himself fully OK with this rowing bit. "I guess I got my US Navy time to thank for that," he said.

"You got small boats training in the Navy?" Thomas asked, surprised.

"Shee-it, no," George said, "Small boats was the best place to make with the girls down in Orlando. You know, on the boating lake."

Thomas said, "Yes, right. So we go at nine. I'll row us out of the Marina and take the first half hour or so on the oars. Saeed, you'll be here in the stern, facing the rower - yes, my friend, the stern is the back of the boat, OK? You'll be in the back facing forward. After the half hour it'll be your turn at the oars, George. We'll be on a heading for a landing near the Meridien hotel in Bahrain. We have to make allowance for wind and tide, but with all our weight she'll be well loaded and pretty stable. Let's just remember we're not in any kind of a race. We only want to get there, and preferably in good order, OK?"

Saeed said, "I been wondering about something, Mister Thomas, why don't we just get us an engine? There's plenty in the shop."

"Two reasons; the first one is noise - the sound of an outboard engine carries a long way across water, even in a bit of a wind. Much more important to us though, police radar picks up metal best of all, the more metal and the higher above the waterline it is, the more it picks it up. That reminds me; we'll stow the guns in plastic bags. They'll be below sea level so they shouldn't be a radar hazard. Radar's very good these days but as I said they'll have problems picking us out of the on-screen clutter tonight. OK, let's sort out our rations. Anything we don't need to take I'm going to dump after dark. We'll be leaving here at nine so get yourselves some rest. I'll take the watch from here on in."

At eight forty five Thomas did the rubbish run whilst the others carried the dinghy outside on to *Jazeera*'s stern deck, ready loaded with the three plastic bags of clothing and the guns plus a smaller bag of food and drink for the trip. Thomas told them to hang on while he went back for the bucket. "For baling," he whispered in answer to Saeed's query. Saeed groaned softly.

Inside Jazeera, beginning up forward, he gradually worked his way back, wiping off all surfaces as he went. Several times today he'd combed the place, looking to remove every visible sign of their occupancy. She looked as good and clean now as ever, give or take the undisturbed signs of Al-Sottar and Al-Muttawi's visitation. After helping the others to carry the inflatable out on to the pontoon he went back aboard to re-enable the security system and lock up for the last time. Or maybe not the last time. His Plan B was still only three parts formulated.

Thomas had to admit that, floating now off the end of the pontoon, the two and a half by one and a half metre inflatable seemed impossibly small for three pretty big guys, and the oars ridiculously toy-like. He turned to his companions with a reassuring grin, shook hands with each of them. "OK now", he murmured. "All aboard who's coming aboard." He got in first, kneeling astride the seat to hold her in against the pontoon. Saeed followed, badly unbalanced and muttering a verse from the Qu'ran. As the big man entrusted his weight to the boat it was all they could do to restrain her from sliding out and away from the pontoon. He said something completely unintelligible as he sat down heavily in the stern, then, "That was some of my Nubian," he whispered. "I was just saying 'I don't like any of this shit'"

"Shut up Saeed," Thomas whispered. "Shut up and just stay still. You're in no danger unless you feel the need to jump around and dump us all in the drink."

George whispered, "If you two've finished dancing and singing do you mind if I fucking join you?" He stepped quickly and confidently into the bows. The dinghy rocked, to the accompaniment of a small cry from Saeed. "So come on, guys, let's hit the fucking high seas." He imitated the subservient cockney accents from old British war movies. "Cocoa, Skippah?"

Thomas let go of the pontoon and took up the oars, swivelling her bows towards the end of the harbour wall with its red navigation light. As they slid past the eye-shaped windows, the dark elegance of *Jazeera*, George whispered, "'Bye, 'bye, sweet lady. Take real good care now. You sure been good to me."

Out in the harbour there was already a solid rock and slap to the motion of the Zodiac. Thomas pulled her along, developing his rhythm, keeping the blades of the oars deep and firm, square on to the direction of stroke. Passing along the rock pilings of the harbour wall he judged they were making a good three knots. If the forecast held, the wind should be adding the best part of another knot as soon as they cleared the harbour. There were one or two gaps in the cloud cover, the brightest of the stars shining through. As they moved out into the void he lined up the harbour wall navigation light with the light from Al-Sottar Marine's gatehouse window. This would take them just about due east. Soon enough the guard would be on his early rounds. The dinghy began to feel the increasing exposure as they moved out of the lee of the land and into the open sea. One of his oars caught the top of a wavelet and showered them with ultra-salt spray. The helping wind blew into his face, loaded with humidity, adding to the sweat that ran from his face and body. The bad left elbow was holding up all right, so far at least. He said, "Those lights, Saeed?" He nodded to his left. "That's the Causeway to Bahrain. It's about five kilometres away. Keep an eye on it, we don't want to get much closer to it than this, OK?"

Saeed said, "I cannot be too sure about this, Mister Thomas. I'm feeling ..." His despairing voice faltered.

Thomas said, "Sure. I know how you're feeling. We all do, first time. It's not a problem. Let it go my friend. Lean out over the side. Get it all up." But the sound and smell of the heavings and retchings quickly made him want to follow suit. He said, "Remember our man, Major General Gordon? Gordon was sea-sick every time he saw water." He had no idea if it was true but it didn't matter. The lights of the Marina and the city were growing more distant, beginning to merge and blend together. Abdul-Rahman's beach house would be there, to the right of the main illuminations. There'd be lots of action on a Wednesday. He tried not to think about it, concentrated on the port wing-light of an aeroplane as it descended like a slow spark from a bonfire towards Dammam Airport.

After a moment George asked, "Who the fuck's this Major General Gordon?"

Another spray-shot hit him full face. Thomas gasped, "Was, George, was; British Army, eighteen ninety odd, killed at Khartoum by the Arabs." He blinked away the salt in his eyes, part sweat and part sea-spray.

"Oh, sure," George grunted. "Nice night for a boat trip, though, skipper."

They were a long way out now and the motion of the Zodiac had become more violent. Thomas thought about how a two and a half metre inflatable wasn't built for this sort of thing, how it was just a cork to float you out to your boat in the harbour, had no keel to combat the constant twisting of an upset sea.

George had to speak up over the sounds of the weather. "You want me to take over yet? I can't see nothing in front. We're going to need your compass. Could go round in a big circle and land ourselves back in the wrong fucking country, else ... Wey-hey..." A wave of some height had pitched them stern up, now they were scudding downhill. "What the fuck's this all about, then?" The Zodiac leaned slightly to port as Saeed sought again to empty his emptiness into the uncaring seas.

Thomas had noticed how, for some time now, Al-Khobar in the distance had wanted to slide to the right. "What this is, George," he said, "Is a twenty knot wind, rising and veering northerly. I'm having to pull her around to my right all the time." He needed to speak much more loudly now and his elbow had started to ache quite badly. "You ready to take over?" He'd taken the oars for longer and had rowed them much further out than he'd planned. He ought now to make a call to Brad. He knew the odds against were falling as fast as this bloody wind was rising and veering. Brad would be sitting somewhere in England, wondering about them. He should be told ... just in case.

"What's the drill, skipper?" George asked.

"I'm going to time it so I can ship the oars and fall backwards into the stern," he shouted. "After my count of three, OK? You climb over me - but fast - and get rowing. Fast, George, fast." He paused, gasping, as the latest shower overtook them, adding to the lake already swilling around his feet. "My count of three, right? Listen to me, Saeed? You have to do some baling, OK?" The shapeless hulk mumbled something, began feeling around in the bottom of the boat with the bucket. "Saeed, my man, stick with it. You are a bloody good man for an accountant." He bent forwards, plunged in the oars for one final

122

pull, shouted "one, two," and, as he clipped the shafts along the tops of the side bags, the 'three'. He flung himself backwards but by the time George scrambled over him and got into position the wind and waves had swung them broadside on, the waves tilting them steeply sideways. Looking now at the New Yorker's broad back, Thomas could sense the man's power and control as he leaned forwards, digging in his left hand oar to pull her around easterly again. The dinghy had half filled with water and Saeed had needed to redouble his baling action.

Complete cloud cover now so no starlight, just the broken blackness of the crested seas and the intermittent keening of the wind. The ribbon lights of the causeway were much closer. Less than a kilometre away now, he guessed, realising also that they were about half way over the straits, because they were about level with the twin restaurant towers on the causeway, one lit red and one green, rising up above the mid-point immigration and emigration platforms. He fumbled with the knots on his plastic bag. "Good to see you weren't kidding, George. You did actually get some practice on that lake," he shouted. He took out the mobile and switched on, adding, "Apart from with the pussy, I mean." The screen on the mobile lit up and after a moment the Bahrain server name, Batelco, appeared.

"Pilot to navigator, where the fuck are we?" George shouted, "Any idea, skipper?"

"Hold on. I'm just going to make a call." His words were wind-sucked away into the blackness. He dialled the number. George's back was rhythmically bending and straightening in concert with Saeed's arm, bucket attached, dipping and swinging and emptying.

Brad answered on first ring. "Hi there, partner! Thank God. I tried you several times tonight but you were switched off. We have a bad line."

"No, the line's good," Thomas shouted. "It's OK, I'm on the Bahrain server now. Listen, we're about halfway across and the weather's begun to kick up some real shit." He held on as one more mother wave attempted to skew and topple them at the same time. He watched George digging in with his port-side oar. "Some real shit," he repeated, "and not bloody forecasted. There's the three of us in a rubber dinghy. Me, George and Saeed."

"Got you. I'm on the nineteenth floor of a tower block. The flags are stretched out straight from here. Red and white. Could probably see you if it wasn't as black as a coalman's arsehole."

"You're kidding, Brad. You mean you're in Bahrain?"

"Yep, Bahrain. Waiting with the hot bath and a bottle of the good old water of life for our hero's return. How's the crew holding up?"

He attempted with his body to shield the mobile from the wind and the sea, which would allow him to keep his voice down. "Great, these boys are just fine. Bit of mal de mere in the back. Listen, Brad. If the wind doesn't veer northerly any more we should be landing somewhere on the mainland. Less than an hour at the rate we're going. Stay by the mobile and I'll keep you in the picture, OK? You got a car?"

"Sure. What if it does veer more northerly?"

"Then we'll pile up somewhere on the Causeway itself. On the Bahraini section, sure, but on its bloody weather side. No medals for that, not on a night like this... Good fun though."

"Right. Really hilarious. See you, pal."

Chapter Eight

An hour and a half out of Khobar, wind gusting up to twenty knots and maybe more. George was doing everything possible with the oars but they both well how much they were being pushed crab-wise, not so much east into Bahrain as south towards the causeway.

Saeed hadn't spoken a word if you didn't count the Qu'aranic mumblings as he leaned over the side, but in between the empty retchings he had kept up with his metronomic baling action and, but for that, they would have been swamped long before now.

The road lights on the causeway appeared and disappeared with the rise and fall of the inflatable. Already Thomas was able to make out individual car headlights. He had to brace himself to keep from sliding around on the slat-wood decking but he was sitting in sea water, getting showered by it, blinking it out of his eyes, holding on to the bags to prevent them from being swept away. He switched on his torch, keeping the light of it well down below the top-line of the side bags. All that concern about patrol boats! No chance, not tonight.

The mobile telephone was in its plastic bag inside his shirt. He took it out, also took out his sketched map in its taped up plastic folder. They were definitely well into Bahraini waters. He needed to understand more exactly where, then he could make a best estimate as to where they were likely to make landfall. He got a rough compass fix at two hundred and twenty degrees on the restaurant towers, drew an imaginary line on the map; somewhere to the north of Al Muhamadiyah island, well inside Bahraini waters.

The seas were raising the boat on high for jets of flying spume to splatter his head and all down his back, then down again, pitching and rushing sideways, front end down. He needed to hold on with one hand, clutching the bags with the other, looking straight into the blackness of the waters with George pulling for his life, for all their lives. They'd bottom out in a brief new silence out of the wind, hesitate then slowly, then more quickly rise once more into the maelstrom. Al Muhamadiyah couldn't be far off now, because the chain of causeway lights were individually identifiable now. It was very dark and almost too late when he picked up the line of white, close in.

He grabbed George's shoulders and put his mouth up close to an ear, shouted, "Pull, George, pull like hell into wind and to your right. We're being pushed back on to a bloody island." He felt George look up from his oars, the massive shoulder muscles re-doubling their efforts. A minute later the breakers were inching past and away. Shouting again into George's ear he said, "Nice one sailor. I have our location now. We're in between the mainland and this little island and we're being pushed backwards on to the Causeway. I reckon we'll be on it in less than twenty minutes if you keep going like you are. But it's upside downtime time if you let up; want me to take over?"

George turned his head to shout. "No problem, I need to lose the weight." Thomas felt the shake of his shoulders. The man was actually enjoying this. "I'm getting as much right hand in it as I can. Figure the nearer the mainland the better when we fetch up on the Causeway, right?"

"Right you are, Mr Schwartz, Keep your eye on Saeed, I'm going to make another call." He huddled down below the level of the air bags for maximum shelter, took out the mobile, holding it clear of the swill and rush of bilge-water.

Brad picked up straight away. "How you doing now, partner? Sounds like you're on the midnight express. Sooner you than me out there."

"Right, it's a little bit bloody hairy. We're going to land up on the Causeway. What's the time, twenty two hundred? Hopefully there's not too much traffic going across. I plan to hi-jack a car. I've a pal lives in Adliya. There's a safe haven there for a bit."

"Great idea, the hi-jack. Come on, Thomas! You can hi-jack me. Don't worry about the rest of it. I have it covered. Listen, I'm on the highway signed Saudi Arabia right now. Tell me what happens when I get to your Causeway."

"I don't suppose there's any chance of my being able to keep you out of this, is there?" There was no reply to that, not that he'd expected one. "OK, then this is what you should do. You got three dinars in your pocket?"

"Sure."

"You'll come to the toll booth before the start of the causeway. Give the man the three dinars and he'll give you an exit card and let you through. Drive on and forget the card, you won't need it." The

126

boat lurched and banged down hard then bumped and scraped across some solid underwater obstruction. Frantically, George pulled on his left hand oar. Saeed's moan reached him even over the wind. "Sorry about that, Brad, I think we just touched bottom somewhere. It's OK now, we're clear again. Not too far to go. Listen, if the guy in the toll booth asks about your Saudi insurance tell him there's no need for it, you're only going to take a meal up top of the tower, admire the wild night, OK? The tourist sight-seeing bit. When you've driven over as far as the Bahraini tower precinct you just turn around and come right back down the other carriageway. Now, the first land mass you see over the side is the island that's now to the right of my present line of travel. Stop the car and take a good close look at your inside front wheel. I should be able to see you by then so I can talk you in to where we fetch up on the causeway. You'll need to go careful. The causeway's mostly covered by CC." He laughed. "Can't have you getting a ticket or anything."

"OK, or 'Roger,' as we used to say. By the way I'm in a white Maxima."

"Understood."

"Good luck... Thomas?"

"Yes?"

"Oh, nothing. Dear mother, having a wonderful time ... be seeing you."

The causeway lighting would reach out for only that final twenty metres or so before they hit the rocks, out of view down there of the CCTV cameras, but any passing motorist would surely see them if he chose to glance down during those few final seconds. They had two choices: either continue to back as slowly as possible stern first on to the rocks or turn her around and charge straight in, bows first. The last way would lessen the risk of their being seen because they would be visible in the lights for the shortest period, but the hit could probably damage the boat and could well hurt them into the bargain. He tapped George's back. "We're going in bows first, flat out," he shouted. "Turn her right around fast when I tell you to and dig in hard. Then the moment I hit your back you fall forwards alongside Saeed. I mean fast. You'll need the boat's air bags to protect you. Hold on tight and hope we hit on top of a wave, OK?"

George said something in acknowledgment but it got lost in the wind as they surfed over what felt like their millionth wave-crest.

The causeway road level was thirty feet above the breakers. He thanked God for the engineers choosing to use a jumbled rock foundation rather than a vertical wall of fitted stones. Clambering up it might be uncomfortable but at least it was climbable. As they drew closer in to the lights he was able to see Saeed more easily. The black man had stopped baling to turn around, seemingly transfixed by the seas that now surged and broke upon the rocks that they were fast approaching.

Thomas punched George's back; instantly the right hand oar dug in and pulled and dug and pulled whilst the starboard oar backed up and the Zodiac Cadet spun almost on its axis and then both oars immersed, stroked hard through water, bright-lit now. They rose, ever so slowly up a breaking wave. He punched George in the back again and flung himself flat to the floor as the bow behind him smacked hard into rock. Their combined weight must have saved them from overturning but even so everything for the moment was chaos. George had just about had time to fall forwards. If he hadn't he'd certainly have been flung into the jumble of massive stones. It was Thomas himself who took most of the secondary shock as his friends were catapulted forward, clutching their bags.

Saeed was first out, scrambling up the rock pile. Thomas shouted to him to stay put while George helped him with the boat. A towering wave rushed in, leaving him gasping, desperately holding on, the thunder of its contest with the rocks filling his head. The forward flotation bags had punctured, which made it easier to hold and ease her up the rocks. When they were finally out of reach of the seas he used his knife to open the parts of the boat that were still inflated. It was now a shapeless mat of dark rubber. They dragged everything still higher, until they were able to sit well down in the shadow of the final breast-high concrete wall, atop it just the Armco railings and the highway. He was retching up what felt like a great deal of painfully salt sea water and his eyes and throat felt burned. Still clutching his plastic bag he leaned forward, the better to evacuate his stomach. The well-rounded rocks up which they'd needed to climb had been sharp with molluscs. His hands were scratched. He looked at the others as they looked at him. The rocks on which they now sat seemed to be heaving like the sea from which they'd come.

"Fuck, fuck, fuck," gasped George. "Guess we made it. You told us it'd be easy, didn't you, skip? No fucking problem at all, was it?" Still able to laugh, he pummelled Thomas's back to assist the evacuation. "Cough it all up, sailor."

Saeed spoke quietly, the deepness of his rumblings almost lost in the wind. "I am very sorry, Mister Thomas. I was very afraid. I could do nothing to help you and Mister George and of that I am ashamed."

Chest heaving, Thomas grabbed for his hand. "You did great, my friend, just great. Damn sight better than General Gordon would have managed." He winced. Saeed's grip hurt like hell. "But for your baling her out we'd all be swimming for it right now."

"But I told you, I cannot swim," Saeed said, not recognising the figure of speech.

"Here's another secret," George said, "Neither can I. And it would have made no fucking difference anyway, not if we was Tarzan and Johnny Wiesmuller both. No bastard could swim in that. Me, I'd just like a quiet chat with that fucking weather man."

"When you boys have finished with your reminiscences let's talk about how we're going to get you out of here." Brad's drawl had come against the wind as if from another place, right above them.

Resisting the temptation to stand and peer over the wall Thomas asked, "Brad? You're here already? How the hell did you know where we landed?" George and Saeed had been shocked into total stillness. "Anyone about up there?"

"Not right now. How? I'm driving down the road in the slow lane according to instructions and I see this pack of drowned rats coming out of the ocean half a mile away. I couldn't have missed you." A car whizzed by and then another. "Fortunately for all of us I was the only one using the inside lane. These boys all seem to be in such a hell of a hurry. But I must have picked up a puncture, if you see what I mean, so right now I'm changing the wheel. There's just the three of you, right?"

"And the boat. We should take it with us and dump it somewhere."

"Stay well down. We might have a problem now." Brad sounded calm enough about it. "There's a slow moving copper coming along here. I hope he's not feeling too nosey."

Thomas heard the slam of a car door. He motioned to George and Saeed to back tight up against the wall. Another voice, raised to overcome the howl of the wind. "You have some trouble here, sir?"

Brad: "Just a puncture, officer. I think I ran over some glass out by the tower."

Voice: "Perhaps we may help? You are British?"

Brad: "Yes, British. It's very kind of you, officers, but there's really no need for all of us to get dirty." A mother of a wave hit into the rocks. Thomas felt the shower of spray on his face. Brad laughed. "Nor even wet."

George had pulled out his automatic, its barrel shone, wet and yellow on blue black in the shadow of the wall. Thomas put his hand on it, shaking his head, frowning. Second voice, sounding equally amused: "We think to call a breakdown vehicle for you, my friend. This is not good night for changing wheels. Your spare, she is OK?"

Brad said, "I bloody hope so. If not, Hertz'll have something to answer for." There was a pause, then, "Yeah, seems fine. And all tools present and correct. I don't have any problem here. Ten minutes maximum."

Voice: "Don't worry about the obstruction, my friend, you are in Bahrain now."

Brad: "Thanks, officers. I like the sound of that. Appreciate the offer, too. Goodnight."

Second voice: "Good night and you are welcome. Welcome to Bahrain."

Thomas heard the car doors shut and the jabber of a starter motor then the rev up and drive away. George was grinning all over his face. Now even Saeed was once more smiling his great, white-toothed smile.

Brad said, "Right boys, one at a time, on my count; over the top and straight in the back of the car. Keep well down."

Thomas said, "I'll be coming up last. What's left of the boat will need to go in the boot. It won't sink so it's going to be a bit too bloody obvious if we leave it here. Do you really have a puncture?"

"The policemen took a pretty good look at it. Just as well I'd stuck a knife in, wasn't it?"

"We're in pretty much shit order here," Thomas said, "Hope Hertz won't mind us bringing a bit of the ocean and maybe a little blood into their motor."

Just the soft hum of the Maxima's engine. So wonderful a near silence after the hours of high wind and white wave. But then Saeed began to laugh his deep bellied volcano of a laugh and George joined in and as the causeway road left the sea and ran on to the mainland past the toll booths Thomas couldn't keep himself from adding to the general sense of relief. "I don't know about you guys." Brad said. "I mean, what's so bloody funny? Are you sure the three of you were in regular jail, not some kind of secure medical institution?"

130

Wedged into the passenger seat-well Thomas said, "Mister Bradley Scott, meet George Schwartz, Olympic oarsman par excellence. And the large gentleman, that's our tame Sudanese, Mister Saeed. Don't ask me about his family name. He never told me it."

"Bin Farsi," said Saeed. He was trying his best to squeeze himself down on the floor behind the front seat. "My name is Saeed Mohammed Bin Farsi, Mister Brad. And I am very pleased to meet you. Why I laugh? I laugh because I am bloody alive and because there is no bloody water beneath me, this is why I now bloody laugh."

George said, "Yeah, ditto. Wow, that was some fucking ride, man."

Thomas looked at his watch. A quarter to midnight. Each time he looked at this watch he saw Al-Khomein standing on the pavement wearing just his socks and underclothes; a fat man crying.

They were passing a multi-coloured children's amusement park. At Thomas' instruction Brad pulled off at the next slip road, stopped underneath the flyover. They needed to change into something dry and less disreputable. George put on his dark grey knee length shorts with a black Nike T-shirt and trainers, Saeed a white T-shirt and grey shorts with the sandals that he complained had never properly fitted his outsized feet. On board *Jazeera* Thomas had managed to restore his own jeans and the Ben Sherman shirt to some semblance of decency and the new sandals felt OK. All their wet stuff went back into the bags and into the boot but the deflated Zodiac came out to be dumped on a pile of fly-tipped rubbish. Apart from the raw blisters on George's hands their cuts and scratches were all superficial. Brad said, "We need to talk, folks. We can drive around and around whilst we talk, or how about something to eat? Anyone fancy a drink?"

Thomas said, "Drink? What's that? I shouldn't think you'd need to ask us, Brad. But first things first, I have to get in touch with my guy about beds for the night."

"Just for once I think you're wrong there, skipper," George said. "First thing first for me is a couple drinks, man. Get all this shit out of my goddam mouth, yeah? What you say?"

"You don't have to worry about accommodation, Thomas, it's all fixed," Brad said, "and anyway, dinner would best be in a pub at this time of night. This is not Saudi."

"OK," Thomas said, "you talked us into it. But listen, Brad, I reckon the police here could be on the lookout for us - you know, pictures and all?"

"I've been here three days," Brad said, "and all I've picked up about the great escape is by rumour from the expats. There's been nothing published and no pictures. Christ, I don't know what a fellow has to do to get famous these days. In any case, you look about two stones lighter and one hell of a lot different to when I last saw you, what with your new non-coiffure et al."

There weren't too many customers left in The Killarney Jug. Three Arabs at the darts board, by the look of them possibly Saudis, two expats playing pool and four more sitting up at the bar with a young woman, bare midriffed, slit-skirted; probably air crew. Thomas blinked, needing to tear his eyes away from the sight of the girl's crossed legs. A couple sat by themselves in one of the darker places. There was a mini-band in the corner doing something Irish. The tall Indian barman with 'Joe' on the green sweat shirt with its shamrock insignia smiled a welcome, his hands wide-spread on the bar-top alongside the beer pumps.

"Good evening, Joe," Thomas said, "I'd like a pint of the Red. And whatever these gentlemen want, and please, one for yourself." He took from his pocket one of his hundred dollar bills, put it down on the bar.

Joe was already pulling the pint. "Thank you sir, very kind of you."

George said, "Thanks skipper. Joe, make mine one of the same and a Jack Daniels chaser." He turned to Thomas. "Hey, I'm liking this already, but I'm just a little bit, what the hell you say - embarrassed?"

Thomas said. "Forget it, money's not a problem. Not yet awhile anyway. Saeed, what about you, big man, what you having? There's plenty here alcohol-free."

Saeed crashed the heel of his hand on to the bar-top. "A pint of the black stuff for the black man, skipper, if you should please."

"Well why not, man; Guinness is good for you," Brad said.

Thomas had suddenly realised how hungry he was. "You still doing food?" he asked. The barman nodded, pushed across the menu.

Brad said. "Hope you guys don't mind but I have some personal stuff to talk over with Tommy here. After you've all eaten, that is, there's no rush. And is it OK with you if I ask my lady to join us? She's just over the road in the apartment." He indicated George and Saeed. "You two guys will be staying with us so I'd like to introduce you, anyway." He grinned at Thomas. "Your skipper already knows my Rose."

Whilst they ate their steaks and fries Brad bought a fresh round of drinks and one for the musicians who'd agreed to stay on for a couple more numbers. One of the group at the bar walked unsteadily over to request the use of the mike. The guy actually knew all the words. As he reached the final, 'and did the pipes play The Flowers of the Forest,' the door opened and Rose was there. She looked stunning, almost literally stunning to Thomas and, he guessed, the other two who had not seen a female other than in their imaginations for some long time. She wore a cream coloured, close-fitting trouser suit with a deep vee neckline that set off the coffee colour of her skin, the black skull-wrap of her hair, the bright cerise of her lips. Brad said, "Rose, meet our guests. This is George Schwartz and this, Saeed Bin Farsi." They got to their feet and in turns shook her hand. Thomas noticed George's wince. They'd have to do something about those blisters. "And no need for me to introduce this reprobate," Brad added.

Thomas touched his lips lightly to the cheek she'd turned to him. Rough beard on smooth skin. The perfume hit hard.

She was quietly laughing. "I know you jailbirds haven't seen too much of the opposite sex lately, but still and all … anyway, don't let me interrupt you, gentlemen."

"Jesus, ma'am," George said, "You shouldn't have used that word."

"No?" she said. "What word?"

"Sex, ma'am, sex," George said.

Thomas said, "So how've you been, Rose?"

"OK, you know. Better than you, anyway, Mister Thomas."

Brad put a protective arm around her shoulders. "She's doing better than OK. She's helping me do the setting up here." He looked at Thomas. "You know, for the Colonel's business?"

Saeed held out his hand. "I am most delighted to meet you, madam,"

"Call me just plain Rose," she said, "And I'll call you just plain Saeed. Please do sit down. May I please have one of your chips, Saeed? Eat up, gentlemen, your food's getting cold."

It wasn't much more than an hour ago that they'd all been fighting for their lives, Thomas thought. Or maybe it was just the Rose effect, he didn't know, but suddenly he did know just how tired he was. He laid his knife and fork side by side on the unfinished plate and drained his glass. "Brad, can we get on with it? Please excuse us folks. We won't be long."

As they sat down in the corner Brad touched his knee beneath the table. "Don't look so bloody worried man," he said, grinning, "Here's something you're going to need, compliments of the Colonel."

The British passport was old and well used and crowded inside with a miscellany of visas and entry stamps. The photo was of another age but it was him right enough, just as real as the name had once been his, "Thomas James MacRae," he murmured. "Well, once upon a time I was once John Thomas Macrae. This is near enough and not too near. Thanks, Brad. I shall never know how the hell he manages to get these things done."

"Nor me. Anyway, the entry stamp says you arrived this evening off the overnight from Heathrow. I've made a two night booking here in the Ambassador for you, Tommy," Brad said. "Your other lads can't check in anywhere without a passport so they'll be staying with us till we can fix it for them. The Colonel gave me a contact at the Embassy. Useful guy there - the old man said he knows you well enough."

"Knows me? I've never been near the Bahrain Embassy."

"One 'Honourable Jeremy Ferris-Bartholomew'? I believe he's recently been promoted, transferred over from Saudi. I just love the Honourable bit. Those secret services boys are about as honourable as Ghengis Khan."

"Secret Service?"

"MI6, unless I'm very much mistaken."

Thomas slipped the passport into the breast pocket of his shirt. "Ferris-Bartholomew, he knows about this?"

"Christ, no. I mean, he certainly knows you were in the Service and he knows I know you, but unless he's a bloody good actor he hasn't made any connection with tonight's thing."

Thomas said, "I thought I'd left all that stuff well behind me." He sighed, took another mouthful of beer. "You must have, too. Well, OK, let's hear it. I know who I am now, but what am I?"

"You're a businessman on what is literally a flying visit. As I say, you check in here at the Ambassador for tonight and tomorrow night. That suitcase in the car is yours. Rose's clothing selection's inside it so don't blame me if you don't like the stuff. You fly off to England Friday night. Well, Saturday morning actually, zero two hundred's your take-off time. Here's your ticket." Thomas felt it touch his knee. "Me, I'm a business man as well, here with my wife and co-director to set up a Middle East branch of Industrial Group Services, that's ISG on your company credit card. You'll find it tucked inside your passport. And in case you're wondering, the job's genuine and the company's a genuine one, set up and owned by the Colonel; we're even making genuine money, would you believe. Good, eh?"

"You know, I can't say how ..."

Brad butted in, "Then don't." He switched direction. "Just how bad was it over there, Tommy?" he hesitated. "You don't sound too brilliant. But there's more help if you want it. Colonel Grenville figures the Service owes you a thing or two." He grinned again. "Whatever, I'm with you all the way, you know that."

"Yes, I owe you, mate, and thanks. Me? Put it down to tiredness. How bad? I'll tell you about it one day. But these guys - this is a pretty good team, Brad. You said there'd been no public news about the breakout?"

"No, not even on the Net. But our friend the Honourable told me a lot of the story. Seems there are quite a number of dead. Bloody battle royal by the sound of it. Police and Army guns v great numbers of nasty guys with not a lot more than the proverbial tooth and nail. Apparently it's unlikely we'll ever get to know exactly what happened but as I understand it the dead definitely included two British. Lots more people injured. I can't imagine why but it seems the Saudis are blaming you, my friend, and after you, all Brits in general plus the Prime Minister, the Queen of England et al. The Right Honourable Jeremy says there's at least thirty of the buggers still out and on the run."

Thomas thought about Darren, down and hit bad, and about Jimmy Bellingham who'd done nothing but stick around to look after his friend. So far as he knew they'd been the only two Brits left in Al-Mahli. He lifted his glass high, looking up to the light through the amber liquid, "This one's for you guys," he said softly, "And thanks for trying."

Brad knew enough not to ask but raised his own glass anyway. "I'll drink to that as well, whoever they are, or were."

"And Manchester United," Thomas said. He could feel the alcohol now.

"All right, and here's to good old Man U," Brad reciprocated, then, "Our man in the Embassy told me you'd been asking about Connie?"

"Right. Any idea what he'd found out?"

"He told me she definitely wasn't on the expected exit flight. He assumes she went out on one of the following ones, after your lads left for England. She isn't hereabouts anyway. The Embassy sent all your compound stuff home to your sister's." He looked up, frowning. "You know, they'd definitely got you down for the final exit, Tommy."

"Yes. I'm really sorry it took all this - this mayhem." Over Brad's shoulder he could see George holding court as if this was his every-night home and Saeed of the injured face, as if he'd stumbled into this new world and didn't quite know yet whether it was a good one or not. And Rose? Rose looked like Rose had always looked; The magnet

135

that attracted all unto itself. He said,"You know, Bradley Scott, your lady ought to be Mrs Rose Scott by now."

"It's none of your bloody business but I'll tell you it's not for want of asking. Me asking her, that is, not the other way around. She's never said no, but she's never said yes, either."

Thomas nodded. He had made up his mind. "Well, let me tell you about my own wonderful wife. Seems she's with a Saudi, a Saudi sheikh in Al-Khobar. Actually said gentleman is, or was, our sponsor over there." The words had formed themselves with great difficulty, had dropped like acid from his lips, and the hurt was incredible.

For some while there was a silence between them and then Brad said, "I'm not even going to begin to ask what you mean by that, my friend. It's too late and we're all too tired and tomorrow is far too much of another day."

But Thomas said, quietly, "I'm going back for her Brad; and for him."

With hardly a pause Brad nodded. "Of course; of course we are," he said.

It was almost two o clock before they'd said all their light-headed goodnights, having agreed to meet at twelve thirty in the Sunrise Café. Brad explained that he and Rose had some things to do during the morning with the setting up of the ISG office. He'd said twelve noon at first but had caught the look on Saeed's face and put back the meeting until after prayer time.

His hotel room was huge. He shivered, adjusted the air conditioning. This would be his first night alone in a bedroom since London, more than two months ago. He went over to the window, looked down on the sweep of a now almost deserted Corniche, following it around the bay towards the distant Pearl landmark and the still more distant lights of the Meridien Hotel, out on its spur of land, his mind making so easy the leap, beyond that, across the straits to Saudi Arabia.

Standing in the shower he realised he was almost asleep. Dried off, still naked, he got into bed under the duvet. Looking for the light switch he noticed the red flash of a recorded message light on the bedside phone. He frowned at it for a moment, suspicious, then lifted the receiver and pressed the button. The voice said, "Welcome home, Captain," and there was indeed a welcome home in the voice of Colonel Grenville. "Something told me you'd make it. I'll be waiting in terminal Four. For now I'll bid you just a very, very good night."

"And a good night to you, too, Colonel." he murmured. He replaced the handset. The room was inclined to sway. He switched off all the lights, his mind in overdrive, the protective darkness his forgotten friend. But now came all the pictures and all the emotions, flashing in, mixing, strangely out of time, parading in and out of focus: Rose and Colonel Robert Pierce Grenville and Sheikh Abdul-Rahman bin Sulaiman Al-Sottar and an unclothed Consuela Maria Carrapaga and his sister Sheila Thornton as a young girl and Darren, down and hurting and Jimmy sitting crying amongst the bodies and the boys oddly grown up and the Sea Fibres horse-racing party. And there was only the night forever, and the faces of all the dead.

Having made an escape from the close proximity of your confinement, the time of greatest danger is when you first come within reach of what you believe to be your safe haven. Try not to break your cover until you are absolutely certain, had said The Book.

Chapter Nine

Sunlight burned a white line down the semi-dark where the curtains didn't quite meet. Sometimes, Connie had issued her soft instruction. 'Come back to bed, Thomas. I am cold,' but now he tried not to think about the woman who had, at that time, known only him. He picked up the bed-side telephone and ordered breakfast. 'Thankyou, that will take approximately twenty minutes, Mister MacRae,' someone said. 'MacRae!' Had he been asked, he knew he would have replied 'Thornton.'

He showered and dried then picked over his new-found clothing. In the bottom of the case was an envelope with a card, on the front of it a picture of a thatched cottage standing half hidden in an abundant overgrowth of summer garden and the words: "Welcome Home." In the centrefold Rose had added in red ink, "Dear Thomas," and some crosses and there was the lipstick imprint of an open-mouthed kiss, which at first he thought quite a clever part of the card's design until, suspecting otherwise, he put it to his nose.

The Gulf Daily News had been pushed under his door. He scanned it whilst eating, looking for any mention of recent events not forty klix from here. There was nothing. Looking out of the window, there were no white-caps on the sea, just low-tide washed out blues where the shallow sandbanks were located and the cobalt strips of the deep water channels. Down below, traffic along the Corniche was moving in sections, snake-like, gathering itself together at the red lights then shooting forward and stretching out on the green release.

At half past twelve he made his way out into the saturating mid-day heat, crossed over the road. Brad and George and Saeed were already there, upstairs in the Sunrise Café. Saeed was now dressed in thobe and ghutra, Saudi fashion. "Good morning people," Thomas said, "No Rose, this morning?"

Brad said, "She's interviewing secretarial staff for ISG. You slept OK, I hope?"

"Like a baby. How about you all?"

George said, "Wonderful, when I'd finished rowing the fucking Atlantic and the room stopped moving, wonderful. Great apartment, real Hollywood, man. You can see from here to eternity and there's this big deep pool right on top, right outside the door of the apartment. We thought we'd died and gone to heaven, right buddy?"

Saeed said, "Perhaps, but I have no interest in the swimming any more. I cannot understand why is that," and they all laughed. The Indian waiter whose name was Salamullah came up, waiting and smiling, whilst they placed their orders. Salamullah repeated the order and disappeared down the stairs. Thomas said, "Let's hope nobody else comes up. If anyone does come, will it be all right to reconvene in your apartment, Brad?"

Brad nodded, "Yes, of course."

Thomas sat back in his chair. "Well, how to begin? I think we can say so far so good. What we need to decide now is what happens next. Brad, while we were holed up I told these guys only that I was going to get myself back into the Kingdom and that I was looking to do that (a) for my own reasons and (b) for money, big money,"

George said, "You just said the magic word, skip. How much is 'big'?"

"Just wait a moment, George. Big money equals illegal equals dangerous. Very dangerous. But I have to tell you, yes, there is the money, but for me personally there is also the man."

George said, "So? You gonna tell us about that?"

"As I said, it's personal, George," he said, "But I'll get around to it. I asked you two guys if you might be interested to get in on the action because I'm going to need a team for what I now have in mind. I know how you Cell Block three guys can perform. So I'm going to outline the plan, then I need a 'yes' or a 'no' from you. If it's a no I just have to trust you to forget this conversation ever happened. 'Maybe' is not an answer from here on in. In or out. You're both OK with that?"

They murmured their agreement and Thomas turned back to Brad. "Now listen to me, Mister Bradley Scott. I'm letting you in on this because you're my friend going back a long way and because no way would we have made it here without you. But you obviously have a good job here and a bloody good lady. I'm not going to allow you to

140

jeopardise any of that, you simply don't need it. These guys, well, like me they do need it, you'll understand that."

Brad said, "There was a time ... but, Tommy, these days I tend to make up my own mind. And hell, the way I see it you always did need a minder." He looked at the others, grinning his film star grin. "First time he starts operating without me some bastard shoots him up. The next thing he's bloody well gone off and married the girl from Ipanima. Besides, I thought I heard 'big money?'"

Thomas shook his head, shrugged.

George said, "OK, let's have it then, skip."

Thomas took a paper napkin and sketched the west facing coast of Bahrain, top to bottom down the right hand side. Down the left, the eastern seaboard of Saudi Arabia. He drew in the causeway as a horizontal connecting line with a circle in the middle. To the north of the causeway, in the hollow of Bahrain's Manama bay he drew a letter X and opposite it, on the Saudi side he put in another X and the initials A.S..

"I think I'm reading you, skipper," said George. "This is us." He pointed to the Bahrain X. "Then this line is the causeway. This circle's their Customs posts, immigration etcetera. But what's with this 'A.S' thing?

"'A.S.' is Sheikh Abdul-Rahman Al-Sottar. That's his beach house. I'm going to come in off the sea and take the house and what I think he has that's mine. And I'm going to take the man himself. He's going to pay me a five million dollar penalty for what he's done and he's going to tell me why he's done it. That's one and a quarter for each of us if you're all in this thing with me." He added another X, a little further south from the beach house. "And this is the Marina and our lovely old Jazeera," he said. "By the way, this was our route last night..." He dotted a line, curving out from the boatyard and then south east to meet the Causeway, indicated the wind direction with a big arrow and a 'W' and the tide with another smaller arrow and a 'T'.

As the waiter approached with his relay of food and drinks Thomas flipped over the napkin and nobody said anything else until the food service was finished. The silence continued momentarily, then Brad picked up his fork, turned over some of his curry. Casually he asked, "You planning on killing anyone, Tommy?"

Thomas said, "No." He hesitated, "But it could happen." He realised he needed some sunglasses. The white light through the window was truly eye-aching. "I didn't start the war, guys, remember that. But let's face it, this thing has developed into a minor war. There's been a hell of a lot of people getting hurt."

"How well do you know this beach house and what goes on there?" Brad asked.

"How well? Very well. I've been there as a guest on a good few occasions."

George said, incredulously, "Let me get this straight. You plan for us to land on the beach and take the house and hold this guy for ransom, is that it? Shee-it, man." He was using his fork to hold his steak whilst he cut it into pieces with the knife.

Thomas said, "Yes, George, that's about the strength of it. Listen to me. Nobody's going to be looking for any worms to turn, if you see what I mean, so we'll have the element of surprise, we'll have it in spades. Remember, any ranking Saudi is absolutely sure of his own safety when he's in his own country." He stirred his soup into steaming life. Pieces of carrot and beans and potato rose to the surface, sank back. "I'm calculating that, to bring it off with a high enough chance of success, we'll need to work in two teams of two, each team in its own boat. There's a lot more detail to plan in but I see the canoes making the return crossing tied together. It has to be on another moonless night and I'm sad to say it but we'll have to have some wind for a bit of a chop on the water. When we get over there we'll anchor up just off-shore from the house and watch what's happening before we go in." He had seen Saeed's change of expression. "Don't worry, Saeed, it won't be like last night. Here we can get the right kind of canoes, pick and choose our timing and so on." The soup was really very tasty. He went on, "I'll be going in on the beach first. There's things I have to do before the main landing."

George said, "Main landing! Christ, the guy's planning some kinda fucking Omaha Beach!

Saeed just appeared stricken. He shook his head. "I would go for you anywhere on the earth, Mister Thomas, but I cannot go back on the sea. This is not possible, you do not know how bad it was for me."

"That's up to you Saeed. But even when you were at your most sick you carried on thinking and doing what you had to do and, I've told you, nobody's going to risk going out again in seas like those last night. We just got unlucky, that's all." He paused. Outside in the road a couple of policemen had drawn up, now sat astride their motor bikes, talking together. "But Saeed, there may be another way that doesn't involve you getting your feet wet." The immaculately uniformed policemen had got off, propped up their bikes, were now walking

142

towards the Café. He said, quietly, "OK, time to split. There's no hurry. George, you first with Brad. I'll follow on with Saeed. We'll be at your apartment fifteen or so minutes behind you. Don't need to make it look as if we're running away or anything. Make sure the building's Security is expecting us, OK? On your way out of here why don't you ask Salamullah to bring us up some fresh coffee? Oh, and the check."

Brad and George went down the stairs. He could hear Brad talking to Salamullah. and George saying something that made the policemen laugh. The policemen climbed the stairs and sat at the opposite table. Through the window he could see Brad and George walking across the road then turning into their apartment building.

One of the policemen looked across, said, "Your friend who go, I ask him, how his car today?" Thomas was genuinely puzzled, must have looked it. "Your friend stop to change wheel on the highway last night. I stop to help but he need no help. One very filthy night, yes?" He and his friend seemed to think this funny but there was no sign of recognition nor of any curiosity. Thomas breathed more easily. He and Saeed drank their fresh coffee, conversing in English with each other and with the policemen. When they had paid the check and got up to leave Saeed bade them good-day in Arabic.

The more fluent officer said, in English, "Welcome, gentlemen. You have yourselves a good day here in Bahrain."

Thomas said, "Yes, officer, is that an order?" which was enough to leave them laughing: Laughing policemen, he thought, Just how wonderful is that?

He had to admit the apartment was wonderful, too.

Brad had retrieved some beers from a massive refrigerator, plus a plastic bottle of water for Saeed. He sat down in an easy chair, said, "So, OK, if it wasn't going to be me, who was your fourth man to be?

"I was thinking about Ben Benedict," Thomas said. "I told you we'd been keeping in touch through the e-mails. Last time I was over in England I met up with him for a few beers. He has his own sea angling charter boat these days." He hesitated, took a swallow of beer. "It doesn't seem to be doing a whole lot for him financially and I'm sorry to say his marriage went all to pot some time ago. Matter of fact he'd asked me about possible job opportunities out here. You know, before they clapped me in irons. Although I'm pretty sure sergeant Ben didn't actually have anything like this in mind but I reckon he'd be well up for it. Remember Iraq?"

George said, "Iraq? What's with Iraq? You guys did get around."

Brad said, "Once upon a time and long ago, George. And Derry - sorry, Londonderry. I remember that well enough. Anyway, Tommy, you won't need Ben because I'll be there, won't I. But tell me more; what happens after we grab this guy? And number two; how do we get away with all this filthy lucre the man's going to volunteer for us?"

"What happens? In the first place you'll all be masked, and at all times, in his presence. All except me. I want him to see me as I see him. "After the op's over we'll be leaving a trail pointing back to Bahrain, but in reality we'll be holed up with our man for a few days, back on board *Jazeera*. It'll be pretty much the same as before, but likely to be more people coming and going."

"Mister Thomas," Saeed asked, "What about it if His Highness wishes to go out on the ocean in his ship while we are ourselves there in residence with this Mr Al-Sottar?"

"'Sheikh,' Saeed. He calls himself a sheikh. The way I know it that's unlikely. About a one in ten chance historically. If the Prince does decide to come we welcome him and his crew aboard and deal with the situation, that's all. I have several contingency plans but there's nothing fixed and firm at his stage."

Saeed asked, "What by this 'deal with the situation,' you mean?"

Brad said, "Tommy means we play it by ear Saeed, you can't script absolutely everything on an operation like this. At least, not at long range you can't. It's too dangerous because you lose the advantage of flexibility – and besides, the enemy has this habit of writing his own script and it's not like yours, right?" He got up and went to the kitchen for more beers and another bottle of water for Saeed.

"Tell us about the money, skipper," George asked, "That's the other thing. Has he definitely got all this dough? If he has will he let it go and if he will, how do we fucking get hold of it without getting caught with our fingers in the till?"

Brad had returned with the fresh bottles. "I suppose you'll be thinking about the McGonigal scam, am I right?" he asked.

Thomas said, "Right first time. I'll be explaining later how it's going to work for us. But George, yes, I can definitely confirm Al-Sottar does have the five millions - and one hell of a lot more besides. Like most other Saudi money it's stashed away in various industrial investments and as cash in Western banks. I should know, I've transferred plenty into his accounts over the past five years. And as for your, 'will he let us have the five'? Well, I reckon he'll make us a present of such an amount if he thinks it gets him any kind of a chance to help Saudi law get hold of us and hang us by the proverbial balls."

George said, "I've got a feeling you guys know pretty much what you're talking about. Yep, all those lovely green-backed dollars. I'm in. So when do we go, skipper?"

"Not immediately. There's a lot of organising and planning to do," he said, "I'm flying to England tomorrow night. I need to do some research there. It's all connected. I don't expect to be there for more than a week, maximum. When I come back I'll have new passports for you two guys. With any luck you're going to be free as a bird - as two birds. We'll firm everything up then. Plenty of time to sort out the boats and all the other gear. Don't forget we do still have the Brownings, right, George?"

George nodded. "I stashed them under the rear seat in Brad's car. There'll be no gunfight at the OK Coral though, guys; not enough shells."

Brad said, "We'll need to tool up properly. That won't be a problem. Our ISG has plenty of armament. Trade samples, right? And I hold all the licences. And by the by, I've got some ideas about the boats. We can be getting on with that while you're away in England, Tommy. And we got George's and Saeed's passport photos done this morning. Here." He took two envelopes out of his document case, handed them to Thomas. "Photos and title page details. Meet our Sudanese friend, Saeed Al-Fonsi and our new American friend Mr George Papacopoulis."

"George, you might have given yourself an easier name," Thomas said. Noting Saeed's concern, he added, "Don't worry, nobody else knows and nobody else will know anything about this. Only the four of us. And that's permanent, no matter what, OK? Brad and I have contacts from our past life, people who are totally guaranteed to ask no questions." He hesitated. "I mentioned the possibility of you not needing to get your feet wet, Saeed. Well it occurred to me that with a new passport Mr Saeed Al-Fonsi could get a Saudi visa in London and just drive on over the Causeway. Brad, you could do the same for that matter. Might be best that way, as a matter of fact. We could hit the beach house from land and sea. You could both return over the Causeway if we reckoned it safe, or if it's not safe you'd have to take the sea route back with George and myself."

"I like this better," said Saeed, "Except it shall never be less safe than over that sea."

Thomas went on, "What about Rose? Do we bring her in on it, Brad? Up to you."

Brad said, "Definitely. She's a great organiser, you know that - besides, you couldn't keep it from her. The lady misses zero to nothing. And if we're going to do a McGonigal we're going to be best off using her as an intermediary. She's scheduled herself to spend the rest of the year here, helping me with the ISG set up."

George shook his head doubtfully. "I'm not too sure about that. Too risky?" He finished off his beer in one swallow. "For her, I mean. But I don't even know what the fuck you guys mean about this McGonigal."

Thomas said, "How about you, Saeed? What do you think?"

"I think I would follow Mr Brad. Nobody knows this lady as good as him. But what about the money?"

Brad said, "Don't worry about that. If she's in, she's with me so we share my corner."

Thomas said, "OK, Brad, we'll talk to her later. But talking about money, I have nine hundred and sixty U.S. in cash and a credit card in my old name that I'm about to cut up into little pieces. I daren't touch any of my old bank accounts until I've sorted out the situation. I also have your ISG company card, Brad. The one in my new name. What are the rules with that? By the way, guys, I am as of now Thomas MacRae. That understood?"

George said, "MacRae? Sure. Me, I have zilch dough. Guess I can get myself fixed up with a new card from the USA. They'll probably want to know why I haven't been paying off the old one, though, and why no-one's been answering their fucking letters. But, hell, it shouldn't be a problem."

"No need for that, George," Brad said. "Minimum exposure, right? Let's keep right down out of sight. I'll lend you guys what cash you want, all on account, OK?"

Saeed said, "I have nothing, but I am expecting soon to receive one point two five million dollars, less my share of our costs. Of course, please count me into this plan of campaign, Mister Thomas."

Brad said, "So that's the four of us in, right? Plus one fair lady to follow." They shook hands, each with the others around the coffee table. "And now we're going to do this thing we'll do it right, starting with keeping the books straight. That'll be you, Saeed, I guess you're the best man for that. I'll even hire your temporary accounting services for ISG if that's OK with you? Just one thing though. Tommy, if these guys agree I think we should divide the take into five shares. You're the boss so you should take two of them and the rest of us one each."

Saeed said, "I agree, but then we should increase our income to six millions of dollars U.S.. Mister Thomas then has two point four and we have our one point two."

George said, "The guy's a financial genius. Agreed by me, boys. I can't see the Sheikh of fucking Araby ballsing himself up for the sake of another mill more or less."

"OK," Thomas said. "So, it's all for one and one for all, is it?"

Saeed grinned. "That was the Three Musketeers, Mister Thomas. We are four in number; not to count the lady Rose."

"Yes indeed, I stand corrected," Thomas said. "How about the Four Horsemen of the Apocalypse, then? Why don't we meet up later for a small celebratory night out. Rose comes too of course," he added, "But right now I'm a free man and I'm going to take a walk along the Corniche and I don't give a damn how hot it is. Just being able to go where the hell one wants to go…"

"Yes. I may come with you?" Saeed asked.

Together they walked out of the air conditioning of the apartment building and past the abstract shape of the Diplomatic Area monument, crossed a dual carriageway at the lights then sat on the sea wall for a while. They watched a bare footed lad fishing his hand-line from the rocks down below. The water was glass-clear and calm. The heat and the humidity and the intensity of sunlight were all but unbearable. The boy had been bringing in a succession of tiny silver fish, hauling in his line hand over hand, taking the fish off the hook, rebaiting and whirling the weighted end around his head to gain maximum distance on the re-cast. Half way through his next retrieve the line suddenly became as tight as a bowstring and then just as quickly went limp and loose in the water. The boy looked up at them, shrugged apologetically. "Fish. Big fish he takes my fish and my hook," he explained, speaking in Arabic.

"Al'lah!" Saeed said, "You told me no sharks in these waters, Mister Thomas."

"That was just a bigger fish eating a smaller fish, not a shark." Without thinking, he had spoken in Arabic. The boy looked up from his tying on of a new hook. "Yes, sir, it was a shark," he said, gravely. "I am a fisherman. I know such things."

Sternly Saeed said, "Be respectful of your elders, boy." To Thomas; "I must go now, soon it is time for prayers and I would like to visit the big mosque here. I have heard much of it. With your permission

Mister Thomas, I shall not join with you tonight. This does not offend you?"

"Saeed, it does not offend me. There are many times when I have wished I could share your convictions." He held out his hand. "Go in peace, my brother. And do not worry anything about the sea." Still the Arabic.

The boy called out, "Sirs, you would like to buy my fish?"

Thomas laughed, spun down a silver half dinar. The boy plucked it neatly out of mid air. "As a fisherman you will make a fine businessman, little one," he said. "You can eat your fish for me today."

George and Brad and Rose met him in the hotel lobby and the four of them walked through into the hotel bar, The Kilarney Jug. The place was packed and the noise level high. Over all the heads Thomas at once spotted Dave and Marie, over here from the compound in Saudi Arabia. They were standing amongst a group of others in front of the bar. So far they hadn't seen him. He grabbed Brad's elbow, turned his back to Dave whilst George and Rose pushed on through the crowd. He explained, "There's some people from Saudi in here who know me. I'll go straight into the gents and then out. Give my apologies to the others, Brad, please. I'll be knocking on your door tomorrow morning, OK? Have a good time now."

By the time he'd got outside George was there, waiting for him. George said, "Then there were two,' right? I figured there are too many risks in places like The Jug and all the fucking restaurants in this place. For me and you both. But do not despair, skipper, Georgie knows some places your friends will never get to. Follow me."

Thomas said, "Why the hell not? Let's find ourselves somewhere dark and crowded with a good bar where we can get ourselves nicely pissed, OK?" He grinned. "Not too pissed, though. We wouldn't want anyone asking you for your papers, would we?"

"Now you're talking my language, skipper. I know just the place. You got any problem with naked ladies?"

The place was on the top floor of a small hotel up some back street in the old City. It was dark enough and it smelled strongly of hot Arabia and the music was Eastern Mediterranean. They were granted a table close to the dancers. All the bare-footed dancing girls doubled as singers. Everything about the girls moved except the fixture of their smiles as they danced to accumulate the garlands that were being so expensively gifted by the audience, exclusively male and predominately

Arab. Thomas raised his glass to his companion. "George," he said, "This is one hell of a long way from Al Mahli, my friend. Cheers."

They drank expensive beers and, later, even more expensive whisky. The mounting bill seemed of less and less consequence as the evening accelerated into the new day. It was amazing how each hour seemed to contain so many less minutes than its predecessor. Thomas knew it was time to go when George tried to invade the dance floor and two substantial sub-continental gentlemen politely but firmly brought him back to the table.

Finally, as the two of them staggered to their feet George made one last despairing attempt at a physical farewell for his chosen one, and the rest was just a blur. Sometimes funny, sometimes angry but mostly just a blur.

He woke up in an unfamiliar panic. With sweat jumping from his forehead, he swung his feet to the floor, sat still on the edge of the bed. His head hurt abominably. Yes, this was his hotel room and he was naked and last night's clothing was scattered around the floor. Madness, bloody madness. He checked his watch. Friday the thirty first of August, ten thirty. He stood up and made his careful way into the bathroom, turned on the shower, stepped gingerly under its spray of sharp needles, needing to clutch the hand rail to keep himself vertical. The bruises were coming out but, checking himself over, nothing seemed broken. He heard himself groaning out aloud.

Having completed his ablutions he searched for and found his wallet. Lucky, very lucky. Credit card and passport were still in it; only three hundred dollars missing. 'Spent,' would be the more accurate word. Could have been worse. He called Brad.

"Tommy! Where the hell are you? How the hell are you, come to that?"

"I'm OK," he said, "If you call being run over by a herd of rampaging elephants OK. I'm in my hotel room." He hesitated, fearing the worst. "How's George?"

"We were beginning to wonder… You weren't answering your mobile. And George? You should know better than me, pal. Looks like he's just had a week on the bloody Somme. He got himself up out of his pit, God knows quite how, but thought better of it and went back. Looks as if he'll be sleeping 'til about tea-time tomorrow."

"Oh, shit."

"As you say. Anyway, before he returned to the arms of Morpheus your man told us about the fight." Brad sounded vaguely amused.

149

"Christ, what fight was that, then? I don't think I need to know about this."

"Shades of Saturday night down on Poole Quay. You were in this Club. George got himself involved in some kind of a fracas and you waded into them like Mike bloody Tyson. You weren't exactly holding back. The opposition's going to remember you, all right. Anyway you got our boy into the only lift in the place and picked up a taxi just ahead of the avenging horde. Just as well you're out of here tonight, old son. I'm not sure Bahrain's big enough for you, what with one thing and another." He laughed loudly. "Seriously, Tommy, I don't think you could have left any bodies behind and let's face it, after six weeks in that Saudi cess-pit you both damn well deserve the odd bender, right?"

"If you don't mind, I'm going to stay in here in the hotel today, do some heavy relaxing by the pool. What time did you say my flight was?"

"Check your ticket, zero two hundred, I think. Why don't you come around here for dinner tonight and I'll run you to the airport afterwards?"

"Only if you promise to keep me away from alcohol. I mean, for ever."

"See you around eight. Be done with the hotel and all ready for the airport, OK?"

He dressed in clean shorts and tennis shirt and open sandals that were slightly on the small side for his feet, then bagged up the dirty stuff, dialled for the Laundry and asked a man called Ronnie for a same day service. The voice on the phone announced that this was Friday and in any case it was too late for same day return. "You said your name is Ronnie?" Thomas asked. "Well, Ronnie, I need my stuff laundered and back here by six this evening. I have an extra twenty dollars. What d'you say?"

"No problem. I'm coming right up, Mister MacRae."

"That's very good of you. You get your money when I get my clothes back, anytime before six."

He picked up the Gulf Daily News and went down to the lobby, bought an Arab News and yesterday's Times and a pair of cheap but stylish sunglasses, then walked through to the swimming pool. As he expected, only the Europeans, especially the airline crews would be out there in this heat. He sat well back in the shade of the building, ordered coffee and biscuits and read his papers, occasionally glancing over the top at the bikini clad girls, slow cooking themselves out in the full glare of the sun. Once, a strawberry blonde sat up on her sun-bed, looked casually around, adjusted her shoulder straps and lay back down on her side, facing him, one knee pushed forward, red finger nails drumming lazily on a well-oiled, honey-brown thigh.

A small piece deep inside the Arab News caught his attention. It was headed, "Prison disturbance quelled," and read; "The Dammam authorities announced that a recent disturbances at Al Mahli prison had been ended. Prison life has returned to normal although it is understood that there have been several injuries over the past ten days." He scanned the Times and the Gulf Daily News but there was nothing else.

Closing his eyes he could still see Darren looking at him, an oddly puzzled look, clutching at his abdomen, crumpling ... Jimmy, sitting on the baking hot concrete shielding the head of his friend from contact with it. He stood up, stuffed the newspapers into a bin. He couldn't help looking back. The blonde had lowered her glasses. He could see her smiling eyes. The hand on the thigh lifted slightly, waved. He nodded, restrained the return smile, turned away.

Up in his room he hung the 'do not disturb' card on the outside door handle and closed and locked the door then lay down on his un-made bed. And soon enough came the hot visions of this dark-skinned girl with her family beside a hotel swimming pool. The girl is watching him through the big window as he talks inside with her father. She's looking over the tops of her sunglasses, smiling, knowing. Her name is Consuela and she has a figure you can feel without touching, one to die for. One, in his dream, he knows he will die for. Because this girl, whose name is Consuela, presents a danger even greater than does her father.

Chapter Ten

Businessman Thomas MacRae had no trouble exiting Bahrain and the early morning BA flight was half empty. ISG Limited had bought him a very comfortable first class window seat. On the screen at the front of the cabin he watched the plane's snail-like progress across an outline of the Middle East. Right now they were overflying Saudi Arabia. He shivered involuntarily. A not so young stewardess happened to be passing. She smiled down on him. "You're cold, sir? Can I get you a blanket?".

"No thank you," he said. She was pretty, age notwithstanding. He grinned up at her. "I was just dreaming about having to make a forced landing in the desert."

She looked at him oddly. "We try not to think about that sort of thing. Can I get you something to drink?"

"How about a whisky? Single malt?"

He adjusted the rake of his seat and the leg rests, put on the earphones, clicked through to the classical music channel. The Chopin together with the Isle of Jura did it. He dozed off, in his mouth the seaweed and heathery rock taste of the Scottish Highlands, in his ears the marvellous piano music set against the background drone of the plane's engines.

After seven hours in the air but only four on the clock, local, he looked down in the early morning on the wanderings of the Thames estuary. England. The country he called home, the one he'd wondered about ever seeing again. Sheila would be getting the boys up about now. How had she been managing to fit them into her life-style, customarily such a day and night thing, especially night.

More thoughts of Connie. Had he really been that disappointing a husband? Boring? Life on the compound may have been hard on her simply because it was so bloody easy, but it was the same for all the wives. As the plane sank low over the rooftops and the gardens and the cat's cradle of roads around Heathrow, skimming the tops of the hangers, connecting with the tarmac runway, he thought of Connie and Al-Sottar together, and of what he would do.

As always, Terminal Four's arrivals hall was at the same time Bedlam and Babel. A kind of cell block three at visitor time but with perfumed, chemical air in place of the prison's body smells.

Colonel Robert Grenville stood out from the humanity that divided and flowed around his six feet three inches of well dressed, silvery good looks.

"I wasn't sure you would be coming in person, Colonel," Thomas said, shaking hands, "It's a fairly unsocial hour. But thanks anyway." He stumbled forward as a great pile of trolleyed, roped up black plastic bags and taped cardboard cartons brushed by his leg.

The Colonel chuckled. "Welcome home, Thomas MacRae. We'd better get ourselves out of the firing line."

In the car park Thomas noted the meticulously coded de-activation of the car security system and the care with which Grenville approached the vehicle. Noticing his interest, the Colonel said, "Force of habit. Or you could put it down to conceit. Why anybody might want to blow up a silly old gardener like me I really do not know." Driving out of the car park, he said, "Thomas, is it to be some breakfast locally or would you prefer to go straight home? You'll be staying with us of course, pro tem."

"They used to do a damn good breakfast at the Skyline, sir."

"Right you are. But I think they've changed the name of the place. It's some kind of a game, now, I think. Every few years at decreasing intervals our hotels like to swap their names around."

Breakfast was still excellent, whatever the name of the place. The Colonel updated him with news of his life, supposedly in retirement. Clearly he'd found a ready market for those hybridised tea-roses of his. It had bcome much more than just a hobby for he'd made enough at it to fund his initial excursions into the field of arms dealing, the main business of his burgeoning new company, ISG.

"But that's enough about me," Grenville concluded. "Shall we get down to cases?" Light blue eyes stared unblinkingly at Thomas from beneath bushy grey brows. "Perhaps first of all we need to establish a definite understanding about your, er, your status whilst here in the U.K."

"Why not? The Saudi police very kindly informed me that there's a warrant out in the UK for my arrest. Thornton's arrest, that is. I need to be very careful. It won't take much of a slip to connect Thomas

154

James Thornton with Thomas James MacRae, will it? So I guess I'll be undercover. Bit like the good old days, in fact." He couldn't resist the slight note of bitterness. His left elbow was reminding him, as always it reminded him when he was tired.

"That's about the strength of it, my boy," the Colonel said. "I was able quietly to check it out." There was kindness and understanding in his smile. "Do I take it that you're on a mission to clear your name? Good Lord, how very melodramatic that sounds."

"I have to set things straight, and bloody quickly. But, Colonel, there's no need for you to be involved. You've surely done more than enough for me already. If you want to know my plans that's absolutely fine but I'm not about to risk bringing you down with me. Should they manage to bring me down, that is."

The Colonel nodded slowly. "Yes, it has been too long a time since last we met, Captain Thornton. And yes, I would indeed like to hear about your plans."

"Perhaps I can get back to that, sir? First, can I ask if you are up to date on what's happened with Paul and David?"

"Your sons? Yes of course. I seem to recall my saying you were not to worry about them. I think you were standing in a shower somewhere at the time." He sipped from his cup of tea. "But first, I really do have to say well done, Thomas. Your escapade, I mean. Quite pleased the old training still comes in handy now and then. I do know the territory you were in and I can well imagine it would not have been much of a doddle." He picked up a teaspoon, added a little sugar.

"We had a fair amount of luck. But I have to admit I'm still trying to rationalise the human cost of it all."

"It does seem the mob took matters into its own hands, you know, after the break out," said the Colonel. "Strong case of the worm having turned, I suppose."

"Has Brad told you anything about my plans now?"

Grenville shook his head. "No, he hasn't, and I wouldn't have dreamed of asking him. 'Need to know', and all that. But back to David and Paul, they seem to be getting on extremely well in all the circumstances. I and my wife - you'll remember Delia?" Thomas nodded; who would forget the lovely Lady Dee? "Yes of course you do. Well, we've been meeting your sister and the boys quite regularly, sometimes over at her studio place in Lower Longstock, sometimes at our house. We're only twenty miles or so away, but of course you know that." He chuckled. "When they visit us the lads like to play with all the old soldiers' memorabilia. David's got all the makings, you know. He's a real take-charge fellow, isn't he? And Paul? That boy can charm all the birds down off the trees according to Dee. I wouldn't doubt it."

"Colonel, what do they know of ... of what happened out there?"

"What they understand is that (a) you have been staying in Saudi Arabia just until you've sorted out some business problems and (b) their mother is waiting for you to finish doing that. It isn't clear and it doesn't matter to them whether she's waiting in Venezuela with her family or back with you in Saudi."

Thomas coughed, frowned. "I can't yet be sure, but winding back the marriage clock is probably going to prove an impossibility."

"I'm sorry. I mean, your marriage is your business, Thomas, but surely, if - I should say after you've succeeded in disentangling yourself from these, well, these allegations?"

"The truth is that I myself don't yet fully understand why Connie is where she is, nor why she isn't here in England looking after the boys."

"I see. Or rather I don't see, but that's not important." He shook his head and signalled the waiter. "We can talk things through along the way. Oh, by the way Thomas, I should tell you that your ISG credit card is good for five thousand sterling a month until you get back on your feet." He held up his hand to cut off Thomas' protests. "You obviously cannot access your private funds at the moment. Think of it as a loan if you like. Bradley will have told you ISG is my company and so it is, but I have a very substantial investor group behind me. It is an arrangement that allows me to use the company's equity and its earnings pretty much as I will." He led the way out.

Thomas said, "Thank you again for all the support, Colonel. It seems you've converted yourself into a businessman far more effectively than have I, après SBS. I surely haven't made much of a success of it, have I?"

"Success is a moveable feast, Thomas. It is in large part a matter of opportunity. And it probably helped that I felt no compulsion to 'get away from it all,' as did you. Being a normal, reluctantly contributing taxpayer here in his native land and being a reasonably free man ... that's what I like to think I spent most of my life fighting for."

"That's a mighty subjective word, isn't it, sir? 'Free', I mean?" The inside of the Range Rover was very comfortable. "You know, when I was first sent to Ireland I was able to do some research of my own. I found out that my family – the MacRaes that is, they'd been fighting exactly the same bloody battle for as many generations back as I cared to investigate. All the way back to the Battle of the Boyne, certainly, and even before that. Anyway, after that first Ireland job, wherever else the Service sent me - Iran, Iraq, Uzbekistan, South America – I always found similar situations. Groups of people fighting over possession of a chunk of mother earth to call their own. Even my father, who was shot and killed by his own side when I was eight years old, you know, he used to send me poems from wherever he was hiding out while they were hunting him down. Freedom? To do what?"

"Quite. Of course we knew a lot about your family history, Thomas." The colonel injected himself out into the four lane commuter crawl of the M25. "You saved a great many lives in Ireland you know; and the ones you took probably deserved to be taken according to any normal standard of human decency. Besides that, you actually succeeded in removing a lot of drugs and hardship off the streets of this poor old country of ours."

"Yes, but really, what did that accomplish? The more stuff we took out of the system the more it put up the street price, which probably led to more and bigger crime and a greater margin of profit for those involved. Thatcher's market forces in the bloody raw."

"I agree with you, Thomas. The way I see it myself, there are only two possible options. Option one is for what we might call 'The State' to go on as it has, fighting a very expensive losing battle The other is simply to let everything sink into a kind of happily catatonic abyss on the grounds of inevitability. Open the floodgates to the stuff. Price comes down. In other words, let the cancer take those it's going to take, without disputation."

"What do you think, Colonel?"

"First thing I think is that it isn't you and I who should be having this discussion. But beyond doubt there are now in this world more nouveau riche coming out of the drugs trades than from all the butchers and bakers and candlestick makers rolled up as one. And on the bottom line there's probably more human misery being delivered by these people each and every day than is being imposed by all the shooting wars on planet earth." He braked to avoid a BMW that had cut across the lanes of close-packed traffic. "My personal bottom line? I think about the drugs pestilence as being a cruel and vicious thing, certainly, but a discriminatory one, too. One that will not take the strong … " He left his words hanging in the air.

Thomas said, "It's all a long way from roses, Colonel. And a very long way from those old Cockleshell Heroes, for that matter."

"Yes, isn't it just?" The traffic had closed up and slowed again. There was a long silence as they stop-started down on to the M3 filter, finally able to pick up speed. "Enough of all that," he said, "Let's talk about your situation."

"OK. I plan just three things, Colonel. Firstly, to see David and Paul and try to explain to them what's going on in terms they can understand without it hurting them. Secondly, the Saudi police claimed I was acting with a firm of boat-builders in Portsmouth on the drugs thing." Grenville raised his eyebrows. "I need to find out who I'm supposed to have been working with. You remember Kit Patterson?" Grenville nodded again. "Of course you must. So you know he's running the Sea Fibres boat building concern down in Portsmouth?"

"I'm very sorry to have to be the one to tell you this, Thomas, but I'm afraid Patterson's dead. Killed in an accident about a month ago. It seems a truckload of timbers collapsed on to his car. Pity. He was a good man."

The news hit Thomas like a blow to the stomach. For a moment there was nothing to say, then, "I'm so very sorry. Kit and I got on very well on the business front. In fact we had a hell of a good time together at Cheltenham races when I was over on a buying mission." He thought back to the conversation overheard from his hiding place in *Jazeera*'s chart room. "I heard that two of his people had been arrested on charges connected with my situation in Saudi."

"Is that so?"

"The Saudis must be in touch with the police here."

The Colonel sighed. "And so it goes on." He dropped the subject. "You said 'three objectives'. So what is your number three?"

"To get back to Bahrain, one week today."

The Colonel pulled in behind a middle lane coach to let an overtaker go by, "Back to Bahrain? You'll no doubt tell me why, should you think it appropriate. Suffice to say, Thomas, having helped to get you out of the Middle East, I would be devastated to see you becoming entangled with all that nastiness again." He laughed unexpectedly. "Having said that, I feel obliged to add that you do bring the whiff of a forgotten excitement into an old man's life."

A man holding hands with a child was walking with their dog along a pathway through gorse bushes alongside the motorway. Thomas said, "How do you think it would it be if I arranged to take my boys out fishing?"

"Good idea." Grenville chuckled. "And I'm more than sure I speak for them in saying so."

158

"You remember Ben Benedict? Sergeant Ben Benedict ?"

"Of course. He's now living in Portsmouth, I think. A number of 'ex's' still keep in touch with each other - and with me - on an informal basis, you understand."

"Ben and I e-mail each other every now and then. He's operating an MFV for parties of sea anglers. I thought I might see if I can book him for a day charter. I'll need to consult with Sheila first but, Colonel, if it's OK with you I'll get my head down for a while before I call her. And I shall need to fix myself up with a rented car." Grey based islands of cloud were moving across the blue of the summer sky and the first rain drops were impacting their windscreen.

"That all seems excellent. Welcome home, Thomas, have I already said that?"

"Yes, and thanks. I think I've said that as well." He watched the passing countryside in silence, fell asleep to the metronomic whisper of the wipers

He woke as their wheels crunched gravel on the driveway. Lady Dee was exactly as he remembered her, as elegant as ever. Her careful grey hair and country clothing made the perfect picture as she stood in the cottage doorway, the Black Labrador they called BB at her feet, older now but his tail waving from side to side. "It's good to see you Thomas," she said, stepping forward to be kissed by him. "And I do love the hair cut. How rugged, and that corn-field of a beard! How very Russell Crowe! Now come on in and make yourself at home. Your bed's all made up. Shall we get your things upstairs?"

He'd showered and shaved and now lay flat out on the bed. The window was wide open. The showers had stopped and the air smelled of England, of the confusion of summer things out there. Eyes closed, he thought of that other window, the one with the grill over it.

A pair of birds, wagtails, he thought, must have produced a late brood in a nest under the eaves of the roof, deep within the ivy. At frequent intervals he could hear the nestlings' upsurge of chirruping excitement. A blackbird warbled his heart out from a station in the tall poplar down at the end of the garden. If ever in this world there once had existed Utopia, it had to be somewhere like this… and again, he slept.

The sun woke him. It had lowered itself down the sky so that the early evening beams were falling on his face. He got up, tidied himself, went downstairs. Lady Dee came smiling out of the kitchen, her hands covered in flour. "Well, good evening, young man. I hope you got some sleep?"

"I most certainly did, thanks."

"You can sit in the living room there and watch the news or read the paper until dinner's ready, or you can come and talk to me in the kitchen. I have things on the go."

"I'll come with you and make a nuisance of myself."

"I'm glad of the company, Thomas. Robert won't be long. He's taken BB for his constitutional." She smiled. "Or that's his story. Personally I'd be surprised if the two of them aren't ensconced in the Black Bull. Robert imagines I don't know how often he drops in there for his pint of beer, and probably potato crisps for BB... I never ask."

"BB; the old boy must be getting on a bit now."

"That applies to the two of them although neither one would know it. BB's almost twelve and that's not bad for a big dog."

"Not at all bad." He turned to look out at the garden. "You do have a lovely home. The Colonel's a lucky man."

"I sometimes think when all is said and done that, yes, we are indeed the lucky ones. It hasn't always seemed that way you know." She smiled gently. "Now, am I allowed to ask you about Consuela?" She brought over two mugs of tea, placed them on the ancient, solid oak table. "Milk and sugar?"

He shook his head. "Neither, thanks." The name Consuela had hit him hard, almost a physical thing.. "I'd rather not get into anything about Connie, Lady Dee, not yet anyway."

"Poor Thomas." She opened the Aga door, extracted a baking tray, lifted off a scone. She placed the scone on a plate with a pat of butter and some jam, brought it over. "Cut that open and try it after it cools a little. You must be starving. I'm afraid supper won't be ready much before eight."

The Colonel returned with the dog at seven, invited Thomas into the living room. "How about a whisky?" he asked. "I have some excellent old Western Isles stuff, or a blended if you prefer?" Holding their drinks they went out through the French windows on to the patio where the Colonel raised his glass. "Here's to you and yours, Thomas." He took a first sip. "Let me show you around the place." He laughed. "Don't worry, it's not that extensive."

Glasses in hand they strolled down the paved pathway separating the lawns from their carefully terraced borders, mostly herbaceous and now in all their glorious late summer maturity. Thick, very tall yew

160

hedges bounded the garden, seeming to make an island of the place. They passed a somewhat overgrown orchard, came up to a greenhouse. The Colonel punched in some numbers to disable the alarm. "This is where I do most of my propagation. There are one or two quite valuable little ladies in here, that's why the precautions. Take it from me there's no more sweetness and light in the world of the gardener than in any other industry these days. I have my main commercial houses down on the coast." Once inside he slipped his hand behind the head of a particularly large, dusky red rosehead, bent to smell it, invited Thomas to follow suit. The powerful scent held traces of vanilla and cinnamon. "This is my latest, if I may employ such a word in respect of about twenty five years of trial and error. She's 'Mea Trallee.' She's going to make us a fair amount of money: Aren't you, my lovely?"

Walking on, the path meandered through an overgrown expanse of nettles, brambles, dog roses. "Have to leave something for the butterflies," he said, "And all the other things that were here before we were. That's my excuse, anyway." He gestured ahead with his glass. "And this is where I do most of my thinking." The path ended on the bank of a narrow, fast flowing river, perhaps only twenty metres from one side to the other. His voice dropped. "There's a nice rise on this evening." Out in the swirl of the current winged insects fluttered and rose from the surface, dancing gold in the low-angled sunshine. A ringed boil in the water told of the premature death of one of them. "There's some nice fish here, Thomas, the browns breed naturally. We eat only the rainbows. Do you fish the fly?"

Thomas nodded, entranced. "Not much lately, but I certainly have done." On the far bank stood the poplar that had been visible from his bedroom window. He realised that the sight of the river itself must have been blocked off by the vegetation. He looked up at the male blackbird, stiff and quivering filled with strength under the liquid outpouring of his evensong, up there on high like some wonderful version of the callers of the faithful to prayer. He thought of old Mubarak Al-Jidha, hoped he still had his precious freedom of the desert.

Grenville said, "We'll have to fix you up with some tackle tomorrow. If it's anything like this we should be all right for some supper. Talking of that, we'll have a fourth to supper tonight, Thomas. I hope you don't mind. I called Sergeant Benedict after you went upstairs. He agreed to wander over to Lower Longstock for a discreet look around. If I were the law and I was on the lookout I might just be

161

watching for you at Sheila's place, yes? Of course I told Benedict nothing more than to try to work out if the local artist was being watched. But he wasn't slow to pick up your connection with Sheila, therefore the boys." A splash, then a larger than usual set of concentric ripples diverted his attention. "Did you just see that? I'd say a three pounder, wouldn't you?" He turned to face Thomas. "Benedict called me not an hour ago. Seems his car broke down right in the middle of Lower Longstock, if you see what I mean. He was forced to spend most of the afternoon in the Moon and Sixpence, just opposite your sister's place. Thomas, he's reporting that he isn't the only stranger in the village."

"Thank you, Colonel, I should have thought of that myself." It had been a shock.

They started back up the path, hearing the sound of tyres on the gravel drive in front of the cottage. "In fact, unless I'm much mistaken here he is, right on cue."

The sandy-haired ex SBS commando stood uncertainly, almost as if to attention. He addressed the senior man. "Good evening, sir. Thanks for the invite. I'm sorry I'm not really dressed for dinner, wasn't expecting it." He turned to Thomas. "Nice surprise to see you here, too, sir." They shook hands.

"Great to see you, too, Ben, but call me anything you like except 'sir'; 'Thomas' will do nicely. It was good enough up on Hill 76, if I remember."

"Yes, sir. Whoops, sorry. But the Colonel's still the Colonel, if you don't mind. Old habits die hard." He grinned. "I heard about your problem in Saudi from some friends at Sea Fibres." He looked puzzled. "They told me you were, well, thrown inside out there?"

"You mean jailed, I think. Yes, I was."

Grenville said, "Gentlemen, why don't we go through to the table? And perhaps we should in deference to the efforts of the chef save the business of the evening until after we've eaten? We need to ingest your information without getting indigestion, if you see what I mean, Ben. If anyone wants to wash up, it's along here, first left."

The dining room was all low, uneven oak beams, creaking wood-parquet flooring, dark mahogany furniture. The glass fronted sideboard and the bookcase and the framed photographs and citations around the walls spoke of this household's military life. Pre-lit red wax candles reflected in the window panes. Outside the window, tree-tops stood in silhouette against the last of the light. Lady Dee closed the curtains.

162

The food was as excellent as Thomas had expected. As they finished dessert Thomas raised his glass to the hostess, "I really do feel someone ought to propose a vote of thanks to you. That was just simply superb."

"Why, thank you, kind sir," she said, clearly pleased with the success of her efforts, "I understand it would have been considerably enhanced as against the kind of fare you've been having of late. But please do not imagine that Robert gets this four star treatment all the time. Most evenings it's just he and I and BB in the kitchen with something simple and a bottle of plonk. It's nice to have the opportunity to practice something a little bit more interesting. Right, I'm going to clear away now." She raised her hands. "No, gentlemen, I need no help. And I do know where my place is, or rather where it is not." She got to her feet, waving away their protestations. "I'm sure you have things to discuss. Perhaps I'll see you in about half an hour? I thought we might have coffee out on the patio tonight." She turned at the door. "And of course you will also be staying here tonight, Ben." It was not a question and there was no mention of alcohol and driving.

Ben opened his mouth to say something then changed his mind, smiling his thanks.

Grenville said, "Right then, down to business. Thomas, perhaps first you'll want to put Ben in the picture?"

Thomas said, "Yes, of course, Colonel." He hesitated, sipped at his glass of port. "Ben, there's been a hell of a lot happening to me but it really isn't all that complicated. In essence one or more of the people at Sea Fibres in Portsmouth seems to have been engaged along with somebody at my boatyard in Saudi Arabia on what was a substantial drug importation and a local dealing operation. Lord only knows, drug dealing is a serious enough matter here, but in Saudi Arabia, well, if I just tell you their landing cards have printed across the top in red letters, 'Death to drug dealers' ... " He went on to speak about being jailed in Saudi Arabia, about what had happened to the boys and, the most difficult bit, about Connie. "I was told my wife had gone to Venezuela to stay with her family. You'll remember Carravaga?"

Ben nodded. "I should just think I do!"

"Connie being back with him, her father, it wasn't the truth. When I was jailed she stayed on in the Kingdom. In bloody secret." He found it difficult to get out the next words. "Right now it would seem she's with my Saudi sponsor. Or rather my ex Saudi sponsor." He took a deep breath, looked down into his bubble glass, swirled and sipped at the warming brandy. "The rest sounds simple even if it wasn't. I

163

managed to get myself clear of the prison before they got around to removing my head. Now here I am. I have some plans, but first things first. Ben, Colonel Grenville tells me you reckon my boys and, or my sister may be under some kind of surveillance?"

"Yes, that's my opinion anyway. I'm very sorry to hear what you just told me. You know ... if there's anything I can do...?"

"You may regret that. There may well be. But look, what seems to be going on in Sheila's village?"

"For cover I emptied my car radiator. As I planned it, by the time I reached Lower Longstock the radiator would have blown, accidentally on purpose right outside the village pub. I knew it would take the local garage the whole afternoon to ship in and fit the new one, so I had a reason to hang around and chat to people. Nice people too, give or take these two hikers."

The Colonel said, "They, I take it, that is, these hikers, they were not so nice, you think?"

"Well, sir, in normal circs you'd be happy enough to take a drink with them but no, I don't reckon 'nice' and I doubt they were cross country hikers either. You've never seen a less sun-burned pair. Seems they checked into rooms at the pub yesterday. According to the landlord they've been asking questions, some of them about the artist in the village. That's your sister, Tom. They tell me she's the only artist around Longstock. Matter of fact I could see her studio or cottage or whatever from right there on my bar stool. Anyway, matey number one says they're interested in her pictures but the landlord gives me his opinion on the side, which is that the buggers wouldn't know a Holbein from a hockey stick." He hesitated. "I got talking to them. Unless I'm very much mistaken they're a couple of Belfast boyos all right. Could be regular Brit coppers, I suppose. You don't know what to expect these days, but I don't think so."

"So it seems we have might have cast our fly on the waters, hooked a brace of piranhas." said the Colonel. "Yet more questions than answers, still."

Quietly, Thomas said, "Tell me what they looked like, please, Ben."

"One was quite old, smallish, nondescript really. Balding, gingerish hair. Number two younger, maybe thirty, short cropped hair like your own. A fit looking guy, called himself Brian. Mind you, I thought he slipped up once over; called the old guy something else, something like Georgie, I thought it was."

"Georgie? ... J J?" Thomas said. "Could it have been J J?"

"Well, yeah, might have been."

The Colonel murmured, "No, Thomas, not J J McCann. That particular piece of poison went the way of all flesh some time ago."

The telephone rang in another room and Lady Dee came in carrying the portable. She said, "It's for you, Robert," but looking at Thomas, as calmly as always, as used as she would be to a lifetime of sudden change, imminent threat. "It's Sheila. She may have something of a problem."

"Good evening, Sheila," the Colonel said, "How can I help?" Even from across the table Thomas could catch the pitch and the duration and the urgency of the response. The Colonel listened, eyes lowered, fingers of his disengaged hand drumming softly on the mahogany table top. He said, "All understood, my girl. Just try to relax. I'll repeat what you've said for the benefit of a couple of friends I have here with me." More high pitched babble then, "Yes, completely trustworthy," then, "No, Sheila. The person you think has tried to break in may himself be a policeman, in which case there's no point in calling them, is there? Two things; One, you must keep this line open and tell me everything that has happened and is happening just as it happens. I mean everything, is that quite clear?" He glanced up as the answer came, smiling his reassurances. "These friends, they're on their way over now, or very shortly will be." Thomas and Ben were already on their feet. "When they get to you they will approach from the back of your house, from the riverside walk. I shall ask you to unbolt the kitchen door only when I know they're in position. Second point, I take it the boys are all right? Not panicking or anything? …. Fast asleep you think? …. Good … Good girl. Talk to Delia now, please. I'm going to brief the others." He handed the phone back to his wife.

"Thomas, Lady Dee rented a car for you to use. It's insured for any driver. What happened was that Sheila was watching television, heard a noise upstairs. Your sister's a clever girl, Thomas. Living by herself it seems she keeps a recording of her own voice plus two others - male voices – in readiness for just such an event. All she needed to do was switch on. She found a part of a window pane had been taken out up on the first floor landing and spotted this fellow hurrying away up the High Street."

Thomas said, "I have to go. Sorry, Ben, this is my party. Best if I handle it myself."

Ben shook his head. "No way, sir. Haven't been on anything like this since you know when. Besides, you'll need me to watch your back, won't you? Like always?" He grinned. "Specially as how you'll be a bit out of practice."

165

Thomas said, "OK then, no time to argue but thanks. Colonel, I have my mobile and you have yours so let's keep in touch."

The Colonel said, "Hold on a minute." He took out his keys, hinged back a framed portrait of the Queen sitting straight-backed, side-saddle in full Irish Guards regalia, then unlocked the wall safe behind it. "You just might need this." He reached into the safe and took out a pistol. Thomas didn't recognise the type. "It's the new issue Sauer P226 semi-automatic. It's fully loaded with twenty rounds of nine millimetre."

Thomas said, "Thanks, Colonel, but I don't think we can risk it. If those people are who you think and they really meant it, they'd have been in there by now and got clean away having done whatever it is they wanted to do. It's more likely they were just burglars, isn't it? God, how I hope so."

Colonel Grenville said, "Are you sure? If they are the boyos … it could get pretty nasty."

"Jesus … I thought I'd left all that stuff behind me." Thomas hesitated, looked at Ben. Ben nodded.

"To hell with it. Sorry Colonel, I think I'll change my mind. We'll go with your pistol," Thomas said.

Chapter Eleven

"Best park at the pub," Ben said, "Saturday night there'll be plenty in there right up to chucking out time. What do you think?" He grabbed the car's hand-hold as Thomas took a bend too quickly.

"Sorry about that. Bit out of practice with country lane driving. Yes, sounds good for an hour or two but we'll need to find somewhere less obvious later. Villages have eyes." He tried to keep the anxiety out of his voice. "Some Neighbourhood Watch worthy calling in the Law, that's all we need."

"What's the plan?"

"You stay with the car and watch the front. I go in the back way. The Colonel told my sister to be prepared to open the kitchen door. She doesn't know about me being out and over here yet so she'll be just a bit surprised when I make my appearance."

Ben said, "You know the lie of the land?"

Thomas could see the raised headlights of an on-comer, the car itself as yet still out of sight. He dipped his lights. The on-comer reciprocated. "There's a footpath behind the cottage. Goes down to the riverside, runs beside the river for maybe half a mile then turns into a wood. From there and through to the car park just off this road it's a regular lover's lane. Best if you drop me off there at the car park. I can walk in to the back of the house along the river. You take the car on to the pub and wait up. I'll call you to decide what happens after that. OK?"

"Sure thing. You tell it, boss, I'll do it."

"Bit too much like Armagh, don't you think, Ben? Except we'd have thought more than twice before moving around under this bright a moon."

"We would that. You'd have had us in the observation post before dark and I'd have been shit scared to move a muscle... unless it had to be the old finger muscle." He grinned.

"If this attempted break in at Sheila's was your Irish pair in the pub, it's least likely they're standard issue cops. The way I see it they could be British Secret Services, MI5, or possibly even the MI6 boys. Everyone and his mate's in on this drugs-busting these days. Or they could just be privateers acting for some very angry guys I left behind me in Saudi." He pulled off into the woodland car park. Under the overhanging branches it was much darker. There was only one other car there, lights off and stationary. The top of a blonde head appeared briefly as their headlights swept through the three hundred and sixty degree turn. He slipped out of the car, closed the door carefully. Ben's departing headlights made the tree shadows dance and swing as he set off along the footpath. In the new darkness there was no way he could avoid snapping the odd twig or miss all the water filled ruts in the muddy track but soon enough he was through the wood and walking the riverside tow-path.

Reaching the outskirts of the village he checked his watch. Ten forty five; he called the Colonel.

"Yes, Thomas, you are in position now?"

"Affirmative. Two minutes from contact."

"Hold on, I have your objective on my other line ..." slight pause then, "Yes, she's OK with that, you can walk right in. Note this, I did just now tell her who would be visiting. I thought she'd had quite enough surprises for one evening."

"Yes. Thank you, sir. I'll let you know what happens." He switched off. There was nothing he could do to conceal his presence from anyone who might be watching the house from back here. He climbed over Sheila's garden fence and hurried down the path past the tool-shed and the overgrown vegetable patch then crossed the lawn with its children's swing and its discarded plastic toys. He opened the kitchen door, closed it quietly behind him. Sheila was pressed up against him in the darkness, her arms up around his neck, and there was the smell of her perfume and the soft push of her breasts. He whispered, "Hi, Sheila, you'd better go a bit bloody careful. I haven't been this close to a woman in months." His lips found and kissed the wetness of her cheek. "But hey, hello there sister woman, how are you?"

"And hello to you, too, brother man. I'm fine apart from being under siege in my own quiet little country cottage." He felt her reach behind him to turn the key in its lock, come up on tiptoes to socket the bolt.

He kissed her lightly on the mouth, held it longer than might have been necessary. "That's much better," she said. "Come on now, let's go

168

through to the sitting room. It's not all that cold for hardy Brits but I've a nice little fire going for my man from the desert. And first I have to call Robert. I shall tell him the eagle has landed." She giggled softly.

He found himself reluctant to release her. "Listen, I'm sorry, you know, about that bastard burglar, whoever he was."

"Oh, I wasn't too worried about him. I was concerned about some other man, my brother actually, the one I hadn't seen hide nor hair of in the last three years."

"Yes? No need is there? I have a call to make as well. My friend Ben is waiting and watching over by the pub."

She led him by the hand, out of the kitchen and across the hallway and into the warmth of the living room, switched on the lights. There was a faint, painterly smell of linseed oil and turpentine about the place. Sheila looked great, give or take the smudged make-up, although he thought that when she smiled, like now, there might have been a touch more crinkling around the light blue eyes than there had been. She was wearing an above the knee length dress, white and short sleeved, her bare legs shapely, spare, slimly ankled. She said, "Take a seat, John Thomas. I have some of that whiskey you used to like; Isle of Jura, right? They didn't make you into a teetotaller or anything out there, did they?"

Thomas sat down on the settee. "No they did not make me teetotal and yes I'd love a little of the good stuff." She poured a good measure into a tumbler. "Hey, I did mean just a little. I have to keep alert if I'm to be any use here. Remember I'm a touch out of practice with the demon drink. But I must tell you, you do look bloody marvellous, Sheila."

She said, "I do? How frightfully nice of you to say so. Anyway there's been no sign of that awful man since I frightened him away." She handed him his whisky, plopped herself down on the other end of the settee, drawing up her legs beneath her, holding out her glass. "Cheers, cousin Thomas," she said. "And before you ask, the boys are fine. You're not having them back, you know."

They clinked glasses and took a first sip, then he said, "Do you know, I'm very proud of you, Sheila. I always was and I am now and I'm very grateful and you always make me feel good. Can we go upstairs to see them?"

"Surely. I hope you won't mind but they both absolutely insisted on having practically all their hair cut off. Bit of a fashion statement I think." She smiled, reached over to touch his head. "Seems they weren't the only ones." She led the way upstairs, paused on the landing to indicate the sash window. She'd taped a transparent file cover over a round, hand sized hole in the glass. She whispered, "I think it was luck really. He dropped the piece of glass on the outside path just as I turned down the TV. My heart was pounding like the old trip-hammer, whatever that might be, but I turned on my 'talking with two men' tape and ran up here quick as a flash. I saw him turning out of the front garden into the High Street. Didn't feel like going off after him. That's when I called Robert."

"This man, you can describe him?" The smell of oil paints was stronger up here. A canvas was propped out of the way against a wall. She'd be using the heat rising from downstairs to help dry it. An estuarine wilderness of clouded dawn greys, muted browns.

"I only caught a glimpse, side on but mostly back view." She shrugged. "As you can see the street lighting out there isn't good. But describe him? He was quite small, wearing one of those Musto type country coats with wide, light beige collar. Light coloured hair. But then there was this other man, across the road outside the pub. I had the feeling they could have been together, you know? He was definitely bigger, younger, had on jeans and a long sleeved check shirt, worn outside."

"The one this side. You told the Colonel he had ginger hair?"

"Yes, could have, but might have been fair. Fair hair. I don't really know." She paused and looked at him. "You think you might know who he is, don't you?"

"No," he whispered, inching open the bedroom door. Light from the landing shafted across David's face as he frowned and stirred, rolled over, sighing deeply. If anything the unfamiliar lack of hair accentuated the young boy's beauty. As they advanced into the silence of the bedroom he felt Sheila take and squeeze his hand. Paul was lying half out of the covers on the other bed, one pyjama clad leg hanging down over the edge. Thomas replaced the foot on the mattress, pulled the duvet up around the narrow form, bent down to kiss the boy's hot cheek. He turned back to David, lightly kissed the boy's forehead. Straightening up, he looked one more time from Paul to David and back to Paul, seeing for this one moment the lost face of their mother, then returned Sheila's hand squeeze, indicated the door.

Downstairs again, he called the Colonel to say he was going to stay where he was. It was unlikely but just possible that the intruder would have another go during the night. He would be watching the back of the house. Sheila's car was out in the front drive so he would use it to

170

rig up an alarm. It would be safe for Ben to go back to the Colonel's place for some sleep.

"Excellent. Good night then, Thomas. I take it your sister's all right with the plan?"

"Yes she is. Good night, Colonel, and thanks again. I'll call Ben now."

He dialled Ben's mobile. Ben said, "Yes, boss. Everything's OK here. Yourself?"

"All quiet on the Western Front. Listen, I'm going to stay here overnight, just in case. I've spoken with the Colonel. Why don't you go back to his place, get some sleep? I'll call you after seven in the morning. Unless anything changes it would be great if you could take over from me tomorrow while I go back and get some sleep myself. By then we'll know whether or not your unlikely pair of hikers have gone on their merry way. Probably singing 'Valderee, Valdera', or something."

"It's not a problem. I'll call my guy in Portsmouth and get him to handle tomorrow's charter, he's done it before for me. Group of executive types from a local factory plus one of their customers. Nice guys. They'll load her up with enough smoked salmon sandwiches and booze to sink her then go awful quiet when she gets out on the 'oggin and starts a bit of a roll."

"You've just reminded me, Ben. Do you have a free charter next week? I'd like to take the boys out."

"You kidding me?"

"No. Monday. That OK for you?"

"It will be."

"Fine, usual rates, of course."

"My usual rate to you is zero point zero," Ben said, "And no arguments please, sir, OK?"

"Good night, Ben"

"Good night - Tommy, sir. You know where I am."

Thomas slid his fingers between the drawn curtains, watched through the slit as Ben drove off. Sheila said, "Now, are you please going to tell me what's going on? This wasn't just some ordinary botched up burglary, was it?" She frowned, uptilting her chin, pushing the hair back behind her ear, sipping her drink. "When Connie called to ask, was it all right for her to send the boys over, she told me you'd got into some serious problems and couldn't leave Saudi or even communicate with anyone. She said she planned to go to South America to try to get her family to help. The lady was in a bit of a

171

state, understandably I suppose. All I could do really was say 'yes,' and, 'what time does the boys' flight arrive?'"

"I can't thank you enough for that, Sheila. The boys were OK on the flight?"

"To the manner born according to the stewardess. They're great kids, Thomas. I thought it best to get them a temporary place at the village school. They start there after the summer hols, that's a week on Monday. They'll be all right, they've made friends with some of the lads in the village already. I hope that's all OK?"

"Perfect, at least until I can sort myself out a bit." He stretched out his legs, feeling the comfort of the room and the warmth of the coal fire and the Isle of Jura.

"So, you're going to let me in on what the hell happened out there?"

He shrugged. "I've done a few things in my life of which I would not necessarily be proud, but I don't think I ever did anything to deserve this thing in Saudi, Sheila."

She said, "Well come on then, tell me. Not coming straight out with it is one of your less endearing habits."

Thomas said, "I'm getting used to explaining the inexplicable. I just went through it with Ben. It's been very difficult but it really isn't all that complicated. I was accused of being involved in smuggling drugs into The Kingdom of Saudi Arabia. Cocaine. God knows this would be serious enough anywhere but in Saudi it just means the big sword. Virtually automatic. I was actually shown one of my men attending his own personal decapitation. They didn't but I hope you will believe me, I didn't know anything, anything at all, about any of this when I was arrested and jailed. Someone must have gone to a lot of trouble..." He leaned forward, better to feel the warmth on his hands and face. "You wouldn't want to know about that Saudi jail, Sheila ... Anyway I was informed that the boys were here and that Connie had gone back to Venezuela to stay pro tem with her family." He looked up. "Seemed unlikely. She hadn't been in touch with her family, the Carravagas, since we got it together."

Sheila shrugged. "Neither of you ever spoke about her family and it didn't seem polite to go on asking, so my female curiosity finally died from malnutrition."

"Anyway, I had an inside tip-off that she'd actually stayed on in the Kingdom, hadn't gone to Venezuela or anywhere else. I have no certain idea how or where or why, but the word is, she's..." He reached out for the words then, as lightly as he could, "she's run off

172

with my Saudi sponsor, would you believe?" He paused, gathering his thoughts. "As you can see I managed to get myself out - escaped is the real word for it - and with my head still attached to the rest of me. Apart from seeing the boys and you I'm here to try to get to the bottom of things."

She said, "My poor boy Thomas. Do you suppose the man who tried to break in here could in some way be connected with this stupid drugs thing? Christ …the rotten bastards."

"Take it easy, sister." He moved across, put his arm around her shoulders. "Most of the Saudi's I know are great. They think about things differently to us but that doesn't make them bad. There's rotten apples in many a barrel. But it's all right now. I'm here and even if someone suspects I made it, only you and the Colonel and my guys in Bahrain know that for a fact. I'm not even a Thornton at the moment. According to my passport I'm now Thomas MacRae."

"Thomas MacRae," she repeated, looking hard at him. "My mother's maiden name goes well for you. But how can I possibly take it easy? I knew Connie was lying. I knew it. When she called me she was, oh, on a different agenda, let's just say. And it's not just hindsight but I'd have laid odds it involved a man other than my brother, in which case she just has to be insane, doesn't she?"

"That's very morale raising, girl, but enough of me. How've you been, yourself? What about mother and father?"

She said, "Me, I'm doing fine. Lots of people want my pictures, thank God." She sniffed and tried a smile. "Without false modesty I think the latest ones actually are the best I've done. Less of the camera in them, more of the x-ray if you can forgive me for a touch of the old arty-farty stuff."

"The one upstairs on the landing, I liked that one. I always knew you had talent. Tons of imagination, lots of technique."

She smiled at him. "Yes? Now I'm getting quite rich, well anyway, by my own standards, I've had the attic converted into a proper studio. Lots of big windows, big light, yes?"

"Good for you," he said. "But there's no lucky new man yet appearing magically over the horizon?"

"Yet? What do you mean by 'yet.' A man isn't essential to human female life, you know, not in the twenty first century, and I've had my bloody fill of husbands, that's for certain sure."

"Two partners? Doesn't exactly sound like the end of the tunnel of love these days."

"Look, any time I want a man I flatter myself I can walk over the road and plonk down at the bar and order a pint. Like moths to a candle, if I say so myself. Give or take the smell of linseed of course." She grinned, shook her head then took another sip of her drink. "I only ever wanted one man," she added, with assumed drama, "and the world said I could not have him. And maybe he didn't want to have me." She looked at him coolly over the rim of her glass, close up.

He tried with limited success to bend his bad arm closer around her shoulders, winced. "That elbow of yours isn't any better then? The bastards. Yet more of them. How could the bastards shoot my brother? Anyway, you were asking – yes, mother's all right, even if a bit lost at sea, things being as they are. You know … poor daddy."

"No. I'm sorry, Sheila. Tell me"

"He can't have too much longer to go, we have to face it." She shook her head, sat in silence for a moment. "Of course mother wouldn't ever do that, would she? Like, face it?" She raised her free hand, gently took the lobe of his ear between her finger and thumb, smiling again. "Do you want to sleep with your pretendy sister but real life cousin, Thomas?"

He blinked, shook his head. "Sheila, I'm here to look after you," he protested, "Not to satisfy any lusts, much as the thought might appeal. We've stayed away from that stuff all this time. Your mother was right … remember, after the sand dunes?" He extracted his arm and sat up at once, all business. "Listen, I'm going to pop outside and do a little work. I need a reel of polyester sewing thread, black if you have it, and your car keys please. I'm going to use your Jeep's alarm to rig up an early warning, just in case."

Sheila found him the cotton and her car keys. He took down a copper bottomed frying pan from the overhead rack in the kitchen then let himself out. For fully five minutes he stood quite still, listening, hearing nothing, then unlocked the Jeep, placed the frying pan on the dashboard, tied the loose end of the thread to the peg-hole in its handle. He ran the reel up and over the driver's rear view mirror and out through the gap of the fractionally opened passenger door window. He ran the reel low down around a gate-post and pulled gently until he could see the saucepan had been lifted, was able to swing freely inside the car. Then he stretched the cotton over to the other gatepost at hip height and tied it off, locked the car and took a moment to examine it. The frying pan hung in mid air, motionless, the thread invisible. The Jeep's interior alarm system would take care of the rest should anyone walk into the cotton. He slipped back inside

174

through the kitchen door, locked up behind him. Sheila was still in the living room, attending to the fire. "All done now," he said, "Anyone coming up the drive is going to get a shock, that's for bloody sure. If your car alarm should go off during the night you must just do exactly what I tell you, OK?"

"Thomas, you are such a very clever boy," she said, looking at him over her shoulder, the white dress tight across her buttocks. "But what could we do about anyone coming in as you did, through the back garden?"

"There's a good moon out there. I wondered whether I could use your studio windows to watch things. I suppose I should really use your tool-shed as an OP - an observation post - but I'm not too keen on that. I'm not exactly equipped for outside surveillance."

She stood up. "So it seems I've made up my fire for nothing then?"

"Afraid so. The guys who just may be out there - well, those guys are pro's. They won't walk away just because they've ballsed up their first try. Come on now, show me your eagle's nest, OK?"

She walked over and stretched up to kiss him, murmured, "I'd love to. Show you my studio as well. But as someone once said, tomorrow is another day, for the eagle's nest. I do love you, you know, and what's more I do think you love me just a little bit. As a woman and not just a cousin stroke sister." She laughed softly.

"Come on, show me the way."

"I may not be the only one," she said, "but I'm the only one who's here. I'll show you my bedroom door on the way up. It won't be locked, so if you get bored with the night view over my lovely little back garden ..."

Through the wide expanse of floor to ceiling studio window he could see everything down the garden and to the river beyond. By moonlight the studio seemed very Spartan. Just a chequer-board lino tile floor covering and a long leather couch and a number of canvas backed folding chairs and finished or part-finished canvasses stacked on the floor or up against the walls. In the centre of the room was a wooden table with a miscellany of brushes in glass jars and boxes and tubes of paint and a couple of rags, flung down like dead seagulls. And alongside the table, an easel carrying a large canvas with the first few outline brush strokes of a picture.

He picked up one of the canvas chairs, carried it across to the window, taking care to position it in shadow but at an angle for maximum observation. Settling down, he recalled his training. *Move*

175

nothing except your eyes. Move your eyes constantly and consciously to keep awake and alert, Fix on something, anything, A branch, a star, a hole in a wall. Think about it. Not too long. Blink. Move your eyes to something else. You will pick up anything that moves in your arc of vision. Practice, practice, practice.

It was exactly three thirty when the car alarm went off. Almost at the same time as the alarm, he saw the deer bolting wildly past the house and down the garden, with extraordinary fluidity leaping the fence, white rump bobbing off down the riverside. He heard Sheila say, "It's all right Paul, stay in bed and go back to sleep. Don't wake David. I'll go and fix the alarm. We'll be waking up the whole village." Sheila was in a shortie, red silk nightdress. She was closing the boys' bedroom door. The wailing rise and fall of the car alarm dominated everything. She looked up at him questioningly, undoubtedly frightened. He smiled put both thumbs up to signal it was all right and motioned for her to go down and turn off the alarm. She switched on the stair lights and hurried down, her bare feet taking the steps two at a time, him following silently. From the hall-stand she grabbed a raincoat and went out and in a moment there was silence.

On her return they want into the darkened living room. Embers of fire still glowed dull red in the grate. He put his arms around her. She was trembling. "Only a deer," he whispered. "I'm sorry, I allowed enough height for foxes but I didn't expect a bloody deer."

"There's lots and lots of them around these days," she said. There was a catch, a definite flutter in her voice, a deep-seated breathlessness. "I'm frightened, Thomas."

Still holding her, he sat her gently down on the edge of the settee. She bowed her head and moved his shirt aside to touch her lips to the angle between his bared shoulder and his neck. For a moment everything froze and there was a stillness and then he realised the shortness of his breathing and the growing thunder of his heart and he raised his good hand to her silk covered breast and felt the softness of it and the fullness within the palm of his hand.

She looked up at him, eyes closed, lips parted.

He shook his head, whispered, "This is absolutely crazy, Sheila. I have to get back up there, OK?"

"If you insist," she murmured, "If you insist."

He couldn't tell her it was no good. He couldn't tell her about his promise to her mother, nor about what not being able to love her had done to him. Until Connie. Nor yet what all the years of being the destroyer or the destroyed had also done.

Chapter Twelve

It woke him with its inanely repetitive chortling. He slipped off the couch, naked, searching for the mobile telephone amongst his clothing on the studio floor. "Yes?"

"Morning." Ben came over loud and clear. "Reckon I must have woke you up. Sorry. You said you'd call about seven and it's half past now, I was just getting a bit worried."

"Don't apologise Ben. I didn't intend to but I just dropped off to sleep. No excuses; maybe a touch of jet lag." He yawned, wandered over to the easel, sat on the corner of the chest of drawers. "Anyway, everything's OK here. Bit of a scare when a bloody deer set my home made alarm off, but no problems."

"You still want me to come over?"

"Yes please, if it's OK with you. Just to be on the safe side you know. I want to go back to the Colonel's place and then get down to Portsmouth, try to find out what I can about what's been happening at Sea Fibres."

"There won't be too much happening on a Sunday. What do you need to know? Maybe I can help."

"I want to find exactly what charges they've laid against the two men who've been arrested, whether they've admitted anything, what evidence the police think they have, etcetera. The bottom line for me is, if they're the ones who've been using my incoming boats to get their stuff into Saudi, who was paying them for it? I've been planning to get in touch with their boss. Another one of our ex's - you know? Kit Patterson?"

"Yes, but he's dead. He was killed."

"Colonel Grenville told me. I wondered about contacting his wife." He could hear the boys now, downstairs, their voices pitched high.

The low chuckle. "He was a bit like you, sir, bit of a legend, like. Matter of fact I went to the funeral. I always try to when one of our lot goes, you know, if it's anywhere near local. The Colonel did the eulogy. See you in about a half hour then."

"Yes, but it's not 'sir', it's Thomas or it's Tom or Tommy to you, remember? You won't forget about the fishing, Ben?"

"Done and dusted. Bait and tackle all organised. The weather forecast's set fair. See you soon."

Sheila had switched on the radio. Even up here he could smell the frying of bacon. He stood well back from the huge expanse of window whilst he dressed in yesterday's crumpled clothing. A solid beam of intense, dust spangled sunlight angled in. Down by the riverside a solitary fisherman drew back an arm, correctly, in one piece with the rod, hesitated, pushed forward from the shoulder. The long thread of silver glinting line unrolled, shot forward, settled on the water. Very good. Beyond the river lay the neat abstraction of woods and randomly wandering hedges and little fields of a country green, gold, warm and fat to bursting under the late summer sun.

Sheila called up, "Are you decent? There are two young men down here, dying to say hello to their father."

"Coming right down," he called back. He opened the studio door and looked down on the upturned faces. Sheila wore a pinafore over a T-shirt and jeans. She'd tied back her hair. David's expression was of worry turning into slow delight. Paul shouted out, "Daddy!" his face a picture of instant, unquestioning joy. He hurtled himself up the stairs to meet his father half way. "You've had all your hair cut off like us, Daddy!" he shouted.

Thomas stroked the crew cut little head. "So it would seem. Hello there, soldier." He laughed, disengaging the six year old from his legs. He picked him up, kissed the excited little face with its now skewed glasses, sat him on his good arm to continue the descent. "And hello to you, too, David. What happened to the Beckham hair, then? Not too grown up to give your father a kiss, are we?" He sat down on the last stair, set Paul back on his feet, gathered up his eldest son.

David said, "Beckham cut all his hair off. I told Auntie Sheila you'd be coming soon for us, Daddy, didn't I, Auntie? Where's Mummy?" He was looking up the stairs as if expecting his mother to be following on down.

Paul shouted up, "Mummy, we're here."

"Hey, hey, let's just take it slowly," Thomas said. "Your mummy's had to go to see her own mummy in South America. She's not very well at the moment. Your grandmother, I mean. Anyway mummy sends her love. She told me to buy each of you a present, just from her. What would you like, boys? Give it some thought, OK? No need to tell me now." He got to his feet. "And good morning to you, too, Auntie."

"Morning," she said. "I do hope you slept well. Doesn't your sister get one too?"

He stepped forward and kissed her cheek. "Yes I slept incredibly well and yes, you do get one too." He looked at her. "Lots of them."

She moved closer to him, stood on tiptoe to return the kiss, but this one was on the lips, briefly.

Paul was tugging at the leg of this jeans. "Daddy, I want a fishing rod. The man said we could fish in the river but we haven't got anything, have we David?"

Thomas said, "It didn't take long for you to think up that one, did it? Let's go talk about it." He looked at Sheila. "Have you all had breakfast yet? I think I smell something pretty good."

"We were waiting for you, weren't we, boys? I had a little difficulty but eventually I did remember where my frying pan had gone. Every car should have one. I hope all you men are nice and hungry."

David took his hand. "Did you see the broken window on the landing, Daddy? Auntie Sheila told us a bird tried to fly in by mistake. It was in the middle of the night. But Auntie Sheila shooed it off and then Auntie's car alarm went off, didn't it Auntie?" He was wide eyed with excitement. "It was a deer, wasn't it Auntie? And it swam away over the river, Daddy."

"What an exciting life you people in Lower Longstock do live," Thomas said.

Sheila had laid the kitchen table for the four of them. She'd grilled piles of sausages and bacon and was keeping it warm in the oven. Now she bustled around with their cereals and the tea and glasses of milk for the boys, then began to fry some eggs. The boys chattered on about their old friends on the Compound in Saudi Arabia and their new friends here and the school they were going to after the holidays and the landlord of the Moon and Sixpence who'd told them they could fish in the pub's expensive stretch of the river provided they would learn to cast the fly under his tutelage.

"Yes, I see. So the publican wants to teach you fly fishing, eh? And just how disingenuous of the man might that be, Auntie?" She pretended to throw an egg at him Instinctively his hand went up, caught at thin air.

David said,"I bet you don't know that word, Paul. I do."

Paul looked troubled. "Oh yes, I do as well," he said. "But I'm not telling you."

David flicked a sugar puff off the table top at him. Paul was up on his feet, small fists clenched in anger.

Thomas said, "Paul, just sit yourself down. We are guests in this house. We can't have any fighting or bad manners. David, apologise please."

"I'm sorry, Daddy, I'm sorry, Auntie," David said, then, with greater reluctance, "Sorry Paul."

Sheila said, "That's all right David." She looked appealingly at Thomas.

Thomas said, "Thank you. So, all right. Now you can tell us, David, what does 'disingenuous' mean?"

"It means you're not meaning it properly."

He nodded. "Close enough. Very good in fact. I'm sure Paul knew that as well. Now let me tell you about another surprise, boys. If you would like to - and provided your Auntie agrees - I'm going to take you out on a boat on an all-day sea fishing trip tomorrow. Would you like that?"

"Oh, that's really wicked, Daddy," cried David.

Paul jumped up, hopping around the table in his excitement, all anger forgotten. "Yes, wicked, wicked," he repeated.

Thomas' mobile sounded. He clicked on. Brad said, "How goes it?"

"Fine. I'm with Sheila and the boys. We're going off fishing tomorrow. How about that? Everything's OK here but I'm keeping well down; there may be watchers about. How about you and the others?"

"Wonderful. Don't worry about them. The Passports?"

"All fixed. Still the great fixer, isn't he, our good old C.O.? Listen, Brad, can I call you back later? Breakfast's getting cold."

"Enjoy. Speak soon. 'Bye now."

"'Bye."

Thomas bent down, laughing, allowing the smallest one to hug him around his neck. "Can I take it we have a 'yes' to the fishing then?"

"Yes," they chorused.

Sheila said, "She hasn't been exactly asked, but of course it's fine with Auntie, just so long as she can come, too. If she's going to be making the sandwiches she might as well have some of the fun."

Paul sighed, said, "Auntie, ladies don't go out in boats sea fishing." Patiently, and with some obvious embarrassment, he explained why. "Mummy told me you have to pee over the side. And when we went before we had to get the hooks out of huge fishes' mouths and put big worms and stuff on the hooks."

Thomas said, "Don't worry about that, Paul, we'll fix up your Auntie with a bucket in some quiet corner. Of course she can come along, and she won't even have to handle any worms." He was astonished that Paul had remembered that last trip; must be getting on for three years ago. Sheila nodded, smiling at the frying pan, basting

180

the eggs. He said, "David, now come round here to me for a moment. I have something important to say to both of you." He turned his chair sideways. The brothers stood shoulder to upper arm in front of him, still and serious. Conspiratorially he gathered them in. They looked up at him. He said, "Nobody must know I'm here. It's a secret between us until I tell you it doesn't have to be. Is that clear?"

David looked doubtful. Excitedly Paul said, "Are you a spy, Daddy?"

David said, "Do shut up, Paul, if he was he wouldn't tell you, would you, Daddy? But Mummy told me you used to work undercover when you were important in the Marines."

"What's 'undercover'?" Paul asked.

Thomas said, "You are not to use that word, 'undercover,' OK? I asked you if you could keep it secret; you know, that I'm here. Can you do that? Can you promise me on your honour?"

"Yes," they chorused, Paul adding a further, "Definitely," in case of any remaining doubt.

Someone was knocking on the kitchen door; two knocks close together and then a longer interval before the third. He said, "Boys, I don't want you to forget, now. Remember, both of you. You promised me. You must remember what I told you about promises."

Sheila opened the door and the Colonel's Labrador came bouncing in, big and black and grey of muzzle, tail wagging wildly, rushing from one boy to the other, leaving muddy footprints on the chequerboard floor. "BB," shouted Paul. "Oh, you're all wet!" The dog stopped and shook himself as if in agreement. A shower of multi-coloured droplets arced through the sun-shaft from the kitchen window.

Ben had followed on into the kitchen. "Bloody hell, I'm sorry about this. The Colonel told me he was very well behaved, like. And he has been 'til he's recognised his friends."

David shouted, "You've been in the river, you naughty boy." He got off his chair, held up his hand, said, "Sit!" The dog sat, pink tongued and white toothed and panting but otherwise statue-like, shining black eyes staring at the boy with an intensity of expectation.

Thomas said, "Right, let's have some order, shall we? Ben Benedict, this is my sister Sheila. And this is David and this other slightly smaller big one, the one with all the muddy paw-prints on his T shirt, he's Paul. Ben's going to be our skipper for the fishing tomorrow," he told them, "I asked him to come over, maybe take you out for a ride around today. I have to go do some business."

Sheila said, "Nice to meet you, Ben." They shook hands. "Don't worry about the floor, Can I get you a cup of tea? Please, do take a chair. How about some breakfast?"

"Mmmm. Sounds good. Thanks."

Thomas said, "Everything OK, Ben?"

"Everything's fine. Great day for a walk even if his majesty here insisting on going in the river for a swim."

"I saw there was a fisherman down there this morning. He wouldn't have been too pleased. How would you like to tell your new crew about what to expect tomorrow? I have to get moving a bit sharpish so I'm going up for a shower and then I'll get off into Portsmouth." David's disappointment was obvious. "Don't worry boys, I'll be back this afternoon. I'll see you then."

Ben said, "My car's back there, in the woods. To give the dog a bit of a walk, you know? We can all walk back to it, if you like. Then you can pick up your Fiesta at the Colonel's place." He looked up at Sheila. "I thought we might go on into Winchester, take a look at the Ghurkha Museum?"

Paul said, "Wow, that's wicked."

"They've got these huge knives, Auntie," David explained.

With some amusement Sheila said, "I shall look forward to seeing them. Big knives have always been objects of great fascination to me. You're sure it's open on Sundays?"

"Colonel Grenville says so."

"Good. If anyone fancies a McDonalds, it's my treat. Not exactly the roast beef of Olde England's Sunday lunch, but no doubt much more appreciated. We can have our main meal tonight when you're back, Thomas. I assume you'll be staying here?"

"My stuff's over at the Colonel's. I'll bring it with me."

David said, "Daddy! I thought it was a secret. Now everybody knows where you are, there's all of us know it and there's Ben and Colonel Grenville - and even Lady Dee."

"Yes, but these people are on our side, David. And they all know how to keep a secret. We all used to work together on things for the government. And you're in it now, too; you and Paul."

There was a small silence whilst the boys digested their father's comment then Ben said, "It'll be hotter tomorrow by all accounts. You'd best pack a sun blocker for the boat - for the boys, you know?"

Thomas went back upstairs. Whilst the bath was filling he sat on the toilet seat to return Brad's call. Brad was at his desk in his new ISG office. Yes, everything was fine and the office set up going well.

They'd put in a bid to rent a secure warehouse in the docks and if it panned out they'd be moving there, lock stock and barrel. With Saeed's help, Rose had hired an Indian lady as book-keeper and general factotum, and they'd already installed a good accounting system into all of their brand new computers.

"How about George?" Thomas asked, testing the bathwater temperature, increasing the flow of cold. With all the steam it was hot in here. "How goes my American Lieutenant?"

"George? Good as gold," Brad said, "I reckon you've got a good one there even if he did rather hit the clubs big time after we took off to the airport the other night. He isn't telling but I think he's made himself a friend of the female persuasion. Since he wore off his hangover he's been keeping a nice low profile, doing the 'U.S. Military man on leave from Saudi' bit, any time he needs to. How are things at your end?"

"The Colonel's been looking after me really well. As I said, he reckons the new passports are going to be ready as early as Tuesday. Complete with entry stamps into Bahrain and with Saudi visas for good measure. He's getting a Saudi visa put in my passport as well. Brad, I was wondering about that variation, a combined land and sea op. The old pincer action?"

"Yes, why not? Timings?"

"About a week. We'll have time for a full briefing, time to set everything up. Any luck with the canoes?"

"Looking good. I have some feelers out."

"I'm going into Portsmouth today. Bit of a sniff around Sea Fibres." He increased the coldwater flow. "I'm more than a bit concerned. My sister's house was raided last night. She's been looking after my boys, you know? Might be nothing to do with the main event but anyway, we're dealing with it. One other item of very bad news is that Kit Patterson has been killed in some kind of a road accident. I don't know if I mentioned it, Brad, but Kit was Managing Director of Sea Fibres. I'm going to try to talk to his wife. You ever meet them?"

"No. I've heard of him, of course, but I didn't know he'd gone. I'm sorry."

Thomas said, quietly, "It wouldn't exactly have been in the Times, would it? Not sufficiently notable. What those guys got up to in Aden and Borneo won't ever be much publicised. Christ, I remember in Borneo I was never too sure who was actually teaching whom about the headhunting. 'Anyway, have to go. I've my bath."

"Goodbye then." Brad chuckled. "Rose is waving at me. Sorry, waving at you. She sends her love, OK?"

"Tell her not to look. I'm naked." He switched off, placed the mobile on his pile of clothes. Before getting in he parted the curtains and looked out over the road at The Moon and Sixpence. A middle aged man, he supposed the landlord and prospective fishing teacher, was sweeping off the front step. The rise and fall carillons of bells reached out to the church's scant congregation; England on any Sunday morning. A time for staying in bed with your wife and your hangover and the News of the World. He thought briefly about the five times a day, every day, calling to prayer in Saudi Arabia, about the near universal response from the universally faithful. He closed the curtains, stepped into the bath. His left elbow was still the same old mess, as much the victim of the surgeon's knife as of Kerrigan's nine millimetre bullet. He tested the bend. Still the same old forty five degrees only, but not too much real pain today. He clenched and unclenched his fist.

Sitting up in the hot water he got the number from directory enquiries and dialled the number for Mrs Anne Patterson. "Locks Heath six nine double one double six." The lady who answered was going on for sixty but sounded older than that; older and more tired.

"Hello Mrs Patterson. This is Thomas Thornton? I don't know if you remember me. I was a colleague of your husband. I was so very sorry − ."

She cut him off. "Yes, I do know who you are, Mister Thornton. I do not know what you think you're doing but I must tell you, I have nothing but contempt for you and for what you have been up to. Please do not bother to telephone me again." The line disconnected.

Still uncommunicative, suffering from Anne Patterson's rejection, he got into the passenger seat of Ben's old hatchback. Sheila sat in the back alongside David and Paul, with BB lying down behind them, room having been found for him amongst all the assorted tools and fishing tackle.

When they reach the Grenville's cottage Thomas got out, stuck his head back in, said, "I'm sorry everyone. You know, being a bit quiet. I had some unexpected news on the phone. Nothing to worry about, though. I just want you all to have a really marvellous day. Here…" He reached into his trouser pockets but all he pulled out were Bahraini Dinars. "Oh, damn it," he said, "I haven't had a chance to get any English yet. Lend me a tenner, Ben?"

"No problem."

"Give the boys a fiver each, will you? I'll settle up with you when I pay the charter tomorrow, OK?"

Sheila had got out of the car, ready to take his place. "Sounds a bit grim, brother," she murmured. "Anything I can do?".

"Nothing anyone can do I'm afraid. Anne Patterson - Kit's wife, remember? – she doesn't want to know a bloody miscreant like yours truly. But thanks; thanks anyway. I'll be seeing you later." He forced a smile, turned to the boys, speaking up. "Right then. I 'll take BB inside. He's quite an old man now. It might get too hot for him in the car. Besides, when you come back maybe I'll have got back myself. We can all take him for a nice walk this evening. How does that sound?"

The Colonel was working down in the greenhouse but interrupted what he was doing to come to the kitchen for a cup of tea and a talk over of events. BB had dropped off to sleep in his bed, close to the warmth from the Aga. There was a wonderfully meaty smell of something cooking.

After their chat Thomas climbed the stairs to put on some clean new underwear, a pair of fawn coloured chino's and a mid grey T shirt. Anne Patterson's response was still bugging him. He shook his head, angry with himself rather than with her as he went back down. Lady Dee was outside the open French windows, picking sweet peas from the patio trelliswork. He stood watching as she laid each of the thin stemmed blooms carefully into her basket. She glanced sideways at him from behind the silver droop of her hair, offered him a large, blotched ivory and burgundy specimen. He put it to his face and sniffed, closing his eyes under the power of its fragrance.

"Well, go on," she told him, gently. "Go on into Portsmouth. Go try to exorcise some demons." Suddenly he wanted her to hold him as a mother might have held him. He nodded quickly, turning away. She called after him, "We're all here for you, you know, Robert and myself. And Sheila, of course. The car keys are on the hallstand."

He paused and looked back. "You won't mind if I move in with them, Lady Dee?" he said.

"Of course not. I would expect you to, Thomas." She went on picking the flowers. "Just be careful, won't you."

"Don't I always? On our way back we might all go for a walk this evening, taking BB if that's all right."

On the way in he formed his plan of action. First, he stopped in an all but deserted city centre to use his new company cash and credit card. It felt good, having real spending money in his pocket. Down by the dockyard he parked outside the high walls of the Sea Fibres factory buildings, walked up to the gatehouse trying not to seem too interested in what might be going on inside. In spite of it being a Sunday there were a number of cars parked outside the offices. A uniformed guard slid back the gatehouse window. "'S'cuse me, mate," Thomas enquired. "Is there a paper shop around here?"

"Just down the road, first right. It's on the corner. They don't close 'til twelve on a Sunday." The man had his own newspaper spread open on his desk, a naked girl's picture visible, all teeth and tits.

"Thanks," Thomas didn't really know why he was here, what he'd expected to get from it. Only that this was where it had all started and if you want to unravel a tangle the first thing you do is find a loose end and go from there. "Is this the place where they make the big luxury yachts?" he asked.

The guard wasn't interested. "Yeah, think so. Don't know nothing about it. I'm only contract, mate."

Nothing gained from that, he drove north to Hilsea. The offices of the Portsmouth News were open but to judge by the car park only on part staffing, this Sunday. Inside reception he surprised a uniformed guard into putting away his Sunday Sport. The man said, "Good morning, I mean afternoon, sir."

"Sorry to bother you," Thomas said, "I wondered whether I could get a look at some of your back issues?"

"What, on a Sunday?" The guard's tone had changed to one of dismissal. "Open Monday to Friday, nine till five thirty."

"Can I help you at all?" Thomas turned to find a bespectacled young man, maybe early twenties, casually dressed, carrying a document case. The lift doors were closing behind him.

"I hope so," said Thomas. "You're on The News, then?"

The young man said, "Bob Morgan. I'm a reporter."

Thomas caught the guard's suppressed chuckle. Aspiring reporter, more likely, right now nearer to tea boy. He held out his hand. "Good to meet you, Bob," he said. "I'm Tom MacRae. If you're a reporter here, can we talk?"

"Sure."

"In private?"

They walked over to the suite of armchairs. Thomas said, "I need to check out the details on an incident that happened here in Pompey about a month ago. The Managing Director of Sea Fibres Limited was killed in a road accident. There's some other stuff I need to know about as well."

186

"It can't wait till tomorrow, Mr MacRae?" The young man had taken a spiral-bound notepad from his case and was scribbling shorthand in pencil. He looked up, nodded at Thomas' expression. "No, so I guess it can't. You wouldn't be here if it could. What's this other stuff, you said?"

"Bob, why don't you call me Tom. Listen, there may be a story in this for you. I can't say till I've seen what you've got on the accident. I also need to know if there's been anything else in the News lately about Sea Fibres." He took a deep breath. "In particular I need to know about some people working there who were arrested on drugs related charges."

Bob Morgan put down his pad and pencil. "That's all in the public domain, Tom. I should know. I did the Coroner's report on Patterson's death myself. And the arrests before that, too. You reckon there's more to this than meets the eye, so to speak?"

"Maybe."

"It's going to take me some time. I was just off." He hesitated, thinking, then, "I usually go up to The Churchillian on Portsdown Hill for a pint and a pie of a Sunday. You know it? We could meet there in a couple of hours time."

How well he remembered the evenings in the Churchillian's capacious saloon bar. The same hand painted frieze ran around the top of the wall, depicting the scene as it must have been viewed from up here on World War Two's D Day minus one: All the ships lying off-shore in the Solent loading tanks and other vehicles and all the big guns, tens of thousands of khaki clad, steel helmeted troops. Truly an awesome array of military might to be arraigned against the doomed, stand-alone Germany. A mad dog at bay against the guns moving in from all sides, right? He took his pint of beer and his beef sandwich outside and sat on the grass amongst all the families. Many of their fathers and grandfathers would have been in the real life version of that painting. He shaded his eyes and looked across to the narrows of Portsmouth Harbour and outside on the Solent proper to the white dots of sailing boats and the distant Isle of Wight.

Lying back on the grass, he felt himself relaxing in the warmth as he watched the scrap-hopeful seagulls wheeling, side-slipping, soaring in the up-current thermal off the side of the hill. The scent of new mown hay was in his head and the chattering of small voices. His fingers entwined themselves in grass.

At the touch of a hand on his shoulder he woke, sat up very quickly, instinctively rolling away from the contact.

Bob Morgan said, "Wow! Sorry, Tom. Didn't mean to frighten you. You must have been pretty hard on there." He sat down and raised his pint glass. "Cheers anyway. You owe me the next one, right?"

Thomas shook his head to clear away the dreams. "That's a deal, young man. Let's see what you've got for me then."

"Hang on a bit. What's in this for Bob Morgan? Apart from the next pint?"

Thomas got out his cash and laid out three twenty pound notes side by side on the grass. "Just for starters, OK?"

"Right." The young man pocketed the money, took a long swallow of beer, wiped the froth off his upper lip. "Interestinger and interestinger," I'd say. "I already knew that old guy - what was his name? Patterson, yes. Mister Patterson didn't actually die of his injuries. That came out at the inquest and I was there to hear it. The guy died of a heart attack when this truckload of teak fell all over his Beamer. The driver was reversing his truck in the Sea Fibres yard, just didn't see Patterson's car. I've got the clippings in here for you. He indicated a clear plastic folder." He paused for effect, took another swallow. "But I just now called my contact to get an update. Didn't mention anything about you of course. It seems the driver of that truck's gone AWOL. Prosecution pending. He's to be charged with dangerous driving whenever they find him, maybe even manslaughter, the Public Prosecutor hasn't made up his mind yet. Trouble is, they think he's most likely gone back to the Emerald Isle. My guy thinks there's something smelly here. The two Sea Fibres guys who they charged with possession? They've scarpered as well. Broke bail. One of them was the sales manager and the other one was production director." He pulled out a clipping. "Buddy Listerone and one Ahmed Pindari by name. The boys in blue are livid, I can tell you that much. They had much more serious, drugs related charges in the offing, apparently."

"I see. Anything else?"

"Well, yes. It's all happening down at Sea Fibres. Seems there's somebody or other negotiating to buy the lot. Only a rumour from the City but … you know? it's all in here." The young man tapped the folder, drained his glass. "Now then, this is a dry old do. And I'd like the cheeseburger and chips, please. With tons of mayo."

"Cheeky bugger." Thomas had to laugh. "All right, coming up. You've done well. They'll make an investigative journalist of you yet."

188

He put another three twenties on the grass and got to his feet. "But I'm afraid you'll need to go get your meal, yourself." A little girl ran past, screaming, closely pursued by a bigger boy and a yapping terrier. "Where can I contact you?"

"It's all in the folder, Mister MacRae. So what's the story? What's your interest?"

"Later, OK? I need to check out your stuff first. But - is there a fishing tackle shop open around here?"

"What? What the hell kind of fishing? Which way you heading?"

"Fly fishing. And I'm going north on the A34."

"Try Rovers in Fareham, the main street. Could be open on a Sunday. That's not much out of your way."

The Winchester party had evidently had a wonderful day. He found them picnicking down by the river at the bottom of the Grenville's garden. With David and Paul recovering from their excitement at his arrival he poured himself a glass of Australian Chardonnay, telling them to go to the Fiesta, bring back whatever they found on the rear seat. They were back in a moment, besides themselves with delight at the rods and tackle boxes, the contents of which were very soon arranged all over the picnic ground sheet for close examination and minute comparison.

Quickly, Thomas went through Morgan's folder. The boy had made a comprehensive job of it, including all the clippings about the accident, the arrests at Sea Fibres and a small piece from the Financial Times reporting on the company's activities. Sea Fibres, it said, was owned by a private holding company in the Netherlands Antilles. At least one of the majors was interested in buying it.

"Something interesting, Thomas?" the Colonel asked.

"Could be; here, have a look. I got a young reporter on to it."

The Colonel scanned the report and clippings. "This lad seems a pretty live wire. Good work for a few hours." He handed the file back. "FT's a bit off beam 'though. That particular ownership won't sell. They're very much the buyers of things, not the sellers."

"You know these people?"

He closed the file, handed it back to Thomas. "Sea Fibres is owned by Maritime and Terrestial Holdings in the Antilles all right. And M&T is owned in turn by a Saudi, name of Al-Sottar would you believe? He paid sixty millions U.S. for it, about a year ago."

Thomas sat bolt upright in his deckchair. "What? You're sure about that, sir?"

"Yes, Thomas, I am very sure. I'm sure you would have found that out for yourself, given a day or two."

The boys were very keen to get into action on the river right away but the Colonel demurred. "There's time enough for that," he said. "After you've learned something about how to use all this nice new kit of yours. After that you can come and scare the hell out of my trout. Thomas, come into the greenhouse for a moment. There's something I want to show you."

The humidity in the greenhouse was overwhelming. Thomas went over the day's events whilst the Colonel listened, fiddling with his roses. When he'd finished, Grenville said, "Well, you know where I am." He straightened up. "Delia tells me you're going to stay with your family, Thomas. Can't blame you for that. Hate to keep on about it, but you will be careful, won't you." The ageless blue eyes were full of understanding. "Look, why don't you give up on this idea of going back to the Middle East? It's history now. Awful as it may be even to contemplate, perhaps even your wife is just history, whoever knows? You have your own future and the boy's future to think about. As for your group waiting in Bahrain, I'm perfectly sure we can have them returned safely to wherever they want to be. And I'm fairly sure I could straighten things out with the necessary people here."

"And where do I hide away for the rest of my life, Colonel? I've really no option but to play out the game, for better or for worse. Forget Connie? I'm sorry but that's not an option." He offered his hand. Grenville's grip was that of a much younger man. He started to say something but stopped, shook his head, changing his mind.

It was after ten by the time the boys got to bed. He went up to the spare room and unpacked and undressed and lay down. It was still hot, boding well for tomorrow. He called Bradley, updating him on events in Portsmouth, but after a while Sheila knocked quietly, came in, locked the door and turned to stand over him. One of the straps of her nightdress had fallen down around her shoulder. Thomas said. "Brad, I have to go now. I have this beautiful naked lady here and I have to tell you what I'd love to do next and how it is not possible for a man of my upstanding character and convictions."

Brad laughed. "In your dreams, friend, in your dreams." He clicked off.

Thomas murmured, "Sheila, dear Sheila."

Sheila said, "I know; just testing." She shook her head, replaced the shoulder strap, touched his deformed elbow. "I should hate you for doing this to me, John Thomas. So why don't I hate you?"

"Look." He had to ignore the pounding in his chest and the dryness of his throat. "Go sit over there, will you. I'm going to tell you things that nobody should be told. Things that might help to explain things, things to take our minds off that other, all right?"

Chapter Thirteen

He parked the car, made his way down to the ferry. It was a beautiful morning. Ben had driven off to Portsmouth with Sheila and the two small, excited boys, taking enough provisions for a voyage to America. He had set off behind them in the rented Fiesta. Ben was to load up at his moorings in Portsmouth then come across the harbour entrance, pick him up from the Gosport ferry pontoon.

Quite soon he spotted Ben's *Moby Belle* making her way across the busy waterway. David and Paul were standing on her afterdeck in vivid orange life jackets, the smaller of the two figures waving frantically. He jumped aboard, immediately went below to keep out of sight. He looked out through the porthole as they dawdled past the Hot Walls then gunned, stern well down, out into the Solent and the English Channel. After a while he thought it safe to join the others up in the overcrowded wheelhouse. The boys' excited chatter competed with the click and hum of the boat's VHF and the occasional voices of other small boat skippers. Looking back over the cream V of their wash at the receding city and its surrounding, ever diminishing coastline, Thomas felt himself relaxing, more than happy to be able to cast off the tensions and the ugliness of the last few months.

After an hour or so the throaty pulse of the boat's engine lessened as Ben swung her round to come bow on into tide, left the wheel to Thomas, went forward to let go the anchor. Fifty feet of chain rattled out through the roller guides followed by fathom upon fathom of rope, whipping away off the coil on the boat's foredeck. To the north they could still just about make out Portsmouth, hanging above it the faint line of chalky green slopes that would be Portsdown Hill. To the west, closer but still more than a mile away, the white slash of cliffs along the coast of the Isle of Wight.

Sheila had decided to forego the fishing rod in favour of doing a little sketching. "All alone on vasty plain," she joked, getting out her materials, "Never to see the land again."

"Don't worry, Auntie," David reassured her, "We aren't very far out and, besides, we aren't alone. Look, there's a big ship coming and there's the other fishing boats that we saw on the way and there's a speedboat too. Look."

Paul added his own reassurance. "There really is nothing to worry about, Auntie."

Sheila laughed. "Oh, I'm so glad about that, boys. Everything must be all right then."

Ben took up the binoculars. "Le Havre Ferry coming in to Pompey and the Navy Coast Guard coming out of Langstone," he pronounced. "Not much wrong with your eyes, lad."

David spoke quietly, with studied deliberation. "There's something biting." Thomas saw the tell-tale twitch of the boy's rod tip and then the juddering as the fish took up the bait and moved the weight along the sea-bed. The reel's ratchet began to click, slowly, erratically.

"Christ; only a bloody tope," Ben muttered. Thomas resisted the impulse to become involved, watched Ben quietly take a hold on the boy's belt. Under instruction, David timed his strike perfectly; the hook was set and the battle was on. At first it seemed a very unequal match but gradually the runs of the fish shortened. David said nothing throughout, shook his head to all offers of help, the epitome of grim, white-faced determination.

Sitting atop the cabin roof, wedged between Thomas and Sheila, Paul was first to see the fish, deep down in the water. "David," he shouted, "I can really see it. It's a monster shark. Oh no! David, I can see its wings." Thomas could feel the small body shaking and soon enough they could all see the dark spread of the tope's pectoral fins, then the paleness of the belly as it rolled and rolled again in its last ditch attempt to escape.

As Ben readied the gaff Sheila sounded concerned. "I can't believe this. It's huge. He's right, Thomas. It is a shark, isn't it?"

"Sure is. A tope: one of the smaller sharks."

Ben called up, "It's not that bloody small, not this one. This is a fifty pounder if ever I've seen one. Keep it steady, David, you're doing just great. Try to hold her while I get the gaff in."

Sheila said, "Oh, must we really? Must we hurt him some more?"

194

As the fishing line parted, David's rod sprang back, straightened, lifeless. They all watched in silence as the big fish righted itself, and with a single sweep of its tail disappeared back into the depths.

"Auntie!" David whispered, the held-in tears and the accusation there in his voice.

"It's not your Auntie's fault, lad, it's mine," Ben said, "And anyway it wasn't a him, it was a 'her.' All the big ones are female. I might have known there'd be some of those buggers about, day like this in August. So long as we were using mackerel we should have had wire leaders on. Anyway, you beat her, didn't you? We would have let her go when we got the hook out and taken the some photos."

David shook his head. "I didn't beat her, Ben. She beat me." He looked up at them. "She was wonderful, Daddy." His voice shook. "But she still has my hook in her mouth. I just hope it isn't too painful. I just hope it doesn't stop her from eating or anything."

Thomas climbed down to the deck, put his arm around the narrow shoulders of his son. "Hey, chin up, soldier. You did very well. I can tell you, the hook will not be a problem. It'll corrode and fall out in no time and you won't even be able to see the mark. Sharks don't feel pain, you know."

"How do you know that, Daddy?" Paul said.

Sheila said, "Had you better get inside the cabin, Thomas? That boat, Coast Guard or whatever, it does seem to be coming this way, doesn't it?"

Ben said, "She's just cruising, being nosy. I shouldn't think there's a problem."

The dull, navy grey inshore patrol boat was still maybe a quarter of a mile away. Thomas slipped off the roof and into the wheelhouse. There was a new rush of static from the VHF and then, with surprising immediacy, "Good morning, Moby Belle. This is the Coast Guard vessel, Venturer."

Ben touched on the radio toggle switch. "Morning, Venturer, this is Moby Belle. Go to channel ten." He re-set the VHF.

"How goes it over there?"

"Just 'the one that got away' so far; big old lady tope. Over." Venturer had slowed but was still coming on. Thomas was ready to slip overboard on the side opposite Venturer. He made the dive sign to Ben. Even in August it was going to be bloody cold. Ben shook his head, held up his hand, palm out to Thomas to stay where he was.

Coastguard. "Yes? That's rough, Moby Belle. Not too many in your party today?"

"No, that's right." Ben toggled off the transmitter, said to no-one in particular, "None of your bloody business," switched on again. "Over."

"OK. Well, tight lines to you; over and out."

They all watched the churn of white water, the smooth acceleration and as Venturer turned away Thomas' mobile chortled. Brad Scott. Pulse still racing, he pressed the on button, said, "Hi Brad. How's she going?"

"Hello there, Mister Mac." Brad sounded relaxed, in control as always.

"Hello to you, too; what's up?"

"Nothing. Everything's 'A OK,' just to hear your wonderful voice. How's it at your end?"

"Good. Bit of a holiday, actually, but just now interrupted by a close encounter with the local Coast Guard would you believe. I'm out on the Solent with the boys and my sister. Ben Benedict's taken us fishing. David just lost a bloody big tope."

"You told me you were off on a fishing trip. Sorry, I forgot. Sounds exciting anyway. You do have all the fun, one way and another. Tell your lad the ones that get away are the ones you remember most. Thomas, your pal in the Embassy, the one with the double barrelled name? The guy's being very solicitous. Rose and I met him by chance the other night in The Jug."

Thomas felt Moby Belle's lift and roll as Venturer's wash hit them. "Ferris-Bartholomew? Cheeky bastard. But how about the business?" He had to resist the impulse to say, 'over'.

"Off like a rocket, actually. If you know how to provide them with the best of anything lethal you've got 'em lining up out here. And our friend the Honourable introduced us to a group of young Brits. Small detachment of our old lot, would you believe, based out here pro tem. Good bunch of guys. Just babies really."

"Do they know who you are or rather, who you were?"

"Of course. Got into a kind of 'tales of the Brecon Beacons' competition, if you see what I mean. I'm tougher than you stuff."

"Be careful, Brad."

"You shouldn't feel the need to say that, Mister Mac." There was steel beneath the light heartedness. "Here's someone wants a word with you."

There was a short silence then George's voice. "How the fuck you going, skip?"

196

"Just fine, George. I'm out on the ocean with my two boys, the sun's shining, everything's bloody good as a matter of fact."

"Can't keep you away from boats, skipper, can we?" The laugh, then, "When you coming back here? It's a dry old do without you." He laughed again. "Fuck, ain't had myself a single good kicking since you left."

"Friday, George, Friday. But don't expect any repeat of that fight stuff. Not when I'm about anyway. Save it for the enemy, right?"

"Right. Listen, we'll hit that fucking friend of yours like a great ton of shit. Hey, this place! It's so damn good I'm thinking of taking up residence. You know, afterwards?"

"Right, you could do a whole lot worse. May be a bit close to the action though. I have to sign off now, George. Say goodbye to Brad and hello to the others for me, OK?"

He pressed the 'off.' Sheila came up behind him, put her hand on his shoulder. "Sorry, I didn't mean to eavesdrop but ... you definitely have to go back? As early as Friday?"

He looked up at her. " Yes, afraid so, Sheila. Unfinished business and I have some guys waiting on me.. Listen ... sit down for a bit?" Sheila sat opposite him, leaning forwards. He noticed that another button on her shirt front had come undone. Or been undone. "All this ducking and weaving, it's not something I want to live with. I don't expect you or the boys to share it, either." The expression in the pale blue eyes had grown seriously attentive. "I have to sort things, once and for all." He reached across the table, took her hands in his. "I am, as the song says, an innocent man, sister. Word of honour. But right now I'm also a marked man."

The blue eyes shone. "I know that. But afterwards? What then, soldier boy, what then?"

David's voice, shouting. "Daddy, come here, quickly, I've got another one."

"I don't know, Sheila. That I do not know. Not yet." He stood up, touch-kissed her forehead as he squeezed by to get out on deck.

They sat out on deck in the sunshine, eating and drinking from Sheila's tuck-box, tossing bits of sandwich to the cloud of screaming gulls that soon arrived to dip and turn around Moby Belle. After they'd finished, Thomas and the boys fished on and Sheila sat up on top of the cabin, making a series of pastel studies.

They timed their departure from the fishing grounds to arrive back at the harbour just after dark. Once underway Ben instructed Sheila and the boys in the steering of the boat and which harbour entrance light to head for, the light growing ever brighter as the dusk deepened. He and Thomas took up position with their cans of beer on the stern gunwhale. Thomas said, "Well, it's been a great day. Here, before I forget." He handed over the seven twenty pound notes.

Ben took the fold of notes and immediately stuffed it back into Thomas' shirt pocket. He held up his hand, palm outwards. "Not from friends, OK? I owe you plenty and not just money." It was a genuine finality, no mere politeness. "Hey, you have some great kids, I envy you." He chuckled. "You sure you have to go back out there?"

For a while he made no reply, then he said, "Nothing I'd like more than to stay right here, but I can't see much of an option." He drank some beer, watching the colours of the sunset over the Isle of Wight. "I really thought I'd left all this hit and hide stuff well behind me. Seems not. I'm too much of a loose cannon so far as those guys are concerned, whoever the hell they all are. And what am I supposed to do about Connie? Leave her and the bloody Arab that wants me dead to their own devices? Come on, what would you do?"

"Me?" Ben grinned in the half light. "Don't ask."

"Ben, It would help me one hell of a lot to know you were able to keep an eye on things here. With any luck it shouldn't be for too long. How about it? Will you think about it?"

"I've thought about it. I guess if you can't include me in on the front line out there with you, then I'll watch over things here. No problem. Be careful, son." Paul had come out with a handful of bread, had begun throwing it up in the air for the seagulls to swoop and catch.

Thomas said, "Just one thing, 'though, and I do mean this, so it's a deal breaker, Ben. Simple. If you can do it then you will accept payment, OK? This is a full time job, pro tem, and there's no way of knowing about how long is the 'tem'."

"I won't argue." Ben ran his hand back through his hair. "Plenty of time to get into details. Changing the subject, boss, I always wanted to ask you what the hell you actually got up to that time, in that pub? You know, Carrickfergus? Maloney? By the time the shit stopped flying on that one I was well away. You know that. How'd you get them coming out after you like they did?"

He grinned. "Damn all to do with politics. The lovely Caitlin Sherry, Ben. I came on to her, like, big time. For a while in there I thought I might have even got lucky, if you see what I mean. For some reason Mister Maloney didn't seem to like that, would you believe?

Suggested we go for a quiet walk. Didn't mention anything about his friends making up the party, of course."

"Jesus… All that shit and bullets. We were bloody lucky when I think about it. I mean, the chances we used to take …" Paul was climbing up on to the gunwhale. Ben catapulted forward, grabbed him by the back of his shirt, deposited him on deck. He turned the little boy to face him. "Listen to me, lad. On this boat I'm in charge and that means what I say goes. And what I say is, the next time I see you trying to stand on the bloody gunwhale I'll tan your little arse for you, OK?"

Paul's head was down. "Yes, sir," he muttered. "I wanted them to take the bread out of my hand." The gulls shrieked and shouted their approval, wheeling around in black silhouette against the last of the light.

"That's all right, then, son. We all have to learn, that's how we stay alive. But never, never under-rate the sea, right? It'll turn right around and bite you. Hard." Thomas had stayed where he was. Sheila was standing in the cabin doorway. She looked stricken, dying to say something, saying nothing.

"No, sir," said Paul. "I mean yes, sir."

Ben looked to Sheila, said, "Who's steering this boat, lady? She's ten degrees off."

"Midshipman David Thornton. That's who, skipper." Down in the cabin Thomas' cell phone started to ring. Sheila was closest, went to pick up then called, "Thomas, it's a lady called Rose for you? Do you want to take it down here or shall I bring it up?"

He took the call in the cabin. "Hey, Rose, how you doing?"

"And hello to you, sailor." Always the laugh in the voice. "Out on the heaving Main again, I hear."

"Yes… Rose? How's things?"

"Oh, I'm fine. Brad's gone out with George, Saeed's still in his room here.

"Brad said you've got ISG up and mostly running?"

"We've got most of the the balls rolling all right. A fellow with gold edging on his robe walked in today, wanted to get hold of a used submarine, would you believe? Brad asks him, straight faced, diesel or nuclear? This sheikh says, 'which is quickest?' Brad says, 'do you mean quickest through the water, or quickest for delivery?' Unbelievable."

"Nothing's unbelievable, not with those boys."

"So it seems. Anyway, I just thought you'd like to know I've got all your paperwork in hand, and what we think could be the perfect mode of transit for the trip from here. Best leave it for you to see when you get here, but it's looking very interesting. We can thank the boys in balaclavas for the loan of it."

"Wonderful, Rose, you know, you do good work."

"Oh, I have my uses. Say g'bye now."

"Yes. It's always good to hear from you, Rose. 'Bye." He disconnected, went back out on deck.

Ben had switched on their port and starboard lights and they were well on their way in. The boys had fallen asleep, Paul on Sheila's lap out on the darkened deck and David down in the cabin, stretched out along the padded seat. Moby Belle ran past Spitsand Fort and the harbour channel lights, passed close in off Haslar point, came in to Gosport ferry pontoon. Thomas jumped ashore and Moby Belle's engine thrummed into renewed life as she performed her slow turn to port and doodled out across tide towards her mooring on the Portsmouth side.

He checked over the Fiesta. No sign of anything amiss. How easily all the old subterfuges, all the old precautions, had clicked back in. He stopped on his way out of town to buy himself a bag of fish and chips, ate them whilst driving north to Lower Longstock. By that time Ben would have got Moby Belle safely on to her berth, tidied everything up, got them all in his car.

At the last minute he decided to park along a cart track beside the woodland car park, then walk in to the cottage down the river as before. Engine off, he checked his mobile, realising he'd forgotten to switch it back on. There was a text message: KEY IN HANGING BASKET BY FRONT DOOR. It was timed at 21.02, not long after he'd left Moby Belle. The second message was timed thirty minutes later than the first. CALL ME WHEN YOU GET THIS URGENT - BEN.

There was no reply to his return call and the ringing of Ben's mobile was matched by the ringing of alarm bells in his head. He walked silently back down the track to the car park. Three cars, including the one of the night before, the light coloured one with all the inside man/woman activity. Behind the wheel of the second car, by the lights of a passing vehicle he could just make out a man fast asleep, mouth open and eyes closed, seat angled well back. Fellow must have retained enough sense to know he'd drunk too much to drive home yet awhile. The third car was an unoccupied Vauxhall

Astra. Thomas slipped through the trees, reached the now more familiar pathway through the wood, hurried along the river bank.

As he moved in the virtual blackness up Sheila's back garden, some element of long ago training made him stop. For several long minutes he stood stock still. He had actually felt the hairs standing up on the back of his neck. Yes, no mistaking it, pitched low but very definitely a human voice. It was coming from the garden shed. He or they would be looking out through the shed's only window towards the back of the house, able also to see past the house, up the drive, out to the road and across to the Moon and Sixpence. Thomas moved with the most extreme care up to the back of the shed. For several more minutes he stood there, unmoving, before hearing it again. It was difficult to catch what the man was saying, " ... he ..... so where the fock's she focking gone, for ....." A second voice said something else that he couldn't catch at all but the Belfast accent had been unmistakable. He considered mounting a surprise attack, immediately forgot about that. Northern Ireland equals guns. He moved back across the vegetable patch, treading with infinite care amongst lettuces dampened by dew-fall. Once back at the river bank he dialled Ben's mobile. This time it was picked up. He said, "Stay cool, Ben, OK? I don't want Sheila panicking but there's a couple of boyos watching and waiting for them, or for me, I don't know which. ... Bastards are in the shed at the back of the cottage. Where are you now?"

"Yeah?" Ben kept his tone of voice casual. "We've only just left Pompey. What's next? What d'you reckon?"

"Take them to the Colonel's, please. I'll call, tell him to expect you. I think it might be best for them to stay there tonight. Then join me over here. We'll wait 'til they give it up and get their arses out of that shed; play it by ear."

"Maybe we should just go in on them? You must be getting more than a bit bloody sick of these jokers."

"You feeling all over aggressive, Sergeant?" he permitted himself a chuckle

"Whatever. But listen, you got my message? I couldn't pick up when you called back. I wanted to tell you, a couple of Her Majesty's Customs and Excise blokes were waiting for us at the berth. At least, that's who they said they were. I wasn't too sure but you know how it is. You ask for proof of office and they reckon that makes you guilty straight away. The buggers were still with me when you called. That's why I didn't answer."

"What did they want? As if I didn't bloody know."

"Oh, they were OK, really. Asked if we'd been out into International waters at all. I said we hadn't, we'd been fishing, etcetera, etcetera. Plenty of evidence for that what with the boys arguing over the catch, who caught which ones, you know? They asked who was aboard so I said me and the boys and Sheila. Said they'd seen us over on Gosport Ferry, asked why was that? I told them, 'sightseeing by night, what's it got to do with you,' so to speak."

"How were they after that?"

"You mean, were they convinced? I shouldn't think so. Now we've gone they'll probably have boarded her just to make sure there was no-one in residence. Easy enough for them."

"Good man." He hesitated. "Ben, don't tell the Colonel what's up. We don't want to involve him any more than we absolutely need to. And bring two torches, the more powerful the better. Best buy them in a gas station. There's a track through a gate into a field alongside the wood where we parked last night. Use that, not the car park. You'll see my Fiesta up that track. Take the footpath along the river. I'll be waiting for you somewhere. If you need to, you can call me. No problem, I've got my mobile on vibration only. But if I don't pick up more or less immediately you just cut the call, OK?"

"Great," Ben said, "See you in about eighty minutes. Gets more and more like old times, don't she?"

"I bloody well hope it don't, doesn't, my friend. More bullets we do not need. And we don't have the Whitehall behind us these days, remember?"

Ben sighed audibly. "This old civvies street's not too bad, really, but …" his voice trailed off.

"I know, sergeant, that I know," said Captain Thomas Thornton

.

Chapter Fourteen

He made his silent way back to the car park. The lovers had gone but the sleeper slept on and the Astra still stood there, undisturbed, its bonnet cold to his touch. This would probably be the one the watchers were using. He unscrewed the valve cap on its front offside wheel, grimaced as he jammed in a twig, the whistle of escaping air loud enough to waken the fabled dead. He jammed another twig into the driver's door lock as far as it would go, broke it off flush then groped his way to a hiding place under cover of the trees.

No such thing as silence in a night-time English woodland. There's a clicking and creaking of trees seemingly to breathe, to talk quietly to each other, the occasional stealthy movement of small creatures through yesteryear's fallen leaves and once the distant mating call of a dog fox. He watched and waited until a car made its turn on to the farm track. A few minutes later Ben's flashlight came bobbing along the road, crossed the car park and set off down the rutted path, a magnet for excited moths. Thomas followed in silence, closing in until he was close enough to tap Ben on the shoulder.

"Jesus!" All the surprise, all that tension in his voice. "Nice one, boss. You trying to give me a heart attack or something?"

"You weren't always all that nervous. Switch off the light. Let's get some night vision back, yes?"

The light went off. Ben whispered, "What's the score now? Here, you'd better have this." Thomas followed his arm, found the torch, felt the weight of it He whispered, "Thanks. I only know they're in the shed and that they're probably Belfast." He had a sense of all the listening woodland things. "I reckon that's their car, the Astra with the brand new flat and the jammed up door lock."

Ben stifled a quiet laugh. "There's someone's going to be a bit pissed off if it isn't. What's the plan?"

"I go back to the cottage. You wait here. You have your mobile?"

"Yeah"

"It's muted, vibration only?"

"Is now."

"Excellent. When they move out of the shed I'll call you. Just one short burst on your mobile. It shouldn't be too long before they realise nobody's coming home tonight. If, as I expect, they head back here for their car I'll repeat my call after thirty seconds. If I don't repeat, you call me, OK? Best keep the phone in hand, Ben. Acknowledge with one double ring call back to me after my repeat, if and when it comes, OK?"

"Right. What then, after that I mean, when they get here?"

"I just want to find out all about them, starting with what they bloody well look like. So we give them the full beam treatment. I want them to know they're well and truly rumbled, so to kindly piss off. If any shooting starts it will be they who start it, not you or me. They won't be able to see much of us past these torches."

"You think they're after you? They know you're here?"

"If they weren't looking for me I think they'd have been in and out and away by now, don't you? They may or may not know I'm around but if they don't it's likely they suspect it."

"Yeah. Where will you be when I get your signal, then?"

"I'll be following them. When they get here I reckon they'll think it's some kids that let their tyre down. While they're working on changing the wheel we'll jump them. The other car over there, the one with the sleeping beauty? That one should have gone but if not all bets are off. We can't risk any innocent bystander stuff, nor any witnesses. I'm surprised the car's still there now, actually. Poor devil's going to have some explaining to do when he gets home." His night sight returning, he took hold of the switched off torch. "Is that all OK with you?"

"Same old stuff, right?" Ben sounded sure of himself now, even faintly amused. "Bit like the strategy for our football match is to score some goals. You know, if the opposition turns up, if they'll let us in on the bloody pitch. Shit, where's the problem?"

Thomas grinned in the darkness. "Ten per cent planning, ninety per cent reaction," he whispered. "Our kind of war, right?" He turned away to proceed down the track, make his way back down the riverside path. Damp night air was rising from the water, no breeze to disperse it. It smelled of freshwater fish and the remains of an English summertime. He thought of Keats walking by this same river, further down in Winchester's water meadows, thinking up his 'seasons of mists and mellow fruitfulness'. The enormous, white-ghost form of a barn owl drifted by in total silence not ten feet from his head. He checked his watch. Eleven o'clock. Taking infinite care to make no noise he made his way to the rear of Sheila's garden shed. Listening intently he heard nothing from inside. They'd either gone or they were real pro's, these two. Now and then he shifted the bulk of his weight carefully from one foot to the other. Nothing but the stillness and the silence broken by countryside night-sounds and the occasional passing car.

It must have been close to midnight when he heard faint voices. The first one whispered, "There's no way, I reckon. Fucked off to stay some place else, so she has." There was a clear enough note of resignation in the man's soft voice. Another voice, softer, less expressive, "Quiet ...... your balls-up ...... our." Our? Or was that 'hour?' Somewhere close by a tom-cat screamed out his sudden, savage warning, the scream turning agonisingly into a yowl of gradually descending volume. The first voice said, "Christ almighty, what the fuck was that?"

The second man murmured something but, again, Thomas couldn't quite make it out.

Just before one o clock he heard more of the soft voices, picked up the sounds of movement, the faint creaking of the shed door hinges. He'd moved around the side furthest away from the garden path. They were making their way towards the river. He'd already keyed in Ben's number. All he needed to do was to press 'send' and put the phone to his ear to ensure it was ringing out then press the off and wait half a minute, then do the same again. Almost immediately he felt the acknowledging vibration.

He had to let them get a lead. Trailing them by a minute or so, he was little more that halfway through the wood when came the raised voices and the explosive sound of two shots, close together. With his flashlight turned on he raced down the pathway and into the car park to the sounds of the skidding of over-accelerated tyres on tarmacadam and the diminishing howl of a car engine. He swung the torch beam; saw Ben on his knees by the disabled Fiesta, someone lying there on their back.

"Careful with that beam, boss," Ben said, quietly. "We have to get this guy to hospital, like pronto, there's too much loss of blood here. Look after him while I get the car, right." Already he was up on his feet and running. Thomas angled the beam away. In the light reflecting off the Astra's paintwork he could see this was quite an elderly man, obviously conscious, lying half on top of a black plastic bin liner. The bin liner had split open, discharging some of its contents of weedy netting and fish, shining silver in the torchlight, one or two of them still gasping and twitching as if in sympathy. The man had been shot twice through the same shoulder. Close range shots, for the holes in the old tweed jacket were ringed with black. Without turning him over to look he knew the bullets would have hit bone and probably splintered and if the man had been lucky and the splinters had gone right through, would have left a large and ragged hole behind them. If not so lucky the whole mess of lead and bone would still be in there. Blood was spreading from underneath man and fish. The voice was faint but full of indignant force, "You bastards. You'm no need to fuckin' shoot me. Christ a'mighty. What for? Bastards."

Thomas said, "Just try to relax, fella, OK? We're trying to help you. We're not the ones who shot you. You're going to hospital." He took off his shirt. Opening out his penknife he began to cut it into strips. "My friend won't be long getting his car. Want to tell me your name?"

The man groaned more loudly, muttered something unintelligible, then, "Jammed up me bloody lock. Bastards. Bloody fuckin' water bailiffs".

Ben's car was coming now, making a three sixty degree racing turn around the car park, pulling to a stop. The man called out again just once, obviously in a great deal of pain, then lapsed into unconsciousness. Ben said, "He's out. Best all around, I reckon. Listen, it was like this. I was on my way home from my girl friend's. She's married so no names no pack drill. I pull in to take a leak and find matey here all shot up. I take him straight in to Winchester Royal. Reckon that's nearest. If I can get away free I'll go straight back to the Colonel's. How's that sound?"

Thomas nodded. "Sounds pretty fair to me." For a fuck-up, he thought. Pretty fair for a complete balls-up.

They removed the old man's shirt and vest, used the strips of Thomas' shirt as bandages. "Pretty obvious he'd been poaching the river. But did you see what the hell happened here?"

"Look, you'd best take charge of this." Ben handed him his pistol. "I never got a shot at them. What happened? The old boy's been down on the river like you say, doing some poaching. He finds his motor's been spiked when he gets back with the catch. That's when our two lovelies happen to come out of the wood. He thinks they're water bailiffs and he's bent down trying to hide. They spot him. God knows who they think he is. You? Maybe the law? I don't know. Anyway the old boy's got up and there's some shouting and the fellow in the other car, the one we thought was just a pisshead? Jesus! He switches on his headlights, gets out, walks up and drops the poor old bugger. Two shots, cool as you like. Doesn't say a fucking word. Then all three are off and away. Listen, boss, the one in the car? That one is definitely a pro. Stocky, red hair I think." He looked up. By the reflected torchlight Thomas could see the self-doubt. "I could have gone in for the one with the gun. Maybe I should have."

"No way, Ben. Just more bodies if you had, maybe yours included. Right, let's move it. I'll be at the Colonel's. Sheila and the boys can sleep there overnight. Those bastards must be long gone, but best take no chances." Red arterial blood was spreading across the old man's makeshift bandaging. "Here, let's get him in." They retrieved an old coat from the boot of the Fiesta, stretched it out on Ben's back seat, laid the unconscious man on it and closed the door.

"What the hell to do with these?" Ben indicated the bag of trout.

"I'll take a couple; no doubt the Law will be glad of the rest. On your way, Ben." Driving back to the cottage he called to alert Colonel Grenville, headlined what had happened. By the time he arrived Grenville was up and fully clothed, seemingly unfazed by the blood covered, bare-chested Thomas on his doorstep. "Well now, come on in." He spoke quietly so as not to wake the household. "Looks like you've rather been in the wars again. I expect you'd like to wash up."

Thomas looked down at himself, nodded. "The blood isn't mine, it's the poacher's. You wouldn't have a shirt to lend me, Colonel?" Everyone else in the house seemed still to be asleep as he crept up to the bathroom.

Refreshed and back downstairs he was presented with a generous shot of Lagavulin. "Here," the Colonel said. "It's not your Isle of Jura but it's from the same stable. And try this for size." The shirt was a thick cotton, boldly checked casual. Thomas put it on, buttoned up, sat down in an armchair. "Your good health, Colonel." He took a good mouthful, closed his eyes, held it without swallowing for a second or two, relishing the fire-peaty, seaweedy character as its warmth drifted through his chest.

As he recounted the night's events the Colonel listened in silence. "I'm sorry about all this, Colonel," he finished up, "I really do seem to bring the proverbial plague on all your houses, don't I?"

"It might have been better had you let me know all of what was going on. Be that as it may, perhaps I could attempt to sum up the overall situation, Thomas. Tell me if I've left anything out: Number one, you have the Saudi police looking to catch and punish you for a capital offence. Secondly, because serious drug smuggling is involved they've alerted Interpol, so you now probably have them in hot pursuit as well. Number three, your supposed contacts in Portsmouth are dead or have disappeared, although they would not have been of much use to you anyway so far as I see. Whether the UK police might also know that Thomas Thorton has reached England is a moot point. If they do, they've quite possibly made the connection with myself and Ben Benedict. Certainly, the arrival at Winchester hospital of a man suffering from gunshot wounds is going to ring alarm bells all over the place." Unexpectedly the old man smiled. "I'm sorry, Thomas, but it does rather seem as if you might have offended the Almighty. On top of all of this - or behind it as the case may be - enter our nasty old adversaries from the North of Ireland."

"The minute I know what's happening with Ben I'm out of here," Thomas said, He was very tired, not just physically. "I don't want to involve you any further than I already have."

"We shall see." Grenville passed that one by. "I told you before, and it isn't too late now, why don't you let me try to handle things for you? Why head straight back to the Middle East and into still more trouble?"

"I think you're forgetting a couple of points, Colonel, the first and most important being that I can't just walk away from my wife and my friends. Then there's the fact of the drugs charges. What am I supposed to do, just ignore them? Hope they'll go away?"

Colonel Grenville sat forwards, seeming to examine him with great care. "Your own involvement with this old poacher's misfortune have been bad luck. I mean, for once in your turbulent career you have not actually been the instigator. We know there's an illegal substances connection between the Portsmouth boatyard and Al-Sottar's boatyard and we believe this Al-Sottar character is somewhere at the bottom of things, but where does that get us? We've talked this through before. Thomas, you have your family to consider. Please take it from me that there is a massive disinterest here, at levels where it matters, in folk who want to damage themselves through narcotics. Despite what you may read in the media the feeling on high is to let them go right ahead. Look, if a closed, draconian society such as Saudi Arabia cannot stop the drugs menace, just what chance do you think we have of doing so here?"

Thomas swallowed the last of his whisky, said, "I accept what you say but I cannot accept its implications. My father, my real father that is, I believe you know he was shot dead when I was still very young?" The Colonel nodded. "Well, in between his activities on behalf of the Unionists my father wrote a poem; actually many poems. But this particular poem I've always carried with me. He called it The Fourth Light and it's about how these so-called 'illegal substances' will turn out all the lights for the person who takes them in an effort to switch them and himself on."

The Colonel smiled regretfully, shook his head. "I'm not going to divert you, am I? But neither you nor I nor anyone else can shield the weak from their weaknesses. They'll have the horrid stuff at whatever cost to themselves and, or the rest of us." Unexpectedly he chuckled. "You know, Thomas, Service lore has it that all the fish in a certain area of the North Atlantic are still on a high, thanks to you sinking the old Los Alamos. You never will know how long it took me to explain what was actually going on – I mean, to the Admiralty, the Government, MI numbers five and six and Uncle Tom Cobley and all. By the way, I must ask you, did you ever tell your Venezuelan lady that the man in the balaclava was actually you?"

"No, of course not. I wouldn't have dared, even if I hadn't signed up to the Official Secrets Act." He grinned through his tiredness. "How and why should a wealthy Saudi Arabian have got himself somewhere between that Venezuelan drugs cartel and the bloody Irish Republicans?" He shook his head, looked at his empty glass of Lagavulin ... Lagavulin? ... "Wait a minute." Something was nagging away at the back of his mind. Something to do with Lagavulin? He frowned in concentration.

Colonel Grenville said, "Yes?" He leaned back in his armchair, steepling the fingers of his hands beneath his chin. "Think. Take your time now, Thomas. Think about it."

Suddenly it was there. It might be relevant or it might not but it was there. Thomas was back on Al-Jazeera, hiding in the chart room, listening to Al-Sottar and Al-Mutawi talking together in the wheel-house. He said, "I overheard Al-Sottar and the police chief talking together. I just remembered them pouring themselves a whisky. That's what reminded me."

Grenville said, "Here, for goodness sake give me your glass. The Lagavulin obviously activates your brain cells."

209

Thomas handed over his empty tumbler. "They'd been discussing … Connie, you know." He took a deep breath. "I still had that in my head when Al-Sottar said something about wanting to get some crates of the sixteen years old Lagavulin, and then, I remember it very clearly now: 'Cheers,' he said, 'When comes the Irishman? Yes, that was it. 'When comes the Irishman?' Then the policeman said he was due that night but might not come with all that is going on, not with Thornton running around loose." He sat up straight. "That was when Al-Sottar asked him why he hadn't taken off my head quickly, just as he had my foreman's; which was nice of him."

The Colonel handed over the re-filled tumbler, shrugged, raised his own, "So, Damnation to the enemy." He sipped the whisky. "Yes, it could make sense."

"What? What sense? There are lots of Irishmen in Saudi Arabia. You know, expatriates with local jobs like myself, visiting businessmen, etcetera."

The Colonel said, "Now I'm the one who should be concerned about the Official Secrets Act. But I think it could be in the general interest so let me tell you, your sinking of the Los Alamos rather loused up the relationships between South America and the Provos. A little matter of who would not now be paying whom for what, if you see what I mean." He stood up in front of the last of the fire, hands behind his back. "Be that as it may, after the Los Alamos, certain non-political organisations, mainly Italian American, moved in and got hold of things. With a little help from some key names in the North, these people have busily been adding very considerable sums to their personal bank accounts."

"Al-Sottar could have got on to this? I have to doubt that. He would really be taking an enormous risk."

"Were it the case, it would explain a great deal. And the risk to an insider might not be as great as you think. The establishment in Saudi is not too different from that anywhere else. It may say one thing and mean another or it may just turn a blind eye. All I'm saying is that you, Thomas Thornton or Thomas MacRae, you should leave well alone. You cannot possibly beat those people, you know that."

"I can sure as hell beat one of them, the one who calls himself Sheikh Abdul-Rahman Al-Sottar." Thomas said. A thought struck him. "Hang on a minute, the young Portsmouth newspaper fellow, Morgan, he definitely told me the guys at Sea Fibres were to be charged with offences relating to heroin. Yet my own charge-sheet referred only to cocaine."

"So, still they come. More questions than answers." The Colonel glanced at his watch. "If I cannot persuade you to change your mind can you tell me exactly what you're planning?"

"Of course." The mobile was vibrating in his pocket. "Hang on." He picked up, saw it was Ben and switched on, holding the phone close enough to the Colonel so they both could hear. "Yes Ben, how you doing? Can you talk?"

"Yeah. I'm on my way. I left the old boy outside Casualty. Sorry to tell you this, sir, but by the time I reached the hospital I'm afraid he'd gone." There was a hardness in his voice, one that Thomas had not heard since Ireland. "I want those guys, boss. Poor old sod, all he was doing was a little bit of poaching."

"I'm sorry too. Very sorry. But be very careful, Ben. We'll see you soon. We'll need to do something fast about the inside of your car and the tyre tracks in the field."

The Colonel had been listening intently, now held out his hand for the phone. "Good morning, Ben. .... Yes... Good... I don't have to tell you this but please don't talk to anyone at all ... You know, if you' happen to be stopped by the police or anything? And needless to say, I too am terribly sorry about how things have developed, but ...yes ... drive carefully." He pressed off the mobile, passed it back, said, "The two of you will need to use the settee and the armchair here for sleeping tonight - unless you're planning to take Sheila and the boys home?" Thomas shook his head. "No, I thought not. Don't forget, sometime very soon I really would like to hear what you're actually planning to do, assuming you make it back to Bahrain."

"I'm thinking about what you said, Colonel."

"Just keep in mind that I do have valuable contacts, ones that are pretty close to the top of the tree. And so does your father; you won't forget that either, will you?"

Lady Dee, dressed in her housecoat, looked in the door. "What's all the talking," she whispered, "Is there anything I can get for you?"

The Colonel said, "Very kind, dear, but no. We'll have another visitor in a minute. Sergeant Benedict. He and Thomas will be sleeping down here. It really is too late for Lower Longstock. Good night."

"Actually it's practically morning but yes, goodnight, gentlemen." There was a hesitation. "There are twin beds in Sheila's room you know. I don't suppose she would mind..."

"Thanks, Lady Dee, but I'm just fine here," Thomas said. "Good night. And goodnight to you, too Colonel. I keep having to say thanks, don't I?"

It seemed only moments before the sounds of tyres on gravel. He'd fallen asleep and the Colonel must have switched off the lights. He heard the front door being opened and closed and then the opening of the living room door.

Out of the darkness the Colonel murmured, "If you're awake, don't get up, Thomas. Sergeant Benedict will use the armchairs. We'll confer in the morning." Just before the door closed again he said, "No talking after lights out now. Good night."

Ben said, "Hello again - and good night, sir,"

"Hello Ben, And it's Thomas, not sir, remember? ... 'Night."

When next he woke it was to the sound of rain on window glass, the boys' animated voices out in the kitchen followed by the surreptitious opening of the living room door and a strong smell of fish. He opened his eyes. David was close up, looking at him wide-eyed over the dorsal fin of a large rainbow trout. David said, excitedly, "Look, Daddy, Paul and me were just looking at our sea fish and these were there. We didn't catch any of this sort, did we?"

"'I,' David, you say 'Paul and I,' not 'Paul and me.'" He raised himself up on his good elbow. Paul was there too, also clad in pants and vest, also holding up a trout. "And good morning to you too, Paul. No we did not catch them. They're rainbow trout and they came from the river." He yawned extensively. "Now put them back where you found them and get your hands washed before Auntie Sheila or Lady Dee catches you. After breakfast I'll show you how to gut all the fish, all right?"

"I know. Same way as you did the bass and the bream, Daddy. But you said the knife was too sharp, we mustn't touch it!"

He sighed. "That was on board the boat when it was moving around all over the place. It's safer here in the kitchen so long as I'm watching what you're doing. Now push off, can't you see Ben's trying to get some sleep?"

"BB wants his breakfast, Daddy," Paul said, "and he wants to go outside, doesn't he, David?"

Thomas said, "Good lord! Well, just go and let him out then."

"Can we go down the garden to the river with him, Daddy?"

"Go. Otherwise I'll be down there myself and throw you both in!"

The two of them ran out of the room, laughing, just as Sheila came in. "I heard that," she said. "What a cruel father you are."

212

Ben said, sleepily, "And good morning everyone. This is like trying to sleep in bloody Piccadilly Circus." He sat up. "What time is it anyway?"

"Almost eight o clock," Sheila said, "I've never known the boys sleep in this late. Me as well. Must be all that good salt air. But Dee's been up for ages. She's out in the garden in her waterproofs and she certainly needs them this morning. So what's on the agenda?"

"I'd like to talk a few things over with the Colonel and Ben, Sheila. Then you and I and Ben here can have a chat. I don't know how up to speed you are?"

"About last night? Dee told me. Dave Fletcher. Everyone including most of the local hotels know poor old Dave Fletcher goes poaching. He's never harmed anyone so far as I know. How is he now, anyway?"

Thomas said, gently, "It's very bad news. I'm afraid he's dead."

"Dead? Oh my God. Oh, I am so sorry." The light blue eyes had clouded over. "Yes, it most definitely is time we talked. Do you mind if I sit in on your meeting?" As she dropped her chin the sweep of hair closed like a curtain, long and dark and shining and shutting off her expression.

"Of course you can." There didn't seem anything else to say to her. "You want to use the bathroom first, Ben?"

"Yeah, all right. I have to say I've had a few better nights' sleep."

Sheila said quietly, "I hope the old man didn't suffer too much?"

"No, he never recovered consciousness after we got him in my car," Ben said. "But I'll tell you, that car's going to take some cleaning."

"Well, I think it's absolutely tragic," she said, "And if those fish that the boys had were the ones he'd - well, there's no way I shall have anything to do with them. I think it's outrageous …" Thomas realised she was on the verge of tears. She went across to draw back the curtains. Raindrops splatted and scuttled down the window glass.

The Colonel came in, looking as if he'd had a great deal more than three hours of sleep. "Good morning everybody. Look here, why don't we all go and have some breakfast and allow Ben here to arise in some sort of modesty. Thomas, come with me first please, just for a minute, I'd appreciate your help in the greenhouse."

They hurried down the garden. It was warm in the greenhouse, very quiet apart from the drumming of the rain. The Colonel at once began to prod around amongst his beloved roses.

Thomas started straight in. "OK, Colonel, so here's how it's going to be. You know I'm due back to Bahrain on Friday. Brad and the two fellows I escaped with, they're waiting for me there. Connie's with my ex-sponsor, this Sheikh Al-Sottar fellow. I'm perfectly certain Al-Sottar can get me off the hook. I plan on making a surprise counter attack, using the same team I escaped with, reinforced with Brad Scott. I tried hard enough, but I couldn't keep him out of it."

The Colonel continued with the roses, saying nothing as Thomas continued. "Look, I need to find out the whole story from Connie's angle. As for Al-Sottar, we'll just be holding him, hopefully but regrettably all in one piece whilst he clears me and pays over his dues."

"Dues, you say?" The Colonel had picked off a dead bloom. He held it to his nose with eyes half closed. "What dues are they?"

"He owes me, Colonel. Whatever happens now, the bastard damned well owes me. And, Brad excepted, my friends out there have to have some sort of a motive other than brother love."

"Just get the scent of this, Thomas." The Colonel held out the withered bloom. "With some of the really good ones their scent is at its best and strongest when they're dying, you know. So, what will it be, my boy, I mean when you have him all to yourself? Extortion or blackmail? Ugly words, both of them."

"Remember how Vince McGonigal used to obtain his finance? Well. I'll be doing the same thing. Al-Sottar paid sixty millions for Sea Fibres so he's going to pay me the six million dollar commission on the deal he owes me as his agent."

"Six millions ... But of course, I suppose you weren't actually involved in that deal."

"Not directly, except I suppose he wouldn't ever have heard of Sea Fibres but for me. He'd have thought his employee the best value agent ever at the time. Don't worry, he'll fall over himself to sign the pre-dated Agreement that makes it official. He'll pay over the money. Yes, I want to hurt the man, Colonel, but only up here and in here," He tapped his head and then his chest, "and he can count himself bloody lucky. Six years ago I would most surely have killed him for what he's damned well done, not just to me but to my poor little Philipino and indirectly to a lot of others including the ones who got themselves killed in the Al-Mahli jail. Even the old poacher last night. It's all part and parcel."

De Grenville sighed. "Yes you would, wouldn't you ... have killed him, I mean. A rose by any other name, Thomas ... You'll recall the SBS motto? 'By guile, not force'? But then, I believe I can see the justification for force in this case."

"Yes."

214

The Colonel had emptied the contents of a plastic sachet into a small watering can with a very long spout, had filled it from a tap, was now sprinkling it sparingly around the roots of his rose bushes. "The thing is, old chap, you've actually been rumbled. The police are already aware that you're around here somewhere. And this dead poacher changes everything. The old manure gets deeper by the day." He put down the watering can, straightened himself up. "Let's go and talk to the others, shall we?"

Thomas said, "Colonel, I think I should bring my flight forward." He hesitated, unsure as to how to say it. "But before I go I'd like to try to work out a safe way to see my father. According to Sheila the old boy's not doing so well."

"I do understand. And I'm pleased, Thomas. Your father's a good man. Actually, so are you."

Thomas smiled. "Thanks for that. Someone else once told me that."

"The UK airports are going to be too risky for you. I don't think you should use them, do you?"

There was a knocking on the greenhouse door. The boys were standing outside in the rain. Paul's clothes were muddily plastered to his slight body. A whisp of water weed trailed down behind one ear. He was trying not to cry. An equally saturated Labrador stood beside them, tail moving happily from side to side. "Daddy, Paul fell in the river," David explained, his voice coming faintly through the double glazing, his hand holding his frightened younger brother's. "It wasn't my fault, was it Paul? BB accidentally pushed him. When are we going to see Mummy?"

Chapter Fifteen

Thomas picked up his youngest, held the soaking wet form close to him, not knowing whether to laugh or to be angry. "It's a damn good job you can swim, Paul. We'd better get you back to the house, have those wet clothes off you." To the Colonel he said, "That's one benefit of being brought up with a swimming pool outside the front door."

"Daddy, when can we see Mummy?" David repeated.

To Paul's obvious indignation the Colonel was laughing. "Forgive me, but have you ever seen those Victorian postcards they used to reproduce? The little cartoon children with the one word caption – 'Tired,' 'Lost,' 'Defiant' etcetera? Well, I think this one must be little 'Woebegone'."

Taking them back up to the house Thomas said, "Soon, David, I hope we'll be seeing your Mummy soon."

David said, "Oh, wicked, Daddy," and then, "Daddy, it was too muddy. He kept slipping back in but the man came to help him get out of the river but he got out by himself."

Grenville saw the question, answered it at once. "Would have been my security, Thomas. Probably Jones at this time of day. I never know exactly who, or where they're going to station themselves."

Inside the house Paul resisted the attempted cosseting of the two women, insisting instead on showering by himself. All too quickly he re-appeared in the kitchen, enveloped in a fluffy white towel. His clothes were drying on the rail in front of the Aga. Whilst the boys had their breakfasts Thomas excused himself, went out to make his calls.

He spoke first to Bradley Scott, asking him to have an Agency Agreement prepared in his, Thomas' name in regards to Abdul-Rahman Al-Sottar's purchase of Sea Fibres Limited. The deal would not be finalised until the end of the month, he said, so there would be plenty of time to have everything properly legalised, including his own signature at the British Embassy in Bahrain and Al-Sottar's at the Saudi Chamber of Commerce. He asked him also to have a Letter of Credit drawn up, maturing on date of share transfer by production of copy documents. He gave him the name of Al-Sottar's bankers. His commission on the deal was to be set at six million dollars, U.S. "Brad, I think we're going to have to advance the program," he went on. "There's a number of reasons, I'll tell you all about them when we meet. I'm going to try to get back overnight tonight instead of Friday."

"Good. 'If 'twere done, 'twere best done quickly, and all that," Brad said.

"If you insist. I'll call you about the flight times when I have them, but I'll be coming out from Paris or Amsterdam. The word is that Heathrow has become rather too hot for me. I'll drive to the ferry at Dover. I wouldn't expect any problems amongst the booze trippers there, not with such a changed appearance and with MacRae on my passport."

"What about George's and Saeed's new passports and stuff?"

"They're ready now, according to the Colonel. All being well I'll have them biked down to Dover. I'll pick them up at the P&O office."

"Good. I'll see you then, my friend. Take good care now." He adopted his pantomime voice. "We want to be rich. Rich, you hear?"

As he switched off, from behind him Sheila said, "Can anybody come, Thomas?" There was still a tension in the light blue eyes.

He took her hands in his. "I wish," he said. "I wish, but there are things I have to do to sort myself out, things I have to do on my own, and there's a certain Consuela, remember?"

"Yes, I know. I didn't think ... oh well ..." She pulled away from him, the worry transformed into a rising anger. She was looking up at him, her chin held high. "And if you once more say the word 'sorry' I'll kill you, brother Thomas. Now get on with it. Call your airline. Just don't forget to tell me and the boys goodbye on your way out, will you?" She hurried back into the house.

There was a flight with seat availability departing Paris Charles de Gaulle at twenty three hundred tonight, arriving Bahrain zero eight forty tomorrow, Wednesday. He made a quick calculation: Two hours plus from here to Dover. Another, say, hour and a half for the cross channel ferry including waiting and discharge time, three more on the road to Charles de Gaulle, then one more hour for the time difference. He'd need to leave the area by two this afternoon. He checked his watch. Almost nine. Dear God, how tired he was.

Sheila, the Colonel, Lady Dee and Ben were talking over coffees at the table. Paul, dressed in his cleaned and dried clothes was on the floor with David, playing with BB. Thomas sat down and Lady Dee poured him a cup from the cafetiere. He said, "Well, this is it. Bottom line; I need to get to Paris by ten tonight." He looked at Grenville. "If the paperwork's all done in time can it be biked down to Dover by four, for me to collect?"

The Colonel nodded. "I can confirm it's finished. I'll arrange the courier."

218

David looked up. "Are we going home, Daddy?"

Thomas said, "No, son, I'm afraid not. Not this time, I have some more business to attend to. But soon, David, soon you and Paul will be coming."

"I'm sorry Daddy. It wasn't my fault, falling in. Is that why?" Lady Dee was busying herself with cutting up a cake. Sheila was examining the inside of her cup.

"Good lord, no. It's just business, Paul. Auntie Sheila will go on taking good care of you whilst I'm away. And Lady Dee. And BB." Sheila did not return his look, just smiled down at the boys. Thomas added, "And Uncle Ben, he'll be with you too."

Paul's arms were around patient old BB's neck. He looked up. There were no tears now. "But Ben's not our uncle, is he?"

Thomas said, "If he wants to be and we want him to be then of course he is."

Ben said, "Why not? But hey, isn't 'Uncle Ben' some kind of rice?"

Everyone except Sheila laughed. David said, not understanding, "Auntie Sheila, does it mean you and Uncle Ben are an item?"

"What?" Sheila was blushing. "Where on earth did you get such an expression? I don't know what you mean, David." It was Ben's turn to find something interesting in his cup.

"Oh, Auntie, it just means you sleep in the same bed as him," David explained patiently.

"Look, that's quite enough," Thomas said. "Ben, I'm so sorry. Mercifully he doesn't often come out with stuff like that."

David now wore his stricken look. He said, "Yes, Uncle Ben, and I am sorry. I didn't mean it." It was clear he didn't know what he had to be sorry about.

Ben said, "No need, lad. It's me should be sorry. Why would a famous artist like your Auntie here want a rough old bugger like me anyway?"

Paul said, "You're not all that old, Uncle Ben, but you shouldn't swear so much." He went back to cuddling BB. Thomas began to correct him. Ben made a gesture, shaking his head.

Thomas said, "Sheila, I was wondering if I could arrange to go and see father this morning? He may not want to see me but I'd very much like to see him before I go. Try and set things straight a bit. Do you think that's at all feasible?"

Lady Dee said, "Boys, I have a box of really lovely old toys that I'd like to show you. Just you come with me while Daddy and Auntie sort out what's happening." The three of them left the kitchen. BB looked up at their retreating backs, decided to follow.

Sheila said, "Going to see Daddy doesn't seem very sensible to me, Thomas. If they were watching my place for you, whoever they were, why wouldn't they be watching over Daddy's hospice? And he's in a pretty bad way, you know." She shrugged. "But no doubt you'll do as you think best."

Colonel Grenville said, "How do you think it would be if I were to go along there ahead? You know, reconnoitre the place? Anyway I'd like a little chat with Sir Christopher. It's been some time since our last opportunity."

"I'm getting really sensitive about keeping on thanking you, Colonel," Thomas said. "All of you in fact. Without meaning to, I seem to have fairly effectively diverted the course of all of your lives. I can only say that I had no plan to do so."

Ben said, "Speaking for yours truly there's no need for apologies. I've been going nowhere pretty fast since Kathleen left, nowhere else than down the pub, most likely down the tubes as well, eventually." He grinned, shook his head, placing his knife and fork side by side on the empty plate. "That was good, very good. Boss, you haven't told me what you're planning to be up to out there but it's bound to be interesting. I know we've been all through this, but if there's anything useful I can do …I can take as much of the heat as you like, you know that. Any old kind of heat."

"Yes, I do know that," Thomas said, "And there may well be ways and means after this - this current situation is done and dusted. Right now, as we agreed on the boat, I really need you to look after things at Lower Longstock."

"Yeah. I told you; that's no problem."

The Colonel said, "Gentlemen, if this new partnership of yours is to have anything like the impact of your last one, God help the opposition."

Ben said, "Right. I'll need a couple of hours in Pompey this morning to tidy things up. After that I'm all yours - I mean your sister's."

Sheila said, "So. Let's get one more thing out of the way. It's simply inconceivable for the good burghers of Lower Longstock not to notice I have another lodger. They're going to draw the obvious conclusion. After all everybody knows what we over-sexed artists are like." There was not much of humour in her smile. Ben started his protest but she cut him off. "Don't worry about it, Ben. To the outside world we are

220

henceforth, and until my brother's notice otherwise, what David called 'an item.' What a truly horrid expression that is, by the way." Quietly she added, "You and I will be friends who act like an item everywhere outside the hearth and home, nowhere inside it. Is that all right with you, Ben?"

Ben looked embarrassed. "Of course it is. No problems. But - I mean, it was only a few days ago my car broke down in the village and I got to asking about you in the pub."

"So? You came in to see my pictures and I had you in bed. Quick as a flash. Why wouldn't I?"

The Colonel cleared his throat. "Right, so that's all settled then." He seemed anxious to pilot a change of topic. "Where exactly is this hospital of Sir Christopher's, Sheila?"

"Hospice, Colonel, not hospital. Father is in a hospice called Dunholme May; you're allowed visits anytime." She gave him the directions. "Shall I give matron a call, tell her to expect you?"

"Good idea. And Thomas, you'd best give me at least a one hour start."

"That's fine. Sheila, if its OK with Lady Dee why don't you wait here with the boys until Ben gets back? That'll leave time for you and I to have a chat."

Ben and the Colonel drove off in their different directions then Thomas walked with Sheila down the garden. It had stopped raining, the sky now a scurrying billow of white and greys and washed out blue. They went past the greenhouse, through the overgrown orchard to the river bank. He took off the borrowed Barbour, laid it on the Colonel's favourite wooden bench beneath the willow tree so they could sit down without getting wet. "Do you still want to kill me for saying 'sorry'?" he asked gently.

She shook her head, cupped hands up to the face beneath the fall of hair. Instinctively he put an arm around her shoulders. Pain from the bending of his elbow came at him like an old friend. He touched his lips to her head. This close up, in the new sunshine, the dark hair sparkled with reds and golds. In silence he watched the crystal play of the river around about its masses of slow waving, sub-aquatic weed.

Sheila's body shook, her voice muffled. "Do you love me, Thomas? Just a little?"

He said nothing for a few seconds, then, "Love? I've wanted to make love with you, always, you know that. And I love being with you. And I've wanted to warn off all your other men, even the ones you more than liked. Well, yes, Sheila. I suppose I do love you as a matter of fact."

She lifted her head, looking through tears for the truth in his face. Unexpectedly she smiled. "So, the hard man can actually say it; wonderful. Well, me too. That's all right then, isn't it?" And he could see again the young girl standing over him in the Highlands sand dunes, all the mystery and all the female in her pretty, rained on face. And now, finally, his world was beginning to spin out of control and it was she who had to pull them both back. "No, Thomas, not here and not now. Probably not ever. I want your body and your soul, my so-called brother, not just your body for these few minutes."

"Yes, I know. Impossible."

She touched his cheek with the tips of her fingers, whispered, "Yes, I love you, Mister Thomas Thornton-MacRae. And it's all right, you know. It doesn't have to happen, does it? Just so long as you come back to us, you hear me?" There were tears in her eyes but she'd begun to smile again and he was ashamed about the power of this wish of his, this desire to break the long standing promise. But Connie, oh Connie! Nothing must be allowed to break the spell of his resolve, nothing should move it out of focus.

Back in the kitchen Lady Dee was downstairs again, playing with the boys and her collection of old toys. Sheila looked at her watch, said, "Thomas, what about the things you left at Lower Longstock?"

"Best keep them there. I'll buy more clothes and a suitcase along the way." In the driveway outside the cottage Paul was in tears, didn't want to let go of him. David just stood there, wondering how best to behave. He kissed them both and kissed Lady Dee and kissed the tears on Sheila's face, squeezing her upper arms.

At the last minute Lady Dee put her head into the car window, whispered, "I don't want you to worry about the boys or Sheila. Ben's a really reliable man and be sure we'll be doing all we can as well. Don't be too influenced by my husband, either, Thomas. Please just do what you, yourself, feel is right." How did she manage, without apparent effort, to convey such a sense of perfectly good order amongst what she and he and everybody knew was chaos? As the tyres of the Fiesta scrunched off down the drive he waved out of the window, glanced into the rear view mirror at the four of them standing there holding hands with each other. He blinked, could himself have cried. Of course did not.

Colonel Grenville must have been watching for him. He strode out of the hospice building and got into the passenger seat as soon as Thomas had stopped. "Nice place," he said. "If you have to be in one of these places, this is as good as anywhere. So far as I can tell and from talking discreetly to Matron the place is not under any kind of surveillance. Look, I've spoken with your father, put him in the general picture. The man's fighting the good fight in there. Can I give you some advice? I think that's what he'd like me to do."

"Of course you can. You often have."

"Cancel out on this proposed raid of yours? I'll talk to the people here, the ones that matter. We can bring your crew into the UK if that's what you want."

"I know your motives are as good as always, Colonel," he said, "But the raid will be a good use of all that expensive training, don't you think?" He turned in his seat to look the old man in the eye. "There's no way I can sit around waiting for them to come for me, and I'm telling you, they will. It's written into their code, you know that. These people have already ruined my service and now my civilian life and as for Connie ... well, I think you'd feel and do the same as me, roles reversed."

"No. I have to tell you that I feel more and more strongly this is an extreme and an unnecessary thing you're doing. Wherever your wife actually is, it's hardly likely she's being held in some kind of mediaeval captivity, waiting for her knight in shining armour. The narcotics thing - that's a complete irrelevance."

"And nothing to do with it. Look, I actually agree with you. Narcotics are a big train coming head on for the human race. Who the hell in his right mind wants to stand in its way? You know I've done my bit on that front and I've had quite enough of suffering the consequences. No, it isn't that. I want the man, Colonel, I want him to clear me and I want him to pay and I want him to understand ... hell, you know what I mean. As for Connie, I guess we'll just have to see how it all goes, sir." Every now and then, irritatingly, the 'sir' slipped out.

Grenville sighed. "You said you're planning to go in from the sea. Do you really think you can get the man out of his home all intact and back across the water before all hell breaks over your head?"

Thomas realised he hadn't told the Colonel anything about his bolt hole on *Jazeera*. There seemed little point in getting into detail now. He said, "Are you a believer in karma, Colonel? You know, cause and effect, destiny, whatever?"

223

There was an untypical hesitation. "Why do you ask?"

"I've often thought about it ... you know, about my personal attempts to meet force with greater force? Falklands, Ireland, all the other places ... intellectual as well as physical. I suppose I mean not just my own efforts, nor even the Service's as a whole. Sowing the wind and reaping the whirlwind, etcetera. Same old story but we all of us go on writing it and reading it, don't we? So, let's get it on, as our American friends are so fond of saying. Take care now, Colonel. And thanks for everything, especially for this - you know, whatever it was you said to my father." They got out of the car. Thomas walked round to shake hands.

"Thomas?"

"Yes, Colonel?"

"Sir Christopher is actually very proud of you, you know. I would be, I mean, I would be, were I he." He sounded uncharacteristically confused. "Just wanted you to know that. Now bugger off, go in there and make the old boy happy, will you? Don't be put off by all the machinery, nor by your father's appearance. There's a good old-fashioned street fighter under all that. Remember it."

A cheerful staff nurse asked him to switch off his mobile, please, and showed him into what should have been a very comfortable, very large drawing room. It was generously furnished and decorated with fresh flowers and was filled with the scent of them. But the high, metal framed bed with its shockingly wasted occupant destroyed any illusion. Thomas recognised the big picture hanging over the hearth with all the discharging cannon and the charging Light Brigade as the one that had hung in his father's study.

Even allowing for the years since last they'd met, Sir Christopher Thornton was virtually unrecognisable. The skeletal head of what seemed an incredibly old man rested against a great bank of pillows. Computer screens and an array of stainless steel and rubber tubes stood guard over the bed. The nurse said, "Sir Christopher, it's your son to see you," sounding as pleased as if it were her own father she was making happy. "We *are* having a lot of visitors today, aren't we?" She turned to smile at Thomas. "I'll leave you to it. Use that press-button to call me if you need me or when you're ready to go, is that all right? Oh, but I expect you'd like a cup of tea?"

He nodded his thanks, advanced to the side of the bed, watching the old man's face as a boxer watches the eyes of a downed but still dangerous opponent. At last he took the bony hand, bent to kiss the wrinkled forehead. Whisps of white hair had been brushed back, were now spread like a halo on the pillows. He could say nothing. There seemed nothing worth the saying. The old man whispered, "It was very good of Colonel Grenville to put me in the picture. You've been in the wars, old chap. I'm sorry. I should have known ..."

Thomas said, "I don't know what ... Father, you say *I've* been in the wars? Me? You look as if you've been ten rounds with bloody Mike Tyson."

The twitch of thin and bloodless lips, then, "Father, you said. Nice. But a father who wasn't around when you needed him, eh?" He moved a hand to dismiss the protest. "You knew I was familiar with Carravaga? Why I wanted nothing to do with him or his - well, your wife?"

"Bad man wanting to buy Amalgamated's armaments? I guess so. It's all history, isn't it?" He bent down again to lay his face alongside the old man's stubbly-cold one and he could feel the life still in there, trapped and fragile as some butterfly fluttering its last against the panes of a sun-lit window. Changing the subject, he whispered, "Auntie Eleanor, she's all right?"

Sir Christopher spoke low and now more clearly, "Eleanor's just fine. You should go and see her. I'll not tell her what the Colonel told me." He tried a smile. "Grenville said he's been trying to talk you out of it. I said you wouldn't change tack. Listen, go and get the bastard, son. Clear our name, certainly, but that's not what matters. It's what you do, not what people think you do. Like that poem you always carried about with you, the one your other father wrote, eh? The Fourth-light? You didn't know I knew about it. Your old Granny Mac showed it to me. Brilliant, I think." He paused to cough, carefully, as if lacking the energy even for that. "Did Sheila tell you she brought David and Paul here to see me? Crackers, both of them, but lovely young boys. Make sure they're looked after, I know you will..."

Thomas released the bony old form, stood up, pained himself by his father's effort to speak on.

"Come here, Thomas," the old man whispered. Thomas bent down once more. "You won't need to worry about them financially. And now ... my Amalgamated shares are yours. Don't feel obliged ... You can do what you like with them. Take my chair if you ever decide to come down off planet Mars." He managed a death's head grin. "Some bloody hopes. Our Saudi friends, I mean. I mean - trying to fit you into their frame!" He attempted a laugh but the laugh had turned into another cough.

Thomas said, "Thanks. The shares I mean. I don't think they see it quite that way, but all of a sudden it seems less important. I don't want to know, but - how long do they say you have?"

"How long? Funny you should ask that, son. It's a bloody obvious question but no-one ever asks it." He turned his head to look out at the sunlit day. "Doctors won't say. As long as I like or as God wills. But you're the important one now. Listen to Grenville, Thomas. He knows a lot more about how things are than he can or will say to you; just at the moment." That awful skull-head smile again. "I may not see you any more, son. Not here, anyway. If I weren't so bloody English I'd ask you to give me another of those hugs. But Christ! Will you? Please?"

Walking back past Reception he was told that someone had been in to leave him a letter. He sat in the car and switched on the engine and read Sheila's note ... *'Dear, dear Thomas. I'm really glad you could see Daddy. Hope he was not too much of a shock for you. At least you now know he's in good hands.*

For all our sakes be careful and come back soon and know that I am with you, my dear brother, and I can still feel you are with me. I love you like a mother and a sister and a cousin and a lover and anything else anyone can ever think of. Think about the sand dunes and about me (please) and about being young. It was the best of all times, wasn't it?'

She had enclosed a couple of CDs for him to play on his journey. The driving was in itself a therapy, the music a real bonus: the City of Birmingham's Beethoven Symphonies four and seven and The Fureys' Celtic Collections. Lovely chalk and just as lovely cheese.

At the P&O office the girl on the desk smiled at him with a little more than ordinary politeness. He returned the smile, showed her his MacRae passport and when she produced his ticket and a credit card counterfoil a young man in black motorcycle leathers got up from his seat and presented him with a small package, asked him to sign. Just in time to remembered the 'MacRae'.

Whilst dropping off and settling up for the Fiesta at the Hertz office, remembering at the last minute to remove his new CDs, he arranged for a similar car to be waiting for him in Calais. He boarded the Pride of Dover as a foot passenger, bought a conversion to The Executive Club lounge. It was almost empty. As the boat pulled out and rounded the harbour wall he sipped his free glass of champagne, having finished it went down to the shops to buy himself a holdall and some new clothing. Once back in the Lounge he read a newspaper,

226

occasionally looking up and out of the picture window. The seas were long and smooth, the big ferry boat developing a slow roll as she left behind the white cliffs of England. He shivered, thinking about the Saudi - Bahrain crossing, thinking about George and Saeed. Giving up the attempt to concentrate on the newspaper he closed his eyes and fell asleep.

He woke to the chortling of his mobile just as the ferry was pulling into Calais. It was the Colonel. "Hello Thomas, can I ask where you are?"

"I'm on the ferry, just about docked in Calais. Something up?" He started walking through to the foot passenger exit.

"There's no easy way to tell you this. Thomas, but I'm afraid they've taken David. Now don't ..."

"What?" A steel band tightened unbearably around his chest.

There was a new tiredness in the Colonel's voice. "When Benedict got back here, Sheila and he and the boys stayed on for a while then went off to Lower Longstock as planned. She called me on her arrival just to say everything was OK, even though the whole village was being over-run with policemen - "

"But, David? They took David? How? When?"

"Less than a half hour ago. Your cell phone must have been out of range. It seems the boys sneaked out of Sheila's place by themselves. They'd decided to go for a spot of fly fishing with their new kit. Paul got back alone, and in some distress. When they'd managed to get the whole story out of him it seems there were two men already down there, eager to give instruction. Paul managed to give them the slip by jumping in and swimming the river. He saw David being carried off."

"Oh my God. What did Ben do? Are the police involved?"

"Thomas, please hear me out. Delia took a message at home on the open land line ... Irish accent, the man just gave a number for you to call."

"Me? Give me the number please."

"Zero seven double eight double six two five nine. Did you get that? Repeat it to me please" Thomas had pressed the number into his mobile. He repeated it. The Colonel went on, "The man told Delia that if the police were called in - "

"Yes, I've got the picture. I'll call now and get back to you. Where's Ben?"

"He's at Lower Longstock. Will you also call him, soon as you can? And Thomas. I would caution against involving the police just yet."

"Thank you, Colonel. Please do nothing until I get back to you."
He closed down, then dialled the number just as a loudspeaker asked
all drivers to board their vehicles prior to disembarkation.

The voice on the phone said, "Thornton?"

"I'm Thomas Thornton."

"You are just about in time, fucker. Identify."

"Military service number?"

"That'll do."

"Seven one treble three six two nine"

"Listen, we've only thirty seconds left to talk. After that this mobile
gets terminated, that is, it gets thrown. Finished. No point in trying a
trace, OK? All right? Ye've a pen?"

"Yes."

"Listen to me. Your boy tells us you're on your way back to where
you just came from. We're glad about that because we want you back
in Saudi and fucking quick."

"I'll need to get a visa - "

"Shut the fuck up, all right? You won't need one. You'll meet the
Saudis in the Bahrain Customs office on the Causeway, right? They'll
see you through into Saudi, understood?" The man paused, awaiting
the answer, shouted, "I said, is that fucking OK?"

"Yes, I shall be there," Thomas whispered.

"Say again, fucker."

He shouted, "I'll be there but what arrangements for returning my
son?"

The man ignored the question. "Ye'll confirm arrangements by
calling Captain Al-Muttawi of the Al-Khobar police, soon as you land
in Bahrain. Ye got that? Right, press in this number to your mobile:
Zero zero nine six six then four four four, eight four seven seven,
seven nine one. Repeat."

Thomas read back the number, then, "What happens ..."

"Shut your face up, ye cunt ye. Just do it, ye know full fucking well
what happens, so ye do. None better. Remember fucking Shergar?" A
pause, then, the voice full of infinite menace, "And Mister Kerrigan
sends you all his best, so he does." The line went dead. As dead as the
great Shergar, in his day rated the finest racehorse in the world but
spirited away by the IRA and never to be seen again.

Thomas Thornton clicked off his mobile, clicked on again to give
the Colonel the bare facts then disconnected and walked downstairs to
join the queue of disembarking foot passengers. As he walked there
was in his mind this blinding rage, this most bitter of hatreds; over all

228

of it this great, overpowering fear.. Not only for the people who had so evidently given up the fight for the unification of Ireland in favour of using their hard learned skills in the interests only of themselves, but for the ultimate cruelty of Abdul-Rahman Al-Sottar.

He knew the savagery that was awakening inside him. You want me, Al-Sottar? Well, you'll have me, or what there is left of me. And if there really is a God in your heaven you shall wish it otherwise.

Chapter Sixteen

Thomas managed to remove that which was inside his head from that which appeared on his face. Calais immigration showed no interest in him.

He called the number he'd been given for the car rental company, advised them of his arrival. Please have the car ready in ten minutes.. He wound his watch forward by one hour to seven o'clock, local. Taking his new holdall into the toilet, he washed his hands and face, changed his clothing without bothering to occupy a cubicle. A man came in, saw him half naked and left without using any of the facilities, but the old lady with the mop took no notice of him whatsoever. When he'd done he had on a pair of beige Daks, a white, round necked T shirt and a lightweight jacket in a mid-brown colour.

He set off in the newly rented Fiat through the industrial suburbs of the seaport, almost physically sick with worry when his mobile sounded: Ben. He took a deep breath, switched on. His voice studiedly neutral, "Hi, Ben," he said, "Anything new?"

"No, I'm sorry. No excuses. To say I'm sorry … I fucked up, sir."

"Well, I think we'd all best get unfucked up in a hell of a hurry, don't you? There are things to be done. And, Ben, I'm still not 'sir'."

"Those bastards … Sheila was just settling me in. We both thought the lads were upstairs in their bedroom. It couldn't have been more than ten minutes. Thomas, the lady's going bloody crazy here."

"Will you tell her that David is going to be all right? Listen to me now. I'm off the ferry and on my way down to Paris. Kerrigan's people have been in touch. Yes, you heard it right, Kerrigan's people. I'm to turn myself over to the Saudis tomorrow and David will be handed back, simple as that. I'll be confirming all the hows and wheres and whens when I call them and I'll be doing that as soon as I reach Bahrain, OK?"

"Oh, sweet Jesus Christ." There was a depth of anguish in Ben's voice. "Whatever happens, I'm going after them, boss. I'm going after those bastards. I don't care what or how long it takes. But you … tomorrow? There's no other way out? Jesus, there has to be."

Thomas felt quite calm now, wanting his own acceptance of the situation to be heard and understood. "No, Ben, there's no way we can get David back without them getting their hands on me. I'm a big boy and my son, David, is not. You and everybody there, you have your own lives to live. The boys will be OK after this, you know that. Kids are so much more resilient - ." He'd unconsciously gained speed, now slowed down and the BMW he'd just overtaken went past. Out of the corner of his eye he could see the driver, impassive, staring straight ahead. He continued. "I have never meant anything more in my life. I want you to promise me; no more blood, OK?"

A long pause, then, "Sorry, boss, I want to do what you want and I'll do my best but no can do with any promises on this one. Somebody has to see to these people." Thomas saw the blue light of a police car coming up fast from behind, said nothing in response. Ben continued, "We know it for sure then? These Irish are working with your fucking Sheikh?" The police car flashed by in pursuit of the BMW.

Thomas shook his head, sighed. "I'd have had you up on a charge at one time for disregard of an order. But the answer's a yes."

"Right; so what do you want me to do now?"

"Just stay there and keep your eyes open until you hear from me, will you? Brad Scott or the Colonel will see to everything for me on the money front." He thought for a moment. "Ben?"

"Yes, boss."

"I'll ask the Colonel to advance you a couple of thousand; 'on account' so to speak. I'm going to ask him to let you have some of that armament back as well. If push should come to shove ... anyway, keep the hard stuff well out of sight. And for God's sake keep yourself out of trouble. We have enough of that already. The Colonel could get a firearms licence for you but I wouldn't recommend it. It's likely to open up the whole can of worms with me and the old poacher and everything." He remembered the young newspaperman; "One other thing. It might pay us for you to get in touch with a young chap called Bob Morgan. He's some sort of cub reporter on The News. He doesn't know why but he thinks I'm sniffing around Sea Fibres because I have an interest in a takeover. Morgan seems to have cultivated an inside track with Portsmouth police. Tell him you're working with me. Ask whether there's anything new, whether they've turned up either of the missing managers, etcetera."

"Will do."

"Oh, and Ben, this reporter kid works for money. A little of it goes a long way with him. I have to sign off now, OK?"

"Right. That's all understood. Over and out."

The turn off on to the A1 for Paris was coming up. He took it then called Brad, who was with the others at an Italian restaurant in

232

downtown Manama but went outside to take the call. He asked no questions as Thomas summarised the situation. "So that's it. There's definitely some kind of an alliance between Kerrigan and Al-Sottar, I was probably just the idiot in the wrong place at the wrong time. Bit like the old poacher fellow, I guess." He'd been keeping an eye on a pair of headlights that had been following him since the turn off, but the car was swinging away into a service area. He waited to see if any other vehicle exited to sit on his tail. Nothing. "They must have been diverting some of the Provo's South American stuff from the UK into Saudi using the boats being freighted in from Sea Fibres. As I see it now my Philipino foreman, Hector, he probably got on to the coke by chance and thought it was mine, stupidly decided to do a little business for himself. The rest we know. Hector may have given them my name when that was 'suggested', if you see what I mean. So at that point I'm 'it'. Connie's just a bonus for them." He switched on his own headlights, gripped the steering wheel in both hands, knuckles showing up white in the last of the daylight.

"Oh my God. They must want you pretty bloody bad."

"Sure they do. It's not just the cocaine op. I reckon Kerrigan thinks I owe him as well. You know how it is. I wouldn't care, but if I hadn't bothered to make a certain phone call the guy would have been dead meat." He was passing the police car. It and the BMW were pulled up on the hard shoulder. "I want this over, Brad, really fast. I can't take any risks, not any more."

Brad interrupted. "What time do you land?"

"Eight forty. I'm on the flight out of Charles de Gaulle."

"We'll see you in the morning, then, OK?" Brad paused. "We're all with you, Captain. Make sure you get some sleep on the plane. We've time to think things through. Maybe we can come up with something."

"No. After David's home safe it's a whole different story. I imagine by that time the old ball will have stopped rolling. For me, that is, but it won't stop you and the team carrying on with the raid if that's what you still want. Ben's dying to join in with you; he could take my place.

"Forget it, Tommy. No you, no way, OK?"

The plane was overflying Saudi, closing in on Bahrain. His sleep had been a thing of ugly, fractured dreams. He raised the window blind. Below was the desert. He wondered about Mubarak Al-Jidha. Would he have found his family - they him? Or would the police have found him first? And he remembered George's 'That was some great old

233

Arab', and smiled in spite of himself. George would have included his usual expletive.

Soon they were out over the Gulf. From here he could see from Saudi across to Bahrain, so small a stretch of sea although it had seemed anything but small that night of not so long ago. He picked up the elegant pencil line of the Causeway, curving all the way across. He could see the exact place where they'd fetched up in the rubber inflatable. As he looked at the central bubble of the border crossing with its twinned restaurant towers and its crowded, two government buildings, something inside him contracted for here it was to be that, so soon, he would surrender his life.

The plane banked and increased the angle of its descent. Half way between the mainland of Saudi and the central border crossing he could see the white of a tide-race, betraying the presence of the bridged-over gap in the hard causeway, in-built there for the benefit of light coastal shipping. A fisherman waved from the deck of his dhow as they came in low over a sea of sparkling indigo, shading up to light buff where the sand banks arose. Thomas thought about Moby Belle and the day out with the boys and Sheila and Ben. He knew David and Paul would never forget it, and when the worst finally did come to the worst, it was that, he decided, of which he would be thinking.

The flight landed right on time. Brad was waiting for him outside customs, grim faced but the quintessential British businessman. They shook hands, saying nothing. Standing outside the terminal Thomas made his call to Captain Mohammad Al-Muttawi. The Saudi policeman seemed as coldly detached as ever. Bored, almost. "Yes, Mister Thornton, I have noted the arrival of your airplane. I believe you are calling me to tell me that you have thought things through and are returning to give yourself up as any so self-less English gentleman should?"

"I'm not interested in playing games, Captain. I'm telling you I shall be in the Bahrain Customs building, on the Causeway, at twenty two hundred tonight. I need the time between now and then to settle my family affairs. I will meet you or your appointed on the Bahrain side. Immediately that happens I'll make a call to Portsmouth in England. Unless my man there tells me he has my son David and that David is safe and well, I shall not be going through into Saudi Arabia."

"Is that so?" Al-Muttawi sounded faintly amused.

"If anything should happen to my son, be very sure about this, Captain, I have put in place arrangements for the same to happen to you and to yours. Is this totally understood?"

234

Al-Muttawi laughed without humour: "You are threatening me? I cannot believe this, you are dangerously unbalanced, Captain, if I may call you by your proper title. Of course I know not about your family and will wish them no harm. Why should I? But it shall be a pleasure to see you. As much of an irritation as you have been to me, for you I have a certain kind of admiration."

Thomas switched off, turned to his friend. "So, my friend; game, set and bloody match, for me at least."

Brad took him by the shoulders. "Come on. Maybe not. We've been burning a lot of midnight oil here. The guys have come up with what I think is quite a promising possibility. But you should hear it from all of us. Let's go. We're meeting up in ISG's new place, a high security office and warehouse in the Docks area. The boys have been great. And Rose, well, she's been bloody marvellous."

They walked out of the airport into the dark night and the burning heat. Thomas felt every part of him awash with sweat.

The silence in the office was funereal. He looked around at the faces: George, Saeed, Rose and Brad. He said, "So. Well, hello, you lot. I'm very, very sorry. How about that for a bloody understatement?." He didn't know what else…

Rose came over to him, stood up on tiptoes to kiss him. "And hello to you, too, skipper," she said, "Welcome back. I've got the coffee going so why don't we all sit down and see exactly where we are?"

Saeed rumbled, "Yes, welcome. Where we are is not important. Where we will be, that is important. This man Al-Sottar shall know how it is to play such games with little children."

Thomas said, "Situation's all too plain. They've got David. I have to go back to Saudi tonight, twenty two hundred. Otherwise they'll kill my son, OK?" He had found it an incredibly difficult thing to say. "Not a lot else to talk about, is there? I just have to settle my affairs, as they say. Try at least to make some final sense out of this whole mess."

"Thomas Thornton, will you please sit down?" Rose spoke quietly, firmly, calmly. "And will you please stop feeling sorry for yourself? It doesn't suit the man. And you lot, you can sit, too. You're neither use nor ornament. Thomas, please tell us exactly what is supposed to happen. There may be nothing to be done but there may be plenty, but you alone will need to be the judge of that."

Thomas sat down.

George said, "The lady said it, boss." He took his place at the table followed by Saeed and Brad as Rose brought the coffee things.

Thomas said, "Well, you know the score. Simple. It's me for my son." He shrugged. "Finito."

Saeed said, "You will have no chances with those Saudi guys on the causeway. So we must make some chances, yes?"

George said, "Hold it a minute, black man. So OK, boss; so you're now in their custody on the Saudi side of the causeway customs. Your boy is safe. What the fuck happens next?"

"Once I'm in police custody and over in Saudi I expect it's going to be short and sweet."

Rose said, "OK, we know all that but the situation is that David's now safe and you yourself will be on the Causeway, Saudi side?"

"Right; as I say, finito."

"So, as Saeed said, how about a swift counter attack at that point? There and then on the causeway?"

"What the hell are you talking about, Rose," he said, wearily. I'm unarmed and surrounded by armed policemen just itching to get it over with there and then. There will probably be at least one vehicle ahead of me and at least another following on behind. I'm on miles of straight highway with the sea on either side. What do you suggest, I do some kind of Schwarzenegger? Take off and fly?"

Rose said, "What I suggest is that we listen to Saeed's idea about a way to hit them and get you away instead of sitting here feeling sorry for ourselves, that's all. You and my boy here are supposed to be trained up to do that sort of thing, and the rest of us aren't exactly helpless."

George nodded. "Too fucking right, we're not."

Saeed spoke quietly, his big ebony face for once unsmiling. "Yes, I think there is one way. In my country, to bring an enemy convoy to a halt, for killing, we would blow a telegraph pole to block the road just behind the lead vehicle. It is easy. ISG has here some remote control tank mines…"

Brad sat forward, grabbed some paper and a pen. "Tommy, don't discard this out of hand. We've been at this all night so let's just think about it some more. I've a gut feel this can be done. High risk but it can be done."

Thomas said, "Hold everything, here. Thanks a lot, but what the hell are you talking about. I'm not taking you guys down with me. No way."

Saeed said quietly, "If it was not for you, Mister Tom, I would already be a dead man I think."

George punched the air. "So we all want to go the extra mile, skipper, OK? And hey, there's the money! Christ, you know us Yankees; don't do no shit for nothing. Do any shit for money! We done it once. We can do it again."

Rose said. "Listen, Thomas. According to our concept you'll be the only one at direct risk. But this is important." She leaned across the table, grabbed his hand. "Did you manage to get hold of Saeed's new passport?"

"Sure. George's as well"

"And it's all visa'd up, as you said?"

"I haven't actually checked it, but knowing where it came from …"

Saeed said, "That is good. So. I shall drive over the causeway ahead of you. On the Saudi side, on top of the hump of the shipping bridge I shall stop my car to attend to a puncture. I plant the bomb in one of those electrical junction boxes. You shall yourself be holding the transmitter trigger. At the right time - "

"Hold it right there," Thomas interrupted. "First thing, Saeed, do you know anything about explosives?"

The black man laughed, slapped his thigh. "Mister Thomas, when I was maybe thirteen, for two years I sleep in no bed unless bombs for pillows, or rockets, or rocket launchers. Russian ones but - "

"OK you made your point. But what the hell do you think you're going to do next, yourself? You know, I've blown the shit out of everything and you're still marooned in Saudi?"

"I shall be carrying out our plan A, boss." He looked to Brad for support.

Brad said, "Saeed's going to be set up to meet with your Sheikh Abdul-Rahman. He's going to try to get himself invited to this beach house, of his."

"And so. If things go bad for you, this man will not live to rejoice." It was Saeed's simple statement of fact.

Thomas sat forward, "You're all crazy. You? You're going to meet Al-Sottar, Saeed?"

Brad said, "Hold it Thomas, let's elaborate a bit. I told you, we've been working most of the night on the possible detail. But before we go any further let's take a look at what we've got in the warehouse, shall we?" The others stayed in the office as the two of them walked downstairs and into the vast space of the warehouse, empty but for two wooden crates in one corner, one of which had apparently been opened. On top of it sat a four or five metre canoe, "Take a look," Brad said. "Our new friends in camouflage have been most obliging.

These are test models. ISG is authorised to quote the Service for building them over here under licence."

Even after the more than ten years since last he'd seen one Thomas knew every detail of the craft that had carried him and a companion into so many training and real-life operations. This one was different, but so what? "So? Some kind of modified Fol-boat?"

"It's called an SFB - Submersible Fol-Boat. You can sit this thing on the bottom, up to thirty feet down, bring it up to surface any time you want. You can even sit in it yourself for up to two hours whilst it's down there. Otherwise it's pretty much the same old canoe, known and loved by all."

In spite of himself Thomas was interested. "Does it work?" he asked, then, "That's a silly bloody question, isn't it."

Brad chuckled. "Work? Does it ever! This one's been on the bottom of the 'oggin with me in it, and I've had it up and down like a bloody yo-yo. You use this electronic gizmo." He pulled something like a miniature TV remote from his pocket. "Water or air pumped electrically in or out, depending if you're going up or down. Submarine style."

"I'm impressed." Thomas couldn't resist running his hand up and down the sleek shape, "But tell me, I'm agog. How does this thing relate to blowing up the bloody Causeway?"

"Right. We'll explain." Brad led the way back upstairs. "Let's get back up to the gang, OK?" In the office he unrolled a sketchmap of the Causeway and the opposing coasts of Bahrain and Saudi Arabia. He had superimposed a circle with the letter B on the Saudi element of the causeway. "That B's the shipping bridge, Thomas. That's where we figure to stop the car you're in. In all the confusion you dive or jump over the parapet into the tide race. How high is it, sixty feet or so?"

Thomas thought for a moment. "I don't know. Maybe about that. But if the tide's running anywhere near peak it's going to be moving me or what's left of me along at five knots or so when I hit."

George broke in. "Shit, you guys are supposed to be up for this kinda Tarzan thing. So let's not talk no more about bodies? We sure Saeed's going to get through to plant the thing? These passports and visas, there's no fucking about with them. They're all computerised at point of origin, right?"

Brad answered that one. "George, the folk who created these documents can hack in and out of any computer system yet known to mankind. In and out like the old fiddler's elbow, anything and everything from your Visa card account to the Presidential think-tank.

238

So don't worry about it. It's all kosher, his letter of invitation, everything, all kosher, OK?'

"Please do not use words like 'kosher' in this place, Mister Brad," Saeed said, as a man of Islam it is an offence to me." He roared with laughter.

George said, "Didn't I tell you, black man? Didn't I say my mother was Jewish?"

Brad continued with his sketch, drawing a dotted line from the Bahrain coast to the bridge. That's George in Folboat SFB1 and I'm right behind, maybe even tied on, in SFB 2. There are a number of built up channel markers leading out from the bridge. They're like mini towers, stand about three metres at high water. There are four of them."

Thomas said, "Yes, that's right. I've noticed them in the past."

"The tide's going to be flowing - that means going north - at its peak - at twenty three hundred tonight." He picked up his marker pen again, marked in the channel towers. "So, while all hell's breaking loose up above, you go with the tide for this, the fourth and last of the mini towers. We'll be waiting there to pick you up, Thomas."

For the first time Thomas smiled. "Yep, just like that, why the hell not? And now you're going to tell me about your tete a tete with my friend Abdul-Rahman?"

Saeed said, "Yes, this is so. I am Saeed Al-Fonsi, for this is the name we agreed for my new passport, yes? I am acting for General Faraq Al-Karoumi, Sudan army, retired, now the big man of North East Africa Sugar Corporation. The General is thinking about establishing a factory in Saudi Arabia for the manufacture of woven plastic sugar bags. Mister Abdul-Rahman's name had been mentioned. Might he perhaps be interested? If so, Mister Saeed Al-Fonsi would wish to come over straight away for a preliminary meeting. He has only this one evening in his schedule." He paused. "Boss, you think he will go for this, he will invite me to this beach house for this?"

Thomas took a moment to think about it, drumming his fingers on the polished table top, the others waiting for his verdict. He took a sip of his coffee, looked up at them, one by one, shook his head."Initially I thought it was crazy. You guys are incredible. But it could work. If he's at home he'll very likely fall for it." He sat back, folded his arms. "So, why don't you call him now, find out, Saeed? I'll give you his office number. He probably won't be there but they'll possibly let you have his mobile."

Saeed got through to the office, asked to speak to Sheikh Abdul-Rahman. The Sheikh was not available. Thomas listened as Saeed briefly explained his mission. Did the manager have a mobile number?

No problem getting connected. The black man rolled out his opening with the others watching his face. Only Thomas had the Arabic. He was impressed by Saeed's ability to make it up as he went along and the responses from the other end seemed positive. Saeed finally stated his thanks and said how much he was looking forward to their meeting. He switched off, brought the side of one great fist crashing down on to the table. "That," he said, "Was hook, line and sinkers as you fishers, you say."

"Hey," Rose said, "Take it easy, Saeed; that's an expensive bit of woodwork you're wrecking."

Saeed nodded. "All good. I have arranged meeting for eight o clock tonight. It is at his beach house."

Thomas said, "You're not supposed to know how to get there, so call him when you get off the causeway, right? Can I suggest you spend at least an hour with Rose on the Net to familiarise yourself with the bare outlines of the African sugar trade? He won't know much about that but he's not stupid. Far from it."

"Mister Thomas, what do you think I was doing when that guy try to hit me for the pay roll in downtown Khobar? I am one of Africa's top experts in the business of sugar!"

"Yeah, it's fucking perfect," George said. "And with you helping the guy drink himself silly in the beach house we've got him cold, right? Only problem is, my friend, you don't fucking drink."

"I shall make an exception on this occasion. Allah, blessings be upon him, will forgive me and most of it will nourish the sand or the house plants, yes?"

"Right, great," George said. "So it's one for the money, two for the dough, three to get ready and go cats go! Plan A, down and dirty."

Out of the silence Rose said, "That's my boys. Why don't we sort out the armament side of things? After that I suggest we get a take away sent in. And then you all really should get some rest. Saeed, you'll be leaving with the big bang thing hidden in your hire car at exactly five o'clock this afternoon. Brad, you and George set sail or whatever you call it at about seven, just after dark. Thomas, you'll leave in a taxi for the Causeway at around nine."

"You'd have made a great general, Rose Feather," Thomas said.

"I just wish you'd let me come with you," she said. "I mean, in one of the boats"

240

George grinned. "No offence but you ever hear of a general in the front line, lady? And you ever hear of one bridge too fucking far?"

"So, gentlemen; your passports." Thomas opened the package he'd been given by the Colonel's courier at Dover. "Just make sure you memorise your new names. Take it from Thomas MacRae, it's not so easy as it sounds. And listen, when we're all done here you'll know what you want to do, where you want to get to. All I would say is, when you arrive there, please destroy these passports. Apply for new ones in your proper names. The originals got stolen, right?"

Both of the passports and all Rose's consultancy documentation seemed in good order. Afterwards, looking around with more confidence than he felt at the tense faces, he said. "OK now, you crazy, crazy bastards. Let's just do it, shall we?" He walked around the table, shaking hands with each of them one by one. Wound up as tight as a violin string, his mobile sounded. The Colonel came straight to the point. The collection would take place at eight pm: precisely twenty hundred hours tonight, United Kingdom time. At that time he, Colonel Grenville, would confirm to Thomas that David was present at the handover point. There would be a codeword known only to the abductors. The Saudi policeman must take over the call and use it to confirm Thomas' recapture. Only then could the handover take place.

Thomas didn't want to talk on the phone about the new plan. He said, "Thanks, Colonel. Please, I know you won't talk to any of your official friends about this. We cannot risk the possibility of things going haywire. Besides that, it may probably sound incongruous in all the circs but I've given the Saudis my word I'll go with them into their country. I'll take whatever comes once David is safe and sound and I'm on the Saudi side of that causeway."

"Isn't that taking one's honour a word too far?"

"Perhaps. But after I'm in their country all bets will be off, right? Goodbye now." Grenville started to say something but he ended the call, looked around. "Brad, George, Saeed, Rose, I've often said it. Life is ten percent the plan and ninety percent your reaction to what happens when the plan doesn't quite work out. If you knew anything about military history you'd agree with that. Am I right, Mister Saeed?

"Sure you are, boss."

"Then let's just go for it."

ISG having an arms import licence and the premises incorporating a high security lockup, the company now possessed some impressive trade samples of modern weaponry. In addition to the anti-tank limpet bombs the locker held SLR's, M16 machine guns, M79D rocket

241

launchers and a wide selection of handguns including the new SIG's and even Thomas' old favourite, the Browning 9mm high power. Brad acted as their armourer whilst Rose ordered tubs of Kentucky Fried Chicken, fries, cups of Cola. The five of them ate and drank whilst talking through the final details of the pick up, the beach assault, the re-occupation of *Jazeera*.

Saeed then called the boatyard, explained he'd been talking to his friend Sheikh Abdul-Rahman Al-Sottar about some business issues. The boat called *Jazeera* had been mentioned. Was she on her moorings, should he wish to take a look?

Yes, the man told him, the boat was there. The Prince had not yet returned from his holidays abroad.

Thomas looked from the office window over the filthy, sun-drenched water of the docks, out over the sea in the direction of Sheikh Abdul-Rahman Al-Sottar's house, or mansion, or palace. It would be facing this way above its carefully tended beach. Connie might be there even now. Tonight, in that house, the Sheikh would receive his business guest whilst awaiting the news of Thomas Thornton's finality.

Chapter Seventeen

He checked his watch: 21.40 hours. Still well over thirty degrees. His taxi's air conditioning system was not fully operational. Perspiration pricked out of his forehead, ran through the stubble-field of his lower face. The radio delivered a bleating shuffle of Arabic music, the staccato rise and fall at one with the desert, visible now only in the arc of headlights.

The traffic coming from Saudi Arabia into Bahrain on the other carriageway was as heavy as it always was on a Wednesday evening but on this side the road was quite clear. As the driver slowed for the causeway toll booth Thomas' mobile sounded. He snatched it up: Ben. Thomas used his forearm to wipe away the sweat. "Hi."

"Bad time probably, but quickly," Ben said. Thomas recognised the background sounds of a car, the quick hiccup of a gear change. "I think we might have sussed out where they could be holding him. David. I was talking to my guy, the one I've left to operate my boat? I'd told him to keep an eye and ear open for anything unusual at Sea Fibres'. Anyway he was out early this morning seining for sand-eels. They've been fitting out a couple of Navy vessels. There were lights on one of them. There shouldn't have been. The yard's workforce is out on strike." Thomas realised Ben was waiting for his response. "You still there, boss?"

"Yes. Can't say too much." He was thinking quickly. "Exchange now re-scheduled for twenty hundred UK. What's your plan?"

"I dropped Sheila and Paul at the Colonel's. I'm tooled up and driving south through Pompey right now."

"Good. Just watch and wait. For God's sake do not go in on that boat. Do nothing until you are absolutely certain David's with the Colonel and in the clear. Even after that, stay out of trouble. I have enough of it for all of us, right." He tried a laugh. It didn't sound genuine, even to himself. "We all need a little luck at this point, my friend. Keep in touch. But I'm going to be off line in around a half hour. So, soon as you have anything …"

"Boss?"

"Yes, Ben? I have to keep this line clear."

"The other thing is, Bob Morgan found out the cops have the driver of the truck that killed Major Patterson. His body came up tangled in a string of crab-pots off Portland Bill. Bob says the guy was a known face in Ireland. And your name was mentioned, by the cops I mean. I was able to check everything out with some of my fishing mates. It's kosher. Matey was well holed. He was wearing the concrete boots."

Outside the Customs building Thomas paid off the taxi. Inside, Captain Mohammed Al-Muttawi was already in position, immaculate as ever in his snow-white robes. Nobody with him; proof positive that the Bahrainis would not permit foreign operations on their territory, not even Saudi police operations, perhaps especially Saudi police operations. No doubt the real welcoming committee would be waiting on the other side. Al-Muttawi got up from his seat, smiling that smile without warmth. Thomas stood in silence, mobile in hand, waiting for it to ring. It rang at two minutes past the hour of ten. It had been a very long one hundred and twenty seconds. Colonel Grenville's greeting sounded tired. The background sounds set Thomas' heart to a renewed pounding for a boy was crying. The Colonel said, quietly, "We have him, Thomas, and he's fine. I'm sitting in MacDonalds. David just this minute walked in with this fellow. The man says he stays here until you're confirmed as being on Saudi territory. Cannot argue if you know what I mean."

Thomas said, "That's clear enough. Stay on the line, please, Colonel, we're going to exit Bahrain now." He got to his feet, for the first time looking directly at Al-Muttawi lowered the hand with the phone, shrugged. "OK, come on then, let's get it over with."

The policeman's smile had warped. "No, Captain, it is I who will issue instructions. You will come." Thomas followed him to an anonymous, unbadged car, got into the passenger seat. Al-Muttawi got behind the wheel, from the glove box took out and held up a dark red passport, the gold embossed British Royal coat of arms shining clear. "You see? You are now Mister Thornton once again. I must have this other of your passports."

Thomas said, "My name is Thornton. You have my only passport. It's right there in your hand."

Al-Muttawi nodded. "I do not believe you," he said. "No matter." He started the car, drove up to the Bahrain Emigration window, handed over the documentation for them both. Their passports were duly stamped and they were out of Bahrain and back into the Kingdom of Saudi Arabia. Somewhere deep down in the pit of his stomach Thomas felt the old familiar sickness, but he could also feel the comfort of the bomb activator, taped high up inside his groin.

Three Al-Khobar police cars were awaiting them, blue lights revolving slowly. One of them took up station ahead and the other two fell in behind as they were waved through the Saudi side of Customs. Once out on the Saudi Causeway proper Thomas spoke quietly into the live mobile, "Are you still there, Colonel?"

"Yes, Thomas, we're all still here."

"I am now in Saudi Arabia. I am going to put an officer of the Al-Khobar police on the line. He will give your visitor confirmation. Is that understood? The policeman's name is Mohammed Al-Muttawi."

"Yes, that is understood." The hesitation. "Thomas?"

"Yes, Colonel?"

The hesitation again. "Good luck, my boy, that's all I wanted to say. May God be with you."

Al-Muttawi pulled in on to the shoulder of the carriageway, signalled for Thomas to get out of the car.

"This is for you, Captain." He handed over the mobile. Two of the uniformed policemen had come forward from the cars behind. The Captain took out a set of hand-cuffs and motioned for him to hold out his wrists then snapped the cuffs in place, put the key into his pocket. He looked quizzically at Thomas, then at the mobile, shrugged, uttered into it a single word then tossed it over the Armco and down into the night. Thomas heard it clattering on rocks before the faintest of splashes. There was the warm slough and slap of wave on rock, the growl of the traffic on the other carriageway, crackling voices from the police car radios as he was searched for weapons, pushed down into the back of the car. One of the uniforms got in behind the wheel. The other policeman positioned himself in the passenger seat.

Al-Muttawi sat with his prisoner on the back seat, talking now in Arabic on his own mobile. He said, "Yes ... yes, all is OK.... I shall call you later ... No, at Al-Mahli." He clicked off and turned to Thomas. "So, now that this business, now it is all settled I thought we might begin with our little talk." The smile had once more disappeared. Only the cruelty remained behind the man's good looks.

245

"You are some kind of shit, Muttawi." Deliberately and for the first time he spoke in Arabic. "When hell freezes over will I have 'a little talk' with you." In front of him the policeman's shoulders stirred uncomfortably. The lights of the Causeway curved ahead, reaching out to the distant glitter of Al-Khobar, a quadruple orange string of them glittering out of the blackness, closing together with the perspective of distance, rising gracefully ahead over the hump of the shipping bridge.

Al-Muttawi said, "As you wish, Mister Thornton. Oh, but I think there has been, regrettably, a problem. So you do have the language. How interesting. It will not help you. It seems you have a father who is known here in high places. This will not help you, either. Such a shame. You wish to know about this that is to happen?"

"No thank you," he said, and all too soon their little, fast moving convoy was climbing the hump. Thomas took a deep breath, reached down to his crotch, double pressed the rocker switch, waited until they were passing the electrical box then touched the activate button. The timing was perfect. They were close to the apex of the bridge when it happened. Even though he'd braced himself for it, the explosion came with blinding, terrifying suddenness, then the fireball amidst a wild sparking of shattered electrics. An adjacent lamp standard crashed down across all three lanes, just missing the leading police car which by then had slewed sideways. Pieces of metal impacted their own vehicle and yet more rained down as their driver braked heavily, bucking and riding the debris. He heard and felt the punctures and then the impact when one of the following cars was unable to slow in time. There was a symphony of screeching tyres and the crashes and bangs of cars on the other, more crowded, Bahrain-bound side of the carriageway. The place was now in darkness, a shambles, and even while the car was still in motion he had opened the door with his manacled hands, had grabbed a dazed, terrified Al-Muttawi by the front of his thobe, piled out with him on to the road, dragged him to his feet, frog-marched him up to the Armco.

There had been times in his previous life when he had known the contents of a few seconds stretch into this kind of a comfortable, slow motion infinity. With his manacled arms tight around Al-Muttawi he could feel the superiority of his strength, could feel the futility of the man's struggles, fancied in the near darkness that he could see close up the horror in the man's eyes as he was bent backwards over the rail. He even thought he could feel the warmth of the policeman's urine just after they toppled in that unholy embrace past the point of balance, began their twisting, turning, accelerating down-rush.

Al-Muttawi began to scream as soon as he had sensed Thomas' intent. The scream continued right up to the hit. It had seemed a lot further than a thirty metre drop, but in mid-air he had managed to manipulate himself so as to have Al-Muttawi's back impact first, had pulled in tight so as to minimise on himself the shock of their entry. Even so the blow was tremendous. For a split second he wondered whether he'd mis-judged it, whether they'd hit on rock rather than water, but then they were down deep into a black, sub-sea roaring and the man in his arms had gained enormously in strength, had stopped his mad writhing, had locked his body solid. He was clinging on to his escaping captive in the way that a man who knows he is going to die will use up everything that he has and all that he is in his single obsession not to go alone to wherever he now will have to go.

Without the years of his training Thomas would not have been able to think with logic, would not have been able to lift his knee as hard as that into the man's groin, whack his own forehead into the man's face with so much levered, underwater force.

He lifted his arms back over the new slackness of the man's head, keeping hold of him with one hand whilst feeling with the other over the pockets of his thobe, searching for the handcuff keys. His eardrums seemed close to bursting. He could actually feel the bunch of keys but could not find his way into the pocket and had finally to give up, thrust away the policeman, kick for the surface. His chest was at that explosive point where he knew he would need to release his breath, breathe in, even though he know also that, were he to do so, it would be salt water and death that would enter his lungs. And at that precise point his head broke surface.

He was able to think only about sucking in those first, huge, hugely precious lungfuls of air, but soon realised how far and with what speed the tidal flow, concentrated through the narrow opening, had already carried him away from the Causeway. Floating on his back, he recalled that it would be another hour before the tide began to slacken, two hours before it would stop, then reverse. He turned over, blinked the ultra-salt seawater from his eyes. He was passing by the first of the channel markers. Its red light was brighter than he'd supposed. The fourth one seemed a long way away. He turned over on to his back again, his manacled hands side by side on his stomach, started to frog-kick towards his rendevouz, being carried rapidly along by the tide. Already the lights on the more distant causeway seemed to be coming on again. Some kind of emergency supply, he guessed. He could just make out the figures of people gesturing wildly, rushing about amongst the oddly angled beams of static headlights.

It would be some time before the confusion had sorted itself out to the point where any cohesive action would be taken. Had anyone of them seen him taking Al-Muttawi over? The bomb? They probably would not immediately suspect an electronically triggered bomb. An electrical fault would more likely be their first assumption, at least until it dawned on them that a police officer and a prisoner were not included in the carnage. Police cars from the causeway island would probably be first to arrive on the scene and then, when they'd worked out what might have happened to Al-Muttawi and his prisoner, helicopters and breakdown vans would come from the mainland and finally all available Coast Guard boats would arrive. The boats would follow the channelled tide path, sweeping the surface with their spot-lights, looking for the bodies, knowing they were most probably wasting their time owing to the height of the fall, the depth and strength of the waterway.

The more important business would be going on up there on the Causeway, he surmised, as they tried to unravel the chaos and pin-point its cause. They'd have had much experience of brutal, high speed, multi-car crashes, for that was the order of most of their days on the highways of the Kingdom.

Saeed! Saeed would have loved it all, he thought, if only he could have seen the results of his handiwork. He kicked on steadily, passing the second and then the third channel marker tower. He knew that his pace through the water hadn't changed, but he could tell he was slowing over the ground as the tide-force slackened and spread itself out from the shipping channel. Stirred up by a gentle night-wind the water had developed a roll and chop. Now and then a wavelet would break over his face, its ultra-saltiness stinging his eyes. He imagined Al-Muttawi's body following him, loose-tumbling down there along the bottom of the channel, death mask face wide-eyed, the first of the sea's flesh-disposal experts already alerted by the scent in the water, crawling off already in unhurried pursuit ... No hurry when the tides would bring it back ...

The causeway was the better part of a kilometre behind him when he sensed a vibration in the water and there was some kind of light-effect and he turned his head, horrified by the on-rushing bows of a large boat. His dive came almost too late. As he kicked down he felt the thrust from the boat's bow-wave pushing against his legs, heard the churning cavitation of the propeller increasing and then mercifully

248

diminishing as the Coast Guard patrol boat carried on towards the bridge. He had changed direction whilst still under-water, now stopped swimming as his head broke the surface. The boat was already fifty metres away and moving at high speed against the tide. The beam of her spotlight swept from side to side as he watched her receding stern. How the hell hadn't they seen him? he wondered. 'Probably not watching properly. Probably'd concluded they were on a fool's errand.

He paddled around in a circle, looking for any other boats. He could see only one but it was a good way away, coming out from Al-Khobar. He was getting close to the fourth channel marker now. In spite of being hand-cuffed the swim in this super-buoyant water hadn't taken too much out of him. He thought of all the training, all the long distance swimming, some of it fully clothed in the cold, cold waters of Poole harbour and the West Highlands sea lochs. He'd discarded his trainers and trousers, was now naked except for the T shirt that he couldn't hope to get past the cuffs and that wouldn't be impeding his progress anyway.

He felt the hand on his back before Brad's goggled face broke water beside him in the bright light of the channel marker. The shock effect of the contact had been almost as enormous as Thomas' sense of relief.

"Dr Livingstone, I presume? Back stroke, yet! So much more relaxing, don't you think?"

Thomas raised his shackled wrists above the surface, treading water. "Hobson's choice, old son." Wondering why he was whispering, he said, "You shouldn't do that; Not good for an old man's heart. But it's great to see you. All OK? George?"

"Everything's fine. It looked like the fourth of July up there. Bloody impressive. George is up top on the marker tower keeping a look out. There are built-in steps and a parapet. We spotted you after that boat bloody nearly ran you down. Buggers must have been half asleep."

The two of them swam together until they were able to stand on the underwater plinth from which arose the mini-tower, its parapet three metres above the sea, the red light positioned above it on a steel pole. "The charts were dead on for once," Brad said. "This tower's built into a bank of the channel that's only a couple of metres underwater at low. You can manage the steps?"

"Sure. No problem," he said. The cuffs chafed away at his wrists as he climbed. A wet-suited George Schwartz helped him over the parapet, muttering, "Thank Christ for that. Get yourself hunkered down here, skipper. Some bastard with glasses on the Causeway could maybe see you in this frigging light. Like some fucking cat-house right?" He laughed softly, sat down beside Thomas, both their backs against the concrete. He'd seen the hand-cuffs. "Shit! How the hell we going to get those things off of you?"

Brad had joined them now. Thomas said, "With some difficulty I should imagine. Well now, isn't this cosy? I guess the invention worked, then, because I see no ships, I mean there's no Folboats floating around?"

"Oh ye of limited faith," Brad said, "Of course they worked. They're lying down there in about ten feet of water, good as gold and nice as pie, all the kit wrapped and vacuum-packed including your wet suit old son. God only knows how you're planning to get it on over those bracelets. I sure as hell don't."

"Neither do I right now," he said, "I hadn't thought about them needing to handcuff me, not with half the Khobar police force being in escort. Should have known. Anyway the keys are in the pocket of a dead man somewhere down in Davey Jones's place. First things first though. We're going nowhere in a hurry, not just yet anyway." He saw the approaching red and green navigation lights, the sweep of a helicopter's spotlight across the surface of the sea. "Get in tight on me under the lantern and keep quite still, faces down and hands tucked away. Your wet suits won't show up much. They're quite high up and they're not likely to make us out under the light even if they do decide to come by here. I shouldn't think they're looking for bodies that can climb steps anyway."

George said, "Jesus, I've said this before and I'll say it again, You guys don't fuck about a hell of a lot."

"Have you heard what happened in Portsmouth, Brad?" Thomas asked. "Last thing I heard the handover was happening but they chucked my mobile in the drink before I could confirm."

"Nice of them. Yes, your lad's safe and well according to the Colonel."

"Thank God. Brad, will you give me your mobile. I'd better call HQ - I mean call the Colonel."

The voice was uncharacteristically strained. "Robert Grenville. Brad, how goes it?"

"No it's me, Thomas, Colonel."

"Well ... a voice from the beyond! Good God, I might have guessed. So what on earth has been happening out there ?"

"Actually quite a lot. More later but I have to keep this short. They probably think I'm dead and gone but the authorities might just

250

possibly be keeping a watch on the mobile servers. I'm in Saudi waters - literally, but don't ask. I've joined up with Brad and George. I left a fair amount of mayhem behind me. Just wanted you to know and to find out how David is and how Ben's getting on."

"Ben's back with Sheila at her place. Your lads are upstairs there and fast asleep, so I'm told."

The helicopter was circling, slowly creeping back. "We have to go now, but I think it may be time to call in the police. I don't want my sons or any of you to become pawns in the game with these people. Right now they're probably thinking all bets are off."

"Thomas, you intend to come back? Back to the UK?"

"No, not yet. I still have stuff to do. Have to go, 'bye."

The chopper clattered by overhead. In the new silence the tide made little rustling and sucking sounds as it parted around the concrete obstruction of the channel marker tower. Somewhere not too far away a disturbed seabird called its shrill alarm into the night. Others answered, near and far.

"I think I picked up what the old man told you, Thomas. It seems pretty obvious he's right." Brad said. "We have to get you back to base in Bahrain, find ways to get those irons off you. We need to tell Saeed to go to ground for a day or two and try again."

"Not necessarily," Thomas said. "We could carry on with the plan, take advantage of all the confusion, the police being tied up and all. Think about it. We have Saeed in position and we're most of the way there anyway. Once we hit Al-Sottar's place we're sure to be able to turn up something to get these things off me. If all else fails we could send Saeed out for a pair of bolt croppers." Another thought occurred to him. "But, hell, there's nothing to stop us reversing the order. There are all kinds of tools on *Jazeera*. We could go there first, stow the canoe, hole up for the day and hit the beach house tomorrow night instead of right now. What do you think?"

"What about Saeed?" Brad asked, "He'll be at the beach house, won't he, all being well? He was supposed to have only the one free day in his schedule, wasn't he?"

"Money changes business schedules. I could call him, indicate the change, suggest he gets a hotel room for the night. I could be playing the General, you know, Saeed's boss, and I'll be speaking in Arabic in case he has company."

Brad looked doubtful but George said, "Yeah, sounds good. Me, I'd go along with that. Be like going home, on our old *Jazeera*.

Thursday night instead of Wednesday ain't going to make a whole shit-load of difference, is it?"

Thomas said, "No, that it isn't. Are we agreed then? Brad? "

Brad sighed. "How the hell did I get myself mixed up with you two bastards? Yes, agreed. Let's just bloody do it." He took back his mobile, dialled Rose in Bahrain. "Sweet lady," he whispered, "The eagles have all landed but there's this one slight change of plan, all right?"

Thomas turned to George as Brad briefly headlined the new concept. "You sure you're still OK with all of this, shipmate?"

"Sure I'm sure. What the hell else can a fella do for his kicks?"

"That's my man," Thomas said. "Christ, I can't wait to get this steel off my wrists."

"Should be getting fucking used to it, skip. The bracelets. Come on, here's a guy bringing up a coupla boats for us."

Brad had signed off, slipped back into the water to locate the tiny floats from which were suspended the wires and tubes down to the canoe's rise and fall system. Thomas could make out the dark shapes of the SFB's, surfacing like twin walruses coming up to breathe. There was hardly a ripple and just the faintest of whirrings as the pumps drove out the last of the water, replacing it with air.

They'd calculated a distance of nine sea miles from the mini-tower to Al-Sottar Marine. He sat in with George in the lead canoe, Brad tied on behind, all three of them paddling. He squeezed his legs into the bottom half of the wet suit that they'd brought for him but until he could get rid of the hand-cuffs the top half was of no use other than as a cushion. He checked his watch. An hour after midnight.

They stopped paddling at about a mile out from the Al-Khobar sea front while Thomas looked through binoculars at the cluster of beach houses, Al-Sottar's place easily identifiable. There seemed to be a number of people out on the patio but he could make out no detail at this range. Removing Brad's mobile once again from its plastic wrapper, he pressed in Saeed's number. Saeed had wiped the address book from his instrument so that nothing of any incoming call would be shown on its screen.

As soon as the connection was made Thomas spoke slowly, his voice deepned, and in Arabic. "Saeed, good evening. This is the General. You are well?"

Saeed picked it up straight away. "Very well, General, Mister Abdul-Rahman is treating me with great kindness. I have also met with more friends here." Thomas thought he could hear a trace of alcohol in his voice. There was a pause, then, "Mr Abdul-Rahman would like to say hello to you, General. May I pass you over?"

"Please do, but first, note that we are holding everything for tonight. We shall be at, you know, the Hotel Jazeera? Our business where you are is delayed by twenty four hours exactly, that is understood?"

"Yes, I understand, sir. I shall find a hotel room here, I think?"

"Yes, please do so. Get some rest. We will proceed tomorrow, as I have said."

"No problem. I shall be there. Here is Sheikh Abdul-Rahman Al-Sottar."

Thomas felt his fist tighten around the mobile telephone as Abdul-Rahman said, "Good evening General. Good to speak with you. You are in Bahrain, I think?" The voice was slurred.

With care he said, "Good evening to you, too, Sheikh Abdul-Rahman. May I offer my thanks for looking after my man?"

"It is a pleasure, General. Mister Saeed tells me you have asked him to find a hotel? There is no need and it is late. He is welcome to stay here."

Thomas said, "Well, that is very kind. I shall of course be happy to leave it to him to make his own arrangements with you. You have some interest in our proposition?"

"Of course. As a matter of fact I think our people could have a significant input. We have contacts here and also in Europe who could have a use for the proposed material. Their product is not sugar and so, General, they are not competitors!" He laughed. "However I understand that their product, too, requires high grade woven plastic sacking. What is in use now is sometimes less than satisfactory, as I am led to believe." He paused, then, "You are not yourself Sudanese, I think?"

Thomas tried to imitate Saeed's rumble of a laugh, switched to English, "Well, yes, I have to confess that my accent is the product of an American upbringing."

"I'm sorry, I should not have expressed my curiosity. That was most rude of me. I shall make it up to you tomorrow General."

"This sounds very good. I shall look forward to our meeting. Saeed will make all arrangements. Good night, Mr Abdul-Rahman." He switched off.

There were no visible lights in the Marina, not even in the guard-room gatehouse, only the red navigation light at the end of the harbour wall as the two SFB's slid on in complete silence through the black stillness of the water and into the marina proper. They proceeded now with extreme caution so as to avoid contact with buoys or other obstructions, finally drifted gently, still in line astern, into the space between the pontoon walkway and the flare of Jazeera's bows. They clambered carefully and quietly on to the pontoon, stretching themselves to relieve cramped muscles, barely able to make each other out in the darkness.

Brad stayed with the boat whilst he and George padded in silence up the walkway, avoiding the well remembered mooring lines. The reserve set of keys was still there in its hiding place. They let themselves into the office, taking care to key off the alarm, switched on their torches at least intensity and made their way through into the rear of the chandlery. George picked out a pair of long-handled bolt croppers. Thomas knelt down, his forearms and wrists steadied on the floor whilst George positioned the pincers and snipped the manacles from each wrist. He stood up, rubbing life back into the welts.

The set of keys labelled *Jazeera* were where they should have been, where he'd left them. They let themselves out, locking the office door behind them, walked back down the pontoon, stopping on the way to lower the broken handcuffs into the water and let them go.

Having removed from the SFB's such of the vacuum packed items as they needed, Brad closed up their mud coloured decking with the special waterproof Velcro then operated the system. They sank the four metres down to the bottom in total silence. Brad made sure the floats were tucked securely away from sign under the pontoon. "That's wonderful," Thomas said, shaking his head in admiration in the darkness.

Inside *Jazeera* it was as if they had not been away. For Brad's sake Thomas ran through their adopted occupation procedures as they sat together in the main stateroom, torches turned down to the merest glimmering. They opened up one of Rose's food parcels.

Glad of the few hours of rest he had managed before setting off from Bahrain, Thomas gave himself the first watch, sitting in the captain's chair throughout the remaining hours of darkness. There was no threatening activity. Soon after the usual marvel of an Arabian sun-blast dawn he could see that the yard had resumed normal activities.

254

At seven hundred hours a bleary-eyed Brad arrived to relieve him of the watch. By that time a few of the boatyard workers were in evidence, the spring of the upcoming weekend in their demeanor.

All the new, unsold Sea Fibres yachts glittered white and bright in the early light. For boats read losses. At least he could now understand the reason for the owner's unbridled profligacy. He thought of his friend Kit Patterson at Sea Fibres, of the good times they had spent together, would never again spend together. And that one last time, at Cheltenham, when they'd both had just that bit too much to drink. What was it he'd said to Sea Fibres' managing director? "So here's your new order, Kit. I only wish we could sell the buggers as easily as Abdul-Rahman likes me to order them. Oh well, guess it's his money. And now it's yours. Cheers."

Chapter Eighteen

They were only a hundred metres or so out from the beach but the canoes would not be visible to the group on the patio. Floating, static, on the calm blackness of the sea in the darkness of the moonless night. Arabic music. Neither George nor Brad had said anything for some time, not since they'd seen what was going on, not since George had made his strangled exclamation and Brad had told him, softly, please to shut up, told him who the woman was.

Thomas sat still, the binoculars up to his eyes. He lowered them and blinked until his vision had cleared, raised them again. Connie was barefooted and bare-chested, dancing for the three of them: for Abdul-Rahman in shorts and T shirt and baseball cap; for a silver haired man similarly dressed who he had recognised at once as being Michael Kerrigan and for someone who had to be Saeed, in thobe and gutra with his back to the sea.

Connie danced well, even if sometimes seeming a little off-balance. She placed her feet in deliberate half time with the fast phrasing of the Eastern music, rolling her hips and shoulders into ever changing positions. Much be-ringed fingers, hands and gold encircled wrists and forearms traced arabesques in the air. All the black hair shifted, gleaming under the strong lights, swinging like a curtain across the sluggish fullness of her breasts. Had he really ever known this woman? Had he ever really known any woman? But she seemed even now so young, so very vulnerable. Thomas remembered how he had loved just to be with her, remembered how totally and how often he had physically wanted her and how thoughts of this woman had so dominated his thinking since incarceration.

Abdul-Rahman took a pull on the last of his cigarette, momentarily lighting up his face. He flicked the thing away in a tiny red parabola from hand to beach, then turned back, full on to the dancer.

Thomas pressed in Saeed's number, saw the big man in Arab dress on the patio lift his mobile. "I'm coming in now, Saeed. This was a wrong number." Saeed shrugged his shoulders as if in disgust.

He switched off then passed the phone forward to Brad, handing him the glasses at the same time. He offered Brad his handshake, turned around, nodded and saluted George, sitting alongside in SFB2. Rolling himself carefully out over the well rounded gunwhale, he slipped noiselessly into the water, and the all-enfolding sea seemed to have and to hold him as its friend.

At first they didn't see him coming, walking up the beach with his bare toes sinking into warm sand, the upper half of his wet suit unzipped, holding the silenced Browning down by his side and, in his other hand, a diving knife. Abdul-Rahman was the first to notice. His eyes opened wide, the having-a-good-time look freezing on his face. Kerrigan must have seen the change of Abdul-Rahman's expression for he turned slowly, still holding his glass, but in this face there was no surprise. "Well, good evening." He spoke with an unnecessary loudness. "It is Mister Thomas MacRae, so it is now." He was slurring his words, but not too much. "Sure didn't I tell them? Didn't I tell them you can't keep a good man down? Not even down in the bloody ocean." He laughed his brittle, semi-psychotic laugh. The music had finished. Connie stood there, swaying on her feet, blank-faced, seeming not properly to recognise him, nor to understand what was happening. Five metres away from the flood-lit tableaux Thomas stopped, his left elbow aching as if in remembrance. "Kerrigan," he said, "Why couldn't you leave me in peace here? Why?" He switched into Arabic, "What I must do now I do for me first and then for you, for you have done enough, and then for all of those whose lives have been poisoned by your presence on the face of bloody earth, including the man here who listens to me speaking in his tongue with so much surprise." Back into English. "Make your own peace with your own God if you have one, Kerrigan." The little speech he had so often mentally rehearsed had sounded contrived, totally inadequate. Abdul-Rahman made to get up. Thomas said, "And you will keep very still. Your friend knows you should be very still." He made a small motion with the Browning held alongside his rubber-clad thigh.

Kerrigan's expression had even now not changed. "Look, Thornton," he said, "Or MacRae or whatever, it don't matter. Tommy: Yes Tommy. Listen, Tommy, we've both done with all those military games, so we have. It's just fucking history. You and me, we're yesterday's men, you see that? We were good for the shit and the

258

blood but we're out of time now. Sure, we have to make the buggers pay, and why not?"

Abdul-Rahman said, with ultimate reasonableness, "Why don't you put down the gun, Thomas. I'd like you to meet my friend Saeed, here."

Kerrigan said, more softly, ignoring the Saudi, "You have a problem with getting rich, Tommy?"

"Oh I have a bigger problem than that," Thomas said, "Much, much bigger; I fall over it every time I see a kid with his hand out sitting in a shop doorway trying to keep out of the bloody rain: Every time I hear of some old lady knocked down by that crazy who needs to get a hold of her pension for some more of your trade-goods. Haven't you worked it out yet? You know, Kerrigan, I could understand it, I might even have been able to accept it when you worked for your so-called 'cause'. Not any more, not when your cause is just yourself and these other animals eating out the heart of every decent society on planet earth, this one in Saudi Arabia included. Not when you find it necessary and natural to snuff the life out of an old man with a sackful of fish."

"Well I have to tell you that was... hell, that was unfortunate; I was very sorry about it."

Connie had finally worked it out. She whispered, "Thomaso? Oh shit, Thomaso, he say to me you are dead." She began to cry and made to move forward and Kerrigan was surprisingly agile for an older man. A split second after she had come between them he overturned the table, bowling her over. She screamed out as the Irishman hurled his glass at Thomas then hurtled across the patio behind it. Saeed rose from his chair but Al-Sottar stayed sitting, very still, with the table gone from before him. Thomas moved his knife hand to meet Kerrigan's onrush, felt how easily the blade made its way into the man's stomach and then up to twist and then back out. See now how shining red the hand that held the knife. Kerrigan had sunk to his knees, clutching at his wound, the life blood swelling out from between his fingers. He seemed only slightly surprised as he toppled forward, face down, his final breath a shuddered puff of fine light sand. Connie moaned once, her hands up to cover her eyes, her elbows pushing in, squeezing her breasts together. Thomas felt nothing, nothing but the rush of a savage joy.

Al-Sottar said, stupidly, "Why you do that for?" He was looking from Saeed to Thomas to the fallen Kerrigan and back again to Thomas. "Allah! You have shit-big trouble now. Oh, big, big trouble."

259

He switched to Arabic. "Five years and you know my language and do not tell me you know? What for, you do not tell me? You were nothing; dead, it would be better for you now to be already dead."

Thomas said, "Speak in English, Al-Sottar, and from here on in you speak only when I want you to speak, is that understood? And when I talk to you, you will answer me." He said, "Just for starters, why don't you take off your clothes."

"What? What the fuck you say?" It was English.

Thomas stepped up on to the marble floor of the patio and turned to the pitch-black sea, raised his arm. "It's cabaret time, Mister. And I said take your clothes off. My wife thinks it time to see you dance, don't you Consuela?" He flicked the barrel of his gun casually across Al-Sottar's face.

The Saudi Arabian put his hand up to his cheek in the place where the blood was beginning.

"Make a good job of this dancing, my 'friend'," Thomas said, "And maybe, just maybe we'll let you keep your balls. Is that OK?" He reached out and removed the Arab's baseball cap, tossed it away. "Easy, isn't it? Connie'll tell you. Come on now; make with the sandals and the T shirt, big man."

Abdul-Rahman shook his head. Droplets of sweat arced outwards in the floodlights. "No," he said. "This is not something I can do. You may kill me as you have killed the Irishman but I shall not do it." Weakly, he tried to smile, switched back into Arabic, "So what now, Mister Thomas?"

"What now?" Thomas placed the tip of the bloody knife at Al-Sottar's throat. The man closed his eyes. Connie moaned again. He turned the blade, edge outwards, cut slow and straight down through Al-Sottar's T shirt and through the waist band of his shorts. It all now gaped open to expose the pale fat and dark hair of the man's chest and under-belly. In one place appeared a thin red line. He spoke to Saeed without taking his eyes from Al-Sottar. "It's quite difficult to do anything when you have to concentrate on keeping your trousers up. How many more are there in the house?"

Saeed looked shaken. "I know this," he said. "There are just two, Mister Tom; two Philipino servants. It's OK, I just cut the phone lines." He picked a mobile off the floor. "This is his," he indicated Al-Sottar. "What you want me to do with it?"

Abdul-Rahman had his share of courage. The Saudi spoke now in Arabic, low-voiced and with great venom. "This is not good, Saeed, if that is your name. You are with him? A man who comes and eats at

260

my table, and is with my enemy, he is the most unmentionable excrement of a dog. Do you still not know who I am? How did you ever think you get the hell out of here?"

Thomas said, "Saeed, Saeedi, say nothing and pay him no attention unless he moves from that chair. Keep his phone with you for the time being. Keep it switched on. Mister Al-Sottar is taking a piss, if anyone calls. He is temporarily unavailable. If he makes a move you can make that 'permanently', and if you do happen to kill him the heart of this world will beat the more strongly." He remembered what Mubarak Al-Jidha had said. "Joey? Joey is here somewhere?"

"Yes, sir." Joey had emerged from inside the house, slightly built and of an age difficult to tell, as with most Philipinos. He was clearly very frightened but doing his best to maintain a smile. "Yes, the old man, Mubarak. He has told me. I was waiting for you, sir. My friend Vitorio is also here, and he too is OK, sir." He was having trouble taking his eyes away from Kerrigan's body. "Sir, the old man would like me to inform him when you are here, with your permission?"

"Yes, Joey, I would like that him to know I am here again."

"Already I have told him, sir, on my mobile."

Thomas smiled. "Yes. Of course you would have, wouldn't you? We forgot to check for any other mobiles, didn't we, Saeed? Let Saeed keep your mobile telephone for a while, OK?

"Yes, sir, that will be no problem." He took out his mobile and handed it over to Saeed,

"What about my friend Mubarak? He is well?"

"Yes, sir, he will come."

Abdul-Rahman was trying to hold together his divided T-shirt. "Who is this old man of yours. Who the fuck is it?"

Thomas said, "I told you, keep your mouth shut." And to Joey, "You must ask him to please keep away. It is too dangerous now. But Joey, you like music?"

"Oh, yes sir, I like to listen to all kinds of music."

"And dancing? You would like to see Mister Al-Sottar dancing?"

Joey seemed doubtful, hesitating, then he cried out as the black figures of Brad and George appeared in the circle of light, one tall and athletic and the other short, immense with muscle. They wore glistening wet black rubber to the neck and helmets with holes for eyes and mouths. They were carrying weapons and had made no sound.

Thomas said, "OK, later, Joey, the cabaret comes later. Right now I need to talk to my wife." He used the identity number, speaking to the taller figure, "Number two, take care of things here for me will you? Take a drink if you want. There's no hurry, I shan't be long."

Brad nodded. "Shouldn't we be doing something with that?" He indicated Kerrigan's body.

Abdul-Rahman said, his voice trembling, still in Arabic, "How many more of your friends. Allah. No matter, you are all dead men." In English, for the benefit of the incomers, "You are all fucking dead men, right." And for emphasis. "Dead men."

Abdul-Rahman flinched as Thomas waved the Browning, "I told you to be quiet, fat man. I wouldn't think you'd enjoy the pain too much." He turned to George. "Number two, why don't you get Joey here to help you find something nice and heavy? And you'll need to clean up the sand. Then maybe you could take this thing out on a boat ride?" He indicated the body. "It's of no more benefit to anyone here than it has ever been anywhere else."

"Yeah, right." George said. The American seemed fixated on the body. It lay there, huddled down as if to protect its own dark blot of bloodied sand.

"Trust me, number two," Thomas said. "Just trust me." He turned to Connie. "Come on, let's get you dressed." He took her by the elbow and steered her into the house.

Her top and her black abaya were in one of the bedrooms. Thomas sat alongside her on the edge of the bed. She was shivering quite uncontrollably, and crying quietly. "I thought you were dead," she repeated, then, "Our sons? What of David and what of little Paul? Please tell me: Oh, there is so much." She was trying to put on her top but was having trouble with locating the right entrance for her head. He laid down his gun and helped her, noticing for the first time the patches of skin on the insides of her arms that had been damaged by needles.

He whispered "Oh Connie, Connie, what have you done, what have they done to you?"

She looked at him stupidly, pulling her hair out from inside the top, shaking her head to let it fall. And how well he remembered this, the way she got herself dressed and undressed. She said, "Abdul-Rahman say you are dead. With the sword, you know?" The crying started up in greater intensity. "He tell me I must stay with him. He say I can have my boys but still they do not come."

"When did it start?" he asked her. Why, he wondered? Why was it that he had to know that? Of what possible use was it now, to know? He took up the gun again and sat beside her on the edge of the bed

262

and put his bad arm around her shaking shoulders. "When did it start, Connie?" he repeated. "Tell me when it started."

"Yes," she said dutifully, quietly, her voice full of remorse real or pretended. "More than one year. It is more than one year. You are away. You go to the racehorses in England, you remember? He called to invite us both to his party." She sniffled and choked off a sob. "Then he tell me it is OK if I go without you to help with your customers. He sends his limo. There were I think things in my drink and he says I do bad things with the men but I cannot remember nothing, Thomaso. He say he will tell you many bad things if I do not, you know..." She stopped, began making little mewing noises. "His driver, he brings stuff around to the villa when you are working and the kids are in school, and sometimes I go with the driver in his car. And he shows me how, with the sniffing and with the needle. But I have to have it." She looked up at him, not crying any more, suddenly full of trust, her eyes unnaturally bright. "He says he love me but I do not think so and I do not love him. I spit on him. What will now become with us, my husband?"

He wiped away with his fingers the thin line of spittle that had leaked from the corner of her mouth and travelled down the small perfection of her chin. Any hatred for her had gone away. Had not his wife already died? How could you hate a dead woman? Gently, he said, "I do not know, Consuela. It is the truth. I do not know what will happen to us now." He thought about the gun in his hand, of the power that was in it to resolve everything.

"You take me with you, OK? When we go? We must soon see our sons, yes?"

The reference to David and Paul pulled him back from the edge. He said, gently, "Yes. But for a little while you just lie here and get some rest." He left her on the bed and walked back out on to the patio. The table and chairs had been replaced. Al-Sottar sat there, bloody, disheveled, still managing to maintain some of his pride. The second Philipino, Vitorio, had joined the group and had brought out some trays of cold snacks. George was not there but the body of Kerrigan had gone and the place on the sand where it had lain had been scuffed over. Thomas took Saeed to one side, spoke as quietly as necessary to avoid being overheard. "You've done a beautiful job here." He paused and grinned. "You know, if there's another River War or anything I'll make sure I'm on your side, as before my friend."

Saeed looked at him, slapped his leg, laughing. "It was easy, Mister Tom. One easy, easy job. More harder when bang-bang on the side of a Russian tank and the thing just keeps coming."

"They booked you in here at the compound gate? When you came back in tonight?"

"Yes, but it was not tonight. It was last night. The guy on the gate is Sudanese. I have not been outside since I got here. Big party then, Mister Tom. Many people and all talking about the pile up on the bridge. I say I am coming over just ahead of it. To miss it, I am very lucky guy, they tell me." He frowned. "Big headache too, this morning, Mister Tom. This alcohol, I think Islam is right. It is a poison for any man."

"You're probably right enough there. Now listen Saeed, I want you to check out of here. If the guard keeps no record of your car number or name it will be so much the better. Could you trust him with that, or not?"

"I think maybe no problem."

"Good. Give it a try, OK? There's a change of plan. I want you to go straight back over the causeway. When you get through on to the Bahrain side go up to the restaurant on top of the Bahraini tower. Keep your mobile open." He stopped, searching for the words. "My wife needs medical treatment. I'm going to ask George to take her in the canoe to the same place on the Causeway where we landed, you remember where that is?"

"Come on, Mister Tom! Never shall I forget it," The red and white chequered ghutra shook around the shining face. "So this is more of that famous ninety percent reaction? It does not matter, for I have forgotten what the ten percent plan was anyway." The smile disappeared. "But George told me about your lady. I did not know. So why you not tell me, Mister Tom? It is nothing of shame and are we not friends and brothers, you and I."

"Yes, we are friends and brothers and yes, I am sorry. Sometimes perhaps we are all too proud. Or perhaps too much afraid of our own misfortunes, Saeed."

"Yes. This I know and shall remember. So, what shall I do when I have your lady in my car?"

"I expect George will make it to the causeway at around three a.m., that's two hours from now. Please take her to Brad's apartment. I'm going to call Rose and she will know what to do, OK? And afterwards you and George can sit tight in Bahrain, await developments there. I don't think it's going to take us long to tie up our agency with the sheikh here and get hold of the money."

In Saeed's pocket a mobile sounded. Saeed was obviously surprised, he frowned. "This telephone is Joey's." He put his finger to his lips, answered in Arabic then, smiling, "Hello my friend, yes, it is Saeed. .. yes, the one in Al-Mahli ... please wait for a moment." He put his hand over the phone, the look of surprise back on his face. "It is Mubarak Al-Jidha, he would like to speak with you, Mister Tom. You wish?"

Thomas nodded, took the mobile, said, "Good evening, Mubarak."

"So, you return to the land of Allah, peace be upon Him." He heard the life in the old man's voice and felt the lift of his own spirits. They exchanged the normal Arabic politenesses and then Mubarak said "This thing without wires into which I speak, it is my son's. It is good?"

"Yes, very good, old father. I hear you well."

"It is not good. I wish to see you. I know you will come back for your lady and I am waiting here with my people, where together sat you and I to talk and where we watched the sun go down. We shall come to you now. I think you need the help of Mubarak Al-Jidha and of his sons."

Thomas spoke quietly, urgently. "Listen to me, father. It will be very dangerous for you and we are soon to go from here. There is no need for you to come. Some day I shall come to you, for that I would like. And I make you my promise."

"You are in that place of boats now?"

He hesitated, "No, I am in that man's house. But not for long. When I go to the place of boats I will take the Al-Sottar who was in this house where you were arrested. Father, you will remember the thing of which you first spoke to me concerning my lady? I must go soon," he repeated, "If Allah, peace be upon Him, wills it, as I have said we shall meet again soon."

"God is Great, my son, and I am happy but I am sad. Go well to find your peace. This thing into which I speak is accursed that it should come between us."

A dripping wet George had come back up the beach and into the ring of light, now stuck up a thumb. Thomas waved back, spoke once more into the mobile. "Yes. I must go now. Goodbye, my friend." He clicked off and gave the mobile back to Saeed, nodded to Brad. Brad took out the syringe and squirted its contents once into the air and advanced with George on Abdul-Rahman. Brad said, "We are taking you away from here. This necessitates you going to sleep for a while. Don't worry about it, you will be all right. You will be safe and may even be well unless you give us any trouble. All understood?"

Abdul-Rahman rose to his feet, trying to hold up his shorts, his T shirt flapping open. Thomas had progressed his textbook understanding of the language in the illegitimate bars of Teheran and the swamp villages of Southern Iraq and in many similar locations but the stream of Arabic invective impressed him. George held him by the elbows as Brad plunged the needle into his arm. The invective stopped almost at once as he was allowed to slump down into his chair.

Thomas gathered the team together, quickly outlined his proposal, asked George if he was up for taking Connie to the Causeway. "That's not a problem, skip," George responded. "But I'd like to come back to the boat with you guys when Saeed has her safe; you could maybe use some help with the raghead."

Thomas said, "Best if you stand by in Bahrain, George. You can give Rose and Saeed any help they need, getting my wife on the plane to England." He turned to the Philipinos, asked them if they would like to come where he and the rest were going, that they would be well rewarded. He didn't want to think about what could happen if the Saudis got their hands on the only witnesses to the abduction of a member of the Al-Sottar family. Vitorio asked him how much money, please, but Joey shook his head angrily and said something sharply in the language of the Philipines, then announced that they had both decided to come along. They would both help out where they could and do as they were told to do. "But, sir' he said, "how we get out of this compound? We are not permitted outside."

Thomas pointed out to sea. "We go out that way, Joey. All except Saeed who's going to go out the same way he came in."

Saeed said, "No way I am going on any more damn water."

"As I said, Saeed is going to drive over and meet you on the causeway, George. You'll hand over my wife to him and he'll take her to Rose. She obviously needs medical attention. I have some ideas about getting her to England. I'd like Rose to take care of that if it's all right with you, Brad?"

"Sure. Once we've got Connie into Bahrain she should be on the next plane back to the UK," Brad said. "Will she have her passport? Maybe we're best advised to try for some support from that guy in the Bahrain Embassy? The lady's actually done nothing illegal, has she? Isn't she just the victim?"

266

"I'll ask her about the passport but I would be surprised if the fat man hasn't got it locked away somewhere. But you're right, apart from using illegal substances she's clean as a whistle. We might well have to involve Ferris-Bartholomew. First let's get her the hell out of here. And I guess we'll need to take some of her stash."

Joey said, "I know where they keep all that stuff, boss. I should get it?"

George said, "You want I should be shipping narcotics as well? Jesus H Christ!"

Brad said, "George, that's the man's wife in there. Or was, before this fellow got his hands on her. So just stop bloody worrying, will you?"

George grinned at Thomas. "I should have known about you, pal. Shit, the minute I saw you taking on that arsehole of a Warden I should have moved my own ass into another cell. But we are where we are so let's do it."

Thomas glanced at his watch. "Time to go boys. Yes, as the man says, let's do it." Brad helped him carry Al-Sottar down to the water's edge, bundle him into the stern section of SFB1. The sheikh's cut-open undershorts had fallen around his calves, exposing his genitalia to the warm night air. Vitorio got into the bow, George took the oars and Brad pushed out, jumped in at the last second in front of the unconscious Saudi. They quickly disappeared into the darkness.

Connie didn't want to get into SFB2 but, with some help from Saeed and Joey, Thomas finally got her to lie prone in the middle section. She moaned softly as he zipped the cover over her. He helped Joey aboard, then turned to Saeed. "Anything happens to me, just tell Rose to inform the Colonel, all right? I'm aiming to get the Agency Agreement all stamped up by tomorrow night. The money gets wired into my off-shore account in Jersey. I've left the account papers with Rose. You're the signator paymaster. Even if things go wrong there's enough in that account for you and George to make a run for your homes, OK?" He breathed deeply of the salt air, stepped out from the beach, settled himself into the canoe and dug in the first stroke of his paddle. The sliver of a new moon was showing now, high in the spangled sky.

The words came softly out of the night. "Go well, Mister Thomas. You are a good man and remember this; Allah akhbar. God, he indeed is great."

Halfway back to the marina Connie stopped her crying. She spoke softly. "I love you, Thomaso."

"You love me?" He imagined Joey, listening up front.

"Yes," she repeated, "I do, I do love you, Thomaso. I would like to see you and where we are."

He stopped paddling, released the decking to allow her to sit up. There was the swell of the sea and he could just make out his wife, sitting there in the darkness and the new silence and the heat and the clammy humidity, looking around. But the sounds of her grief began anew, the dreadful choking back of sobs. "And David and Paul I love," she managed to say, in between.

"Best not to talk, Consuela," he said. "Not now." He dug in the paddle and swung the canoe around, feeling the warm breeze on the right hand side of his face. They were back on track, moving towards the harbour light.

"Where do we go?" The plaintive voice. "Please, I am afraid."

"Where are we going?" he said, "We are going nowhere. You are about to leave Saudi Arabia, Consuela. And for the time being you must be very quiet. Do you understand me?"

"Yes, husband," she said. "I do."

He lowered his voice for they were quite close to the marina now. "George is going to take you across the water. My other friend, Saeed, is going to meet you in Bahrain. He will take you to Rose. You remember Rose? She's waiting to help you."

The sounds of weeping stopped and then, less meekly, "You have Rose in Bahrain?"

"She is there, with Bradley."

There was a pause but the crying did not re-start, then, "I saw Bradley on the beach." Another pause. "This Rose, you always like her I think." It had not been a question and in her voice was the hope of some small triumph.

"Just shut up, Connie. Shut up and say your prayers, all right?"

"Thank you, Thomaso. Oh, it will be so good to be again together," she said, and then he could hear the dawn of panic in her voice. "But, but I must ..."

"Consuela, I know what you 'must.' We've brought all that gear of yours. Joey told us where the stuff was and where your passport was and it's all in your bag up front with some clothes and your make up and wash kit, OK? Now for Christ's sake shut up."

They nudged into the shelter behind *Jazeera*'s bows alongside the other SFB, recently arrived. As they did so Joey turned around and whispered, "Oh, sir, this is Sheikh Al-Sottar's ship."

"No, it's the Prince's boat, Joey."

"No sir," Joey spoke with shy conviction. "I have learned Sheikh Abdul-Rahman, he buys back this ship *Jazeera* from the Prince. Some more of the Irishmen have come to work in the marina for the sheikh. It is these men who have taken *Jazeera* out on the sea three days of last week." Thomas could hear the puzzlement, the rising worry. "And Sheikh Abdul-Rahman, he was talking with the Irishman. They were to go soon in this ship to Dubai. He says they go there and then go to somewhere."

"What did you say? Where - where did you say he is to go after Dubai?"

"I think he say to go in this ship to Spain, sir."

Spain? What the hell was going on now? But he had no more time to pursue it until he'd got everyone except Connie and George inside *Jazeera* and had sent SFB2 to the bottom. He helped his wife into the front of SFB1. She'd been well warned and now was silent. George had taken his place and now sat in readiness, crouched over in the stern paddling position. Thomas whispered goodbye and take care and pushed her off, once again into the night.

Later, down now in *Jazeera's* dimly lit stateroom Thomas remembered his wife's final words. She'd turned to him, her face just a paleness in the dark. "Please, you will be good to me, Thomaso?" she had whispered. "I am so afraid. Please be good to me, my husband, for you I love." Brad interrupted his thoughts. "Home again then? Some wonderful bloody home for you, Tommy. What do you want me to do with this?" He indicated the unconscious Al-Sottar.

"I think we'd better keep him up here. Right, home again as you say, just like old times. Only this time we can do what we like. There's no need to cover our tracks. Joey reckons the boss here has regained the ownership of *Jazeera*, reckons he's planning a trip to Dubai, then off around into the Med in her would you believe? Joey, why don't you and your friend rustle us all up something to eat. Something cold. But I've told you the rules. No cooking, no noise, minimum lights."

Al-Sottar stirred restlessly. Thomas said to Brad, "When he wakes up we need a couple of signatures from him, plus we finally have to get to know exactly what's been going down here. If they're still trying to remove my head I might as well know the full what for."

Brad said, "We'll have to hold on to him until the money clears, whatever else. Only the local bank can do the priority clearances."

Thomas said, "Joey, do you know when Mister Abdul-Rahman planned to set off?"

269

"No sir."

Thomas nodded. "I don't reckon on anybody noticing his absence before mid-day at the earliest. He often sleeps over at the beach house and nobody would disturb him there. He rarely troubles his office with his presence, and never before mid-day. But if *Jazeera*'s going to have some sort of a crew coming aboard ..."

Down on the floor, in the near darkness of the stateroom Abdul-Rahman Al-Sottar was making small noises, beginning to try to sit up. Thomas thought of his wife, now maybe a mile out on the sea, and of what this man had done to her or with her. He thought of this man's wasting of the life of the mother of his children. And of their father's life, should he have his way.

Chapter Nineteen

Jazeera rocked ponderously on her mooring. Thomas sipped his coffee, trying to rid his mouth and throat of the taste of salt. The stern light of a police launch was making fast along the coast against the first faint tinge of red on the eastern horizon. A thousand callers of prayers would be readying themselves now. He looked at his friend. "I reckon it's going to be a fine day for a little piracy."

Brad frowned. "Piracy? What the hell are you thinking of now?" He was holding his hand over his live mobile.

"I need a few minutes with our guest. Let's talk it through after that. George should be almost there. By the way there's no need for you to put on the hood any more. Might frighten the man." He laughed. "Besides, the hood makes you look suspiciously like you're breaking the law."

Brad shook his head, grinning, resumed his telephone conversation with Rose. On the floor of *Jazeera*'s main stateroom the untidy bundle that was Abdul-Rahman Al-Sottar groaned and stirred.

Thomas had a momentary vision of Captain Mohammed Al-Muttawi, his thobe billowing pale in the tideflow, caught up on something, the swarming of the crabs ... And the Irishman, Kerrigan, down there as a near neighbour. No ashes to ashes, just straight back into that chemical soup from which all life has come ... He shook himself out of it, looked at his watch. They'd fallen behind time. You plan, then you try to carry it out and see where it's going wholly wrong. So you revise it or make another plan altogether. Repeat as before; the human condition.

Brad finished speaking, handed him the mobile. He could hear the sleep in Rose' voice. "So, good morning, skipper. And 'yes' is the answer apropos your not so good lady wife. I'll take charge of her. Assuming the boys get her to me in one piece I'm going to fly her to London, call the Colonel, ask him to fix a nurse and ambulance for when we land. There's this place in Surrey, supposed to be excellent if you can afford it."

"I can afford it. You'll go with her?"

"She can't go on her own. Maybe won't want to go at all." She hesitated; "Brad says everything else is on track?"

"More or less; but listen, you're sure? About going along with Connie?"

"I'd rather hear your more than your less," she said. "Especially with George and Saeed still somewhere out there unconnected. But assuming they make it, I'm sure I'm sure. Not entirely little girl lost you know and by the look of it the poor lady needs all the help she can get."

"Thank you, Rosie." There seemed little else to say.

"If you call me Rosie, Thomas Thornton, I'll call you Tommy. I know how much you like that and you know what I think of sweet little 'Rosie'. 'Bye now." He waited for her to click off but back came the voice again, perhaps a little smaller; "Look here, Thomas Thornton. Be very, very good. Won't you? Please? I wouldn't want anything to go wrong at this stage in the game - for either of you." There was a pause in case there was anything more but there was not. The line clicked and purred. He switched off the mobile, handed it back.

The man on the carpet had tried to move too quickly. Now he rose, staggered, fell down, his voice thick with the sedative. "Thomas? This is you? For God's sake…"

He said, "We're not ready for you yet, Abdul-Rahman, nor you for your God. Why don't you just stay where you are." He walked across to the portside window, began to dial Saeed.

Brad picked up on the good cop bad cop straight away, full of sympathy for the captive. He said, "Look, the guy's going to be OK on a chair, skipper. Come on, man. Let me help you up."

"You fuck off," muttered Abdul-Rahman.

Thomas' call was picked up first ring. "This is Saeed. You are OK, yes?"

"All OK. Where are you now?"

"No problem. I am eating chicken sandwich in the big red tower. The red one. Mister Tom! This is Bahrain. It is very good to be back here again."

"There are people there around you? Or can you talk?"

"No people to listen. Only the ears in the air maybe. Who knows this?"

"Possible but unlikely. Well done, Saeed." The police launch had turned north, disappeared from sight. Now only the dark sea, the spars and masts silhouetted against a still star-strewn sky. "You had any problems getting through?"

"No, but the man in Saudi, he sees my immigration date and the time of my entry. He tells me I am very lucky. He says there was a big accident not too long after I went through. I said I was very sorry to hear it although, myself, I had always been a lucky person, I was born lucky." The laugh boomed and rolled like distant thunder.

"Right, I believe it."

"I do not truly think so. How is it I get myself in Al-Mahli? What time you think George will be, uh, meeting?"

"Must be very soon if all's well. I'd best shut down. We've spoken to Rose and she's OK with everything. Call me back when you've made the pick up, is that OK?"

"Yes, Mister Tom, it is understood."

No sooner had he switched off the mobile than it vibrated like a live thing in his hand: George. "Hi Brad, is that you?"

"Go ahead, George. Thomas. I have Brad's phone just now."

"Thomas, baby! I wanted you anyway. Your lady's been going a bit fucking crazy here. I had to unzip the thing, let her sit up. She says she has to speak with you."

Thomas could hear the sobs, growing louder in his ear. "Thomaso, this is you?"

"Connie for Christ's sake shut up, will you. Everything's going to be OK if you just let George take care of things and keep yourself still and quiet."

"But if you are not coming I am not. I cannot leave you any more. You are my husband." Her tone changed, grew small again. "I have to take a pee now, Thomaso. What can I do?"

He exploded. "Jesus Christ! You're worse than a bloody kid. Just take your pee, for Christ's sake. The canoe won't damned well mind and nor will George. Put him back on the line now."

George said, "Hi again. Yeah, she's calmed down a bit. Listen, I'm going well, I think. Right opposite the towers, I guess about thirty minutes to touch down, max. No sign of any hostiles."

"There'll be full radar cover, but you don't make a big target and at four a.m. you have every chance ... listen, I reckon a change of tactics. It's going to be getting light pretty soon. Home straight in on the Bahrain tower. Saeed's parked there right now. He's up in the restaurant. Call him. The sooner you can get Connie out of that boat, and that boat out of the water, the better."

"Yeah. OK, skip. Makes sense. Wish us all good luck."

"We always seem to be saying that, don't we? Yes, good luck to us all then."

"Hey, you never told me what about the boat. You want I should lose it?"

"Land the passenger, push it out a way and then use the remote to submerge it. I'll get its owners to retrieve it later on. They won't have a problem."

Brad had re-settled the silent Abdul-Rahman on the settee that curved around three sides of the table. Thomas closed the phone, told Brad he was going to take a turn outside; he wouldn't be long. He needed time and space in which to think and perhaps their guest could use some thinking time as well.

High up on *Jazeera*'s flying bridge, out in the open air, he leaned on the rails, looking east into the false dawn. So far, so good. With Kerrigan out of the equation the European end of the cocaine ring was going to be dead or at least badly damaged. But how soon would it be before market forces re-exerted themselves, normal service be resumed? He shook his head. The Colonel was probably right, maybe just a matter of weeks. There was this definite air of futility about it all. But Abdul-Rahman? He wondered how the man would take what was to come. He breathed in deeply of the briny air.

What now was it that he, Thomas Thornton, really wanted from Sheikh Abdul-Rahman bin Sulaiman Al-Sottar? He'd wanted his wife back for a start. But OK, he'd got her or what was left of her even though the bitterness of her betrayal still lay like the early signs of a long-term illness deep inside him. Always would, probably. And yes, he'd wanted the return of the good name of the businessman. What exactly was that to a man whose name and whose station had outworn so many changes? And then, the thing he'd tried so assiduously not to consider; the money. Could he personally take Al-Sottar's money under threat, however 'legal' that taking might be, however filthily ill-gotten the money? He didn't need it, Sir Christopher had made that plain enough. Different for the others.

Revenge? Yes, revenge. A strong enough motivator, but how very bitter a dish was that? More questions than answers as, in silence, he paced the deck, keeping a watch for any sign of activity.

Some kind of personal peace, perhaps? Perhaps to find it as the first of his fathers had in the end found it, in his poetry? He thought

274

about his own poetic efforts at a time when half his list of quasi-military targets remained alive and kicking, himself no longer caring … In the far distance he could see the necklace of causeway lights … he wanted only to be done with this, to be over there with Saeed and George and back in a western world of freedom, however illusory with its computer data, its billions of cameras, laws, rules, regulations, passports, political and social correctness.

He thought about Al-Sottar again; about how the capacity to deliver cruelty, most especially without the need for any personal courage is, in a man of any race, so terrible and so terribly sad a thing with which he has to live.

Between here and the causeway, a long way out, he could see a pair of navigation lights, both red and green visible, therefore moving towards him. Probably a fishing boat trawling for the Gulf's famous prawns; those fat and juicy clearers up of carrion from the bottom of the sea. No, she was travelling too fast for a fishing boat. Must be another police launch or the coast guard. About a half mile out she turned ninety degrees, headed north. Relieved, he took a final deep breath of steamy, night scented air before returning to the stateroom and the cool sterility of its air conditioning.

By common consent George and Saeed had left all their weapons on *Jazeera* before they'd left on their missions. The M79 rocket launcher, the grenades, the spare SLR and the handguns were all stacked away in the galley. Brad had an SLR cradled in his arms. He was sitting, munching on an apple, opposite the ragged Al-Sottar, a torch on ultra low power set down on the wide table between them. "Hello there," he said. "All quiet on the western front I hope? I asked Joey to sort out some clothing for your friend here. He was beginning to feel the AC, poor man."

"He was? He is? You're right with the new clothes, we should do our best to keep our clients comfortable."

Abdul-Rahman said, "Clients? What's with clients?" His voice was one of unadulterated loathing. "Fuck you, you think you're smart enough to do this crap?"

Joey came in carrying an armful of clothing. Thomas said, "Joey, I'm sorry, take that stuff away. No new clothes for the fat man 'til he decides to speak decently. Why don't you make us some coffee - just the four of us. The 'sheikh' here doesn't want a thing. Then tell Vitorio to come in here with you. We need to set you two up on watch whilst we do business with our new client." He turned to the Saudi. "Sheikh,

275

if that's what you really are, why don't you move your arse around so a man can sit down?" He indicated the bend of the U-shaped settee. "Not rushing off anywhere are you, sheikh?"

"I need the toilet."

"I have some papers for you to sign, then we're going to take your lovely *Jazeera* out into International waters. You don't deserve it, but you have my word you'll be OK if you do exactly as you're told. Also when you've told me everything, and I do mean everything, about what in hell has been going on here with me and the coke thing. That all understood?"

Abdul-Rahman said, triumphantly, "You cannot sail from here without papers, you fool. You would not get far if you try."

"Quite right. I think you have the papers. Where are they?"

"Fuck you. I have no papers. But how can I think straight and understand when I have to take a piss."

"In a little while. Business first."

Brad finished his apple, placed the core carefully into a giant glass ash tray. "The guy's only been trying to bribe me, Tommy. Would you believe that? Fifty grand for me, raised to ten times that if Mister Thomas doesn't figure in anything any more, if you see what I mean."

"Is that right? Pretty cheap then?" It didn't matter that Al-Sottar was hearing. "Brad, I've decided not to bother with my share of the agency. I don't need it and there's plenty of charities that do, plenty of people trying their best to pick up the pieces left behind by all the weary bastards like this piece of work."

"Right on, and understood." Brad chuckled, the dimmed down torchlight making a frightening mask out of his smiling good looks. "The girl and I thought that's where you'd get to. And you can count our shares in on the donation, please; less our expenses of course."

"Great. I think it's right. The other two are going to need their shares and I'm comfortable with that if you are."

Abdul-Rahman spoke as if he had finally scented the bait in a possible trap, had decided to try sweet reason. "Look, you are going to tell me what is with all this agency, Thomas?"

Thomas took out the waterproof packet from inside his wet suit vest, extracted the papers and laid them on the table. "All in good time," he said, as the Philipinos came in with the coffee and biscuits. He motioned for them to wait. He said, "Right now its time for a coffee break, then it's mounting the watch time, taking a piss time and time for the business of the day, well sorry, of the night. Isn't this just jolly? Remember what you told me, Mister Abdul-Rahman? About

276

how, for men of your faith, money is not so important? Well, in that case I don't think this next bit's going to be anything of a problem for you." Al-Sottar was saying nothing, just watching them with their cups of coffee. Thomas tapped his forefinger on the papers and grinned. "Hello. As you know, Sheikh Abdul-Rahman, I'm your agent as regards all Sea Fibres business. This is our contract. Sign right here, please."

He had become very tired by the time the windows began properly to lighten. In spite of himself he had to admire Abdul-Rahman's fortitude. Even in a totally losing position the man had tried to go on making deals, tried to squeeze out every last drop of self-advantage. But finally he'd signed. He'd even said he'd help get them to Bahrain if it meant they were out of his hair for ever. They must recognise the danger to themselves in hanging around here, he told them. The balloon would be going up any time now. In fact as soon as the cleaners arrived at the beach house and found him missing.

"Found you missing?" Thomas said, wearily. "What you, the guy who'd take off for a little heavy R&R in Dubai or somewhere without telling anyone, even your poor little wife, arrive back umpteen days later without need for explanation? That's a joke."

Vitorio interjected at that, quietly, with utmost politeness. "Excuse me sirs, but Joey and me, we are the cleaners."

Thomas had thought the small figure in his bright red shirt and blue jeans was asleep in the big, white leather armchair. "Yes, I see. Thanks, Vitorio. Go and ask Joey to come here, will you. You stay where he is and keep a good watch out, OK? Remember the signals I taught you." He turned back to Al-Sottar. "Nobody's going anywhere from here until the bank transfer's happened and the agency agreement is on its way into safe keeping."

Joey came in. Thomas said, "I want you to take this in to the bank. You know it?"

Joey glanced at the address on the envelope, nodded. "Often I go there for the sheikh."

"Right. When you've made the transfers and delivered this other envelope to the couriers you come back here with the confirmations. Is that all OK and understood?"

Joey said, "Yes, sir. But the guard on the gate here, sir, what do I say to him?"

"Nothing. Take off your shoes and walk down the pontoon. Keep behind the boats, out of line of sight of the guardhouse. At the shoreline you'll slip off to your left. It's only twenty metres to the wire and the tide is dropping. You'll find a hole to get through on to the public beach. You come back through the main gate. It'll be full daylight and open to visitors by then. Sheikh Abdul-Rahman is going to give you a note clearing you to collect something for him from this boat. Brad, can you write it out for him to sign? Thanks."

He turned again to Joey. "The bank opens at seven thirty and the courier at eight. Here, take your mobile. Quick as you can my friend. You and Vitorio are coming with us when we leave here. We're going to get you both back to Manilla with enough money to set yourselves up."

"Thank you, sir. May I now call your friend in the desert? Tell him all is good?"

Thomas could see Al-Sottar's badly hidden interest. "No. Please do not mention anything in front of this man. You must call nobody except us, here. Joey, this is very important." He scribbled Brad's number on a scrap of paper. "Call this number once when the transfer is accepted and the confirmation is in your hands. Just say, 'transfer complete' if everything's good, OK? Then call us once more when the courier has the other package. Say 'I'm on my way.' Nothing more."

Thomas watched from a discreet position alongside Vitorio in the wheelhouse as Joey slipped down the pontoon to the shore, darted to his left, got quickly through the wire, walked casually along the tideline carrying his trainers, to any early morning observer just another dark-skinned, early morning beachcomber.

He called to leave a carefully worded message for Rose on the Bahrain office answerphone, updating her with the unfolding situation and the revised destination for the money, then returned to the stateroom.

Al-Sottar stood up in his new clothing, stretching himself. "Now it is better," he said. "We are back working together, mister Thomas. I would now like to talk to you about some serious business."

Wearily Thomas said, "Nice try. You don't give up easily, sheikh, I'll say that for you. 'Together?' Don't ever even think about it. I've had some of your kind of 'togetherness.'"

"Consuela?" said Abdul-Rahman, "You talk of the woman? I am sorry but she is not worthy of it. There are many, many more as that one. Sure, I make a mistake. I should have trusted you, should have brought you in on it. Kerrigan, he was to blame. It was Kerrigan who wanted you ..."

278

Brad saw what was bubbling up, moved hurriedly to head off the explosion, muttered, "Stay cool, Tommy." He turned to the Saudi. "Listen, why don't you make a start by telling us about everything that's been going on? Then we can judge where we're going to be with it, right?"

Abdul-Rahman said, "Yes, gentlemen, sure I will. I knew we could do some business."

An hour of questions, half answers and cross-questions later Thomas was tired of it, and physically very tired. He stood up and stretched himself just as Brad's phone warbled out its imperative. Brad listened, nodded, said, "Well done." He switched off, looked up. "Transfer completed."

"Good." Thomas turned to the Saudi, "You've told us very little we didn't already know and frankly I can't be bothered to ask you anything else. I just want you out of my sight once and for all. There's an inflatable with outboard hanging on davits over the diving deck. You're going to be in it and on the ocean once we're far enough on our way to where we're going. God only knows why I don't -" He shook his tired head. "Brad, I'm going up top to check on Vitorio, OK?" But as he opened the door there was this light of an amazing intensity and then the blackness of the end of the world and he was alone, nowhere, images swimming up at him and going, fast and slow, leaving fragments to play with his fears, fuel the on-rushing terror without time … without time … without time … But he thought, as if from a great distance he might be able to hear …he clung to the voice as someone drowning might cling to an unexpected floating object. The voice was closer now. "You OK, Tommy?"

He opened his eyes in a head that seemed not to belong to him, that seemed to be resting in his friend Brad's lap. He tried to sit up, not recognising the groans as his own. The space he occupied was swimming then stabilising then swimming again. "My God … What the hell happened?" His voice had been a hoarse whisper. He moved his eyes around. "Christ. This is the chain locker? Feels like I've been hit with the bloody anchor …"

"Yeah, well that's right." It was only the shadow of the man's usual grin. "It's all just gone just a bit pear-shaped, partner. You opened the cabin door and there were these two guys and the roof fell in on you. You were out cold and I got myself shot before I could do too much." He sounded oddly resigned, very tired. "I'm sorry but our two friends are dead meat, Tommy." Thomas followed his eyes. The Philipinos were lying alongside them in this small space, one of them half across the other, Vitorio on top, facing up, his eyes and mouth open, two surprisingly small patches of dark red blood disfiguring the light red shirt. Brad whispered, "They didn't deserve that. They'd done nothing."

For a long moment Thomas could neither say nor do anything at all, then, "I should have stayed where I was, in Al-Mahli. Was it really worth it all?"

"That's not the question," Brad murmured. "And it doesn't have any answer anyway."

"Who the hell were they, do we know?" Thomas sat up, looked at his watch. "I've been out for two hours?"

"That's right. Near as I could make it out these guys used to work for Sea Fibres in Pompey. Must have been the UK end of things, set up by Kerrigan and Al-Sottar. I've heard people coming and going. They must be loading stuff or repairing something. I wanted to tell you... about the trip..."

"Take it easy, Brad, you don't sound so good." For the first time he noticed the roughly fashioned tourniquet tied tightly around his friend's still rubber-clad left leg.

Brad said, "No? Not all that brilliant ... guy in the lead got me in the thigh. That was OK, though, six inches down from all the vital bits, thank God." He tried a laugh. "It was this other one, the one through the kneecap? Pretty good aim from all of six inches. The guy must have taken lessons in Belfast, so he must." The imitation accent was poor, the grin weak, the pain very obvious. "In case ... listen, in case I ... Tommy ... they're planning to take us out to sea and drop us off, you know, nicely weighted and still alive and kicking. Before that the bastards will be wanting you to tell them exactly who knows what about what. Al-Sottar, he remembered the comment about your old man in the desert. Hey, these guys know how to ask the questions, Tommy ..." His eyelids fluttered, then opened wide again. "They already tried it with me ... they'll be having another go."

For the first time Thomas noticed the state of the fingers on his friend's right hand. He said, "Try not to talk. You always did talk too bloody much. Let me see that tourniquet." Brad had tried his best to use one handed the end of a reel of five millimetre nylon rope. Thomas loosened the knots, saw how fresh new blood immediately welled up from the thigh wound, exiting through the holed, black rubber wet suit. The knee was just a swollen lump. There was nothing with which to cut away the rubber so he re-wound and tightened up

280

the tourniquet, shaking his head. "Christ, I'm sorry, Brad... that's about as stupid a thing as I've ever said."

Brad's voice was faint but serious. "Forget it, man. Goes with the territory. The territory I chose all by myself. Listen, this is important. I managed to pick up some of what was going on when they thought I was spark out on the floor up there." Thomas started to tell him again not to try to talk, just to rest, but his friend shook his head. "Tommy, for once in your life will you just please, please listen? This boat is loaded. I mean really loaded. She's fitted with a part double skinned hull. We're sitting here on three tonnes of pure heroin. Three fucking tonnes!" As if shocked by his own seldom used expletive he stopped, his face contorted by pain. Thomas loosened the tourniquet again. "We know all about them bringing in cocaine using the old Provo, Sea Fibres, South America connections...." He lapsed into a temporary silence then tried a grin. he went on, his voice weaker... "Guess the bastards just got unlucky with you. I mean, shit, they could have found an easier fall guy. Anyway, quite apart from that -"

From out in the engine room came the consecutive whirrings and chortles of the two great diesel engines, then the steady purring as of one great, contented cat. "All ashore that's going ashore," Thomas whispered.

"I have to tell you more ... the Kerrigan connection, that was coke. Seems now they've only contracted to buy pure heroin from the Afghans - from the Taleban, for Christ's sake. Stuff's coming out through Iran. Al-Sottar's ex Sea Fibres guys? It was them made the pick up for Al-Sottar in mid-Gulf the other day. Joey was right, they're planning to take off with it ... the Med ..." He lapsed again.

Thomas said, "Brad, can you hear me?"

"Course I bloody can." There it was, the twist of a smile; relic of their earlier, happier days together. "We're talking billions, Tommy, bloody billions. And listen, I'm sorry but I've got to tell you. Grenville's somehow involved as well."

"Christ, Brad, ..." He couldn't find the words, but a great anger bubbled up inside him. Brad lay there, white-faced, eyes tightly closed. Thomas remembered the Colonel's 'options' ... 'Go on as we are, fighting a very expensive losing battle against them ...probably more of a delaying action ... or accept the inevitable. Open the floodgates to the stuff. Price comes down. Criminals go out of business.... Let the cancer take those it's going to take anyway, without disputation.' He said, "I have to get out of here, find a mobile. What did they do with yours, Brad?"

"Forget that. Zapped." He groaned once, softly. "Get out? What do you think you're going to do, bite a bloody hole through the hull?"

Thomas looked with infinite care around their confines, again and again coming back to the solid teak door, locked and certainly bolted from the outside; unbreakable without tools and without time. He examined the hinge fixings; countersunk brass screws. Hope began to rise. "I need some sort of a screwdriver," he muttered.

Brad whispered, "Make that a large scotch as well, will you. Vitorio .. he was asleep up top when they came aboard. Can't blame him … but they knew … they knew we …" His voice trailed away.

Thomas felt *Jazeera*'s first movements, heard the easy rise and fall of her engines as she was jockeyed out from her berth. His head was still sucking in pain but his mind was back together now. Brad's pulse seemed OK even though he was in very bad shape. Fresh blood continued to seep past the improvised tourniquet.

Thomas stood up, put his hand out to the wall to steady himself, peered out of the porthole. They were idling past the lines of moored boats. By the time he'd searched every nook and cranny for some kind of a tool they were out in the open sea. But there was nothing; nothing he could use to loosen the hinge screws. The engines now revved up. They would be doing eight or ten knots, just an idling speed for *Jazeera*. He could feel the slow side to side shifting as she cut through the swells. He looked up. High on the wall by the door was a fire extinguisher. *'Look for and find anything that might become of future benefit or advantage however slight. In the right hands a ball point pen can become a key to a door, or a lethal weapon.'*

Brad's voice was almost inaudible. "Why don't you take a look through their pockets? The Philipinos?" His all too pale face was etched deep with the pain.

There was nothing on Joey other than a bit of paper money and a few coins but in Vitorio's trouser pocket he found his answer, a small, bone handled all-purpose pen-knife. Carefully he inserted the main blade between door and frame, smashed the handle sideways with the palm of his hand. As he'd hoped, the blade had snapped in half, had become, in effect, a screwdriver. He worked on the top hinge first. The thing about teak wood. It was self oiling, easing the entry and withdrawal of screw fixings. Before long the hinge was held in place only by the last few turns of the final screw. He got down on his knees to do the same with the bottom hinge, then took down the fire extinguisher, released the nozzle pipe. Sitting on a coil of rope, directly in front of the door, he folded the screwdriver back into the body of the knife, laid it along the roots of the fingers of his right hand and made a fist. Between his fingers he inserted three of Joey's coins.

Brad's voice was the faintest of whispers. "Looks like you're up for a good night out in the East End, mate."

The pitch of the engines had changed and he could feel *Jazeera* settling herself in the water. They would be several miles out to sea now, doing a bit of fishing so far as any observers were concerned. "Wait for it," Brad whispered, "They'll be coming. Won't want any sign of us on board when they exit Saudi waters. Possibility of being custom searched ..."

Voices on the other side of the door. Thomas got himself into an American footballer's one kneed crouch. The instant he heard the working of the outside bolts he flung his shoulder at the hinged side of the door. The man in front took the full impact, went flying backwards into the starboard engine, his Uzzi spinning up and over the top. Those milliseconds... The second man had been covering the unlocking of the door, standing well back against the wall in case of trouble. They were pro's but the man's weapon was all wrong for this situation. He could see the Kalashnikov coming up in slow motion. Using the fire extinguisher as a combination shield and battering ram Thomas hurled himself ahead. Just before the impact, the extinguisher exploded in a white storm of foam and the sound and smell of the firing of the Kalashnikov was a violence in itself, an almost physical thing in the enclosed engine room. The extinguisher smashed back into his chest under the impact of the bullets but he carried on forward, pushing the jaggedly split metal into the man's face, then followed through with an underarm, knuckle-duster right to his balls. As the man screamed, Thomas wrenched the gun from his grasp. Within the new and strangest silence there was no plea for mercy in voice or on the man's face, just surprise and a great deal of blood. He fired twice when once would have been enough. The first man was trying to get to his feet, slipping in the sea of foam. He might have been trying to get his hands in the air, probably knew that he, too, was already dead.

Thomas looked at him, the moment seeming frozen. "OK. How many more?"

The man actually tried a grin. "Fuck you, MacRae." He had a strong southern English accent but the features and complexion of the Eastern Mediterranean.

Brad's voice came from behind, in the chain locker. "No, Tommy, no more. Only Al-Sottar. The guy here, he's called Buddy Listerone.

He's the one got something against other peoples' knee-caps. Likes to shoot at them from behind when they're lying down."

Thomas said, "Well, I can't say it's been good to meet you, mister Listerone." He tightened on the trigger. The bullet drilled a neat black hole just over the bridge of the man's nose. He crumpled and fell quietly, as if tired, as if to go to sleep. Thomas turned back to Brad. "That's it, I'm going to say hello to Al-Sottar. I'll be back when I've seen what's upstairs. Just hold on tight now." He gave the Kalashnikov to Brad, retrieved the Uzzi and checked its loading. Full magazine. There was no sign of the leaks in the hull at the places where bullets had impacted but from one of the holes he noticed the emission of a steady trickle of white powder. He wet his finger, touched the powder, rubbed it across his gums, at once feeling the numbing down effect. Heroin.

Outside the slippery mess in the engine room he took off his trainers. Bare feet would be better. Moving with extreme care he found the stateroom empty, as was the galley and each of the bedrooms and bathrooms. That left only the wheelhouse plus all the outside areas. He spoke quietly, reasonably, through the wheelhouse door. "Come on out, Abdul-Rahman. Your two guys are gone. Our deal's still on the table. What do you want to do? If I have to come in after you and find you're armed I want you to be sure about this; you are a dead man. It's make up your mind time."

For a few seconds there was no reply, then, "You have killed ...?" His voice tailed off. "All - aaah. But how may I trust you?" The voice told both of his fear and of the danger that could come from a man who was all that afraid.

"Money, Abdul-Rahman. You can trust me for money."

Abdul-Rahman laughed shakily. "Ah, yes, of course, but it will not work, Thomas. We are out at sea and I have just called the Khobar police. It is you who should now worry. There is no way you can run and hide, not any more. So, big mistake, you see? Coming back here. Give yourself up. I shall tell them it was all down to them. These guys you killed, they were the ones who were to blame. For everything."

For the second time in half an hour Thomas' shoulder hit a door with all his weight behind it. This lock gave way at once. Al-Sottar had been standing just inside, had taken the brunt of the impact, was now sprawled out on the floor. He was holding a gun. Thomas nuzzled the Uzzi up behind his ear. "Come on now, no more games, friend. Just drop that thing and get up. You're going to call them back, OK? You'll tell the police there's no problem. If they keep on coming anyway

284

you'll tell them to stay clear, that you're being held at gunpoint. Tell them if they attempt to board *Jazeera* you will be killed. You have that?" Through the wheelhouse windows he could see what appeared to be a pair of fast police launches on their way out from Khobar and another from the direction of the Causeway. All three of them were as yet a good way off but, to judge by their crisp white bow-waves, not for long. There would be more boats and there would be choppers, too. Warships even, probably. He repeated himself. "Right. Get up on your feet now and call them again. Tell them to stand off, not to come any closer. No hidden messages. I have the Arabic, remember, and I'm listening. If I go, you go, I hope not in the same direction, OK?"

The police boats kept on coming in spite of their acknowledgment of message number one, but stopped dead in the water after Al-Sottar had delivered the second. They were still perhaps a half kilometre away. Thomas switched off the radio transmitter.

"And so, what now, Mister Thornton?"

"We're going to wait till after dark then make a fast run for it. I'm going to lock you away whilst I bring my friend upstairs. I have to see to him, get him some help as soon as I can."

Al-Sottar said, "It was not me. Such men not my friends; they were simply my men."

"And whose man have you been, Sheikh? Robert Grenville's?"

"You know this?" the man whispered. "How you know this?" But he went, unprotesting, into the wheelhouse toilet.

Thomas turned the key in the lock as the RT sounded, a voice speaking Arabic coming across loud and clear: "*Jazeera*, this is Saudi Police Boat R18 and I am Captain Ziad Al-Bandari. Please re-advise your current status... Sheikh Abdul-Rahman, are you receiving me? Over."

Thomas switched to 'send', spoke in Arabic. "Don't bother us, Captain. The Sheikh will be OK provided you keep your distance." He turned on the boat's radar, glanced up at the screen. "That means you and everyone else, especially including helicopters, is that quite understood?"

"Who are you please?"

"Who I am is not your concern. Your concern is the life and welfare of Sheikh Abdul-Rahman Al-Sottar. Please switch off now. I'll come back to you when I've worked out my requirements. Why don't you do some fishing, we're going to be anchored up here for quite some time."

"Fishing? What with fishing? You - "

Thomas switched off the VHF. *Rule one in defending a stand-off. Stay calm and quiet with minimum dialogue but always lead such dialogue as takes place. Introduce irrelevances so as to give the attackers something inexplicable to spend their time and adrenaline on trying to understand.* He went below, wading through the billows of fire extinguisher foam, reddened all around the crumpled bodies of the dead men.

Brad was conscious. "So, can I take it we have regained control, Captain?"

He grinned down into his friend's face. "Oh yes. Maybe we're getting there, maybe we're finally getting there."

"What happened with Al-Sottar?"

"Locked up tight. No problem. But it's a stand-off. We've got half the Saudi police surrounding us and pretty soon now the other half will be here as well. But relax, Brad. Go with the flow, save your strength." He worked as quickly and as carefully as he could to cut away the wet suit, carefully examining the wounds, trying not to let it show in his face that there was no way this leg would not be amputated, even if he managed to get the man to a hospital. He went back upstairs to the galley, brought down the medical emergencies kit, stopping off at the stateroom cocktail cabinet for a bottle of Lagavulin and a couple of tumblers.

Down in the chain locker he poured out the whiskeys, gave one to his friend. Brad said, "What's this then, party time? I was only joking, before ... " He raised his half full glass, downed it in one, shuddered.

Thomas said, "That's no way to treat an eighteen years old Lagavulin, Lieutenant." He re-filled the glass then washed the bullet entry and exit wounds in Brad's thigh, doused them with iodine, applied a clean bandage. Finally he covered the wound with Elastoplast. By that time Brad had lapsed again into semi-consciousness. He dabbed at the shattered knee-cap, hoping all the metal bits had come through. They should have come through at such short range. Brad's eyelids fluttered and opened. "Relax., my friend," Thomas said. "I have a plan."

Brad muttered, "Oh, shit. You have a plan and you're asking me to bloody relax? Shit, that do hurt, Tommy."

Thomas looked at his watch. Five hours to darkness. "Hurt? You know what they used to say in the Service? 'It's good to hurt; means you're still alive.'? Look, I'm done with your thigh wound. I'm doing your knee now and then I'll take a look at your fingers. It's going to hurt plenty more. I have some chloroform here. You want out?"

"Why spoil things by vomiting over everything, probably including you? Do your worst but do be gentle, kind sir,"

"Yes, right. And after all that, it's going to hurt some more. I'm going to get a dry-suit on you. We'll be taking to the ocean a bit later on."

Brad murmured; "Oh, hell. Just what I need; a nice little swim before dinner."

"That's what friends are for, Bradley Scott," Thomas said. He was picking pieces of bone from the mangled thing that once had been a knee joint. "That's what friends are for, right?"

Chapter Twenty

"Yes, this is Captain Ziad Al-Bandari. What now may I do for you, Mister Thornton?"

"Nice one, Captain. You know me. Good, so you know I'm not playing about here. I want you to organise a helicopter to lift a man off this boat, take him to the military hospital in Bahrain."

"Yes? And if I agree, what then?"

"The injured man will confirm to me that he is safely arrived. That same chopper will then return to *Jazeera* to take off myself and Sheikh Al-Sottar, together. At Bahrain airport a fixed wing airplane plus one pilot - and nobody other than he - is to be fuelled up for four thousand miles minimum, pre-cleared for immediate take off."

"That is all?"

"Yes." Thomas looked through the wheelhouse windows. The Captain's Saudi Police Boat R18 was one of the closest of many vessels now encircling the static *Jazeera*; more an armada than a mere flotilla.

"Understood. Give me some time to organize things. I shall get back to you."

Of course he knew he wouldn't get what he had asked for. He might get Brad to hospital but even on that trip the chopper would most likely be full of guys in masks pretending to be the movie version of the SAS. At any rate they would prevaricate until after dark before they made their planned assault. According to the book, willpower and clear thinking crumbles in direct proportion to tiredness and lack of natural light. So, less risk for them.

This Captain Al-Bandari took his predictable time, his predictably obfuscating messages coming in at intervals as the afternoon wore on. He used the time to get Brad with great difficulty and much more pain into a dry suit and then up the companionway. He left him sitting on the floor, his back against a bulkhead alongside the doors that led out to the aft deck. He made a return trip to the diving kit locker, took two sets of scuba bottles and breathing apparatus, strapped one on Brad, left the other loose alongside him, then returned to the wheelhouse, passing through the stateroom. He hesitated there, then picked up a pre-loaded M79 rocket launcher. Already the light was failing. *Jazeera* and her escorts had drifted well to the north on the tide but the tide had now turned and was running south, taking them back towards the still distant causeway. He switched on the VHF. "Police boat R18: Captain Al-Bandari, you are receiving me?"

"I am receiving you, Thornton. The Sheikh, he is still safe? Please put him on the line now. We must hear him before the helicopter is permitted, you understand?"

"When you confirm that my instructions are being carried out I shall consider your request. Confirm please."

"The helicopter for the injured man will be above you in fifteen minutes."

"And the fixed wing intercontinental?"

"It also has been arranged with the Bahraini authorities exactly as you requested."

"Captain, my friend will be on open mobile telephone to me throughout his trip. By the way I have heavy armament on board. Should there be any deviation your boat is the first one to be targeted. Captain, do you understand this? It is most important for you to understand. I have your position at three hundred and five degrees from *Jazeera*, range nine hundred metres. This is correct?"

"Well, if you should say so, Captain." For the first time there was a note of uncertainty in the voice of the policeman.

Thomas unscrewed the side window fastening, opened it wide, receiving into his face a blast of super steamy air. "Then stand by," he said. "This will not endanger you but if there has to be any more, that next one most certainly will." He picked up the rocket launcher, took aim on a point twenty or so metres forward of the drifting police boat. He'd always been surprised by the relatively feeble shoulder kick-back when the trigger of an M79 was pressed, but the mighty sound inside the enclosure of the wheelhouse more than compensated for that. For the few moments it took the rocket to reach its destination he could hear nothing else. The sea erupted ahead of the police boat and Thomas' hearing returned in time to hear the end of Abdul-Rahman's scream. He unclipped the hand mike, placed it close to the ventilator on the door into the chart room, said, "Take it easy, big man. Say something nice to your friends."

There was an equal measure of terror and hatred in the muffled voice. "This is Sheih Abdul-Rahman Al-Sottar. I am safe, Captain. Please do exactly as this madman has requested."

Thomas said, "Thank you Sheikh. You may now go back to sleep. Captain Al-Bandari, kindly instruct your vessels to switch off all lights except their port and starboard navigation lights. There is nothing for you to see that cannot be seen on your radar and as you no doubt are aware your spotlights are not helping me at this point. I need to be able to observe clearly the state of the incoming helicopter."

He waited for their response as, one by one, the surrounding spotlights were extinguished.

"Mister Thomas?" Al-Sottar's muffled voice had lost all its remaining bravado. "What are you going to do? We need to talk about - about everything. About Colonel Grenville, your friend?"

"Just shut up, Al-Sottar. If I hear your voice again I'll shut it up, OK?" Thomas made quite certain that the VHF was turned off then turned on the recording machine. Speaking in Arabic, slowly and deliberately: "This is Thomas Thornton on board Sheikh Abdul-Rahman's boat, *Jazeera*, addressing Captain Ziad Al-Bandari on board Saudi police boat R18. The time is now twenty forty five and the date Friday seventh September. I am sure you and many others will be recording this. Do not interrupt me. There is a change of plan. Stand down the helicopter. My friend is too badly injured. We are now making for the Bahrain side of the causeway administration island. We shall need a car for the military hospital and then to take myself and the Sheikh on to the airport where the plane will be waiting for us as previously agreed. Now, Captain, I have no way of knowing whether or not you yourself are involved with Al-Sottar, as was your colleague Captain Al-Muttawi, but I am about to tell you and any other listeners everything I know about what he has been going on here… " Speaking in clipped military reporting jargon, leaving out only the name of Colonel Robert Grenville, he headlined all that he knew. Finally he said, "And so I must say goodbye. I can only hope that what I have told you will be of some help, for I personally have no quarrel, indeed I have much respect for The Kingdom. Your ways are your ways - the ways of Allah, peace be upon Him. If, however, what I have just told you is of no help then there is indeed no hope for you." Whilst talking he had been setting the automatic pilot on a direct course for the Saudi side of the causeway. He added a post script. "Naturally I hope for the same salvation for my own country, although I find this more doubtful. Personal freedom can so easily promote anarchy, can so quickly become a shelter for the wicked, can it not?" He switched off, re-wound the tape, unlocked the toilet door.

Al-Sottar at first refused to come out. Crouched in the far corner, he spoke in Arabic, his voice shaking, pitched high. "Please. Please, you stupid, stupid fool. They will not let you get away." Thomas realised the man was close to tears. "We are both now condemned men."

"Condemned? What, you too? Welcome to the club, sheikh." For some reason Thomas felt vaguely ashamed in the face of the man's break down. "If you want to come out and take your chances, then you'd best do it right now. Otherwise you'll be going down with this boat."

"What? What is this? What about going down?" Abdul-Rahman got quickly to his feet, came out with his hands up high. Thomas turned and switched on the recording machine and the VHF and turned the key to start the engines. He pushed the throttles far forward, used a pen to wedge them in their slots against the return spring, felt the instant acceleration trying to fling them backwards as *Jazeera*'s propellers grabbed water, settling her stern, raising her bows. He pushed Al-Sottar out of the wheelhouse with the muzzle of the Uzzi, locked the door, pocketed the key, raced aft to the recumbent Brad. Quickly he had the door to the diving deck opened and he was carrying Brad out into the dark, dropping the two of them without hesitation over the side of the boat's stern, down into the maelstrom of *Jazeera*'s wake.

Uncertain about his friend's state of consciousness he kept a firm hold on Brad as they tumbled together through churning seawater. The roar of *Jazeera*'s engines was fast receding. He blew out the mouth piece of Brad's skuba kit, inserted it into his mouth, felt and heard Brad starting to breathe the bottled air. He did the same for himself with his own kit, took Brad under the armpits, kicked for the surface.

He lifted up his goggles. *Jazeera* was caught in the beams of many spot-lights, making at top speed for the causeway and already halfway there. Even the fastest of her pursuers wouldn't get to her in time, even if they were trying to do so, which did not seem to be the case. Having been taken by surprise by the speed of events, few of them were even moving. And right now they would be listening to the RT and this mad Englishman with his crazy story, not knowing that it was a recording, waiting for him to slow down, dock the boat against the causeway.

Abdul-Rahman would have time in the concentration of searchlights to save himself by releasing the boat's inflatable, or just jumping ship. They were too far away to see or hear anything in detail. Brad muttered, "Well, that wasn't so bad, old mate. You haven't lost your touch, thank God. But they'll be back looking for us when they cotton on." An orange and white explosion split the causeway on the far horizon, the sound of it following on a second afterwards. The silence returned and the night was shot through only by the wavering of spotlight beams.

Thomas coughed up seawater. "I don't think so; not til they've finished picking up the bits and pieces, none of them ours." But there was still this sadness, the special kind of sadness that all men should feel over the death of a fine boat. "Let's go, Mister Scott. I reckon on three hours to Al-Sottar Marine, swimming mostly on the surface but down at ten feet on the bottles if there's any sign of activity. I'm going to tie you on to me but try to hang on to my belt. That way I'll know you're still conscious. If you can use the other arm to help us along, so much the better.

Brad said, "Sounds good except for the heading for Saudi bit."

"Bahrain would be three or four times further. I like a nice little swim but ... Christ ... "

"Yes. Wait though, listen to me a minute." Brad's words were faint but were full of whatever it was that made the man. "If anything happens to me. I mean if I don't make it and you do, I want you to know none of this is down to you. You did what I would have done. I did what you would have done, OK?"

"Isn't the water lovely, daddy?" Thomas said.

"Oh, shit. Be serious will you ... And about Rose, Tommy - "

Thomas blinked the salt water from his eyes. "Here, shut up and stick this back in your mouth. Let's take a look down below again, shall we?"

Exhaustion ... He dragged his unconscious friend out and on to the beach adjacent to Al-Sottar Marine. Sitting on the sand, he unwrapped the mobile phone from its plastic protection, called Mubarak Al-Jidha.

One of Mubarak's sons, the one named Fahad, arrived an hour later, helped him to get Brad up the beach and into the back of a battered old pick-up. Thomas got in and laid himself down beside his friend to keep him warm and to prevent him from rolling around too much during the journey. Fahad covered them both with a tarpaulin smelling

293

rankly of goats or of other animals, drove out to Mubarak's new desert encampment. Brad had still not regained consciousness.

The pick up had stopped. Hearing voices, Thomas sat up and looked around. A second youth, expressionless, stood in their way, a rifle slung across his back, nothing about him moving in the headlights except his robes and the red and white gutra that flapped and wrapped itself around his young-bearded face in the night breeze of the desert. Fahad stuck his head through the cab window, turned back to Thomas. "Do not worry, this is my brother, Abdullah." Without a word the lookout, Abdullah, got into the passenger seat. They drove on a little way further and into the encampment.

Mubarak Al-Jidha was sitting under the lamp-lit awning of one of a group of otherwise darkened tents. Thomas got down from the back of the pick-up, stiff muscled now, barely able to walk upright without staggering. He salaamed in response to the nod of the head and the words of formal greeting and bent his head for the kissing. He could see the hint of a smile in the craggy old Bedouin's watery eyes. The air and the man smelled of the residual heat of the sand and of cooked foods and spices and of live animals. "Yes, I knew you would come when it was finished," Mubarak said. "Although I did not think it would again be as a fish."

"So I have come: But it is not finished, father, although I am myself almost finished. And my friend, who needs much help."

"Yes." Mubarak nodded and pointed to the two young men. "You have met these worthless ones?" The pride in his voice had belied the adjective. The young men nodded, unsmiling still. "Do not worry, they know you only as infidel and do not yet know you as you are." He sighed and spread his hands, added, "That is, not who you are as a fish, you understand. But yet, insh'allah, they may learn as we all must learn. Come, let us carry down your friend to the tent so that we may decide what is to be done."

Thomas said, "I am much afraid. My friend is ..."

Mubarak clapped his hands. "Fahad, bring some proper clothing for Mister Thomas. Abdullah, help us with this man."

They placed Brad on a pile of blankets and cushions in one of the tents and cut away the dry suit. Great clots of blood and small, bright splinters of bone fell away with the fabric from around the wreckage of the knee. Thomas looked at the pale-drawn shell of a face, got down on his knees to cradle the man's head and shoulders in his arms. But there was this awful coldness, this lack of any responsive movement. He was unwilling, unable to acknowledge to himself or to

294

any of the others what he knew to be the truth. All the tiredness, the futility, the overwhelming ugliness washed over him and something inside almost broke free. Desperately he shook his head.

Speaking softly, Mubarak said, "Do not do this thing, Englishman. Do not fight your grief. Grief is good when it is shown. Grief is there by God's grace, may peace be upon him, to help you in this time of your need. Remember that you are with me and with all men who live, as I, and they, with you. And remember also that good men who no longer live are better than any of us or all of us who do live." Thomas looked up into the old man's face. The face was all shadows in the light of candles; a face made as hard and cruel and as understanding as the ancient land into which it had been born. He nodded, reached up to touch Mubarak's hand, laid down the thing that had been Bradley Scott. He got to his feet.

Mubarak murmured, "We must perform the burial quickly, as is the way. And in case of any visitors and before corruption can begin." He laid his hand on Thomas' shoulder. "Corruption comes to all of us but that should be a private thing that should take place out of men's sight below the ground, thus shall be witnessed by Allah, peace be upon him, alone."

Fahad brought for Thomas some Arabic clothing. He divested himself of his wet suit, folded it up, put on the thobe and the headwear and the sandals and pocketed Brad's mobile and his Browning. Fahad and Abdullah, working in silence, wrapped the body in a blanket, tied it with rope, slung it across the neck of a protesting camel. The small train went out into the night to a place some way off that had evidently been well selected, for the digging was easy in this place and did not have the shifting looseness of the dunes. In spite of his overwhelming tiredness Thomas insisted on doing all the digging, on Mubarak's instructions going down a full two metres, in this way, it was explained, frustrating the wild dogs of the desert.

They lowered Brad into his resting place by the light only of the stars and the first thin crescent of a near-dawn moon. Then Thomas took out the Browning. Extending it high above his head he squeezed the trigger. The crash of the single shot broke the still air of this new day, echoed back several diminishing times from the steep faces of sand dunes near and far. The she-camel stamped and snorted her panic, trying unsuccessfully to escape her halter, but Abdullah held on tightly, placed his hand on her muzzle, spoke quietly to her, blew softly into her nostrils.

Thomas dropped the gun into the grave. With the others looking on, in English he spoke the parts he could remember of the Anglican funeral service, afterwards filled up the grave and leveled it off as best he could. He looked around in the first faint flush of dawn for a stick or some other kind of a marker but there was nothing except the stones that Mubarak and his sons had gathered together. They spread these stones across the grave then piled them over with the sand and grit of that place in the desert. "What is left on earth of this man has been well marked by Allah, peace be upon him," Mubarak murmured. "And this, it is enough. But you have buried the gun with your friend, Thomas?" he asked. "Why is this?"

Thomas hesitated, truly not knowing the answer. It had been an act of spontaneity. "In my life there have been many guns and other weapons, father," he said. "Too many. Now, no matter what may happen, for me there will be no more."

The way back to the encampment was traveled in silence. Once there he was shown into a tent, bare inside but for a pile of rugs. He removed his Arab clothing and lay himself down. He remembered the mobile, knew he must speak to Rose. By now, whether she was in England with Connie or still in Bahrain awaiting a flight she might have heard of the destruction of the boat. He checked his watch: It was Monday the 10th of September, 05.20. He didn't want to call anyone, knew himself to be a dead man in the eyes of the world outside, wanted it to be that way.

He thought of what Brad had told him in the water, and then he thought of his sons as the mobile slipped from his fingers.

He had seldom been in so intense a depth of sleep but when he woke he put on the thobe, ghutra and sandals that had been provided, went outside into the glaring heat of the early evening sun. Mubarak was seated in the shade of his tent's awning, alongside him his sons and half a dozen other males of varying ages. The old man lifted his hand. He returned the greeting, walked off into the dunes to effect his ablutions. When he returned, a pitcher of water was waiting for him in his tent, together with a bowl in which to wash himself.

When he had finished he walked over to the seated group, offered them his salaams and the usual exchange of politenesses, spoke to Mubarak. "I have a message for my friend's wife. I will write it down if you have paper and pencil? And then perhaps one of your sons will take it for me to the office of the courier in Al-Khobar. This is acceptable?"

296

"Of course. But I think you will be hungry." Mubarak indicated the spare cushion by his side, the one Thomas knew to be the seat of honour. He sat cross legged, waiting for the old man to take the initiative, in front of him a carpet of many faded colours, arranged on it a bowl of dates and a single glass and a jug of the cultured camel milk they called laban. And another jug, this one of water, shining clear and bright, refracting the sunlight.

"You will stay with us, my son?" asked Mubarak. He poured some of the laban into the glass, set down the glass in front of Thomas.

"Yes, if you will permit it I will stay."

"Soon, perhaps within one moon, when it is cooler, we shall go south cross the desert. And you? You wish to be with us?"

Thomas poured himself a glass of water to go with the laban. "I have many things left to do, father, but I shall try to come with you." He selected a date with the fingers of his right hand, put it into his mouth.

Mubarak chuckled. "Is it not very strange? When first I saw you in that place of Al-Mahli I knew we were of a single blood."

"There was a man, a man of England like myself," Thomas said. "His name was Kipling. He wrote of a boy to whom a tiger spoke. The tiger also said, as you, 'We are of one blood, you and I.'"

"This is so?" The old man nodded slowly. "Kipling." He rolled the word experimentally around his tongue. "You must teach to me this language so that I may understand how it is not strange that a tiger can talk to a boy." Thomas smiled, reached for another date. From one of the tents came the crying of a baby. Quickly the sound changed to one of snuffling and then, once more, the silence. "You hear the newest of my daughters?" In Mubarak's voice the pride came first and then the satisfaction. "I will tell you that I was myself born whilst the great Ibn Saud lived, yet still does the old man Mubarak make sons and daughters. This one I have named Tooma." His face pretended a hardening. "Understand that this name for the new one is not to do with you, Mister Thomas." He raised his hand and clicked his fingers. "So, you have slept deeply and you are very sad and now you have need of a woman to help to bring back life," he said, and before Thomas could intercede Abdullah spoke for the first time, his face still with that same disturbing hostility. "My father, I welcome this man because he has brought you back to us and because it is our way to treat all visitors with courtesy. But can our ways and the ways of our women be understood without an acceptance of the one God?"

Thomas looked to the old man. "If I may be permitted ... I do not know the answer to your question, Abdullah bin Mubarak Al-Jidha, but this I do know, that any man may try for understanding. This was the way of your own people in the beginning. Were you in my country I would help you with our ways and you would understand and live with them whether at first you liked them or did not like them." He tried a smile without response, finished off his laban in one swallow. "And now, if you will excuse me, I have a letter to write."

In the tent allocated to him he took from the woman who said her name was Noor the offered paper and the ball point pen and he wrote:
Jeremy
I am sure you will have had details of my message from the boat, Jazeera. *As you now see I did not die in the incident but until I can get to speak to you it is extremely important you do not reveal my continued existence, especially to your contacts in Saudi Arabia and even more so to anyone, even Colonel Grenville in the UK. The reasons for this will become obvious in a short while when I give myself up to you in Bahrain. For now, let me just say that I did not reveal all in my final message.*

I am very sorry to tell you that Bradley Scott has died of gunshot wounds. His killers were dealt with by myself whilst I was on the boat. The reason for this letter is to ask you to find Brad's partner, Rose. I believe you met them both recently in Bahrain. Rose will be waiting a flight to England or might have already gone. PLEASE ensure she receives the enclosed letter just as soon as you possibly can.

He signed the letter, tore the sheet from the pad, folded it once and started a new letter on a fresh sheet. He wrote...

My dearest Rose.
I am for the time being unable to telephone you or anyone else and so am writing in the hope that this message reaches you promptly. It is very difficult, the hardest message I have ever had to write and there is no easy way to write it.

Your partner, my friend Bradley is no longer with us.

You may already think you know that Brad is dead and you probably thought that I had died with him on the boat, but in fact we both escaped from the boat, although Brad had been badly injured by one of Al-Sottar's men, and we managed to make it ashore in Saudi. He was still alive when we reached land but he died later from shock and loss of blood. I am quite sure about this because early this morning I buried him in a private place in the desert. One day, if you and/or his parents should wish it we may be able to bring him back to England.

I accept that you will most likely have nothing but hostile feelings for me and that you may not be at all interested in what I have to say about it, but I'm saying

298

anyway that Brad was a very good man and you know he was my friend, perhaps my only long time friend. It saddens me beyond words that all too often my friends have been hurt by association with myself, and now you, who would be amongst the last persons I would ever wish to see hurt.

There are other things I have to tell you but, Rose, you and Ferris-Bartholomew are the only ones who know I am still alive. I have had to tell him in order to get this letter to you. By all means tell my sister Sheila but for very good reasons on no account should anyone else know that I am still alive. For the time being at least.

Goodbye. I could say so much more but anything else right now seems - anyway, my love goes with this to you, as ever, unwanted or not ...

He signed this letter, too, folded it inside the one to Ferris-Bartholomew, wrote 'Private and confidential', then 'Jeremy Ferris-Bartholomew, c/o The British Embassy, Bahrain,' on the outside of the fold. He went with the letter back to the gathering. Fahad listened to his instructions and strode off to the pick up. With any luck he would make it to the DHL office before they closed, there to see it safely sealed into the courier's plastic envelope and sent on its way.

Soon enough he would have to decide when and how to follow it. Right now all he needed was to be on his own. He went back to his tent, lay down on the cushioned carpet amidst the smells of smouldering incense, of spiced food grown cold, of the hot sands of the surrounding desert. Thoughts came to him, a mélange only of the good people in his life. Thoughts of David and Paul and Sheila and her sister and her father and mother, and Grannie Mac. And of Bradley Scott of the famous smile. And of Rose Feather. He was so tired. He wondered without real interest how that could be. The girl-woman, Noor, must have extinguished the oil lamp and now the silence and the darkness was absolute. He could tell only by the vibrancy of her perfume that she had come to comfort him and at last there came a kind of peace. He knew how alone he had been, sometimes even when with another or with others; even with others whom he thought he might have loved. But now he did not feel himself to be alone and the relief of that was a physical thing. Here were the lips of a woman, the lips to brush away the tears that finally had come. And this was a dream that was not a dream for neither this woman nor he felt any need to say anything as the night and the making of love and the sleep, or the waking, and all the dreaming went on for ever and for ever. And there was such a word-less tenderness. And he knew by the light filtering through overhead canvas that it was

299

the new day and that he really was awake and that the woman whose name was Noor had finally left him.

Chapter Twenty One

Mubarak had made an all too obvious attempts to take Thomas' mind off things by asking him and his son to ride out to check the camel herd. But the time that he and Abdullah spent together was not comfortable. The young man's silent moodiness, even hostility, went well beyond any normal young man's angst.

They returned late in the afternoon. As they reached the top of the sand dune overlooking the encampment Abdullah turned to him, the wire from the earpiece of his beloved radio extending incongruously into a pocket of his thobe, his face without expression. He pointed down at the sprawl of tents. Thomas had already seen the dusty white Mercedes and the man now sitting with Mubarak. Whilst he was not unhappy to see Saeed he did not want to think nor to talk about what had happened, nor about any of the problems or tensions of that other world.

Abdullah kicked his heels into his camel, charged off down the slope, thobe flying, rifle bouncing on his back. Thomas' gutra snapped and blew around his face as he followed more slowly. One of the boys took the camels away. Saeed had got to his feet. This was not the largest of his grins, but as they embraced Thomas felt all the power of the man. They spoke together in Arabic. Saeed said, "I have much to tell you, Mister Tom. But first I may say you are looking like he of the movie, 'Orence of Arabia, yes?" He smiled more widely. "Did I not tell everybody who thought you dead that I would find you? I … about Mister Brad … Mubarak Al-Jidha has told me. I am very sorry."

Thomas said, "Yes. My wife? She is OK, Saeed? Back in England now, do you know?"

"Yes, sir. Everyone is well except for this sadness of thinking that you and mister Brad are gone."

"I have written to Brad's lady and a British diplomat. Now they and you are the only ones who know I am not dead." He led the way out of the late afternoon sunshine into the shade beneath the awning of Mubarak's tent, accepting the old man's invitation to sit.

Mubarak said, "I must apologise for the attitude and the behaviour of my son. I have said, it is not you who is not liked by him. It is the talk of Islam and the ancient fight against the infidel to which he has been listening."

"It is of no consequence, father," Thomas said. "And I, too, am tired of such things. I bear your son no ill-will. He is a young man as yet uncertain of his strength, of where he may sit alongside his father." He turned to Saeed. "But, everything is good, you say?"

"Yes. You wish to hear more?"

Thomas continued to speak in Arabic. "I have wished only to be here from one day to the next day as the guest of this, my father." He indicated Mubarak, sighed. "However, I know I must soon step back from the sanity that is here into all that other madness." He smiled to take from his words any edge not intended for Saeed.

Saeed said, "Yes. I too think the world is a madness. I have no wish to disturb you. However, please know that I shall be where you are, Mister Tom, wherever that may be." As if in contradiction an F16 warplane with the markings of the Saudi Royal Air Force flashed low over the surrounding dunes, the sound of it blasting their ears after the sight of it had gone, and then came a second fighter and this one pulled up into a vertical climb. They watched the silver glint of the lowering sun on its laid-back wings, slow-rolling, heard the camels grunt and stamp in panic.

"Truly a madness" Mubarak said. "But how strange is a world of mankind that tries to become its own God." He recommended the fingering of his Qu'aranic beads.

Thomas said, "Yes, it is so, my father. Saeed, I am sorry for any rudeness. I have no wish to offend for you are my friend. Please tell me." The man with the scarred-teak face, hooked nose and unsmiling eyes had appeared, holding a silver, curved-spouted dallah of Arabic coffee in one gnarled hand and a clutch of small, unhandled cups in the other. The dates were of the best new-season kind, half of each one pale and hard and crisp to the bite and the other, more ripened half, dark and soft and very sweet. Some of the women were moving around in the encampment, fetching and carrying and readying things for the meal to come. Thomas could tell which one was Noor by the swell of her figure and by the set and the swing of her shoulders and by the quickness of her dancer's step and by the change in the beat of his own heart. "What of George, Saeed?" he said.

"George is planning to leave Bahrain, go home to America. He plans to find his father, perhaps with the money to start this thing called a fishing lodge." He grinned. "Like all others he thinks you are dead. Many men are looking for what remains of that boat on the rocks of the causeway and in the surrounding waters. Thus far they say they have found only some parts of several men, one seemingly a Saudi and some others who were not Saudis although they cannot be certain of that." He finished his cup of coffee. At once another one was poured for him, another date offered. "Yes, the thing with the money transfers? It is all done, Mister Tom. All is well for George and for myself and my family." He picked a date, put it into his mouth, turned to spit the stone on to the sand.

Mubarak picked at his teeth with a twig of cinnamon scented wood. "Thomas, do you believe you will wish to leave this place in order to return to your own land? I have heard it is very cold in this land of yours."

Thomas said, "I will need to think about my situation, father. But know that I am content to be here with you and your family."

"Yes, especially with some parts of my family, I think." His face betrayed nothing.

Thomas got up. "If you will excuse me I return to the dunes for a little while, there to find my thoughts. Saeed, you will go back to Bahrain?"

"With the permission of Mister Mubarak I shall await your return and your decision. It is best. You know of the support that I am eager to give you." The dark eyes gleamed. "Also, the Colonel has told Miss Rose that he will have employment for me at his company. This employment will be in my profession as accountant. The Colonel has asked me to go to England for discussions about this."

Thomas switched into English. "Good for you, Saeed. I am very pleased."

Saeed said, "What little it is that George and I have done, I do not believe we have not done it simply for money. This you must know."

Thomas nodded, squinting out towards the setting of the sun, for a moment not trusting himself to say anything, then, back into Arabic without consciously being aware of it. "Thank you. But your family will be able to join you in Bahrain, Saeed, which will be good. About

303

what you have done, and also George, I shall say only that no man could wish for two finer companions when his night grows dark. And another, also. This one as my father."

Mubarak was still seated, still fingering the tawny beads. "Yes, it is good to have such companions. However there are times when a man has to travel without companions if he is a man and is not a woman to be afraid."

Thomas nodded, asked Saeed for the use of his mobile telephone, to please wait where he was. He took the mobile up to the crest of the closest of the sand dunes, finding sufficient strength of signal to enquire after the number of the British Embassy in Bahrain. He dialed the number, asked for Ferris-Bartholomew. He saw the girl-woman, Noor, scrambling up after him with a jug of water. He thanked her, turned his attention to the mobile. The girl on the switchboard would not at first admit the presence of Jeremy Ferris-Bartholomew but quickly agreed to put him through when he gave her his name.

The familiar voice. "I say, Thomas, this is really you?"

"I have every reason to think so." Thomas sat down cross-legged on the sand, the breeze plucking at his gutra.

"I just told my young lady she'd got the wrong name. Poor girl's terrified. Thinks she's been speaking to a ghost but I've given her the old keep 'keep schtumm' warning. I hadn't expected to hear from you so soon. Yes, I had your letter this morning, and what a lovely surprise. Before you ask, I've already sent your enclosure on per secure e-mail. No-one but the lady will read it."

"Thank you. Do you know where she is, when she might receive the letter?"

"I understand at any moment now, if not already. She's staying with Colonel and Lady Grenville. Yes, the very same as mentioned in your note to me. Anyway, I called and cautioned her personally as per your request. That was less than an hour ago. Told her to stand by for the letter."

"How was she?"

"Oh, about how you would expect. I was so sorry ... " Smoothly he changed the subject. "So, where the devil have you got to now, Thomas? A lot of important people will actually be dying to know, once they understand you're still alive and kicking. You're getting to be a bit of a pimpernel."

"Let's just say I'm with some friends in Saudi. An illegal immigrant, naturally."

"Saudi? My God, Thomas, you certainly have got, as they say, some balls. But the good news is that perhaps you are not so very illegal after all. The authorities in Saudi and the chaps in the UK are now quite satisfied about the, um, the potential miscarriage of justice, as it were." There was a hesitation, then, "Hold on a tick.... Yes, I've just been given the latest from London." There was a short silence on the line, then, "Seems everyone's more than willing to accept the old self-defence stroke miscarriage of justice scenario. So your break-out from that Al-Mahli place, what happened on the causeway with the bent policeman who couldn't swim, and so on and so on. All of it forgotten, yes?"

The news should have lifted him. "What about the boat, Al-Sottar etcetera?"

"You mean the *Jazeera* accident? What would Thomas Thornton, Esquire, have to do with that?" The question hung in the air. He continued, "This man, this Sheikh Abdul-Rahman Al-Sottar, apparently he died as quite a hero. Single handedly killed a couple of very dubious characters who'd inveigled themselves into working for him out here, plus another two bad boys from the Philippines. Seems he'd discovered these characters were planning to use his lovely boat in order to smuggle the Taleban's heroin into Europe, would you believe?" The light laugh. "Apparently the stuff from this ex-motor yacht is still permeating everything on land, sea and bloody air all around the point of impact on the causeway."

"I see." He didn't, not yet, but he knew he would have to pull himself up from the depths of wherever he'd been since he'd buried Bradley Scott. "Jeremy, could you get me safe passage over the causeway and on a flight to London?"

"Nothing easier old chap. Consider it done. Just give me a couple of hours. I've got your number, will call back."

"I'll need to talk to you about a UK visa for a couple of my guys. And about those Philippinos you mentioned, the ones on board Jazeera? I need a contact detail for their families in Manilla. There's something I have to do for them, is that possible?"

"Yes, Thomas. It is not, as they say, a problem. You do seem to have been having a bit of a busy time of it. To be frank I'll be damned pleased to see you safely out of my bailiwick, then we can all go back to sleep around here." He chuckled. "Just take it easy, old son. Give me the word whenever you're ready."

"I will." He switched off the mobile. Noor was watching his face through the eye-slit in her head covering. She whispered, "Now you will leave, English?"

"Perhaps, but not now, sparrow, not yet." He reached down and took her small hand, cool and desert brown, the back of it covered in the traditional henna-dyed designs as old as the peoples of Arabia. The hand responded lightly but the eyes were downcast. He said, "At some time all have to leave, sparrow. We must be happy that we are sad when such a leaving happens, for if we are not sad at the leaving then the being together has meant little. Is that not so? There are some things about which I have to think but I shall come back and then we shall see..." Down in the encampment one of the men was beginning the call to maghreb prayers, the scale-running of the voice high and pure and compelling, the words of the Qu'aran distinct and strong.

The she-camel, the one called 'Osira'ah' was saddled and waiting. Thomas had learned that camels were all as different one from another in behaviour as in appearance and he knew now how best to encourage this Osira'ah, for whom already he had developed an affection. He leaned far back in the saddle as she lurched to her feet, back legs first, then kicked her into a grumbling walk. Already the air of the desert had cooled. Later it would be cold. He rode comfortably into a sky suddenly of indigo washed by streaks of pinks and reds and purples and the effects of the music of the mahgreb and of the sunset and of the words of Ferris-Bartholomew had combined within him into a single strange, uplifting sadness. There was only the plod and scuffle of Osira'ah's great split-plate hooves on soft sand and the rank, hot smell of her and the feel of her body movements beneath him as he settled to the heave and the swing of her ground eating motion. So quickly the explosive painting of the sky had faded, was finished, and already it was dark.

He became conscious of the soft-thumping, long striding gallop of the camel of his follower long before Abdullah had ridden up. He had stopped Osira'ah. From some way back the young man had been calling his name into the night.

The messenger was breathless with the speed of his travel and the importance of his news. "I have heard it on my radio. My father Mubarak told me to come after you and to tell you. There has been something in America. Something of airplanes which have crashed from the sky into many large buildings." His voice was full of fear and yet of excitement and of something else. "It is said that this is done by we of Islam and of Arabia."

Thomas sat there, very still, listening to the outpouring of detail, doing his best to extrapolate the real from the supposed. Abdullah said, "You will return with me now?" It was more of an imperative than a question..

"No, my brother, I am not yet ready to return," he said. The she-camel Osira'ah shifted, her bellies rumbling quietly. In this newly moon-lit place of awesome shapes made by nature from the desert sands Thomas knew that he should feel some fear, did not.

"Yes. So, what will come now?" Abdullah shouted. His excitement had escalated into a barely concealed hysteria. "You, infidel, you will fight Islam? There will be war."

For the first time Thomas wondered whether there could be any self-induced or artificial reason for the young man's mood swings. He said, "Abdullah, always with men there is the forming of hatreds and there is war and hurt and there is the planned and unplanned administration of death. And yet for those amongst us who are not insane, Abdullah, there is also the necessary caring and there is respect, for still we are each others' brothers and each others' sons and we are all each others' fathers." He sighed deeply, feeling the tension, still strangely unconcerned. "Oh, but is this not a madness? This respect being the only way for a man to know that he himself is not insane? Is this not such a glorious madness?"

Mubarak's son unslung his rifle and worked the action to lever a bullet into its breech. He drew himself up in the starlight. "Perhaps it is so. But I am Wahabbi. I am a warrior commanded thus by my people and my people by Allah, peace be upon Him." He was whispering, more in control now but with his voice cracking. Thomas realised the boy was close to tears. He felt the explosion of the shot, might have felt the tiny wind of the bullet as it passed his face. This was a useless way for him to die although it did not seem too much to matter. Unmoved and unmoving, he watched with detachment as the young man tried to lever the next round into the breech, saw, as if in slow motion, the silver arc of the ejected shell case. Abdullah was rushing it and getting it wrong and it was taking fractions too long but finally the rifle came up again and Thomas spoke quickly, still in the Arabic, meaning it. "This time aim truly, my brother, but know that I love you." Then there was the shouting and the crash of another gun and there was Abdullah, unmoving in the saddle, his rifle still raised and pointing.

Mubarak closed up in the moonlight, stopped his camel, looking at his son in silence, his own rifle angled up amongst the stars. He said, "Worthless one, had I tried to kill you, you would now be dead." He turned to Thomas. "I am truly ashamed and truly sorry."

"This is all right, old father. I believe that there is everywhere a madness loose in the world this day, is that not so?"

"Yes, but it is not my son Abdullah who has tried to do this thing to the guest of his father, nor is it Abdullah who gloried in the abomination of today, though perhaps, as I am told, it may be an evil place, that place that is called America. No, the fault is with the cowards who hide in the mountains, they are the ones who have done it, they are the ones who seek to destroy the light of the world with their poisoned words and with the poison that they take from flowers. And it is they on whom God shall now turn his back." The old man urged his camel to kneel. It bent forward, knelt down with its usual pretended protest. He slipped from his saddle, looked up at his son. "Come down here and talk with the father of your blood, Abdullah," and to Thomas, "Go now, Mister Thomas Thornton. Go in peace and in as much of safety as God will provide, for in you I have found another son. Is not God truly great?"

The she-camel grunted as Thomas dropped down out of his saddle on to the sand, took Mubarak into his arms. "Yes, I shall go," he said, "I shall have to go, for there are the sons of my own blood in England, also, and there are others who may need me to help them destroy those of the mountain flowers. But there has to be a passing of time and with your permission, father, and if it be the will of God I shall one day return and travel with you and your people, southwards into the place that you call the Empty Quarter, the place that you have told me is not empty, but is filled with the presence of Allah, peace be upon Him."

"Yes, this is so. Do not wait too long. I have told you before that a man may not live forever."

Thomas forced the camel Osira'ah to her knees, re-mounted her. She bore him aloft and he turned her head towards the east, towards Saeed in the encampment and then, after that, to the causeway across to Bahrain. As he rode, swaying easily in the saddle, he thought of what evil may have happened in America and he thought of Mubarak, his saviour twice, that third and the most innocent of his fathers.

He thought also about the hardness and the kindness of his second father who now lay dying but who had dealt in the delivery of death all through his life; and he remembered as well his first father, his real father who had been dead all of these years but who had caused and had willed the death of others. So many deaths. Riding the night sands he remembered his first father's poem, the one he'd received at his school after his first father had been killed, the one he had for ever afterwards carried with him, the one called 'The Fourth-light.' The poem he knew by heart. It told of the lights that burn within all human beings: the first-light which is that of God and the Universe and the second-light which is a person's world and their country and their race and the third one which is their family and the love of their family. And as he rode on, he thought about the fourth-light, the one that, his first father claimed, is switched on within each man and each woman when each is born, the one that will lighten the way for that person and, perhaps, if it is strong enough, to a greater or a lesser extent for others.

Thomas Thornton remembered that his first father had written that this fourth-light cannot be put out whilst its owner lives except by a man's own attempt to change or falsify that which a man actually is, and that a life without this fourth-light is a life without any meaning.

But in the normal course, his father's poem had gone on to tell him, the fourth-light will not naturally fade until its person dies and after that the fading can last for a matter of hours or for a thousand or thousands of years; and sometimes, if only very rarely, this light will shine with such truth and such strength that it will not be extinguishable for so long as the foot of Man shall walk upon the face of his mother Earth.

Saturday, September 16th 2001

Planters and Reapers

He comes through Heathrow immigration and customs. ISG's new Middle Eastern Finance Manager is with him, although in a separate channel, the one for holders of passports other than UK. And George Shultz, on stopover on route to America. He rents a car and with Saeed and George he drives down the M3 to the Colonel's cottage.

He had not pre-announced his arrival but the Colonel, who had by now learned of his survival, must have been informed for they were all there: David and Paul and Sheila and Ben; the Colonel and lady Dee and the dog, BB. All of them, that is, except Rose. On the Grenvilles' patio, barbeque coals are glowing and a champagne bottle angles out from an ice bucket. Thomas reels back under the combined assault of David and Paul and the dog, for a moment quite unable to say much. Then he straightens up to introduce George and Saeed, decides to shake hands with the Colonel and of course with Ben, kisses and is kissed by Sheila and Lady Dee who take him to one side to tell him about Consuela. She is in good care, they say, although she's very likely to be an on-going problem. Her face downcast, Sheila confirms what he already knows, since Ferris-Bartholomew has told him, namely that Sir Christopher finally passed away. The funeral service has been put back until tomorrow in view of Thomas's expected arrival. Sheila tells him that Aunt Eleanor is very much affected by her husband's death, which is why she isn't here.

Thomas has never learned to call his aunt 'mother' in the same way that he used to call her husband 'father'.

He hasn't decided how to handle the next bit, especially in view of this strange mixture of sadness and happiness. But after he has enjoyed one of the Colonel's steak sandwiches and drunk a little of the champagne and has got everybody's attention, with David holding one of his hands and Paul the other one, he tells them, he hopes without histrionics, as much as he can tell them of his feelings about Bradley Scott. He says nothing about the manner of his death, only about his burial. He says things that he truly means, and he speaks with some emotion also of his second father, and he cannot say these things without adding something about what, so recently in New York City, has happened to everybody's world.

Colonel Grenville says a few simple little words in response, finally telling everyone that he and Thomas will take a walk by themselves but to carry on, please, with the cooking and everything, for they are all more than very welcome. "Everyone enjoy yourselves," the Colonel says. "We won't be long."

The two of them walk in an uneasy silence down through the orchard to the riverside and along to the seat by the willow tree. Here there is the smell of the weedy, fishy river and of wood smoke from somewhere and of fallen apples rotting in uncut grass. Bees and fruit-eating wasps compete noisily with each other. The two of them sit down side by side on the wooden seat on which he had last sat with Sheila, his forbidden sister. Sunlight glitters on soft rippled water, faster moving after the rains.

The Colonel says, "Well, my boy. You did it. You have my total congratulations." He coughs. "I must thank you for keeping me out of it. Thus far at any rate. Might I ask if that will remain the case?" He smiles, the light blue eyes unsmiling. "I mean, do I need now to fall on my sword or anything?" He sounds quite nonchalant, as if the answer could only be of passing amusement, of limited academic interest.

Thomas pulls off a stem of grass, bites into it, tastes its early autumn sweetness. "Look, Colonel, it's all finished, done, history. I know you were only acting for what you thought were the best of reasons."

Colonel Grenville shakes his head. "Finished? Oh, no. But about the involvement of Al-Sottar with Kerrigan and company? I hope you'll take my word for it that their cocaine operations were all completely unknown to me. I suppose the fellow thought to try a bit of running with the hare and hunting with the hounds. Not that this is of any consequence now, of course."

312

"Kerrigan wanted me dead," Thomas murmurs. "Probably just as much as he wanted the profits." He could hear music coming faintly from the cottage. Beethoven's pastoral. "But you say it isn't finished? Why not?"

The Colonel bends to re-tie his shoe-lace, straightens up and sits back, adjusts the angle of his panama hat. Suddenly he leans forward, "Look! There's the big fellow, right over there." He's pointing. Thomas sees the place in the water under the far bank close by the reeds where a large fish has just boiled. Quietly the Colonel says, "I am authorised to tell you what I'm about to tell you. I hinted at it when I met you at Heathrow although no doubt you thought at the time it was all simply theory - your old Colonel's private flight of fantasy. Oh, and in case you're wondering, Bradley wasn't a party to things any more than were you. You said it back there, Thomas. Bradley Scott was a very fine man - and a damn good manager by the way."

Thomas can hear the distant, unmistakable voice of George, the boys' shrieks of excitement, hopes George hasn't lapsed into his usual vernacular.

The Colonel says, "So, without getting into all the details and certainly without naming any names, here it is ... Some while ago a number of people, people of rank far senior to my own in the government, in the law, in industry, in the media and in the military got together, in total secrecy of course. They were and still are convinced that the plague of narcotics was bringing the country to the point of anarchy. They decided as a group to take radical counter-measures. Fire with fire and all that. They would - sorry, will - open the flood gates to heroin imports, in fact actively encourage and even execute such imports. The basic idea, as I hinted, was to knock out the criminal barons simply by removing their motivation. Their profits in other words. At the same time all those who may be weak enough to do so will be able to afford to satiate themselves on the stuff, happily, in peace and with least disturbance to the rest of the community."

Thomas interrupts, shaking his head. "Colonel, this is just bloody crazy. It's the gamekeeper turned poacher, big time!"

The Colonel smiles his iron smile. "Perhaps, but not crazy, Thomas. It's a fact. None of this is in any way 'legal', of course. Westminster would have neither the long sightedness nor the public support for that. At least not until years ahead, when the thing has long been a fait accompli. But fortunately it isn't Westminster that runs much of this disunited kingdom of ours. and some, myself certainly included, might say thank the Lord for that. Look, huge amounts of money, massive funds have been made available." He looks down, repositions the rose in the lapel of his blazer. "For the past two years several of us, working as a team, have been setting up the various operational components. Our group calls itself, 'The Planters', and now we would like to know if you would consider joining us, Thomas."

Thomas can feel the adrenalin flow, the first signs of a new danger, an overwhelming urge to cut this single sided conversation, move away. But for now he says nothing.

"Why The Planters?" the Colonel says. "Because what we're doing is very similar to the way in which the old tea trade was constructed. You know, some of our forebears went to the east to set up plantations. Others organised the shipping and importation and still others all the internal processing, distribution and sales. In other words, industrial chains of linked up, independent business cells, united to create and then to satisfy the craving of the public for infusions of tea leaves."

Thomas can hold his silence no longer. He bursts out, "Tea and heroin? That's a bit like comparing a liver cancer with a head cold, isn't it?"

"Quite possibly." Unimpressed, the Colonel resumes his briefing. "I will continue. Al-Sottar was just one of our procurement people. We have in place half a hundred contracted grower/producers/exporters like him and half a thousand main and sub distributors. This is a strictly cellular structure - actually it's a bit like Mister Bin Laden's in that none of these people know anything of each other and nothing at all of The Planters. However I should perhaps add that there are some intimate groups overseas, none of them Middle East, by the by, who are aware of what we are attempting. They're looking on with great interest." He pauses for questions but Thomas has none to ask. "Finally I should tell you that nobody connected with The Planters is set to gain anything; I mean anything at all, discounting the satisfaction of changing a greater into a lesser evil." He sighs, looks around as if for any sign of a change in the weather. "So, by no means are we, as you put it, 'finished,' Thomas. You have merely disrupted one strand of many, although on the separate issue of cocaine you've done the Saudis a service. I believe, as a result, that you'll be welcomed back there. Not that I imagine you'll wish to take them up on that."

Thomas speaks quietly but with as much force as he can muster. "Well, I'm pleased about that! Welcome back? Good Jesus Christ, I spend most of my military years risking my life fighting the bad boys with the drugs, on what seemed a weekly basis, getting shot up to hell by way of thanks, and now you tell me it was all a waste of everything anyway! But no worries because I've been of help to the people who a few weeks ago wanted to take off my head!" Abruptly he stands up, takes a few paces along the riverbank. "My God, Colonel, there is no way I will get myself into this Planters thing. In fact I should right now go straight to the police."

"Yes, is that so? Perfectly understandable but do take it from me, neither you nor I could stop things. Ditto whether either you or I live or die. Please do sit down again. Difficult to see you against the sun."

He sits down and the Colonel turns, looks him in the eye, straight, unblinking. "Should you really decide to go public with this, be quite sure the story will never see the light of day. At best you'll spend the rest of your life telling it to the nurses in Broadmoor." A grasshopper alights on his sleeve. "And what a waste that would be," he adds, softly. He kills the grasshopper with a quick nip of his forefinger and thumb, flicks it out into the current, watches for a take. "Billions will be spent on bringing in the stuff. It'll be dumped on the market at the price of aspirin. And be quite sure the general public will learn nothing about it." He pauses, frowns, goes on, "I'm afraid some of the halt and the lame will, as I say, fall by the wayside. Much as they're doing just now, in fact, if more quickly."

Thirty metres downstream a trout lips the surface, takes the broken grasshopper, submerges with just a circle of ripples remaining in temporary evidence as Paul runs out into the clearing from the overgrown trail, yelling in triumph. He's closely followed by his brother. "Here they are, David," he shouts. "I told you they'd be here, they're watching the fishes."

Thomas wants to tell his sons to go back to the others, away from this danger, but there's nothing much more to say or to do here. He gets to his feet, bends to encircle the tops of the backs of the legs of both his sons with his good right arm, stands up with some difficulty. He loves the soapy smell of them and he can feel their burgeoning strength and when he looks at them close up he thinks how he would die for whatever it is in their eyes. All the trust, yes, and the love, and some kind of, well, of veneration for God's sake. He says, "Colonel, thanks for putting me in the picture. I've already forgotten about it."

"Daddy!" Paul exclaims, "You can't forget everything already."

In the tall rushes lining the other side of the riverbank something moves. Then a water rat is swimming out into the current, nose in the air, v-ripple behind him, oblivious of their presence until Paul sees that his father has seen something and looks and squeals in excitement, and then nothing.

The Colonel looks up at him, removes his panama, nods, smiling. He stands to offer his hand. The hand is warm, strong, confident of its owner's position, understanding.

With Sheila in her own bedroom and the boys in another and Ben in the third, Thomas has inherited Sheila's studio couch. He is still wondering about Sheila and Ben, not that anything between them should be a worry, he tells himself. A harvest moon shines powerfully through the huge window and he needs no other light with which to see and to dial her number, listen to its calling, hear it stop. "Yes, Mister Thomas? It's me," Rose says.

She sounds weary but he can tell at once that it's all right. He takes a quick, deep breath. "Will you talk?" he asks. The voice seems not quite to be his own.

"Not about Connie because you'll know all about that. Not about Bradley, either, not yet anyway. For the time being your letter told me all I had to know and I'm doing my best ... but I'd like to talk to you about... like, anyway, what are you planning now?"

He closes his eyes. "Oh, Rose. Well, you know, I made at least one very good friend in Saudi Arabia."

"The old man of the desert? Mubarak Al-something?"

"Mubarak Al-Jidha. He'll be taking his people down into what's called The Empty Quarter. Nothing there, only desert, camels and tents. Nothing and everything. I'm invited - I'm thinking of going along with them, making some space, maybe taking the boys with me."

"Why?"

"Why go or why take the boys?"

"Both, but the boys?"

"They're of an age to learn. These people have something worth the learning. Perhaps it's time we all paid more attention. You know, after New York."

He can hear the sigh. "Saudi Arabia! We can't keep you off that damned causeway, can we?"

"Someone once told me we need more of them. Causeways I mean. No man should be an island and all that." He tries a laugh. "Anyway I do miss my lovely Osira'ah." Rose is not doing any laughing. "Osira'ah is my she-camel," he adds.

"How long will you be gone?"

"Six months or so. Time for the divorce to come through, get Connie back to her own people, anyway." He sits up on the couch. From here he can see down the back garden and past the toolshed to the bankside pathway, the moon-silvered river.

Rose says, "She could have a claim on the boys, you know that?"

"In her bloody dreams. She won't ever get near them, Rose. I'd rather have them grow up out in the desert."

"You're not concerned about her family? Aren't they bad people, Thomas? Brad told me they were."

"Yes and yes, but I can't change that. All of us have to live with our history."

"OK. And me? What of me?"

"I hope you might mean 'us'?"

"Yes."

"Oh Rose, Rose, Rose," he whispers. The pale, slow beating shape of the barn owl is ghosting down the nearside bank of the river, looking for something to kill.

"Will you write me a poem, please?" Rose says, softly. "One as good as that one of your father's, the one you carry around all the time? But can it not be about hurt? Please?" Without waiting for any answers she adds, "Fare thee well then, Mister Thomas."

And there is no hurt, only hope, in the click and in the dying of the telephone.

Printed in the United Kingdom
by Lightning Source UK Ltd.
135056UK00004BA/4-6/P